The Norsunder War, Book III

All Things Betray

SARTORIAS-DELES BOOKS

HISTORICAL ARC
"Lily and Crown"
Inda
The Fox
King's Shield
Treason's Shore
Time of Daughters (two volumes)
Banner of the Damned

The Young Allies as Kids Series
The CJ Notebooks
Senrid
Spy Princess
Sartor
Fleeing Peace

A Stranger to Command
Crown Duel
The Trouble with Kings

The Rise of the Alliance Series
A Sword Named Truth
The Blood Mage Texts
The Hunters and the Hunted
Nightside of the Sun
Sasharia En Garde
The Wicked Skill
Ship Without Sails
Marend of Marloven Hess
Seek to Hold the Wind

The Norsunder War III

All Things Betray

SHERWOOD SMITH

BOOK VIEW CAFE

BOOK VIEW CAFE

Published by Book View Café
304 S. Jones Blvd., Suite #2906
Las Vegas, NV 89107
www.bookviewcafe.com

ISBN: 978-1-63632-113-4

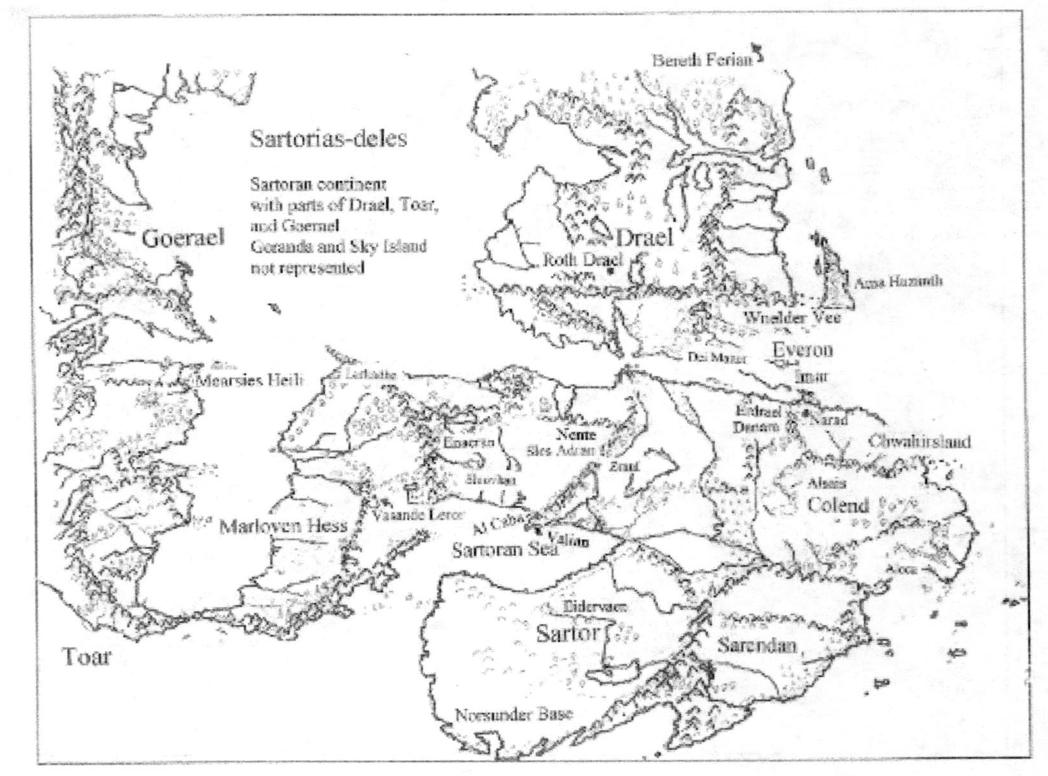

Sartorias-deles
Sartoran continent
with parts of Drael, Toar,
and Goerael
Goranda and Sky Island
not represented
Goerael
Beneth Ferian
Drael
Roth Drael
Azus Huzanih
Wnelder Vee
Everon
Imar
Dei Matar
Entrael
Danain
Narad
Chwahirsland
Mearsies Heili
Larlaithe
Nente
Sles Adran
Enaeran
Alsais
Colend
Zand
Sharban
Acoa
Vaaande Leror
Al Cibar
Valian
Marloven Hess
Sartoran Sea
Eidervaen
Sartor
Sarendan
Toar
Noesunder Base

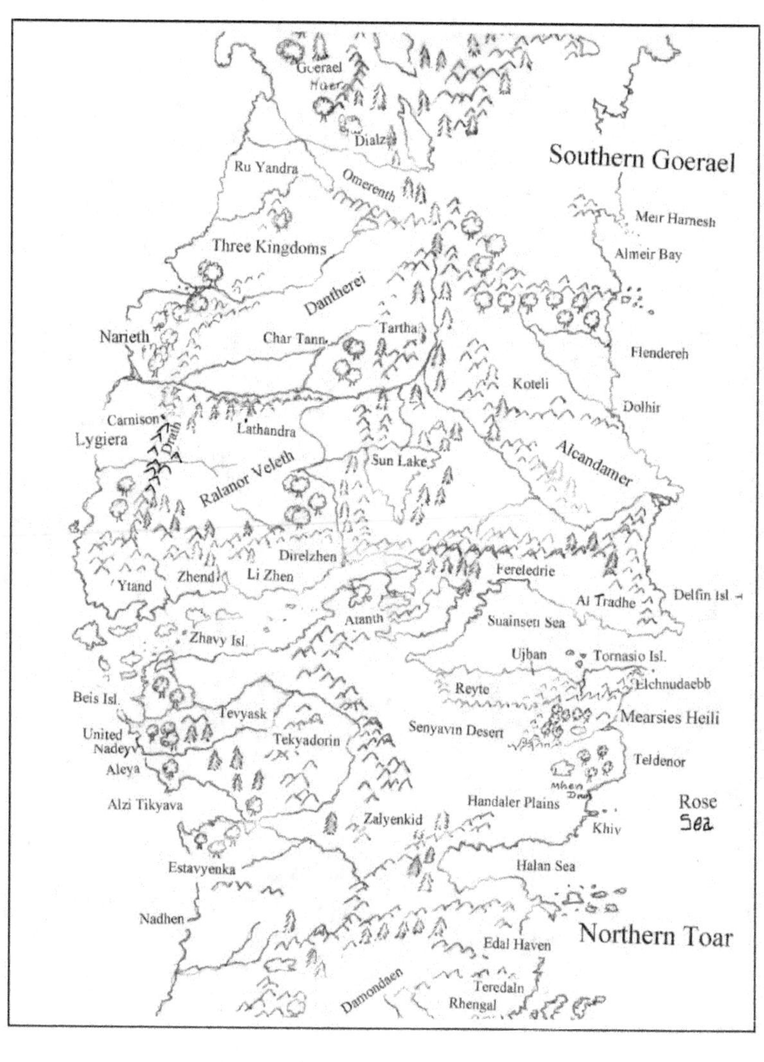

Goerael Huera
Dialz
Ru Yandra
Omerenth
Southern Goerael
Meir Harnesh
Almeir Bay
Three Kingdoms
Dantherei
Narieth
Char Tann
Tartha
Flendereh
Koteli
Dolhir
Carnison
Drath
Lygiera
Lathandra
Alcandamer
Ralanor Veleth
Sun Lake
Direlzhen
Fereledrie
Zhendi
Li Zhen
Ytand
Al Tradhe
Delfin Isl.
Atanth
Suainsen Sea
Zhavy Isl.
Ujban
Tornasio Isl.
Reyte
Elchnudaebb
Beis Isl.
Mearsies Heili
Tevyask
Senyavin Desert
United Nadeyv
Tekyadorin
Teldenor
Aleya
Mhen Drun
Alzi Tikyava
Handaler Plains
Rose Sea
Zalyenkid
Khiv
Estavyenka
Halan Sea
Nadhen
Northern Toar
Edal Haven
Damondaen
Teredaln
Rhengal

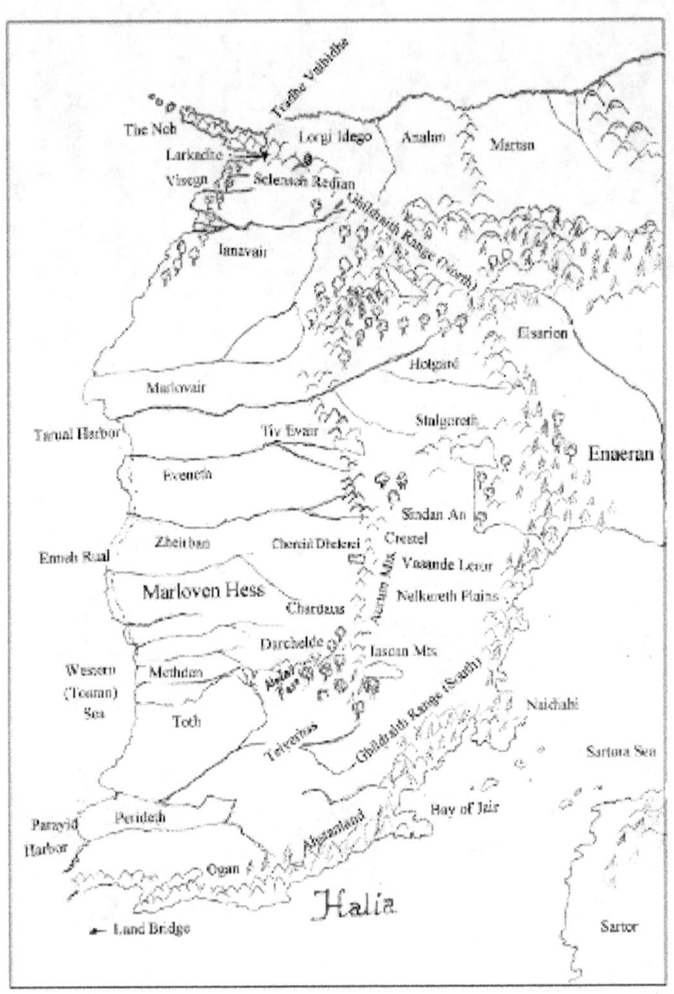

Trader Valbidhis
The Nob
Larkadhe
Lorgi Idego
Anahm
Martan
Visega
Selenseh Redian
Ghildraith Range (North)
Innavain
Elsarion
Hotgird
Mardovair
Stalgoreth
Tarual Harbor
Tiv Evair
Emaeran
Evench
Sindan An
Crestel
Zheirban
Chorsid Dhelerei
Vaaunde Leror
Ennda Rual
Nelkereth Plains
Marloven Hess
Aurum Mts
Chardaas
Darchelde
Jaszan Mts
Western
Methden
Andahi
Pass
Ghildraith Range (South)
Naidahi
(Toaran)
Sea
Toth
Telyerhas
Sartora Sea
Bay of Jair
Parayid
Perideth
Harbor
Abraznland
Ogan
Halia
Land Bridge
Sartor

DRAMATIS PERSONAE

NOTE: Norsundrians, Ex-Norsundrians, and Detlev's boys at the end.

Name most frequently used comes first, so sometimes first name, sometimes last, sometimes nickname.

LIGHT MAGIC MAGES AIDING THE ALLIANCE

Erai-Yanya Vithyavadnais: One of a long line of mages dwelling in the ruined city of Roth Drael. Trained partly by the northern Mage School at Bereth Ferian, and partly by Tsauderei, she works independently, her specialty magical wards. She has one son, ARTHUR (see BERETH FERIAN). Erai-Yanya's student mage is the Marloven exile Hibern Askan.

Evend: [deceased] One-time colleague of Tsauderei, King of Bereth Ferian (a courtesy title only) and head of the mage school there, he surrendered his life to bind rift magic from being used in Sartorias-deles by Norsunder. His place as titular king was taken by ARTHUR.

Igkai: Hermit mage living on the peninsula on the Sartoran Sea. An oddball all his life, he is a friend to birds and animals — and tolerates humans who do well by animals.

Lilith the Guardian: A lower ranking mage and what might be called an officer of rites and rituals in Ancient Sartor, which was as close to a government as they got. She had one daughter, Erdrael, who was killed along with most of the rest of the population when Norsunder tried to wrest control of the world, for reasons explored in a volume to come. Her name is a modern adaptation, and she found herself trying to combat Norsunder on this and other worlds around the sun Erhal; she comes out of hiding beyond time whenever she finds evidence that Detlev has been in the world, acting for Norsunder's Host of Lords.

Mondros "Rosey": Big, bluff, and bearded, he began life as an exiled son of the disgraced Glenereth family, warlords of Ralanor Veleth. He studied magic, aided by Gwasan Sonscarna, Princess of the Chwahir, whom he married and had a son, REL (see SARTOR). When Mondros made it his life's goal to defeat Wan-Edhe of Chwahirsland, he stashed Rel with a trusted friend, where Rel grew up a part of the family, until the urge to travel caused him to take to the road. Father and son found one another relatively recently.

Murial of Mearsies Heili: Recluse mage, living hidden in the western wilds of Mearsies Heili. Born a princess, she supported the transfer of the throne to her niece CLAIR (see MEARSIES HEILI) on the death of her sister. Protecting the kingdom from a distance, she has seen to it that Clair got magical training.

Oalthoreh: [deceased] Head of the northern mage school in Bereth Ferian

Randon Amdrelya: Originally from Vandary, Randon is an accomplished mage who did the Child Spell when around thirteen, to avoid limiting expectations of his culture. Travels around looking for kids to rescue.

Tarael of Drael: A morvende mage of a Drael geliath, captured by the Host.

Tsauderei: Oldest of the senior mages, independent of the two leading mage schools, living in a historic mage retreat located in the mountains bordering Sarendan and Sartor in the Valley of Delfina.

FROM OFF-WORLD

Caris-Merian Rhoderan of Geth-deles: "Rhoderan" is a name adopted by her father, the disinherited and disgraced Harold Dei, who tried to take the throne of Everon a couple of times before he was booted off-world. He had three children, the middle one being Caris-Merian. She came to Sartorias-deles's northern mage school to study magic right before the invasion. An accomplished singer and a scholar, when she is not seeking revenge for her brother's death.

Les (Leskander) Rhoderan of Geth-deles: [deceased] elder brother to Caris-Merian, and a problematical figure in his home archipelago. He discovered vagabond magic, and tried to weaponize it, (he said) in order to win freedom for the underaged and poor. Very charismatic.

Mildred of Geth-deles: a martial artist.

Zairna Raadi from Sri Fortnu: A worldgate traveler and beginning mage, born a prince in a very problematic kingdom; a dragonflower inked into his neck and curling up over one ear testifies to serious rituals. Ditto the diamond earrings he never removes. Ended up at the Northern School of Magic.

June from Earth: From a parallel of Earth in even worse shape, who got caught in someone else's conflict. Has been traveling through Worldgates since, and become a sort of magical lightning rod without knowing. No matter how far or fast she goes, she cannot outrun her own shadow.

The Young Allies and Others,
Listed by Kingdom

Alcandaamera

Charlana, Queen of Alcandamer: A mage of sorts, possessor of the double crown, which distinguishes between lies and truth.

Ama Hazanth

Crow (Prince Marseth Ghandorjien): Crown prince, keeper of the Fire Ruby (which wards storms from the island)

BARBAN

Dara, Leela, Yovres, Honey-blossom: vagabonds, present day

Ancient Tower that once had a window to the past, and to residents from the world Elesh Orom-alsh, guardians of the Fifth Protection of Alsheya (the cup Ethe)

BERETH FERIAN

Arthur (Yrtur) Vithyavadnais: He adopted the nickname Arthur after his rescue by young world-gate crossing friends. Son of mage Erai-Yanya, he early showed great ability in learning and magic, but he was unhappy living in isolation. He was adopted as heir by Evend, the former head mage of the Bereth Ferian Mage School, and presiding King of the loose federation headquartered at Bereth Ferian. After Evend's death, Arthur shared this courtesy title with Liere Fer Eider in her persona as Sartora, the Girl Who Saved the World.

Evend: (see Light Mages)

Liere Fer Eider: Also known as the Girl Who Saved the World, she was the first of her generation to be born with *Dena Yeresbeth*. At ten years old she left her small town to escape being captured by Siamis, who had extended an enchantment over the world, which Liere later broke. The enchantment is generally known as The Lost Year, as most lived in a dream world while it lasted. She was lauded by all, and given the cour-tesy title of Queen in Bereth Ferian, a title with no powers or responsibilities whatsoever — but which still chafed her unbear-ably. Liere was the poster child for Imposter Syndrome until she went to Geth-deles for five years to study magic, and re-turned recently.

CHWAHIRSLAND (AKA LAND OF THE CHWAHIR)

Dirk Sonscarna: Son of the problematical Kessler (see below), on the verge of teenhood. Has Dena Yeresbeth and considerable martial arts as well as magical knowledge.

Jilo: Son of a lowly one-syllable sergeant, heir to elderly *Prince Kwenz Sonscarna*, he finds himself acting king of Chwahirsland, after Norsunder's removal of the previous king, who had ruled for more than a century. What that means is, he is slowly poisoning himself trying to remove the toxic accretion of dark magic enchantments over Chwahirsland, and especially its capital.

Gwasan Sonscarna: [deceased] Princess and mage, married a disinherited swordsman from Ralanor Veleth who later became the mage Mondros (SEE Mages). Their son is Rel the Traveler (SEE Sartor)

Prince Kessler Sonscarna: (SEE also Ex-Norsundrians) The single living descendant of the ruling Sonscarnas, who were systematically killed off by Wan-Edhe, blood relations notwithstanding. Prince Kessler escaped at a young age, made his way to a martial arts group where he mastered military arts. He allied with a Norsundrian mage, Dejain, and began to assemble followers for his plan to remove all hereditary rulers of the world and replace them with his followers, chosen solely on merit. When defeated, he was forced into Norsunder by Dejain, who betrayed him.

Wan-Edhe (born Shnit Sonscarna), King of the Chwahir: Descendant of the ruling Sonscarna family, has ruled for close to a century. A powerful dark magic mage, he has managed to create a powerful citadel in the heart of his kingdom where time itself is distorted in his effort to ensure that he will live and rule forever. He killed off his family and descendants, including his brilliant heir, Princess Gwasan; only his grandson Kessler escaped, but years of abuse told on Kessler's emotional landscape.

COLEND

"Bee" (Aural) Keperi: Chief scribe to Shontande Lirendi. Being blind, he does all his work by memorization.

King Carlael Lirendi: [deceased] Regarded generally as Mad

King Carlael before he was assassinated by Efael of Norsunder. He was as beautiful as he was strange. He mostly existed in a world of dreams imposed by magic, from which he emerged now and then, very alert and very aware. There was a regency council made up of the chief nobles who oversaw the kingdom when he was unable to respond to the world around him, and they ruled until very recently, refusing to relinquish power, though Carlael's son Shontande had come of age.

Prince Shontande Lirendi: Son of Carlael, King of Colend, and new king.

Karhin Keperi: [deceased] She was a teenage scribe student in a small town in the west of Colend, who volunteered to function as the center of the young allies' communication network. An indefatigable letter writer, she first met Puddlenose of the Mearsieans, and gradually got drawn into the Alliance; she was murdered by one of Detlev's boys, and she is still missed.

Lisbet Keperi: Younger sister of Thad and Karhin.

Thad Keperi: Red-haired brother of Karhin, also a scribe student, but much less passionate about the scribe life. Very social, and friend to all the Alliance; he and his brother Bee are very close to Shontande Lirendi.

ENAERAN

Adon Marsael: Distantly related to the royal Elsarion family, tried to take throne. Allied with Norsunder in order to keep the throne.

Andri Malcolin Elsarion: Inherited his throne very recently, after years of civil war.

Gared Inmael: Close friend and adoptive brother of Andri Elsarion: Gared's father, the Elsarion Master of Horse, took in Andri when he was disinherited. The boys grew up together.

Marten (Martande) Eldias: Lifelong friend to Andri Elsarion.

Baras Parael Otobris: [deceased] The new king's Commander of the King's Guard.

Thadara Otobris, Duchas of Merith: The new king's Chief Minister and treasurer, who has her eye on marrying Andri and sharing his throne.

Trevor Macael Elsarion: cousin to Andri, from what had been the main branch of the family. Holds the rank of duchas in Elsarion, a very old province.

EVERON

King Berthold and Queen Mersedes Carinna Delieth: [deceased] Former king and queen, survivors of rough earlier years. Mersedes, daughter of a con man, became one of the Knights of Dei, dedicated to protecting the kingdom. They were both killed (at different times) by Henerek of Norsunder, who had come from Everon, and had been booted out of the elite Knights of Dei for countless crimes.

Prince Glenn Delieth: [deceased] Heir to the throne of Everon, and convinced that a strong army solves all questions, especially the threat of Norsunder attacking; he died in a duel with David, one of Detlev's boys, after forcing the fight on him.

Hatahra Delieth (Tahra), Queen of Everon: Younger sister of Glenn, passionate about numbers, and in her unrelenting hatred of Detlev and his boys. When the war begins, has two children, Jessan and "Carl" (Berthold Jessan, and Mersedes Carinna), and three infants: Madelon, and twins Sedron and Glenn.

Roderic Dei: Commander of the Knights of Dei, once defenders and protectors of the realm. The Knights were decimated in the war Henerek brought, and Kessler Sonscarna finished. Roderic Dei survived to serve as regent for Tahra Delieth until she reached the age of majority.

IMAR

Fer Eider family: Liere's mother, Elen; one of Liere's brothers, who owns a pastry shop. Has two sons and a daughter: Lesim, Milnat, and Marga.

Marga Fer Eider: cousin to Lyren-Sartora, niece to Liere Fer Eider

Tolia: baker, Marga Fer Eider's best friend. ERAS, harbor-worker, Marga's male best friend. Both regarded Marga as their beloveds.

MARLOVEN HESS

Crystal Ingrid Montredaun-An: [deceased] Daughter and heir to Senrid, the king. Five years old. Her chief passion is dogs.

Daltan: Cobbler, middle aged. She is a resistance leader.

Forthan, Retren: [deceased] A young man from a farm background, Forthan is the best of the leaders to come out of the military academy. He became Harskiald, a resurrected title that means trusted commander in chief of Marloven Hess's standing army; before then, commanders in chief were appointed per mission. Struck his banner at Aladas Pass before the defeat of Marloven Hess.

Hibern Askan: Light magic student, tutored by Erai-Yanya of Roth Drael, who learned in the northern mage school. Hibern was disinherited by her family.

Indevan-Harvaldar Montredaun-An, previous king of Marloven Hess: [deceased] Second son of Kethadrend, and raised to be a scholar. Indevan was, like his elder brother, skilled in martial arts, but he was never competitive. His leadership was entirely through a likable, easy-going nature and intelligence. He traveled to the neighboring lands, where he conducted himself so well and so knowledgeably that he did a great deal to lessen the negative Marloven reputation. Married the King of Telyerhas's daughter, Lesra. Had one son, SENRID, [see below] before he was killed by his younger brother Tdanerend, who was appalled at his ideas about limiting royal power and disbanding the army in favor of a militia defense.

Kendred Montredaun-An, Prince of Marloven Hess: [deceased] Eldest son of Kethadrend, son of the grim Senrid who caused the various treaties to be made limiting Marloven Hess. Trained in martial arts at a very young age, sent to the academy too young. He had too much of his grandfather's angry drive, and when his father failed in various forays against those treaties, Kendred tried to rally the young Marloven heirs around him to take the throne. He ended up escaping over the border at a gallop with a company hot on his heels. Had two sons, both of whom he sold after unsuccessful plots. Changed his name, became a pirate before joining Norsunder, dead by age thirty.

Keriam, Janec: Career military man, Commander of the Marloven military academy, also titular head of the Palace Guard. Acted as guardian and foster-father to Senrid, protecting him from the regent as much as possible.

Senelac, Fenis: Wife to Retren Forthan, and head of horse training for the military academy, equal rank to the Master of Horse in the city guard.

Senelac, Jan: Cavalry Captain in the army, now chief of Senrid's coverts.

Senrid Montredaun-An: Young king of Marloven Hess, a mage studying both dark and light magic. First friend to Liere Fer Eider, and second to make his unity in *Dena Yeresbeth*. The Marloven army is one of the most formidable in the world.

Stad, Indevan (Van): Second in command, Marloven army

Tdanerend Montredaun-An, Prince of Marloven Hess:

[deceased] Third son of Kethadrend, raised to be "shield arm" to his brother Indevan. Tdanerend was short-tempered as well as short-sighted, and uncoordinated. He tried to learn magic, but where that came easy to Indevan, as well as everything else, he had trouble learning, and eventually surrounded himself by toadies and the traditionalists who were uneasy at the changes Indevan contemplated. He married Caras, the second princess of Telyerhas, and there, too, he was unfortunate: she was ambitious, despised him as much as he came to despise her after she tried to scorn the Marlovens into setting up a court. He killed her first, before he took out Indevan and Lesra. His daughter, Ndand, was Senrid's chief companion. Tdanerend tried control spells on her, meant for Senrid, which motivated Senrid to master magic at a young age so he could fix his cousin. Tdanerend went over to Norsunder before losing the kingdom, and then his life. NDAND left the kingdom to become a musician.

MEARSIES HEILI

Aurora of Mearsies Heili: Clair's small daughter, already showing signs of being a wanderer, like her Uncle Puddlenose.

Clair of Mearsies Heili: Young queen of Mearsies Heili, a small agrarian polity on the northeast corner of the continent Toar. Niece of the hermit-mage *Murial*, and cousin to the wandering boy known only as *Puddlenose*, she has adopted a group of girls, most of them runaways. Her right-hand and designated 'heir' is *C.J.*

C.J. (Cherenneh Jenet): Found by Clair, who traveled through the World-gate, C.J. is from Earth, adopted into Clair's gang of runaways and rejects. She learns magic fitfully, and is generally regarded as the leader of Clair's gang of girls.

CJ's Gang of Girls: Falinneh and Dhana currently wear human form but are not actually human; Seshe has a mysterious past, suspected of being a runaway princess (which is actually correct); Irenne thought the world was a stage and she was the heroine of the play, which got her killed by accident by one of Detlev's boys, but she is still very much a presence among the girls; Diana is a martial artist and forester; Sherry and Gwen are followers. They are a very tight found family.

Mearsieanne: [deceased] Once Queen of Mearsies Heili, on her return to the present time, she stepped in and in the nicest way possible, shouldered aside Clair, her great-granddaughter, in order to show her how ruling ought to be done. After the invasion, she bound Mearsies Heili in a protective lattice-ward that was tied to herself, then she walked into a Selenseh Redian and surrendered her life, binding the enchantment onto her. The key is Clair.

Murial: *(see Light Mages)*

Puddlenose of Mearsies Heili: Bereft of family at a very young age, thus no one knows what his actual name was. He was abducted and used by The King of the Chwahir in his complicated plots, he was rescued several times by Rosey (Mondros, see LIGHT MAGES). He wanders the world, determined to have fun. His chief companion is a world-gate wanderer from Earth named Christoph, but sometimes he's joined by Rel (see SARTOR). Gradually he traveled on land less and on the sea more, until he was made second in command by Captain Heraford of the *Tzasilia*, former privateer.

REMALNA

Bran (Branaric) Astiar, Count of Tlanth: brother to Meliara, wife NEE

Meliara Astiar, Queen of Remalna: children Alaraec and Elestra

Nadav Savona: Vidanric's oldest friend and chief aid, son Nadav

Vidanric Renselaeus, King of Remalna: children Alaraec and Elestra

RALANOR VELETH

Flian Elandersi, Queen of Ralanor Veleth: was a princess from Lygiera, distant cousin to Garian Herlester of Drath.

Jaim Szinzar: Brother to the king, and nominal leader of the army, though Jason commands in action.

Jaimas Szinzar: Younger child of king and queen

Jason Szinzar, King of Ralanor Veleth: [deceased] military background, inherited the throne, and the care of his siblings, at a young age. His chief rival is PRINCE GARIAN HERLESTER OF DRATH

Jewel Szinzar: married to the King of Lygiera, MAXL ELANDERSI, has several children

Liara Viana Szinzar: Eldest child of king and queen

Markham Glenereth: disinherited, technically denied the Glenereth name, though the king intended that to be temporary. Liege to the king, a martial artist of superlative skill.

Lexan Glenereth: son of Markham Glenereth

SARENDAN

Darian Irad: [deceased] After his defeat in a vicious civil war, Darian Irad stepped down from the throne and ended up as a military consultant on the sister-world Geth-deles. On his nephew Peitar's assassination, Darian Irad insisted that he was a regent for Peitar's son Darian, and not a king: he had gone to Geth, where he married and had a family.

Darian Selenna: son of Peitar Selenna, and heir to the throne.

Has Dena Yeresbeth.

Derek Diamagan: [deceased] Charismatic leader of the revolution, a commoner who wished to overthrow all the nobles, and institute common rule. He was a far better speech maker than he was an organizer; his revolution was a disaster. Close friend of Peitar Selenna until his assassination by Siamis, at that time nominally of Norsunder.

Lilah Selenna, Princess of Sarendan: [deceased] Younger Sister to Peitar. She, with friends *Bren* (artist), *Innon* (a noble-born accountant at heart) and *Deon* were deeply involved in the revolution.

Peitar Selenna, King of Sarendan: [deceased] Reluctant king who would rather study magic, he came to the throne after an especially vicious civil war. He, nephew to the former king, Darian Irad, was one of the leaders of the revolution, but advocated non-violent means. His accession was a compromise between the commoners, who adore him, and the nobles, who recognized that at least he is nominally one of their own; on his assassination, he was, at his own order, replaced by his uncle.

SARTOR

Atan, (Queen Yustnesveas Landis V): New young queen of Sartor, after the oldest kingdom in the world was removed from time by nearly a century. She was found as an infant on the border by Tsauderei the mage, and raised by him before the enchantment was broken. She began her queenship as a mage student with little training in statecraft, but well-read in history.

Gehlei: Former guard in the days before Sartor was enchanted for a century, escaped with the infant Atan. Raised Atan to age fifteen along with Tsauderei the mage.

Hinder and Sinder: Morvende (cave dwellers), friends of Atan.

Julian Landis: born Julian Dei, she is Atan's cousin who wore the Child Spell for a considerable time. She relinquished it on Atan's promise that she would not be considered an heir, nor a princess. She is a wanderer by nature, and was happiest when staying with Dtheldevor of Wnelder Vee's gang.

Mistress Veltos Jhaer: [deceased] Former chief of the prestigeous Sartoran mage guild, until the enchantment the foremost mage school in the world. Now a century behind. She was further burdened by guilt for having lost the kingdom to enchantment, she left the guild woefully behind as they struggled to recover their old prestige. Assassinated by Efael of Norsunder, she was replaced for a time by Tsauderei the mage.

Old Helas: One of Rel's city guards, left from before Sartor's 100 year enchantment. Along with BEAK, a young guard.

Rel: Known as Rel the shepherd's son, and more widely as Rel the Traveler, he was happily raised by a guardian in Tser Mearsies until wanderlust caused him to leave home. Met Puddlenose of the Mearsieans, and consequently became tangled in some of the Mearsieans' adventures. Friends with Atan, and one of the Rescuers. He was the only outsider ever invited to join the Knights of Dei in Everon; in the previous volume he discovered his parentage (SEE Mondros the mage), which he is still trying to process.

Rescuers: The name given to a band of children who had lived in a magic-protected forest during the enchantment. They sheltered Atan before the enchantment was broken. Ostensibly highly regarded as heroes by the Sartorans, there are the aristocratic Rescuers, and the non-aristocratic, Rel among them.

SLES ADRAN

Bartal na Shagal, King of Sles Adran: Allied with Adon Marsael of Enaeran, and Norsunder.

Chantala Shagal: Niece and heir to Bartal, daughter of Chantal,

Bartal's sister. Cared for by her elderly nanny MARIANA, who was Chantal's devoted nanny.

Haries: Last name of the pair of artists who shelter Chantala na Shagal during the war.

Kinarde, Arandos: Sarendan-born Norsundrian placed as watch-dog and then commander over Bartal by Norsunder

Navor Mandracar: army commander and close friend of the king.

Master Orthal: runs an art school along the river. Other artists in training: LEMETH, LISI.

TELYERHAS

Havlan Casarod, King: Family the most direct descendant of the Cassadas, who were regarded as visionaries (or mad). Son of a queen known for her lack of skill at ruling but her genius for music, he had two sisters, LESRA and CARAS, who married Marloven princes and ended up dead. A scholar, he has a consort, who is also a scholar but he handles a lot of minor ruling issues. Has a son and a daughter.

VASANDE LEROR

Kyale Marlonen: Adoptive sister to Leander, relishes being a princess, and is jealous of Leander's attention.

Leander Tlennen-Hess: Like Senrid, a young king, though of a tiny polity that historically belonged to the Marlovens, then broke away four centuries previous. Leander and Senrid have a lot in common, and would be friends, except for Leander's jealous stepsister.

Llhei: [deceased] Sarendan-trained nanny (sister to Lizana, nurse to the royal children of *Sarendan*), governess to Kyale, remained after evil Queen Mara Jinia defeated.

Alaxandar: Captain of royal guard, quit under evil queen Mara Jinia, protected Leander.

LAND OF THE VENN

Erenlara Sofar: Barely into her teens, princess of the Venn until her brother's death in the invasion. Has Dena Yeresbeth.

Kerendal Sofar: [deceased] Was king of the Venn, until the invasion. He committed suicide rather than submit to a blood-binding forcing him to act according to Norsunder's will. Met Rel the Traveler [see SARTOR] the one time he was able to escape Venn and his duties, as a young boy.

WNELDER VEE

Dtheldevor: Daughter of a privateer (some say pirate) who was killed when Dtheldevor was small, but not before she was taught martial arts. She became the champion for the young prince Murgeh Troiad, sailing against pirates infesting the shores, and helping to fight off an enterprising Norsundrian.

She has a hideout called Dthel Rendm, on one of the hundreds of islands off Wnelder Vee's coast. She did the Child Spell decades ago; in lived time she is in her late seventies. She accepts kids on the Wander on her ship and her island, but her most loyal shipmates are: Sarmonwilda, born a dawnsinger; Sharly, a centaur from the northern reaches, and Sidres, another centaur; Gloriel and Peridot Warren (twins, from Earth, born with mundane names) and Joey and Ellen Warren.

Her most frequent visitor who doesn't live with the privateers is Julian Dei Landis of Sartor.

Troy, King Murgeh Troiad: erstwhile king in Wnelder Vee. Though kingship is little more than a title — the guilds do what little governing is required in small, very rural Wnelder Vee — he resisted even that much, preferring to wander the world and master music, and kept the Child Spell in order to avoid royal duties. Actually considerably skilled as a bard.

NORSUNDER

Aldon: Military leader with a thirst for warfare, the bloodier the better. Wants to command the invasion in order to foster eternal war.

Alsaes: First came to notice as Kessler Sonscarna's companion in Kessler's plan to take over the world. Given a mortal wound, surrendered self in exchange for bloodknife spell to preserve his life. Extremely vain. Dyes hair blond to hide Chwahir origins.

Benin: [deceased] Ambitious mage, his specialty the soul-bound (people caught at the point of death, their wills bound to the command of whoever holds the soul-bound magic). Benin tends to not wait until potential soul-bound are dead in order to experiment.

Bergan: one of Imry Llyenthur's staff, along with COLLERON, and Duin [see below] These are all typical flunkies, though Bergan sells info to whoever will buy it, most of all to Aldon.

Bostian: Ambitious Norsundrian military captain, obsessed with making himself king of Sartor.

Connanre of the Host of Lords: A charismatic musician. It's still unknown if he was turned or born without a vestige of conscience. He was the one who precipitated the Fall of Old Sartor by turning one of the rituals into a bloodbath, it is said to win the attention of Yeres. He is the Host's master spy.

Dejain: [deceased] Mage specializing in dark magic, one of a succession of Norsunder Base commanders, who tended to be summarily replaced by violence. Now deceased

Duin, Fassler: Imry Llyenthur's chief aide-de-camp. Born in Chwahirsland.

Efael: Considers himself one of the Host of Lords, the authors of Norsunder. Has a penchant for cruelty. He is the Host of Lords' chief assassin, bloodhound, interrogator, and errand boy; he and his sister Yeres consider Detlev their rival for a seat among the Host of Lords.

Elzhier: One of Connanre of the Host's best spies. She joined Norsunder as a young, angry teen.

Henerek: [deceased] Ambitious low-ranking young Norsunder military captain, originated in Everon. Wanted to be one of the Knights of Dei, but was cashiered due to excess cruelty, drunkenness, and inability to follow orders. Led a brutal war in Everon, now deceased.

Host of Lords: Authors of Norsunder, existing beyond time, readying for a second try at taking the world. Or worlds. Why, and who, they are will become clearer in succeeding volumes.

Hyath: Very young, ambitious, and cruel mage studying under Yeres.

Ilerian of the Host of Lords: Currently wears the shape of a beautiful and promising morvende, though morvende did not come out of their caves until a couple thousand years after the Fall of Old Sartor. The story put around is that his turning was Detlev's first act on emerging from Norsunder-Beyond. Ilerian is the architect of Norsunder he founded Norsunder-Beyond using the life of the architect, Sfenaraec.

Imry Llyenthur: Shares field command of invasion with Efael of the Host. A mage and a martial artist, he has Dena Yeresbeth. He's essentially a strategist.

Lesca: Apparently lazy steward in charge of Norsunder Base. Overlook her at your peril.

Svirle Treloar of the Host of Lords: He was heir to Yssel and still uses that title though Yssel is long gone. His underlings address him as "Lord Svir", the word 'lord' being an ancient title. He was the organizer of the Fall of Old Sartor, recruiting and forming plans. He is the ultimate in assumed privilege: nothing he does could be wrong because he deserves the world. It was he who lured Ilerian to the world, then discovered that he could not control this fascinating entity, so he exerts himself to function as go-between between Ilerian and everyone else.

Theronezhe of the Host of Lords: Their military chief.

Yeres: She and Efael, her brother, were born off-world and so thoroughly and spectacularly corrupted that they caught the attention of Svirle of Yssel, one of the authors of Norsunder. Yeres is a powerful mage. She and Efael gladly execute the errands that the Host of Lords, steeped in evil, consider too distasteful.

Ex-Norsundrians

Detlev Reverael ne Hindraeldrei: Chief visible mage and sometime military leader, answerable to Norsunder's Host of Lords. Born four thousand years ago, has lived in and outside time ever since. Like his nephew Siamis, has Dena Yeresbeth. Left Norsunder in 4753: much speculation on both sides as to why.

Kessler Sonscarna: Renegade Chwahir prince with considerable military abilities, forced into Norsunder as a result of treachery by the mage Dejain. Hates Norsunder. (See *Chwahirsland* below)

Siamis Reverael: Nephew to Detlev. Formidable mage, and like Detlev, has Dena Yeresbeth. Left Norsunder previous to Detlev, after furnishing the means to free the Venn from an eight-century-year-old binding of their magic. Adopted Yanli, the last descendant of someone Siamis was close to on his first visit to Sartorias-deles. He has reason to believe that the woman, Isa Cassadas, was pregnant with his child before he was forced to return to Norsunder. They were both teenagers.

Sveneric Reverael Hindraeldrei: Detlev's son, trained with the boys.

DETLEV'S BOYS

Adam: Artist, formidable talents in Dena Yeresbeth, artist until his hands were ruined by Efael

Alaki (Ferret): Acutely observant, aware of overlapping worlds, spy

Curtas: [deceased] Strongly responsive to line and harmony, especially in building

David: Captain of the group, best in most areas

Erol: Chwahir born, plucked off a battlefield. Excellent at stealth

Edde (Noser): [deceased] Taken from another world, at best a mascot

Laban: Volatile and longing for what he cannot have, a Dei descendant

Leefan: Quiet, strong martial artist, cousin to Rolfin

Mal Venn (MV): Martial artist, studying magic, excellent sailor

Rolfin: Cousin to Leefan, superlative martial artist

Roy: Strong Dena Yeresbeth, mage and scholar

Silvanas: Martial artist and horse master

FOR MORE INFORMATION . . .

Visit the Sartorias-deles wiki at http://reqfd.net/s-d/

I fled Him down the nights and down the days

I fled Him down the arches of the years

... I fled Him down the labyrinthine ways

Of my own mind, and in the midst of tears

I hid from him, and under running laughter.

Up vistaed hopes I sped and shot precipitated

Adown titanic glooms of chasmed years

From those strong feet that followed, followed after

But with unhurrying chase and unperturbed pace,

Deliberate speed, majestic instancy,

They beat, and a Voice beat,

More instant than the feet:

All things betray thee who betrayest me.

—by Francis Thompson, taken from "The Hound of Heaven"

PART ONE

Norsunder-Beyond

TIME IS DISTORTED THERE. Its measure is meaningless within it. And yet, much as its authors strove to master eternity, there was still some correspondence to outside events.

It is time to return to Hibern of Roth Drael, slammed into Norsunder-Beyond by Ilerian early in the invasion, to be dealt with at his leisure, before Kessler warded Sartorias-deles from such transfers.

It seemed to her that she had been walking, and walking, and walking, until she consciously heaved a huge sigh.

The heavy air of Norsunder did not stir.

She seated herself on a featureless stone bar. Pressing her hands down hard against its rough sides, she subjected her surroundings to a kind of desperate, close scrutiny. Rising panic demanded some kind of touchstone to reality. She rubbed her fingers against the gritty cement, concentrating on every sensory detail. It was too uniform a gray to be granite, despite the feel. It was about three feet high, twenty or so paces long. No discernible purpose.

The ground beneath her sandals was compressed, slate-colored dust. Gritty dust. It stirred when she kicked at it, and hissed when she ran her feet over it. The dust seemed to hang in the air before settling. It left no prints. Yet it did not cling to the hem of her gown.

A chill tightened the flesh along her upper arms. The air

around her was still, cool, and though she was wearing a light summer dress she had a feeling she would sense nothing different had she put on a heavy woolen winter gown before disaster overtook her. The chill was due to fear.

Her shoulder still ached, at five distinct points, where Ilerian had taken hold of her and thrust her—here, into Norsunder, the stronghold, for millennia, of the enemy.

She spoke out loud. "How long have I been here?" The sound of her own voice flattened, like the dust around her. She could almost see the distortion. She wondered if someone standing five paces away would have heard.

Very well then. She had tested the senses, all but taste, and...

She sniffed. There was no smell.

She bent, and sniffed the granite, expecting grit, or moss, or mildew, or dry rock: nothing.

She dropped her head into her hands, struggling to calm the frantic throb of her heart.

After a time she raised her head with a defiant jerk, and glared at the dull, dark horizon. "All right. If no one hears me, then why not speak aloud? I do not think much of your plans, Norsunder. In fact, I'm getting sick of your lack of direction. Sick of lack of air, lack of space, of perspective, of time—" Her voice trembled.

She got up and began walking again.

It seemed she had been walking for endless hours. She didn't really ache physically, but she got so bored she thought she ought to, so when she spotted one of those stone bars, she would sit and rest. But sitting was not restful, so eventually she would get up again.

And walk.

And walk.

Her surroundings remained featureless gray, stretching out for a day's journey—or a year's. Or maybe she was walking in a circle. She felt constrained, yet in all her walking she had yet to reach any kind of boundary. The 'sky' curved eternally overhead, lightless and impossible to measure. Could she touch it if she jumped? Or was it limitless, like the sky above the world? There was no light source anywhere, yet she could see herself and a certain way ahead and around and behind.

No hunger, no thirst.

Panic-panic-panic. Again she forced the stale air into her

lungs and slowed the heartbeat crowding her throat.

She began to walk faster.

On arrival she had seen people. In fact, she retained a confused image of buildings—or some kind of squarish obstructions—before she realized that Ilerian had unaccountably not come through the transfer, and she had run to escape before he appeared. Fear had given her the illusion of speed. She'd lost sight of those buildings, or whatever they'd been, almost immediately.

It would almost be a relief to see someone, she realized, though anyone she would find would be an enemy.

"What I must do," she said out loud, "is to find a way out."

Lengthening her strides, she watched the placement of each sandal, the passing of dusty ground beneath her feet. One, the other. One. The other.

Onward.

One

LARKADHE, A PLEASANT CITY once fortified, not far from Lindeth Harbor, was where Imry Llyenthur, commander of the military side of the Norsundrian invasion, had unaccountably chosen to set up his headquarters.

Just after dawn Llyenthur arrived in the room he'd adopted as a study to find his aide Duin waiting complacently.

Llyenthur didn't look at all like a Norsundrian commander. Impatient of appearances, he was dressed in his customary baggy tunic, the laces untied, loose long trousers, and soft-weave mocs instead of riding boots. He almost never wore weapons, at least not visibly. His hair grew in neglected sun-bleached light brown locks straggling down his back, but Duin and the rest of his staff had learned — the hard way, as everyone did in Norsunder — that he was stronger, faster, smarter, and much meaner than any of them. He was also moody, and his sense of humor and his temper were sometimes indistinguishable. Though they complained about him with creative invective behind his back, they respected his temper — and his ready fists — enough to follow his orders with care and exactitude.

He dropped into his chair and began sorting the pile of reports that lay on the desk.

"Two captures today," Duin began.

"Only two?" Llyenthur murmured, eyes scanning rapidly down the second sheet of the report. Duin wouldn't be so smug if the bags had been flunkies. "Who?"

"Couple of kings. Hier Alverian—"

"Good." Llyenthur turned to the third sheet.

"—and! Andri Elsarion of Enaeran." Llyenthur glanced up from his reading as Duin went on triumphantly, "This one knows where the cap-list whites who were in Mearsies Heili are hiding, and what's more, he's got instantaneous communication with them." Duin smiled in triumph as he laid down the report he'd been keeping to himself.

"What's this?"

"While Elzhier was poking around the Enaeraneth capital, trying to pick up Elsarion's scent, she stumbled on a loudmouthed brat, one of the inner members of his old gang. She cultivated him for a week, got him drunk, and he started bragging about this magic paper that Elsarion kept hidden in the city there. He'd come in every so often, write on it to Liere Fer Eider and the queen of Sartor, among others."

"Detlev?" Llyenthur asked, fanning himself gently with Duin's report, which he knew would go into exhaustive, and irrelevant, detail.

"Him, too. So said this brat. Anyway, she thought he was lying until she found out from an unrelated source that Elsarion showed up in town every week or so for some obscure purpose. Another drunken revel and the brat revealed where the paper was hidden at least part of the time. She set up a watch last night, got a patrol from me—not from Marsael—and when Elsarion showed up at dawn, they nailed him."

"And the paper?"

"On him. No one has touched it."

"Very prudent. And our friend Adon Marsael?"

"Knows nothing. She said when she commandeered my patrol that she had orders from you to act completely on her own."

It was a question as well as an answer. "Yes," Llyenthur said. "Where is she now?"

"Went to find Liere Fer Eider. That brat said she's in Sles Adran organizing the resistance efforts there."

Duin didn't expect, or want praise. He wanted an edge on the other aides.

Llyenthur tapped his fingers meditatively on the pile of

reports for a few heartbeats; he'd always expected the lighters to put together some kind of comms, but not so soon.

"Better have him up now. Other concerns will have to wait." He picked up the reports, and began scanning them much more rapidly than before.

Duin went out at once.

His disappearance from the room removed him from Llyenthur's attention. A very short time later, just as the reports had been separated into two stacks, the sound of scuffling outside the study heralded Andri Malcolin Elsarion's appearance.

He was flanked by several big gray-tunicked guards who thrust him into the room and then at a sign from Llyenthur effaced themselves, shutting the door firmly behind them.

"Andri," Llyenthur said, trying not to laugh. "Make yourself comfortable. As much as you can," he amended, eyeing with increasing amusement Andri's battered and tattered appearance. "Perhaps I ought to have asked Duin how my patrol fared."

Andri grinned, slowly flexing the mangled left hand that Llyenthur's resident medic had just finished wrapping up. "You can still use a couple of 'em."

"A couple of them," Llyenthur repeated, miming the round eyes of someone Properly Impressed. "My, my. But here! Have a seat." He indicated a nearby chair, and his amusement increased at the speculative expression in Andri's face. "Please! You really would be better off not trying to prove the truth of your formidable rep just now."

Unquestioning surrender was not part of Andri's nature, but neither was he suicidal. He was in a tower with an unimpeded hundred-pace drop beyond the window. A squad of rather annoyed armed guards waited right outside the door. Andri had a broken hand and a skull that ached from the sword-hilt blow that had felled him earlier, ached so much that his eyes seemed to rattle in his head every time he blinked. And this Llyenthur character was lounging back in his chair, completely at ease—which Andri recognized as a warning. You didn't even have to note the muscle definition where his sleeves pulled against his arms, or the obvious strength in those long, loosely clasped hands.

Andri sank into the chair, and stretched out his scruffy booted feet before him. "You're more spindly than I thought," he admitted.

"Spindly!" Llyenthur exclaimed, glancing down his own length as if in amazed discovery. "What? I'd say we're much of a size, you and I. We'll have to try a couple of falls when that heals up, if you like." He indicated Andri's broken hand. Then he paused, his green eyes going distant in focus. When he went on, the friendly expression was still there, but his tone flattened. "I've waited a long time for an opportunity to talk to you. What I'd really like to hear is your opinion of the organizational abilities of our mutual friend, Adon Marsael—"

Andri made no attempt to hide how unexpected he found this question, but just as he opened his mouth to answer a dark flicker in the air presaged transfer magic. A tall, sharp-faced young man dressed in black appeared, familiar to Andri from the bad old days as Efael of the Host.

Efael glanced at him, then turned his faint, unpleasant smile on Llyenthur. "I'll let you know what I find."

He gripped Andri's arm and they transferred out.

Llyenthur went to the door, opened it. "Duin!"

The aide appeared a moment later, his eyes searching the room in mute question.

"Efael," Llyenthur said, picking up the smaller of the two piles. "Find out if Alvar Zhendarei has a paper, or if he knows anything about them. And send word to the rest of the trackers." He waved the papers in a gentle salute at Duin's frustrated expression, made the transfer sign, and vanished.

Two

AS SOON AS THE transfer malaise released Andri, he attacked.

Efael was hoping for just that. After flooring the already-battered Andri with excruciating expertise, Efael signed for a couple of waiting guards to pick him up and hold him. He turned to speak to the commander while Andri blinked, his vision swimming. He'd heard enough references to the beauty of the place the Host had taken over to be considerably surprised to find himself in a windowless, heavy stone-walled room with dank, cold air. Just after he realized he might not be in Imar at all, his attention was caught by the commander's stiff and fear-sharp voice: "Yes! It will be done!"

Efael turned his attention to Andri. "Where's this magic paper?"

"Magic paper?" Andri repeated blankly, though he knew it was a losing gambit. Llyenthur's goons had seen him cram it into his breast pocket when they'd attacked, and sure enough Efael glanced that way.

"Get it out," he said.

"'Fraid I can't reach it." Andri held up his bandaged hand. "You'll have to get it out yourself."

"Get it out with your right hand," Efael said. With that he established that he wasn't going to touch it.

"No."

Efael said, each word distinct, "You're going to take it out, and you're going to write to Yustnesveas Landis, or Detlev, or whoever's at the other end."

"No."

This time Efael smiled with anticipation. "Lock him up," he said to the commander. "Have some fun. But I want him to be able to see, and to write. And keep him pretty for my sister."

Since the Host had been forced to remain in the flow of time, Yeres had become increasingly sensitive; it was the smells of torture more than the sight that disturbed her. Bodily secretions, but mostly any sign of decay, infuriated her, for such things were the inexorable reminder that every day she had to spend in the world doing things like eating and sleeping made her one day older, and unless she was vigilant, it meant she was one day less perfect.

Efael left Andri Elsarion to the rough hands of the guards, and transferred back to Narad. He walked into their suite in the heart of the fortress, where the distortion of time was strongest. Here, Yeres had forced that disgusting, reeking old wreck to turn over his own suite to them. "If you want escape from time," she'd said sweetly, "then you had better double your efforts here, don't you think?"

She had also forced Wan-Edhe to import the trappings of a semblance of civilization, lengths of painted fabric to cover the bare stone walls, golden fixtures such as lamps and leaf-shaped tripods to hold glowglobes, a bed big enough for both brother and sister when they were in the mood, and trunks of silk for clothing. More gold arrived by the wagon-load, shaped into belts and pins for her draperies, and earrings and crowns as ornaments.

She looked away from her polished mirror. "What?"

"They have a comm system. But it seems to be closed circle."

"Like the lovers' lockets of the days of Tivonais?"

"Yes. Though this is paper."

Yeres pouted prettily into her mirror. "I do miss Tivonais."

Efael had been hearing that for centuries, and it was no more interesting now. "Then you should not have killed him," he said—as he invariably did.

Her usual rejoinder was that it was impossible that he should have any other man or woman after he'd had her, but repeating that was a reminder of the dreary drag of days, and she turned, angry, for she'd actually been able to forget time while inventing new and pretty clothes.

"Yeres. I want your help getting the key to this comm paper."

"What do you want me to do about it?"

He smiled. "It's Andri Elsarion."

"Oh!" She was interested now—she hated it when her marks got away.

"I have to go set up the wards for Detlev. Because I mean to force Andri to write an invitation."

"Can I watch?"

"You can do better. Have fun with Andri while I do the magic, but leave him able to write. Or you can help me: I want tight wards, mirror wards so that Detlev cannot escape. It will take effort."

"Bring Andri here."

Efael sighed. "And risk Wan-Edhe getting at him? You still haven't found all his tricks. He could slither in from anywhere in this shit-hole."

She debated arguing. She hated going out into the drag of time, but when Efael got like this, he'd remain stubborn, and maybe even keep her from the fun. "All right."

Andri was stuck in a bare, windowless cell, lit day and night by a single glaring glowglobe. His arms were shackled behind his back, the metal of which grated painfully against his wrist-bones every time he moved even slightly, and these irons were attached to the wall by a length of heavy chain which was not quite long enough to permit him to stand erect or to lie down. He was very rarely given anything to eat, and scarcely more frequently allowed sips of water before being shackled to the wall again.

Despite her promise, a week of magical mind tortures was all Yeres could spare, after which she fled back to Narad and examined herself feverishly for the tiniest sign of aging. As she was the physical equivalent of twenty or twenty-one, it was unlikely she'd find any—though in the culture she had come from, women often had a raft of children by that age. But she was obsessed with preserving her youth. Nothing was as important as that, until the Host found the way to eternal life at last. Nothing.

Efael was also prevented from spending much time

playing in the dungeon. There was one demand after another, like watching that shit Imry Llyenthur, who seemed to have lost all interest in Andri Elsarion, much to Efael's disgust. There were also Svir's demands, which must be dealt with promptly: they still had not broken through to Mearsies Heili, despite a massive cordon of ships almost hull to hull. And there was that whitehaired prettyboy Jehan Merindar somewhere east of Sartor's continent, sabotaging Efael's eastern fleet. Those idiots in the ship yards could not build fast enough!

It took two weeks before Efael could get back to Andri.

He distrusted whatever magic was on that paper—but there was no true control spell that would force people to do what they were told, outside of reducing them to soul-bound. Who were nothing more than animated corpses, no more aware of what they were forced to do than rocks. Efael could have killed Andri to make him a soul-bound, except that these were so very boring. Much, much more fun was the humiliation of constraining an annoying prisoner to surrender to his will, fighting a battle they could never win.

The only spell available was a partial stone spell, that is, a spell that would freeze a target who took an undesired action. This spell was not always trustworthy if the target fought hard enough. Efael had discovered that it was far more successful when the target had been physically weakened—such as Andri was now.

"Get the paper out, and dip your pen," Efael said, and began to pulse the stone spell.

Andri fought it. But the only movement that did not freeze him into a painful numbness was when he moved in the direction Efael wanted. Pulse. Pulse. Pulse. He was sweating and nauseated as his hand reached slowly into his pocket and retrieved the grubby paper, and laid it on the board. Pulse. Pulse. Lightning lanced through his brain, but not enough to hide Efael's smile of pleasure, the unblinking dark eyes as he watched Andri's fingers close on the pen. Pulse! Andri dipped it into the ink, jerking his hand so the ink well spilled—but a guard set another one down.

"Write Detlev's name," Efael began.

One last surge of resistance enabled Andri to draw a line, right to left.

And the paper vanished, as Siamis had promised.

Efael turned away in disgust, releasing the stone spell

compulsion. Andri's head fell forward onto the lapboard with a hollow clunk.

"He's yours," Efael said, which made one of the guards grin and the other rub his hands.

Efael transferred back to Narad to complain to Yeres—while back in the dungeon, the guards grabbed Andri by the arms to drag him down to their play room. They got midway down a hall when a tall, thin assassin in black led three more in. The guards barely had time to draw breath to shout for reinforcement before they choked to death on their own blood.

Andri roused briefly. His resistance was purely symbolic as the new ones in black grabbed by the arms. He was saved further heroic but futile efforts as his vision smeared into darkness. A woman stood directly in front of him, staring intently up into his face. She seemed to be waiting for him to focus on her. His vision comprehended a round face and brown eyes.

She said in an urgent voice, "We're here to get you out. Do you understand? If you can move at all—"

Some of Efael and Yeres's nightmares had begun like this, but Andri would have tried escape until oblivion took him. He couldn't talk but gave as firm a nod as possible, then he ventured a step—

"Carry him," the woman said to the burly man holding Andri up.

She moved to the cell door, peered out, then waved. They left.

It wasn't until they were halfway down a corridor and Andri had counted four or five doors that he made a protesting movement. The man stopped. The woman whispered, "Something wrong?"

Andri worked his lips. "Others?" he croaked.

"And how will you get out?" The woman uttered a soft laugh. "Obviously we'll have to come back in. Right now you're the only one marked for execution. Let's go. The Norsundrians are all at the other end, but for how long—"

She broke off, leaving the obvious unstated.

It was a grim journey, but Andri did his best to remain awake and cooperative. The spiral staircase finally did him in; the flickering torches and his swimming senses smeared together and out he went.

When he came to, it was to find himself lying flat on a

cushioned surface. Darkness was soft on his eyes after the eternal glare of that cell.

Out of that darkness came the flicker of a candle, and a moon-round face. "Here. Drink this."

Some warm and savory broth went down—and stayed.

"Ahhh," Andri said, with utter conviction, and then he slept.

A couple more brief awakenings, which always brought more of the tasty hot broth.

Andri opened his eyes one morning and realized who he was, but not much else. His mind, now awake, flooded with questions. Movement showed he was still weak.

"No, don't try to get up," came a familiar voice. It was the woman again. She'd been there for most of his awakenings, but not all.

She had a cloud of tightly waving dark hair pulled off her wide brow, and heavy-lidded, almost lashless brown eyes and pale skin. She appeared to be a few years older than Andri. A quiet, controlled face.

"Who are you?" Andri croaked.

"Does it matter?" she replied. "You can recover here, and when you feel better, be on your way. Or if you decide to join us, I'll tell you more."

"Underground resistance?"

"Yes. As to why I'm here, I too am out of action for a time, so to free up the others I play nursemaid." She held up a wrapped arm. "We were hoping you might have some information on Norsundrian movements, or know someone who can help us in our work. We thought you were foreign, though you seem to speak Scaerth well enough."

Andri grinned a little. "I'm Enaeraneth, and the language comes easy because of a spell."

She pursed her lips, then said, "You want to sleep? If talking tires you I'll go."

"No. I'm awake for a time. Wouldn't mind some listerblossom, though. Green kinthus, if you have it."

She got to her feet, her slinged arm moving easily against her. "I'll be right back."

Despite his words, he fell into a light doze, but woke again when she reappeared carrying an enameled cup from which a pleasant-smelling steam curled up.

She set the cup down and helped him prop himself up on

big straw-stuffed pillows. "Those will cover you if they search, and we'll hope they don't sit down," the woman said with a low laugh.

Now that he was sitting he looked around. He was in a low-ceilinged room with a wide window adjacent to his couch that looked out over a vegetable garden. A burly man stood guard within view, his attention off beyond the edges of the whitewashed walls of the house.

Andri wrapped his fingers around the cup and watched the gleam of sun in drops of dew on leaves, blossoms, and the slow-hopping progress of bumble bees around a plant with bright yellow flowers. Butterflies flickered here and there—

His reverie was broken by the woman. "So," she asked, "how did you get caught?"

Three

Sles Adran to Ghildraith Mountains (North)

LIERE FER EIDER ELSARION took out her magic-paper—at last, an answer, after two weeks of silence from Andri. There was always a lag, as he refused to carry it with him, but this was by far the longest silence.

However, when she looked at the paper, instead of Andri's messy scrawl, she found a neat, small, unfamiliar script:

> *Liere: can you meet Detlev at the Selenseh Redian south*
> *of Ideygo? He says you know how to find it. Sveneric.*

Liere slapped her inner pocket, where the magic-paper she was supposed to give Detlev still resided. At least it was not wintertime. And Andri had even told her there was a back way to that Selenseh Redian that would not involve trying to find the wary flying folk—a route that the Norsundrians apparently didn't know about.

Three weeks later, she stepped down onto a cliff-ledge in the mountains between Shingara and Ideygo, and drew a long, tired breath. There was the cave.

The summer air so high in the mountains was clear, the light sharp, the sun warm on her face and arms. Shrub-greened rocky crags towered above, and beyond them layered clouds tumbled toward the east. The air on the cliff was so still that her mocs crunched audibly in the dirt. She half-expected some hideous apparition to manifest itself between her and the entrance to the Selenseh Redian, or Imry Llyenthur to step smilingly out once again, but nothing happened.

Cool air smoothed her cheeks and brow and caressed her sweaty scalp as she passed into the Selenseh Redian. She scouted mentally, finding no traces of human minds in the vicinity. Apparently Norsunder had given up patrolling the area, in favor of deploying their strained resources to trouble spots.

She walked into the glowing jeweled cavern, enjoying the pure, healing air. Magic tingled along her limbs like friendly fire and she danced a few steps, using cleaning magic to divest herself and her clothing of grit and grime mid-whirl. Then she sat down and pulled out her paper (which seemed the crisper for the cleaning magic) and wrote a quick note to Lyren-Sartora.

> *I've reached the Selenseh Redian. I'll write you again*
> *before I depart, or if I discover anything of interest.*
> *You?*

She received a cheerful reply from her daughter, whose quest for a magical artifact had been unsuccessful—a legend long disproved—but at least she was now safely back in Mearsies Heili with the rest of the gathering refugees.

Liere then tried to write to Andri. Her husband. Husband! Heat flooded her nerves, pooling deep when she thought that word. Their wedding, and their time together had been so brief, the memory seemed almost ephemeral. Well, her emotions had been so overwrought, especially coming so soon after—

No. The argument with Senrid had ended. He had offered the first toast at their wedding. Everything was good between them, even if it wasn't the same. But nothing ever stayed the same, right?

She dashed off a determinedly cheerful note to Andri. Time passed with no words appearing on the paper, and she sighed, wishing he trusted magic enough to carry the note with him instead of hiding it and traveling to it when he wanted to write to someone. What was going on in Enaeran that kept him from writing for well over a month? She would have been there by now, with him, if she had not been effectively summoned here—

No. She would not worry. Andri was remarkably adept at survival. And he was on his home ground, whose hideys and byways he knew better than anyone, having spent so many years as an outlaw.

She decided to catch up on shorted sleep, and settled down at the boundary of the soft, soothing light given off by the jewels. Cool air flowed in from the cave entrance some fifty paces away. She spread her cape over herself and curled up.

Liere started awake, and discovered Detlev walking to the entrance to look outward. "You're here!"

He turned back, and she laughed. "Drat! I toiled across three countries just to see the mustache and long hair that CJ has been cackling about. Did she make it up?"

Detlev smiled. "I got rid of the mustache. As soon as Imry saw it, it had outlived its purpose. The hair I still have." He obligingly turned around, and she saw the brown ponytail hanging down his back.

She was trying to reconcile the sight of Detlev, the villain of old, now with long courtier-length hair instead of the squared-off military haircut that was common among most Norsundrians.

Detlev said, "The short haircut was sufficient for my role at the time."

Liere folded up her cloak. "In the days of old Sartor you had long hair?"

"And up until relatively recently. Would you like a catalogue of my customary garments?"

She looked up, startled, to discover that the fearsome Detlev was making a joke.

"Not needed," she said briskly. "Anyway, you requested that I meet you here. Well, here we are. And I have one of the Siamis papers for you, though it occurred to me halfway up this mountain that surely you knew about these papers long before we did, and you probably have one already."

"I knew Siamis was in the process of making them, but I was elsewhere when he decided to bring them out. Thank you. Tell me about what you found in Enaeran and in Sles Adran." He slid the paper inside his tunic, and sat down on the ground within sight of the cave entrance.

Liere clasped her arms tightly around her knees. "Andri is spreading his resistance organization out from Shiovhan, and at first I helped, till he asked me to go to Sles Adran. I haven't heard directly from him for at least a month. He never trusted the magic-papers." She rocked back and forth. "I tried mind-call, but he was thoroughly blocked. Of course that's not surprising, these days. He was never adept at mind-touch even when there wasn't any threat of the Host listening. But he has always had a very good mind-shield."

"And Sles Adran? What did you do there?"

"Contacted the resistance, and tried to convince them to swap Princess Chantala Shagal's name for Andri's, which is what Andri wanted. We still cannot figure out how Andri's name got mixed up there. I also went to visit Chantala na Shagal, as Andri asked me to make sure she was all right. He wanted me to do it instead of him checking as he's still wary about a plot to match Chantala with him. It was her devoted nanny who admitted to the plot, but Andri doesn't know how many were in on it. And he suspects that plot might be why his name came up so much in the Sles Adrani resistance."

Detlev, as usual, looked inscrutable as he said, "Did you meet with Chantala na Shagal?"

"I did. And though she seems rather unworldly, I think she understood me when I asked if we could put forward her name. She said that she had administered Denwy, which I understood to be large and important, and so she would do her duty in Sles Adran if called to it. She might be more of a scholar and a poet than a wily ruler, but Andri and I both think she could rule Sles Adran if helped by good people. Anyway, the artists she's living with have helped her a lot. Though they modestly attributed her blossoming to the friend of her youth who recently returned to the village to help her."

Detlev inquired with mild interest, "Did you meet the friend?"

"No. What would be the point? Do you think the Norsundrians would waste a valuable agent on Chantala? And if they did want her, why leave her there?" There was no change in Detlev's face, but instinct nevertheless prompted her to speak. "Do you think the Norsundrians are involved there?"

"No. Go on."

"I was busy setting up lines of communication in Sles Adran and talking up Chantala as queen until Sveneric contacted me and said to meet you here." And she waited expectantly.

His smile was brief. "My turn for news. First, one can transfer from one cave to another. Most of the time. Though Norsundrians bent on mayhem still cannot get in. That is, they could, but they invariably find the magic…overpowering, let us say."

Liere gazed at him in surprise. "That's kind of disturbing. I mean, that the caves descry intent."

"To a degree that none of us comprehend. But the burn of dark magic doesn't help with access."

She accepted that. There were so many weird forms of existence in the world, she had no trouble believing that the Selenseh Redian would be, well, sentient in some way otherwise impossible to describe. "What have you been doing since you discovered that you can get around via the caves?"

"Visiting people and monitoring the Host from a distance," he said. "And Imry's organization as well."

"Should I spread the word about the Selenseh Redian transfers?"

"For now, it is best to keep it to yourself. It is important that the Host (and Imry) detect no mass movements of key people toward the Selenseh Redians."

"Then you don't want just the Norsundrians not to know about the cave transfers, you don't want anyone to know? Not even friends?"

"Not everyone, as yet," he agreed. "Let them continue to rely on their skills to elude pursuit for the present. I'm telling you because I suspect you probably would discover it on your own. And it would be understandable to want to share."

Liere considered that. The Selenseh Redian were all in mountains, six of the seven far from human settlements. The one in Mearsies Heili was the only one relatively near. People didn't think about going to the caves, ordinarily. She turned to Detlev. "They aren't secret in themselves. Norsunder knows about them. CJ was telling us not long ago about Imry Llyenthur sending half an army to chase you and David into one."

"All correct. Norsunder knows that the caves are capable of a certain amount of physical restoration, let's call it. They also know that time cannot be trusted."

"Siamis." Liere drew a deep breath. "When Tsauderei sent him to the cave, and he vanished for a year, wasn't it? Almost a year. He came out almost a year later, and he turned against..." *You.* "Norsunder. Of course Norsunder was watching, too." She wondered how much of a shock it had been to Detlev for Siamis to turn; her own pet theory had been that that was when Detlev began to turn against Norsunder himself. No one believed her, not that many years before his actual withdrawal from Norsunder in 4753.

She flicked a troubled glance at Detlev, trying to find a diplomatic way to frame the question, but he went on, "You will, no doubt, be moving back and forth for larger plans. I encourage you to use your stealth skills to get in and out of the caves for now."

Liere turned away and began picking at a bit of mica in the stone without seeing it, as her mind tried to race along several paths at once. "The Fall. The Host didn't destroy the Selensch Redian back then, right?"

"No, they did not, but they diminished magic so much that the caves were inaccessible for millennia."

"They won, but they didn't win," she said slowly. "The only ones who won were those who destroyed things to be destroying. But that wasn't the Host. They wanted something magical, something obviously powerful, am I right?"

"You are."

"And so they withdrew beyond time, to wait. But they are here now, so what they want is here?"

"They were actually on what might be called a scouting foray, and to watch the invasion that Efael initiated. But Kessler decided to ward them, forcing them to remain within time's boundaries."

"And no one knows why?" she asked.

"No one knows why," he agreed.

"But you have guesses?"

"I do. Which I will share if I get any evidence that supports them."

She frowned. "We all 'knew' as well as we know anything about Ancient Sartoran days that there was lots and lots of magic, and the war was terrible beyond any of ours in present records. I guess I've picked up Senrid's view that most of that is historical hyperbole."

"Efael agrees, which is why he precipitated the attack."

"But you don't agree?"

"Efael and I agree on very little."

All her instincts insisted there was something missing here, something very old, and very dangerous. He knew what it was. He might even be what it was.

In the distance, a night bird uttered a long cry, and she shivered.

Four

MAKING A GREAT EFFORT, Liere dismissed her speculations. Why scare herself?

Somewhat acidly, she said, "What *can* you tell me? For example, the status of my friends?"

If he knew the cause of her change of mood, he gave no sign. "Siamis is in Mearsies Heili still, and is aware of arriving refugees. Which friends are you concerned about?"

"How about Jilo? Did David find him?"

"Yes, and I believe their travels have proved profitable for both."

"Arthur?"

"Siamis says that he's in Mearsies Heili."

"Senrid?" She walked toward the cave entrance, then sat down, looking outward.

"Still in Marloven Hess, as far as I know." Detlev joined her.

Liere rubbed her hands up her arms as she gazed toward the strip of moonlit sea beyond Lindeth Harbor. "No further news of Hibern, I suppose?"

"No."

She tightened her grip on her arms. "You're sure Siamis's information is correct? I can't believe it! That she would challenge any of the Host. She was with us in Lisdan shortly before she vanished, and gave no sign of that kind of desperation."

Detlev replied, "I do not know the circumstances of disappearance, except that Ilerian was searching in western Colend about the time she was there."

Fear tightened its grip on Liere's heart. "So you know something of what the Host had been doing?"

"They have settled in Imar, as you probably know. Svirle tested Kessler's magic with quantities of his own—meant to draw Kessler—and Efael and Yeres used their own methods to try to hunt him down. Meanwhile Ilerian is building magical wards there."

"I see," she said, looking around again as if to reassure herself. Talking about the Host in this beautiful place seemed even more sinister, if just by contrast. She turned Detlev's way again, and said, "Imry Llyenthur told me he is David's brother, and I saw enough of the resemblance to suspect he wasn't lying. He wouldn't be the one of your boys who left, would he?"

"Yes." She could hear his amusement. "That was Imry."

"Then you know him."

"Very little any more. I saw nothing of him after he left."

"Why did he leave?"

"Several reasons, spoken and unspoken."

"Such as?"

Detlev laughed. "If you are really interested, I will show you my memory of our last conversation.

"Yes," she said instantly—more to see how much she could get from him, but she was also intensely curious. "Unless." She flung out a hand to halt the memory-share. "There's some horrible act involved."

"No." He laughed. "Merely talk."

Detlev offered mind-contact.

Liere was given the perspective of someone seated at a desk adjacent a window that looked out over water. Shipboard? Silvery light streamed in, reminding her of the quality of light over Geth-deles.

Then suddenly Imry Llyenthur was in the room, facing the desk, nudging against furniture and picking things up from the desk, examining them, and tossing them down again. He was immediately recognizable, though Liere had difficulty controlling her mirth at the unprepossessing differences between Imry-then and Imry-now. He was rake-thin, in ill-fitting clothes, blond hair waving down into his eyes and wisping out over his ears in wings. Bony hands never still, with large knuck-les emphasized by redness. Liere thought: *Either he chewed them or he fought a lot*, and Detlev's thought drifted back: *Both*.

Imry looked up abruptly. He said, "I'm leaving. I came to tell you."

Detlev replied, "Leaving the houseboat? The island?"

"Leaving *you*." Imry picked up Detlev's pen, flipped it in the air, and caught it again with the other hand.

"Since you are free to do what you like, you must have come to announce it for a reason."

"I hate being this age." Imry's voice cracked and squeaked on the last word, which caused him to laugh reluctantly. There was no resemblance at all to David in his bony, lightly freckled face with its brightly nasty green eyes, but for a fleeting, unpleasant instant—when he laughed—the corners of his mouth and his chin reminded her disturbingly of Senrid. "And I hate being held back!"

"So you've said. And I've pointed out I haven't held you back. I do withhold the things for which you're not ready."

Imry flashed a quick grin, jabbed the pen toward Detlev, and then flipped it spinning into the air before catching it. "So you say! But who's the 'you'? I'm tired of waiting on them."

"You're not waiting on them. Each is developing at his own pace, and each has different strengths, but as a whole their progress is steady. And you are not as far ahead as you think."

Imry snorted in comprehensive disgust. "You're deluded. Look at 'em. Laban's barely adequate with anything he touches, Adam's as squeamish as a lighter, Roy's just a lump, David moons and messes with books. MV's all right—or would be if he had a mind of his own, but he just parrots Siamis, who is a walking, talking turd."

Detlev said with some amusement, "You will find the regulars to be, as a whole as well as individually, even more disappointing."

"Maybe, but I won't have to baby 'em along. I'll be telling 'em what to do, and when they get in my way I'll rip 'em apart, and get promoted for it. Don't give me your shit about an army being stronger than one person—"

"But you still do not yet appear to perceive the distinction. I'm not forming an army, which is one mind controlling a number of trained bodies. You will act as a unit. Your strengths will be the greater for being the sum of each of its parts. But you must first learn cooperation and mutual trust."

"Trust!" Imry's voice was vibrant with bitter scorn. "What I see is MV and me waiting around while Adam learns to count his fingers and toes and not cry about missing the number."

"Adam may one day surprise you—"

"Yeah! By getting caught by a party of old women." The pen snapped in Imry's fingers. "He's a dolt. They all are, and you won't even let me kick some sense into his head. I'm sick of wasting time I could be learning magic. Instead you have me coddling them along."

Detlev said, "You may be the most advanced in weaponry, you certainly are the fastest, but you are not the smartest. I assigned you on basic-skills training to teach you patience."

Imry tossed the pen fragments onto the desk, his gaze wide and unblinking with anger. "Nor am I the strongest. You make sure of that, don't you."

"I have explained how keeping the Child Spell will be an unparalleled advantage in the field. And how that in turn will protect your autonomy."

Imry snatched up another pen and snapped it in two as he said with such disgust his voice cracked twice, "If we're as good as you promise we'll be we'd force our way up the ranks pretty fast and get autonomy that way. There's something else, something you're not telling us, I know it. And the only thing I can think of is, if we grow up you'll lose control over us."

Liere couldn't hear Detlev's laughter but she felt it—and underneath it, far down, she sensed his awareness of loss.

Imry flushed angrily. "I'll be back, when I've done what I want, then we'll see which of us was right."

And as Imry obviously waited for an answer to this challenge, Detlev said, "Yes, I expect we'll meet again, and we will see who was right. But if you change your mind in the interim, I'll always welcome you back."

Imry punched his fist into the back of a chair once, twice. "Your terms or mine?"

"Mine."

Imry slammed the door behind him, and the contact ended.

Liere gazed up at the distant, peaceful stars overhead.

Detlev said, "Have you an observation to offer?"

"You were sorry to see him go," Liere said.

"Yes."

"Speaking as a lighter, good riddance. Adam, Curtas, most of the others made the transition, didn't they? I remember those two especially were well-liked before we discovered the connection to Norsunder. But I don't think we would have liked Imry at all. I suppose your regret was mostly that he'd start a general exodus among them?"

"No, there was no danger of that." She could only see his profile against the blue of the lightening sky in the east, but she sensed a brief pulse of amusement. Then he was neutral again. "My failure was entirely with Imry, who resisted being part of a group from the first day I brought him."

"From where? I mean, what kind of person was the father, who gave up not one but two children! And David was a baby, yes?"

"Yes. The father was extremely smart, extremely cruel, with—or you would have heard more about him—a taste for luxurious living that outstripped his ambition. A woman who thought an exiled prince would make her a princess tricked him and bore Imry; he killed her for it, was going to kill the child, then changed his mind and decided to make the boy into an assassin to send against his father. You can imagine how terrible Imry's early life was. When I encountered them, Imry was a small, beautifully dressed malevolent nervous fury not quite five years old, who knew more ways to kill someone than many grown assassins. But then the grandfather he was supposed to assassinate died, and that plan went out the window. David was...the result of another plot that also ended with that death. I bought them both."

Liere breathed in the scent of pine as she assimilated the wretchedness of two innocent lives that ought to have begun with shining promise. "His name? The father."

"Kedran Llyenthur."

"No, before."

"Kendred Montredaun-An."

Imry Llyenthur's HQ - Larkadhe

When Duin saw who had appeared, he dropped what he was doing and—hiding his annoyance—asked, "Shall I summon Llyenthur?"

Elzhier shrugged, not bothering to hide her own annoyance. "Here's what he sent me for," she snapped. "Cram it up your ass." And she tossed a closely written paper onto the relay desk.

Duin met the eyes of the guard at the door, who went out to slip the word to the two waiting couriers that their wait had just been extended. Then Duin gritted his teeth, laboring to keep his face composed, as Elzhier pushed his papers aside and sat on the part of the desk at which he'd been working in order to stare at the big map.

Duin muttered the contact spell, and time began to stretch.

Elzhier completely ignored Duin as she continued to study the markers on the map, but Duin knew if he touched that carelessly tossed paper she'd round on him fast enough. So he simply sat and waited.

Then Llyenthur appeared, and Duin's nerves jumped as he observed the tight mouth and narrowed eyes that indicated his commander was in a temper.

"Elzhier," he said. "I trust you're here for a reason?"

She glanced at him, her contempt obvious, and jerked a thumb down at her report. "There you are. After a week of the most boring, tedious time I have ever wasted. Augh!" She went on scornfully, "Days and days of listening to that damned Elsarion fool blather on about his boyhood, and that piddling civil war. A few laughs when he got to the tangle with Marsael— but not enough to make the whole worth sitting through." She shrugged.

Llyenthur listened, smiling, without touching her report. "I believe I told you that Andri Elsarion likes girls, and girls like him. You must admit you're more winsome than I am. Or Duin, here," Llyenthur went on in a soothing tone. "You did what I asked, despite your distaste for the assignment?"

"Of course!" Her scorn changed to affront at this slur on her professional ability. "I was perfect. Or why bother in the first place? I sat and listened to him spout on and on about his worthless life, even to stories about some old crone singer he likes—" Her voice was suspended in revulsion.

"Then let us see what you produced." Llyenthur picked up the paper, and read it all the way through without commenting or changing expression.

Duin silently retrieved and reorganized his papers as Elzhier watched Llyenthur with a smug tilt to her chin. Let her be wrong, Duin thought. Just once.

Llyenthur finally laid the paper down, his brows rising.

"Tell me, Elzhier. When he mentioned his romances, did he give you names?"

"No," she said with relief. "Just sickening nicknames, like Doll Face and Rose Bud and the like. Why?" she asked, snapping the word out.

"Because this is trash," Llyenthur stated, and Duin rejoiced to see him give the arrogant spy that particular smile he had come to thoroughly loathe the sight of. "No, more than that, it's a joke."

Elzhier gasped, and Duin turned his back to hide the grin he could not suppress.

"He either figured out what was going on or he never trusted you. Senrid in Seth Aron, organizing an army destined to march on Larkadhe... Elzhier, you've been snowed."

"What?" She said through her teeth, "I'm going right back there now and I am going to strangle that turd in his sleep."

"If it will relieve your feelings to return please do so, though I strongly suspect from the look of this that he will be gone."

"Nonsense. He could barely get out of that bed."

"He talked to you precisely as long as it took for him to recover enough to do just that. Try to find him! But if you do, I want him here. I'm beginning to think Andri is —" He broke off, and looked Duin's way. "Attach Wilsar to Adon's service, Duin. Elzhier. Vent your spleen in a search, if you wish —"

"If he's gone, I'll find him," she promised.

"Whether you do or not, return tonight. I've something else for you, and far more to your taste."

She carefully performed the transfer spell, and vanished.

Llyenthur raised his gaze from contemplation of Elzhier's report, and smiled again. "A waste, Duin. If Andri's mind stayed intact through Efael's entertainment, he must have a mind-shield second nature to breathing. And what is more compelling than that, more even than weak as he was — and he was! I saw him when we smoked the guards right after Efael abandoned him — he figured out my little ruse. He also, despite Elzhier, and my people, managed to contact Detlev, and I strongly suspect it was one or more of my former brethren who pulled him out. They are the only ones who could get past Jarias's team."

Llyenthur picked up the report and dropped it onto the grate in the fireplace where it rested on several crumpled sheets discarded by Duin earlier. "Adam organizing a communication network of old women ... Detlev's been biting at my heels long enough. He must know I've got the message. I hope he decides on a confrontation soon."

And, thoughtfully, he half-lifted a hand toward the cold grate. He said nothing, nor did he move, but bright flame flashed with shocking suddenness and roared up the chimney, shriveling the papers greedily.

Duin decided to ask for an explanation some other time.

Selenseh Redian - Ghildraith

Liere said, "Senrid knows, I take it. About Imry being his cousin?"

"Oh yes. David told him about them both not long after we left Norsunder."

Liere's first thought was that Senrid never told her. Then, squaring her shoulders in the darkness, she thought firmly, why should he?

She dismissed the tangle of regrets, unanswered quest- ions, and discoveries made too late. She turned her mind to the various things she had learned this day. She looked at the timing, the lessons. All of what Detlev had told her was true— she knew that—but instinct became conviction. He had yet to tell her the whole truth.

The early sun lanced its rays across the valley, banishing the stars as it painted the mountains with striations of gray and gold and red.

She rose and went back into the cave. Detlev followed her. He had waited this whole time. For? She studied him closely, then said, "Where now?"

"Did you not intend to return to Mearsies Heili?"

She let her breath out in a rush. "I knew there was something. It's Andri, isn't it? Your summons—even your question about Sles Adran—you're watching for him, too, and he got caught, is that it? But he's all right. And he turned to you for help, and not to me. That's it, isn't it?"

"Yes. He's safe, And he is with MV now," Detlev said. Then he told her what had happened.

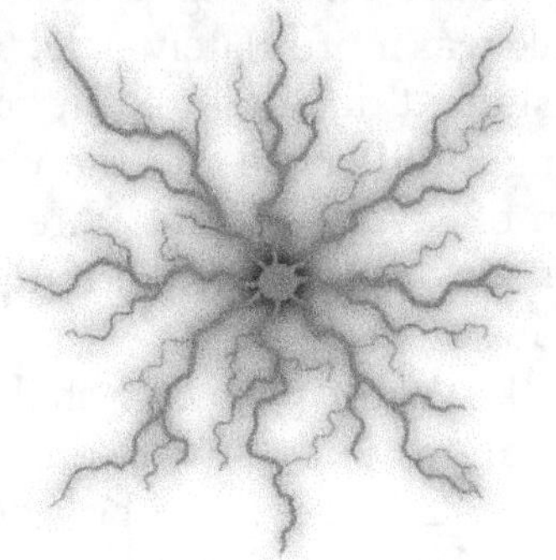

Five

Mearsies Heili

A SUMMER STORM SMASHED over the Toaran continent, pouring warm rain for half the night, to end just before dawn.

No one liked this weather except half-human Dhana, who of course would be out dancing in it.

CJ had become restless.

She cocked her head, listening to Aurora and the Delieth children, who were already awake, and racing up and down the stairs, their shrieks echoing through the palace. CJ mooched off in search of Clair, who had been continually surrounded by visitors ever since her return from Imar. She poked her head into the throne room, which had turned into a kind of giant parlor. The white palace was filled with refugees, and people tended to congregate there, it being the biggest room.

CJ was still not used to seeing those borrowed Arusian tapestries on the walls, beautiful as they were. No one had taken them down after they were put up for Andri and Liere's wedding. Clair seemed to like them, as well as everyone else. Same with the flowering plants in pots everywhere, and the cushions on the floor, which made for cozy groups. Changes, CJ thought, were okay everywhere else, but she didn't trust too many right at home.

It was far too early for free court. Atan, Clair, and Tahra

Delieth sat on cushions near the dais steps, reading over some papers that looked suspiciously like ledgers. Ugh.

Erenlara Sofar's golden head was turned toward Sherry and Falinneh, who traded off telling some story. One side of the Venn princess's face was inordinately pale, the other bruised by the blow she'd sustained during a recent border skirmish. She had taken to joining Puddlenose and the volunteers who went out under cover of every storm, threading through the Norsundrian blockade to escort in the refugees Siamis located by his ceaseless scans.

CJ stared at the Venn princess, shaking her head in a mixture of admiration and envy. Eren was good with weapons—better than CJ ever would be. She'd even gone back to fight the next day, but over dinner that night she'd fainted, while passing a bowl of cheese, her face landing smack onto her plate. She'd been the first to laugh when she came to after a few heartbeats, but it was a pained laugh, and the discovery that she also had three cracked ribs had caused both Atan and Tahra to confine her to the castle.

She was good at everything, but CJ had seen how the careless friendly overtures from the others girls had caused Eren to brighten like flowers after a rain. Whatever her life had been like in order to make her into this extraordinarily beautiful and adept girl, loneliness had been a big component, a loneliness made worse by the death of her grown-up brother.

Before he'd left, Sveneric had said to her, "Erenlara could use a friend when she goes north again."

CJ said, "I think so, too. But it can't be me. I'm not going anywhere without Clair, ever again."

Sveneric's expression shuttered. "Of course." And he never brought up the subject again, which made CJ feel guilty.

She'd been assuaging that by trying to entertain Erenlara, and make sure she got the best desserts and snacks. That reminded her. She'd promised to show Eren her records from past adventures. She suspected that Eren was too polite to ask twice, so CJ backed up and transferred down to the underground hideout, where she kept her drawings and writings, to see which one to offer first.

Dhana drifted into the room, which meant the rain had let up, and once again it was hot outside. "Writing more records?"

CJ scowled. "I still have to write down my trips with Dirk and Randon, but somehow I can't start. Anyway, I'm actually here because I told Eren she could read some. I started lookin' at 'em. Good for toughening up the stomach."

Dhana laughed. "Got mine there, too?"

"All of 'em, Clair's as well. I started reading and remembering, and being disgusted at the mess I made—"

"Ah, don't bore on about what a bad job you did in writing them."

"But it's true."

"But you'll never finish rewriting those things. And who cares how it's written, so long as it's written?"

"But it *does* matter. I was so wrong about people. About what happened. And I left out so much. Of course, a lot I didn't know at the time. Maybe I ought to go back through and add notes..."

Dhana sighed noisily, impatient with CJ's pickiness. Her memory as a human was clear and yet not; it took only the feel of wind and sun, of rain and snow, to bring back images and emotions felt during those times. Human senses bounded human memories. "Here we go again," she said, giving another loud, noisy sigh. "Mind if I quote along?"

"Only if you get the insults right." CJ forced a laugh. "I also half-promised to let Randon read 'em, because he liked hearing about our adventures while we were traveling, but now I'm not so sure."

"Written wrong again?" Dhana crossed her arms.

"Naw, I don't think he'd care if I made mistakes, or forgot to describe something that ought to be described. And I know he'll like the insults. But I'm not so sure about letting him read about old Pilo when he was a villain. And then, it's weird, but I never put in much about the good times. I seem to get paper and pen and ink out mostly after something nasty happened."

Dhana shrugged. "Jilo knows we all feel differently now. Including him. That journal is like a drawing. Of a time. One we cannot return to. Or have again."

CJ rubbed her eyes, trying to find words for what she meant. Strange, how Dhana was just like them most of the time—but then every so often there'd be this reminder that she was not quite human. Though you wouldn't believe that, looking at her pointy-chinned girl face, the splash of freckles across her nose, her mostly-blue eyes, the thin blond hair kept short at shoulder length so she wouldn't have to trouble with it. Dhana sat not like another girl would sit, flopped or curled. She leaned in a light, arrested curve, looking somehow as if she were about to take a step and fly.

Such a difference from her non-human form! CJ had been trying unsuccessfully ever since she first met Dhana to describe that form. The closest she could come was the lines inside a diamond's facets, except Dhana curved with the current. A live diamond? No, that sounded stupid — like somebody trying to be a poet, and only succeeding in being a pompous twiffler.

CJ shook her head impatiently. "I tried to write down Clair's birthday, a long time ago," she confessed. "This was before Mearsieanne came, and it was just us. I wrote down everything we did and said — I sat in the corner so nobody saw me taking notes. I described us all. Even me."

Dhana grinned, wishing she could see how CJ described herself. CJ was so short and skinny and definite. Her long, straight black hair, her stark blue gaze, her expressive face that never masked what she was thinking — what did CJ say about that? Probably something like, "I wore my usual green skirt and white shirt and black wool vest." And that's all, because she'd never see herself the way the rest of them did.

CJ scowled. "I went to bed thinking I'd done a good job, but when I reread it in the morning, it was just stupid. I didn't get down how Falinneh looks, how her voice sounds when she tells her dumb jokes, because that's what makes 'em funny. Then there were all the subject changes. I don't know, it was us but not us — not the fun, the coziness of the Junky when it's raining and we're safe inside with good food and no grownups telling us that making fun of villains isn't proper language, and oh, I threw it in the fire. I wrote it again, adding in all those things, and it kept getting longer and longer, and finally I was even boring myself, so I figured, if anyone else read it, instant coma."

Dhana shrugged. "Who cares what anyone else thinks?"

"But I wanted so much for someone in the future to know how our lives were back then, when the Chwahir were the worst villains we faced. And they weren't really all that bad, except when Wan-Edhe would come and order them to do horrible things or die. I wanted to remember how it was when Irenne was still with us."

Dhana's smile flashed. "How much she and I used to argue?"

"I didn't put in a lot of that," CJ admitted. "Now I don't

think I could. It doesn't seem fair to her memory."

"Why not? We liked to argue. Making up was fun, too. She was always so dramatic. So what are you going to do, toss 'em all in the fire?"

"No! Too much work went into them! I am going to rewrite them one last time, I decided, if we ever get this nasty war over with." CJ threw the journals back on their shelf. "And if Eren really wants to know, we can tell the stories out loud. Together."

CJ returned to the white palace's throne room, partly to speak to Eren, but she still wanted to see if last night's border patrol was back yet—and she still needed to talk to Clair, but not around all those listening ears.

She peered toward Atan and Tahra at the same time that Clair spotted CJ, then joined her. CJ dropped onto a hassock and eyed Erenlara, who had her arms pressed across her middle. "Their singing giving you a gut-ache, Eren?"

"Hey," Falinneh protested, as Sherry giggled.

Erenlara's laugh was rather insubstantial but mirth showed the more brightly in her quirked blue-violet gaze. "It is that there are such songs. We Venn do have songs of enmity, and of challenge, but they are very formal in their, how do you say it? Their invective. But not such songs, which are funny. Or if we do, I never was permitted to hear," she added, her head tipped to one side.

"Which insults did you like best? I hope it's the ones I put in!"

"This was a song in which Detsie—Detlev? He meets a goat, and a—" She gasped, pressed a hand again over her aching ribs.

Sveneric drifted up, noiseless as always. "If my father ever meets a goat, you can be sure he is polite."

"What if the goat isn't?" Randon asked at his shoulder.

Falinneh said, "Then he turns it into a human before it bites him!"

"Oh! You are back from the coast patrol?" Eren asked Randon.

"Just got back."

Atan, who had stayed up all night, turned toward the door expectantly, thoroughly aware of the absurdity of staying awake all night while Rel was chasing Norsundrians off the coast, while she had slept every night during the long winter months while he was chasing and being chased all over the Sartoran continent.

Randon began detailing the latest patrol. Clair's attention was on the signs of restlessness in CJ. She also suspected the cause. She learned over and whispered, "We can catch up on the patrol report from Puddlenose. Why don't we get a tray of berry juice for everyone?"

CJ nodded vigorously.

Soon the two Mearsieans sat side by side on the low terrace wall outside the kitchen. The strong breeze that dispersed the clouds overhead rustled the garden flowers. Birds cawed or twitted with musical abandon. They heard delighted shrieks from the towers high overhead, as Aurora and the Delieths chased and were chased.

There was never any question of amity between CJ and Clair being disturbed, but understanding had been strained during the horror of their recent experiences.

Clair watched CJ digging her toes into the mud and considered what to say. They'd been friends for many years, ever since CJ had left Earth forever to join Clair's gang. The girls all had embraced the Child Spell, and—most of them having escaped from bad backgrounds—had bound themselves into a family. But even families eventually grow up, and the invisible but perceptible tugs against that spell were there for some, if not for all.

The immediate subject was how much the two of them had hidden from the other while both were in danger. "Shall I say it first?" Clair began.

"Say what, that you will never go back to Imar, or anywhere near them?"

"I already made that promise," Clair said. "You heard me. And I meant it. I also know how much I endangered everyone here, since the wards protecting this kingdom are keyed on me. All I can say in my defense is what I said before: I really believed no one was better fit to find out exactly where the Host is staying than us, as none of the Host know us. All the mages have wards and traps waiting for them."

CJ said, "I can kinda see how, once you were there, and you found out they had prisoners, you didn't want to just leave people there. It was the same with Randon and me. We went to check on Caris-Merian, and next thing we knew, we had to help David the poopsie escape the clutches of that stinkard Llyenthur, and then we were running for our lives. We didn't mean to get into danger of being croaked. It just happened." She sighed. "What scared me was finding out how much danger *you* were in. You didn't say anything in your letters. But I didn't either, so I'm not pointing the Flying Finger of Doom at you, oh no."

"The fact remains I did endanger everyone," Clair said

"You didn't mean to," CJ said loyally, and because she knew Clair was right, she switched the subject to something less uncomfortable. "Here's the weirdest thing of all. I kind of like ol' Detsie-poopsie-potsie!"

"I never hated him. Once I actually met him, during the time I was a prisoner on the fifth world. He never tried to make me a Norsundrian. Instead he forced me to examine my convictions, right at the time I was doing that anyway."

Neither of them mentioned Mearsieanne.

"I hate thinking of that time, and I can't help wondering what business was it of his," CJ muttered.

"What business is it of anyone's? Is it Llyenthur's business to ruin kingdoms who never did him any harm? Was it Liere's business to figure out what was wrong with Caris-Merian, and to warn Detlev?"

"I don't know. I just hope you don't listen to that Siamis."

Arrow to the mark. Here was the true problem: change. As always CJ saw to the heart of things, even if she didn't understand what she saw.

And it hurt. Clair hid the pangs of regret, of guilt, of grief, aware that the invisible arrow was change. Not just change, but her lifting the Child Spell so that she could pass puberty and come into her own as a true adult, rather than half of one.

Clair knew it was going to happen. The tug had been imperceptible for several years now, mild enough to ignore as restlessness, as the call for action. Since Siamis had forced her to face the truth, there in faraway Imar, she'd known she would have to tell CJ someday that she was going to finish growing up—that it felt right to do so. But not quite yet. Certainly not during this horrible war.

And Clair shoved the entire subject away with long practice.

"I'm glad you're not mad at me." Clair sighed. "Anything else?"

CJ wrinkled her brow, not wishing to be perceived as being nosy, but she was genuinely worried. "Well. It's Dhana," she admitted. "This is about the fourth day she's spent more and more time in the water than out of it. And though she's always been moody — almost as much as I am — lately — " She stopped when she saw Clair grin. "She's come real close to picking fights. Ahhh, you're not surprised. You noticed too. Is it the war? Is she going to give up being human?"

"Goes back farther than the war, I think," Clair said. "To the time she and Roy went into Norsunder to find that magic thing that bound the Fifth World. She had to use her innate magic. She was struggling to stay human while wanting to revert to her natural firm. Norsunder has that effect."

"Is it because *she* hates change? She hated it when she thought Diana was going to join Dtheldevor's gang."

Clair did not point out that there was someone present in this conversation who loathed change far more than non-human Dhana. "She will discover that change is inevitable," she said gently.

"It doesn't have to be," CJ said stoutly. "We've had good years, and we can have lots more good years, if everybody stays safe."

Clair's straight brows went up, the only dark color above her hazel eyes and below the glistening white hair. "CJ, one of these days none of us will be here. But change doesn't all have to be bad."

CJ whooshed her breath out. "It's Norsunder. It's all their fault! Oh, I know, I know, not everything, or everyone, is 100% evil or 100% good. Though I don't know about that Efael, or those other creeps in the Host. They sound 100% evil to me."

"Perhaps the question is about capability," Clair said slowly. "War brings out the worst in some, who were considered good citizens before. And brings out heroism and generosity in others, who might have been less good. But I think Dhana has seen the truth of the fact that fear, as well as anger, makes us humans cruel. She sees how much Norsunder is in us all?"

CJ hated the turn this conversation had taken. "One thing I know for sure. There's no Norsunder in *you*." She ran back into the throne room, as Clair followed more slowly, after asking the kitchen staff for some of the berry juice they kept in chilled jugs in the ice room.

Clair entered through the back door just as CJ's bright, clear voice resonated through the throne room, "The pirate mustache! It's *gone*. Now no one will ever believe me!"

As Clair shot through the door, she glimpsed new arrivals framed in the double doors at the entrance to the throne room: Detlev and Liere.

The entire room had gone silent. Then Detlev, who had worn many guises over the centuries, said, "I will attest to the existence of the mustache to any who ask."

Liere pointed up at Detlev. "He still has the hair."

Everyone began talking at once, some laughing, before a shriek brought them all round to see Lyren-Sartora bounding into the room, arms wide. She charged straight at Liere and nearly dropped them both onto the floor as she hugged her laughing mother.

Intensely curious, Atan glanced from Liere and Lyren-Sartora to the former Master of Evil to see how he took this demonstration of sentimentality. Detlev looked as inscrutable as ever—and his attention wasn't even on Liere and Lyren-Sartora.

Atan turned her head to see Erenlara of the Venn gazing up at Detlev, her pale face emphasizing the steady solemnity of her dark blue eyes. It was Detlev who turned away, a broad smile transforming his face as Sveneric hurled himself into his father's arms.

Atan sensed a presence at her side; Rel had come in, and dropped down beside her. "Is Erenlara another Detlev hater?" she asked. "She never mentioned Detlev destroying anything in the Land of the Venn, or assassinating anyone."

"Not that I know of," Rel said.

There were levels to the haters. Both Rel and Atan turned toward Tahra, who still sat near the throne, her body tight with hostility as she set aside the ledger she had been working on and stalked out, her voice echoing sharply as she summoned her children to go straight to their chambers.

The Delieths vanished without making a ripple. Atan, tired from sitting up all night, and unwilling to admit it, was aware for the rest of the day how the atmosphere had intensified. She watched from a distance because she always did, but when she and Rel were alone, she said, "Was all that high hilarity due to Liere or to Detlev? It couldn't be caused by him."

Rel sank back on their bed, and crossed his powerful arms behind his head. "Beg to differ," he said. "It was precisely Detlev. You had to notice how everyone stilled, then he made the joke about the mustache, and Liere picked it up. Next thing, they were all yammering questions."

Atan frowned as she took out her hairpins. "You think he did that on purpose?"

"I do."

"Why?"

Rel shrugged massive shoulders. "So they'd yammer their questions."

Atan dropped a pin, and gave Rel a skeptical look. "I don't believe it. Why would he ever want to be pestered with inanities like, 'Do you have a secret army?' and 'How can we get rid of the Host?'"

"I think he picks up a lot by what questions people ask. Moreover, he can then ask a question here and there when everyone is already talking. Gets a readier response from those who might not say anything if he asked for a private interview. If they talk to him at all."

Atan considered that. "You mean, he used that joke, weak as it was, to…level the social expectations?"

Rel shrugged again. "Possibly. He can read minds, but I can't."

Atan began brushing her hair so briskly that it crackled. "Why is it," she said finally, "that when I use laughter, I think of it as perfectly benign, though I haven't always felt benign. But when I think of Detlev using it, I assume his purpose has to be sinister?"

Tsauderei, the old mage who had raised Atan, had taught her to laugh. Then he'd taught her that a queen's laughter could be a weapon, and it could be a tool. *Laughter is a natural leveler,* he had said. *It can diffuse tension. It can bind a disparate company. For a moment, when everyone laughs together, there is no distinguishing gender, or age. There is no duchas nor commoner. But laughter can also be used to enforce hierarchy, especially when those at the top use it against those at the bottom. When you become Queen of Sartor, you must always remember why you are laughing.*

"There's no getting past his reputation," Rel said. "He has to know it. Maybe he wanted to get Tahra laughing."

"That will never happen," Atan said. "I know some consider me humorless. And I am, compared to some. But Tahra has no sense of humor whatsoever. With her, the world is drawn in lines and numbers. This side is evil, that side is good. Detlev could save the world tomorrow, and however long she lives, she will be waiting until her last breath for him to turn it all to evil.

Because she will never forget or forgive Detlev for raising those boys, one of whom killed her brother."

"In a duel." Rel shook his head, and as she finished tying off her braid, he said, "We're probably both wrong. If Detlev wanted to talk to anyone, surely it would be you. And he wouldn't crack jokes to do it."

"Not I. There's nothing I know that would be of the least use to him. Surely he'd want a report on the rescues through Remalna. The secret harvest plan."

"He'd be better off talking to old Tsauderei if he wants to know about that," Rel said. "Tsauderei might be completely confined to his chair now, but his mind is as fast as it always was. It was his idea to set the refugees to secret planting, and he even told me the names of scribe chiefs in order to get the word out, which reduced me mostly to a message runner, like the old days before scribe desks." He shifted up onto his elbow. "Blow out the lamp, will you? We've got a night to ourselves. The sky's clear. Looks like maybe for a few days. At the end of which, I'll have to return to Sartor."

Atan doused the light, then crawled into bed next to him, saying,

"Let's not talk about Sartor. Or Detlev. In fact, let's not talk at all."

He uttered a low, villainous chuckle; the sheets rustled, and she gasped.

Six

HAVING BEEN UP FOR a day, a night, and another day, Rel and Atan had retired early. Most of those who sailed with Puddlenose had also retired, but the rest were vitally interested to have so infamous a person as Detlev among them. Even more infamous than Siamis, who so far, at least, came around very rarely, and never stayed for meals.

But when Janil, Clair's steward, asked Detlev if he was staying for supper, he said, "If it's not too much trouble, thank you."

Such politesse from a name that had only been spoken in whispers—usually preceded by curses—unnerved her, so she only bowed, and then cornered CJ. "You were traveling with that Detlev recently, I understand. What does he eat?"

"Good question," Falinneh exclaimed. "What do you serve a Master of Evil for supper? Even a former one?"

CJ snickered. "He told me and Randon that he likes everything except vegetables boiled into mush. But he'll eat it if there's nothing else."

Janil gave a nod. "That will do fine." And she bustled off.

CJ was perfectly ready to go off and ask what his favorite meal was, but when she finally spotted him in the hallway outside the library, he seemed to be deep in conversation with Mildred, the martial arts teenager from Geth-deles, who always dressed in black.

Was he recruiting her? CJ shied off again, afraid to be perceived as a poke-nose, but she was not the only one side-eyeing Detlev, wondering what he was there for.

More were gathering in the dining room than usual, but Detlev was not among them. Neither was Sveneric; those curious to witness the Evil One using a fork like everyone else had to squash their curiosity.

CJ encountered Mildred early the next morning, each of them racing in opposite directions on the stairs. CJ hopped to the side, and Mildred halted, putting out her hands to steady spindly CJ lest she tumble down the stairs. "Sorry," she exclaimed. "I am sorry, me."

"It's all right," CJ said, and then, because they were alone, "Last night. Was Detsie trying to recruit you into the poopsies?"

"The what?"

CJ reddened. "Uh, his group. You know, Roy and the rest of them—"

Mildred chuckled. "Ah! I remember. What you call them. No, no, I think there is no more recruiting—and it was so even when I used to scrap with some of them, ah, in the wanderers' city, on my world. When we were about your size."

CJ goggled at her. "You did? And you survived?"

Mildred laughed inside at CJ's appalled expression. "Eh, one or two were very rough. Very. But they never called me Snake Eyes. There were some there who did, ah, you know, behind my head? Where I could not hear? Except that I could."

CJ said skeptically, "They were *nice* to you?"

"One or so, the little one who was always covered with chalk, yes. The blond, quiet one. Curtas, yes, I remember his name. Adam and Curtas. The rest, eh, they called us all shitbirds, turd-sniffers, you know, the insults of that age. But that was everybody, from the rich ones to the ones who ran from very bad masters. You see?"

CJ, who vividly remembered the Earth version of school-yard bullies, said, "Oh, I know what you mean. They were stinkers, but not *snobs*."

Mildred twitched a shoulder, then said, "Detlev, he asked me to do something. I will go to do it now. There is no sailing, Puddlenose said, for days. It will be clear."

Avidly curious, CJ followed her the rest of the way up the stairs. "Can you say where you're going?"

"An island very far. The one Arthur went to. There is

someone wavering between Norsunder and not. Detlev says, I am the best person to help, that in ways he is like I was. Ah! I know what he means, I. And I shall do my best. CJ, would you do me a favor?"

"Sure!"

"Find Arthur. Will you ask him if he'll talk to me, and if so, bring him to my room? I'm going to pack a few things."

"Okay."

"Thanks."

CJ started down the stairs, then Mildred's voice, low and terse, stopped her. "CJ?"

CJ looked back over her shoulder. Mildred leaned down over the stair rail, her black hair swinging close to her face. "In case I don't get back. Find David, to tell Dak what happened about Caris-Merian. He's the only one who can convince Dak it wasn't his fault for not being able to stop her."

CJ agreed, her shoulders up under her ears.

It being directly after breakfast, CJ was confident that Arthur would be in the library—but for once he wasn't there. CJ looked all over that floor, then decided to ask Roy, as he and Arthur were rooming together.

CJ ran to the old upper ballroom, unused for over a hundred years. It was now the weapons practice room. A number of the refugees who patrolled on Puddlenose's fast tri-masted *Lheit* were there for practices once again overseen by Rel, just as it had been last fall when they were all hiding in Lisdan. Why does that seem a thousand years ago, CJ wondered as she scanned the room. But some things feels like yesterday. Like Irenne's death.

Roy was in the middle of a bout with wooden knives, fighting against Puddlenose as Arthur watched. CJ slunk over to Arthur, and as soon as she whispered Mildred's request, he went.

CJ turned to leave, for she could see at a glance that those there were far beyond her rudimentary skill level, but she slowed when Puddlenose dropped his knife, hooted a laugh, then said to Rel, "Lost again. Hey, Rel! How 'bout if you challenge Detlev?"

"Whew! That's a hot idea," Randon exclaimed as Roy—who was putting his knives in the rack—laughed.

Rel looked faintly surprised. "To what? An eating contest?"

"A swordfight!" Randon rolled his eyes in Overstrained

Patience.

"Why?" Rel leaned on his blade. "Doubt there'd be any difference this time from the last."

"What?" Puddlenose croaked. "What? When? Why wasn't I there?"

Rel rubbed his chin thoughtfully, then said, "Two, maybe three years ago. Maybe longer. It was when I went to see that house Curtas made for them."

"And?" Randon demanded.

"And what?"

"Who won?"

Rel's lips twitched faintly at the row of bloodthirsty faces. "He did."

Randon said, "Meaning no insults to anyone, but he's stronger than *you*? Seems to me he's half your size."

Rel lifted one massive shoulder. "Don't know. Faster with a blade, yes." And, seeing them all waiting for an explanation, he added, "It's Dena Yeresbeth, isn't it?" He addressed Roy, who shrugged. "Makes his control that much better. Anticipates movements, moves less, so he exerts less. The difference is slight at high skill levels, but slight is all that's needed. Who's next?"

Remembering Eren's reaction to Detlev earlier, CJ stole a glance at the Venn princess. There was no alteration in the blue-violet eyes or pensive profile at all. CJ found herself hoping that Eren wasn't a hater like Tahra, though she would never say so, aware that a lot of people thought she was the Olympic Champion grudge-holder herself.

CJ escaped at a run — almost crashing again, this time with Arthur, who was just coming in the door. They steadied themselves, both laughing, and she said, "Mildred got what she wanted?"

"Wasn't much I could tell her. I just transferred back from sending her through the Selenseh Redian," Arthur said. "She'll be able to sneak out without anyone seeing her."

CJ nodded, thinking, here's another who knows the secret of the Selenseh Redians. And *I* didn't accidentally blab!

She continued downstairs, this time at a decorous pace. Clair wasn't anywhere in sight. Eventually CJ was distracted by a chase game some of the younger ones suggested, now that the weather had cleared up, and went off to do that.

Clair was unaware of being sought. She had known that Sveneric had been giving Erenlara magic lessons in the alcove.

She was surprised to hear the rumble of masculine voices, and poked her head in to discover Detlev and Zairna in there with Sveneric. Eren was not there.

Clair began to back out, but Sveneric said, "There you are! Zairna was giving Detlev a more detailed report about Imar, which neither of us are likely to see." He indicated his father and himself.

Clair hid a pulse of panic. It seemed too convenient to find them all here. Had she been under some sort of compulsion—

Stop it. Stop it. She had seen compulsion in Imar. There was no compulsion here. It was a reasonable request. She knew that there were deadly wards awaiting Detlev in Imar, and of course he would want to hear an eyewitness account.

Zairna was just finishing up his description of what had happened. Clair was glad that he'd reached the end. She did not want to relive that experience any more often than she had to. Her dreams were bad enough.

Detlev looked up then, his gaze compassionate. Clair pressed her lips together. Did he know? How could he? She did not talk about those dreams to anyone, not even CJ, lest some of the more powerful minds pick up her worry. For CJ would worry. And her mind-shield wasn't always as effective as she thought it was.

Clair knew her own limitations. She would not go outside her borders again. She knew she could not prevail against millennia-old evil. She would *never* go back there.

Detlev said, "Thank you, Zairna. I've not yet conversed with Siamis at any length, but I gather he suspects there's a way in."

"I believe he is right," Zairna replied, with quiet conviction.

The import of his words exploded darkly inside Clair's mind. She looked down at the floor—her floor, in her home—and clasped her hands behind her, because she could not hide trembling fingers.

Breathe out. In. Pinch skin between fingernails.

Her focus stayed in the here and now. Sound, light, murmuring voices exchanging comments on alterations in Imar's geography rapidly rewove into sense: no one was forcing her to go. Nothing would happen to her here. And if anything she knew could help, she ought to share it.

She raised her eyes, and discovered Detlev watching her.

He said, "Do you have any additional observations to make on what you found in Imar?"

"No," she said. She nodded at Zairna Raadi. "We discussed what we saw, afterward. I think ... I think his statements will be clearer than mine."

"Can you tell me more about Yeres's attempt to trap you?" Detlev asked. "And the phantoms you saw, passing from there to here?"

Clair's mouth dried, but her voice stayed steady. She liked that. She listened to herself describe what she'd revisited in dreams far too often since. She did not describe her own fog-headed state of mind when she woke from the worst of those dreams. How sometimes her mind seemed stretched between Norsunder's otherwhere and the world around her.

At the end Detlev thanked her, and then a group of Clair's own friends appeared, bringing June.

"Found her," Dhana said to Sveneric. She indicated June, the off-worlder who, like CJ, had once lived on Earth. Teenage June was wary, distrustful: her experiences on Earth had scarred her far more deeply than CJ's had.

Clair backed up, closing her eyes.

A way in.

Ice stole through her veins and bones. That meant a way past all the powerful magic ringing the Host in order to stand face to face with them in their own citadel. Before one could begin an attack.

The urge, stronger than anything, to demand that Detlev and the others promise not to share this information warred with her inclination to keep silent, to stay neutral. Invisible, so *They* far away in Imar would never see her. It was far too easy to imagine CJ going with despair in her heart, to forestall the Host attacking Clair...

Breathe! It's just imagination! Yet she felt as soul-chilled as she had while standing in that hell-lit foyer of the castle in Imar.

"Yes, I do recognize it," Detlev was saying to June. He had taken the ancient silver cup briefly into his hands, turned it over, and now gave it back. "It's one of the five Protections of Alsheya. The fifth, in fact. The Protections were the focus, the lens of the magic of the Alshi on our fifth world." Seeing varying degrees of incomprehension in the faces around him, he went on, "Elesh Orom-alsh was — still is, no doubt — a world outside Erhal's system. There were a number of Alshi both in Sartorias-deles and in the fifth world. In the years before Svir began his assault on Old Sartor, a few of them had come here to observe, to learn, to teach."

His gaze rested last on June's round face. Clair noted the stubborn line to the girl's chin, the knit brow below the mat of brown hair. As if in answer to a question she was not willing to voice, he said, "The castle you described was probably their center on this world. I met the Guardian twice, both times elsewhere. I suspect what she was hoping for in setting up that enchantment the way she did was someone from her home world to free and use it some day after she was gone. But she also allowed for out-system-born people in case the rescuer might not be an Alshi."

"I've had no magic training of any kind," June said.

"But you've the potential to learn. More specifically, your mind was able to comprehend the time-bridge as she conceived it."

With the subject change, the poisonous overlay receded from Clair's mind. Relieved, she said, "No one else seems able to use that cup, except for the way it acted in Imar. Which was none of our doing. But is that it, that's its virtue, to remain invisible to evil, and to render people around it invisible?"

"I expect there's more," Detlev replied.

June eyed him. "Does that mean you don't know how to work it?"

"I was not taught it." Detlev touched the rim of the ancient silver cup. "As I said, I only met the Guardian, both times briefly. From what you describe, it sounds like the protective magic was set up over a scry stone with extremely powerful magic over it, a kind that does not currently exist, except in Norsunder-Beyond. Which is the mirror image of this magic, the cost quite deadly." He pointed to the cup, and smiled. "In the meantime, it holds water, doesn't it?"

Gwen's voice came from behind. "Hoo-ee! That thing is huge! I'd rather drink out of my hands!"

June said, "For practical purposes, it's better for holding paperclips, or pens."

"Socks!" Gwen—of course—had to offer more ridiculous suggestions.

Clair studied the cup, wondering if Detlev's suggestion was less innocuous than it had sounded. It was not his way to pressure this wary off-world girl by saying something like *This cup is incredibly powerful, and we could use that power – IF you figure it out.*

As jokes and laughter eddied around her, June scowled at the cup in her hands. Her pose unsettled Clair, evoking memory of that upstairs hallway in the Dei manor, the way her mind began to slide into that weird half-dream existence, as if she stood on the edge of a chasm, staring into—

Stop it. Fool! Of all the people in the entire world, you are the only one who is safe, she scolded herself. *Your kingdom alone is unassailable.*

She walked out, and was grabbed from behind by two small hands.

"Jessan and Carl aren't allowed to play. Why not? The rain's gone." Aurora sounded cheery, but her green eyes quirked in question.

"Have you asked permission very, very politely?" Clair said, trying to sound cheerful.

It worked. A flash of brown feet and flying white hair, and Aurora was gone, followed by Dhana and Gwen.

Clair turned, to discover Detlev waiting for her attention. "Have you considered the likelihood of the Host attempting to lure you out?"

Clair's lips parted, then closed. Private she was, but she wasn't foolish—or a liar. "You saw it?"

"Yes."

Not invisible. She hugged her arms against her, chilled again. Just a short time ago she was determined never to utter any of these words, but his question, so direct, so unjudging, had disarmed her. "Maybe my feeling that I've been poisoned isn't so fanciful?"

Detlev's brows quirked. "Siamis explained that, did he not?"

She sighed. "Right. And yes, before you start in on the lecture, I know I should never have left Mearsies Heili in the first place."

"Why did you decide to go?"

A shock of anger bloomed, then died when she realized that his question was not an accusation. It was a real question, implying there might be a reason she had not seen.

She took a long, steadying. "No, I never thought of them somehow worming the idea into my head. But if." Disgust made her shiver. "If one of the Norsundrians had somehow planted a compulsion in me, when? And why wasn't I aware? I haven't been in their hands since I was on the Fifth world with you and the boys, and I know you protected me from the real villains. Nor have I had any mysterious bonks on the head. Well. Obviously I have some thinking to do, and forewarned is forearmed. Anything else?'

The hint of challenge in her voice was met with neutral inquiry. "You're keeping an eye on crime patterns, even petty and widespread?"

"Of course," she said. "I'm well aware of the possibility of their sending in some skunky lighters who bypass the border enchantment, but can be controlled from the outside. And I already — long since — took precautions."

"Then you're ahead of me," Detlev said, smiling.

Clair knew when she was being humored, but she also knew she'd asked for it.

What she didn't suspect was how deeply troubled Detlev was by what Clair did not say.

Siamis, listening on the mental plane from the Selenseh Redian, said: *Can you bring her here and use the dyr?*

Detlev replied, fast as a flick of wings: *Don't need the dyr. She is as clear as water. Also, if Ilerian has found her, he'll know if I use the dyr, and that I am here, which is sure to increase the danger to everyone else.*

That was the threat: Ilerian would be as easy to grasp as poisonous smoke.

Detlev added: *You are going to have to be vigilant.*

CJ burst in then. "*There* you are. What's going on? Poopsie powwow? Wait, no poopsies here."

"Exchanging observations," Detlev said.

CJ crossed her arms. "Do you have any to share with us? Or are you going to stay all mysterioso?"

"I face many of the same constraints that you do," Detlev said — and Clair was glad to see that he answered CJ without sarcasm. "A general observation only, that the Host are restless. Feeling the pull of time."

CJ smacked her hands and rubbed them together. "Good! I hope they all get lumbago. Does it weaken 'em?" she asked fiercely.

Detlev said, "Not in any way you can count on to work to your advantage, should you meet one. It may force them to a confrontation sooner."

"D'you think that's what Kessler wanted to happen?" CJ asked, her blue eyes round.

"Impossible to say. Siamis reported that Kessler said little when they teamed up to free the prisoners in Imar. And he vanished afterward. May I look at your situation map?"

"It's Atan's," Clair said. "I'll go get her." She left—glad to go—and CJ ran with her, a sympathetic, comforting presence.

Atan arrived in the library, having just come from an unsettling interview with Tahra, whom she'd found dressed in traveling clothes, a pack in hand.

"The ledgers are up to date. Clair's heralds are more competent than I'd expected. This kingdom will be able to accommodate the influx for a year or two yet. I hope to be back by then."

"From?" Atan said.

"I cannot tolerate that man's presence, and how the rest of you defer to him," Tahra said—for her, evenly. "I am going back to Everon, to evaluate and to organize my people in reclaiming my land from the enemy. I will take the paper Siamis gave out; I can tolerate him, as long as there is no proof he's under Detlev's command." Then, before Atan could speak, "I commend my children to your care; teach them statecraft and history, or whatever you deem proper for royal children. The only thing I asked is that you do not let that man, or his spawn, anywhere near them. Promise me." She stopped, staring unblinking at Atan through eyes with the same distinctive Landis shape.

Atan stared back, fighting annoyance. But Tahra was who she was. She was unlikely to change. And how much would Detlev even be around in future?

"Very well," Atan said.

Tahra nodded, her tight shoulders relaxing. "If I die, use your judgment on how long to maintain a regency for Carl and Jessan." She stretched out a hand, ruffled fingers through Carl's unruly bangs, and touched Jessan's pointed chin. She raised the same hand, and did the transfer magic to the Selenseh Redian; magic dazzle and wind made the children blink.

Atan stared down at Carl Delieth, the thin, small, intensely serious child whose painful sensitivity made everyone who knew her feel protective. Her twin, Jessan, ranged himself next to her as if to defend her. Four dark eyes looked up at Atan in expectation.

"We'll be all right," Carl said in a voice stiff and high with effort at control.

It was then that Clair found her. "Detlev wants to look at your map."

A short time later Atan blinked at Detlev, who stood with Sveneric. Rel had just turned up, having come from his practice salle. They watched Detlev sweep his gaze over the map. He apparently did not have to study it to comprehend the whole.

He looked from Rel to Atan, then said, "This is a formidable blockade."

"I don't think our representation here is even complete." Rel touched the rows of markings indicating Chwahir ships sailing in eternal blockade, each a cable's length apart from the next. "Norsunder adds more ships all the time."

"Wan-Edhe's obsession to be the first to gain control of this kingdom will suffice to keep the Chwahir out of other battles," Detlev said. "Until Efael finds a new target. Tell me about your hit-and-run tactic against the blockade."

"Siamis helps with scanning," Rel said. "We use the magical fog that hides the border from view to get into position, usually during storms. We break through weak points in the blockade and harry the enemy long enough to allow refugees to come in. I don't know how Siamis finds them—probably the same way he finds weak points in the blockade." Rel tapped his head.

Atan then said, "Do you have corrections to offer?"

Detlev gazed down, then shook his head slightly. "As far as I know, you have the main of the Chwahir navy ranged against you at present, as commanded by Wan-Edhe, with Efael supervising. Khanerenth's young king, who has years of privateering behind him, is doing his best to keep Norsunder's fleets on the run in the east, as you have indicated here. Counterbalancing that, Llyenthur successfully holds the Sea of Storms and the waters south, between Goerael and Drael, through his enchantment on the Venn. As well as the Sartoran Sea."

Sveneric looked in silent question to his father, as on the mental plane, Siamis said: *Are you going to tell them what we're holding back? The outlook is so grim.*

Detlev replied: *Not yet.*

To Rel and Atan, he said, "It looks bleak, with Norsunder in control of all shipyards, and only one effective fleet on the far side of Sartor. But there are stirrings within the Chwahir, the most numerous and best controlled of the fleets."

"Jilo," Rel said.

"Yes," Detlev replied.

Seven

Yaldar to Larkadhe and various points

WHILE DETLEV LISTENED IN on strategy sessions in Mearsies Heili, dropping a suggestion here and there, there were strategy sessions elsewhere, some with him as subject.

One of which was what both assumed to be a private meeting between Yeres and Connanre of the host. It took place when she desired, in places she liked; it never would have been the other way around.

Connanre knew it, and acknowledged it, but it no longer drove him to bitter despair as it had long, unsettled centuries ago. He sensed, these days, that he was winning. He could feel the change. And now he just about had within his grasp the means to—

Magic transfer: *She* was here.

His hand ran over the strings of the harp and sent a fanfare chord shimmering into the bright afternoon air. They met in a garden of the sort she loved as a setting for her games.

Yeres's black eyes were marked with exhaustion, but her cheeks were pink and she whirled around with her customary butterfly grace before perching next to him on a rock. A shining lock of dark hair fell across one green silk-covered knee; the strong sun touched the rich red highlights gleaming among the dark strands. In the temporal world there were smells. Her scent was a mixture of salty sweat, and a hint of her favorites ambergris and musk, left from her trove in Norsunder-Beyond, for they were impossible to find here. But she stored her clothes in spikenard and rosewater. He breathed it in, finding her proximity an enticement.

"Four hours late." She laughed. "You *haven't* been here the whole time?"

He lifted a languid hand. "My day's labors are done. I have left only a suitable ballad to compose. There's a competition tomorrow in Ellora."

He prided himself on being the least affected of all the Host by the drastic change in their circumstances.

She studied him, her lips curved in a sardonic laugh. "As well you are required so seldom. Narad still stinks, until I can force Wan-Edhe to do what I want there. But it's a diet of knives in Imar."

"The gentle brother?"

"He's the worst." Yeres wrinkled her nose. "I've been avoiding him of late. Which enrages him further." She made a gesture of world-weary prettiness. "He's like an incendiary device about to go off." Her breath escaped in sudden mirth. "Currently scowling and growling about wanting to take over from the Little Shit Imry. I've been cheering him on in that!" She clapped her hands lightly. "It'll be fun to watch those two go at one another's throats. By the way I've sensed your hand in what I thought was merely a game. Why? And why did you call me?"

He plucked an ancient melody on his harp, and when she paused to listen, he caught her hand, and pressed a kiss into the palm. Would she bide for a dalliance? No, it was always when she chose, not he, and never where it would cost her time. "I want you to separate with me, Yeres. I've the wherewithal, I believe."

She smiled at him, then pulled her hand away. "Are you really going to be tedious about the cozy progression toward a shared old age?" Her voice sharpened with spite.

"I know something no one else knows," he said, and exulted in her little intake of breath, her parted lips.

"Oh, please tell me it will kill Detlev."

"It will, but it required careful handling."

"Tell me, tell me!"

"He has made two very great blunders. And I have discovered both."

Her eyes widened. "What?"

He shook his head, aware that the prospect of a shift of power would kindle her passion. "Not yet," he said, knowing she'd come back to him. And that would anger Efael, who disliked any trespass on his possessions. "Not when you're so much in residence."

She said coldly, "I hate being put off. *Tell* me."

"I will. But not yet. First you must get Efael's attention off you, in earnest."

"I want whatever it is to trap Detlev alive. It would be such a present for Ilerian, and Svir would be forced to stop pouting and give us complete freedom."

"I think we can."

She clapped her hands again, then leaned forward to give him a lingering kiss. But then, laughing, she disappeared, leaving Connanre sitting on his rock contemplating the power of desire.

Presently he rose, and transferred all the way to the north of Goerael, to the winter garden outside the fortress on Erdrael Danara's border that Efael had been frequenting. Then, in full view of Efael's hand-picked guards up in the two main windows there, he absentmindedly made the sign that would send him to Imry Llyenthur's stronghold in Larkadhe.

And back to the heady warmth of summer. Connanre leaned on a balcony rail in the fragrant afternoon wind, and looked down with interest into the garrison courtyard.

As yet no one had seen him, which made him smile. A gentle reminder you've nothing to hide, Imry? he thought, easily picking out the tall, thin figure with the flying light brown hair and white shirt and brown trousers (liberally printed with dust from falls) from the uniformed martial elites. Laughter, shouts, the ring of weapons reverberated sharply up the stone walls.

Connanre watched a brief, violent struggle. There was a tangle of arms, legs, flashing blades, and Imry backed away, laughing, as one of his men lay huffing painfully on the ground, fingering his bleeding chin where he'd just been nicked with Imry's knife.

Hoots and laughs rained on the two men from the ring of watchers. Imry prodded the prone one with the toe of his boot. "Up, Shurstan. Give us your report from Khanerenth! Have you found their fleet yet?"

The sound of the familiar voice made Connanre's smile

widen. He genuinely liked young Imry. Connanre bore him no grudge for having been one of Detlev's pets, or for his later cocky attempts to trespass in his own domain. He'd given the boy a couple of salutary lessons and they'd worked together successfully since. Too bad his own present plans necessitated Imry's destruction.

Connanre hoped he'd be able to see him before it happened, to explain why it was all Detlev's fault.

A circle of faces turned upward, and Llyenthur gave him a mocking salute with his knife. Connanre raised his hand in a lazy return-salute. He'd so much rather set Efael up. But one must use what is at hand.

Efael. How'd he scorn this scene. The scuffling, the fun. When he exerted himself, it was sudden, real, and always as violent as possible. Efael didn't care who he killed. He just liked the killing. Imry seemed to have some scruples in that regard — a practical attitude these days, not wanting to waste your own forces, when backup was still penned in Norsunder. Connanre liked practicality. It was refreshingly unpretentious.

He transferred to the hard-packed dusty ground, and indicated a nearby dark-brown blotch. "Using prisoners?"

Llyenthur shrugged, wiping his face on his sleeve.

"How do you get 'em to fight? Offer 'em freedom?"

Llyenthur grinned. "If they win." He lifted his voice. "Merry-bells!"

There were some grimaces, and one or two sharp laughs of anticipation as Llyenthur tossed his blade across the courtyard to thud into the post next to the rack where they kept the practice weapons.

"And if they do win?" Connanre asked, as one young warrior, with the resigned face of one who has been fore-chosen, turned his back on a knot of his peers, one of whom tied his wrists. Another, with a chortled imprecation in what must have been the language of his origin, produced a necklace of clashing little bells and dropped it over the tied one's head.

"Then they're mine," Llyenthur said. He rubbed his nose and sniffed, watching idly as four other men were blindfolded and given long, thin, wicked-looking canes, one for each hand.

Connanre watched with more interest as the remaining warriors formed themselves in a rough square around the five. Llyenthur added cheerfully, "Which is the most useful form of freedom, eh? What's going on?"

"A visit, merely," Connanre said.

The watchers started shouting goads and spurious encouragement to the men in the square. The one with the bells endeavored to move silently, nearly was slashed by one of the blindfolded ones swinging his cane, leaped to the side—and his bells rang sweetly. "I see they've finally recovered from the epidemic," he commented.

The canes whirred on the air. The one with the bells on moved as stealthily as he could as three blindfolded ones converged, swinging, on his old space. Imry coughed, then choked on a laugh as one fellow had a cheek laid open; another heard a cane coming and blocked it with his. A shout of approval went up from the watchers.

"Finally," Llyenthur said. "The question of who is going to feed Kessler his own entrails when we do catch up with him has the ranks divided a thousand ways." He paused as one of the watchers, impatient with the slowness of the action, gave the belled one a thrust between the shoulder-blades. A shout rang up the stones; the canes hummed. Struck. "Don't tell me, you're bored?" Llyenthur turned to study Connanre.

Those mordant green eyes were remarkably acute, but Connanre had the advantage of millennia of practice. He gave a languid shrug. The dust from the battling men drifted near, and Llyenthur sneezed, which caused a hacking fit. Unable to control it, he transferred them up to his room in the castle.

Connanre followed, smiling with sympathetic amusement as Llyenthur poured out and drained a glass of water. Then, dropping the glass on the tray, Llyenthur said, "Whoever finds Kessler and gets the drop on him, I have promised myself I will be there to watch."

Connanre laughed appreciatively. "It'll be Efael, of course."

Llyenthur grinned. "So he says. And he has assured me of an unimpeded view of the fun."

Connanre liked Imry much more than he liked any of them. Sadly, Yeres didn't.

And so, dismissing regrets, Connanre began a mild conversation about winter planning and training, into which he dropped certain well-chosen and oblique lies.

Unnamed Village to Efael's Lair

While Connanre went to set up Imry Llyenthur, Yeres went to find her brother.

Efael was halfway around the world, standing in the smoke-choked darkness and staring at the smoldering rubble of the village he'd just had torched. She looked at his empty hands, and laughed.

"You lost Adam." She laughed again. "Again."

His rage was heavier than the smoke-clouds, and darker. She kept laughing, unable to stop, for she loved seeing him in a rage. She waved her skirts at a red-cindered something that tumbled crazily near her feet. How she adored the prospect, the setup, the execution, the reaction! Firestorm anger was better than wine, better even than tincture of poppies. It fueled her amusement, and kindled her passions; it never, ever, touched her beyond that. The angrier Efael got, the more she shivered with anticipation, hugging herself.

"Now we know why Detlev insisted on training them on a world in real-time." She stated the obvious because she had a purpose.

And he was long familiar with her methods.

He looked around. The crisis had ceased long ago. There was nothing here—nothing. The flames had burned down to soundlessness, the silence oppressive.

He gripped her wrist and they transferred to the ancient, shadowy borderland castle that Yeres recognized with a stifled sigh of disgust, once she recovered from the jolt. It seemed that this secret castle of Wan-Edhe's was becoming Efael's favorite lair. She hated its darkness, and its smell of old blood. Equally, she was tired of the wrenching speed of his transportations.

"And so?" He crossed his arms.

"How about a lamp?" she snapped. "I am not fond of scrabbling around in the dark when I needn't."

"You want to see my face. Why? I'll tell you what I think."

She heard the oblique warning and hugged herself tighter, laughing without sound. And sensed, with increasing delight, how the sight of her twirling around reassured him.

He dropped into a long-backed wooden chair near a window that looked out over the bleak Chwahir landscape. It was morning here, just barely. In the distance northeastward lay the dark bumps of the Chwahir capital, Narad.

"This is such a stupid place," she said with heartfelt irritation. "Why pick it out so often?"

"Because Wan-Edhe hates my being here," he replied with his old, familiar malicious pleasure. "Where have you been?"

"Spying for Ilerian." She spoke the lie with readiness, and boredom.

The weak gray light touched some of the contours of his face. That was enough to show her he believed it. Strange, how though she could find him whenever she wanted she was able to ward him when she didn't want to be found. Or, maybe they both had the ability to ward the other, but until recently — this unnaturally long imprisonment in real-time and space — they had not had occasion to play-duel with wards?

"You were going to say something about my having lost Adam's trail." He propped a boot up on the table. "Or are we back to how Sveneric went to ground in the teeth of my hunt?"

She lifted a shoulder — she'd gotten her fun out of teasing him about that. "They're rats. Of course they have rat holes." She perched lightly on the arm of his chair, and twirled her fingers in his fine, dark hair, so much like hers. "I too have been learning things," she said confidingly, and bumped her hip against his shoulder. "Tying actions to dates."

"You think I'm right?" He slid his arm possessively round her waist.

"Mmmm ... I'm still ambivalent. But I will say this. If you decide it's a waste of time to catch another one of Detlev's pets and pry the plan out of him, you might consider an alternative."

Efael said nothing.

"I still maintain the rest of them will be as ignorant as Adam was," she went on, playing now with the laces on his shirt. "If Imry really was provoked into leaving by previous arrangement with Detlev, surely Detlev would have planned for exactly what you are doing now."

"Imry has the old magic, I'm nearly certain of it," Efael said. "Also. He had Detlev trapped three months ago — and let him walk away."

"Svirle was watching. He said they made it into a Selenseh Redian. Which could have swallowed them for *years*." She sighed. "I know what you're going to say. The days seem long when you're in them, and the seven years between Imry leaving Detlev and Detlev betraying us was time enough for any sort of plot to be set up. How stupid that sounds! Well, let's suppose you are right—and I hope you are, what fun it will be!—you're still not getting very far."

"Svirle told me to keep out of Imry's magic and out of his process of command. He said I was interfering too closely in both."

Yeres's breathless laughter trembled insubstantially on the still, heavy dawn air. Her brother's peevishness, Svirle hawk-watching Imry, all provoked irrepressible streams of amusement. When she could speak, she patted the top of her brother's head once. "Well it is kind of thunder-footed to be examining Imry's main dispatches and monitoring his spells. He knows he has eight eyes on him. Ten, if you count Connanre."

"What's your suggestion?"

"Trick him, of course." She laughed again.

"Trick," Efael repeated scornfully. "You trick him. If I'm right—"

"You still have to convince me!"

"—I shall praise him with great praise."

Yeres dissolved in delight at the sudden switch to their home language, at the still but deadly tension in Efael's strong, pale hands. His fingers slid to the tiny buttons on the front of her bodice. She let him get so far, then she struck his hand away, aware of his intake of breath. They never kissed, ever. Sex between them was pure rut; they understood perfectly that exquisite knife's edge between pleasure and pain.

She whirled to her feet. "I'm hungry!" she proclaimed. "And I am not going to eat here."

And she transferred out.

Efael sat where he was, staring out at the barren land, glare-lit in the morning light. Was Yeres trying to spin him into another of her games without telling him what it was? Probably. But then from time to time she had liked sending some promising and ambitious favorite against him, in order to watch Efael win. He smiled.

Yeres smiled also. If he came after her, she had him.

She strolled into the breeze-cooled terrace at the Dei manor, and gave Svir a mirthful "Good morning!"

Of course she had him. She always had.

⸺⸺⸺⸺

On the border of Ru Yandra – Goerael continent

Elzhier the spy walked inside the tavern that had been designated as a rendezvous, clutching her shawl close about her against the chilly rain, the first sign of harvest season coming.

No one inside gave a slow-moving, bent-shouldered woman more than the briefest of glances. She shuffled her way across the room and slid into a booth on the other side before pushing back the damp shawl.

The other two people in the booth looked up. The big slab-faced man with hair the color of brick exchanged a look with Elzhier that involved a why shrug on her part and a snorting breath on his. Neither was a mind reader, but years or more or less cooperative action had evolved their own signals.

The third person was Connanre, he of the mild, mobile face and the voice and demeanor of a bard. Connanre observed this passage with interest, then he leaned out to signal the harassed tavern keeper.

"What?" the latter snapped a moment later, and glaring sweatily at Elzhier. "Your third finally here? You want those platters now?"

"Hungry?" Connanre addressed Elzhier.

"No." She waved a hand. "Hot wine."

"Two platters," Red grunted.

"Got it," the tavern keeper barked over her shoulder, already halfway across the increasingly busy room.

Connanre faced Elzhier. "Did anyone follow you?"

"No one." Elzhier folded her shawl, and pushed her hair back. "I even tried a lure."

"Remarkable." Connanre smiled.

Red exchanged glances with Elzhier, and both shrugged.

Red said in his flat, grating voice," You're assuming that Llyenthur trusts us."

"He doesn't?" Connanre asked. "He seems to be extraordinarily busy — not just with keeping the strike troops busy, but with his own games with Detlev. Speaking of whom, it has to be at least one of his boys busy tearing up Chwahirsland right now; Wan-Edhe is like a maddened bull, demanding the return of his people. Efael is trying to force Imry to send his coverts to root out the troublemakers, who are specifically targeting Efael's command structure along the coast. Imry insists he has no more coverts. Imry needs diligent, obedient spies. I'd like to send him some. Unless you've given him cause not to trust you, I think he's going to assume that you are diligent, obedient spies."

His soft, musical voice stayed pleasant, but Red and Elzhier both showed with tightened mouths that they heard the implied threat.

Elzhier lifted one shoulder in a shrug expressive of annoyance. "I'm sick of tracking for him. I'm done."

She stopped as hot wine and food appeared and were unceremoniously thumped down before them. As soon as the server was gone, she said, "We come and go freely enough, and there are no discrepancies between orders to field commands and progress markers on the map at HQ. Everything, in short, is transparent except whatever thoughts are crawling between his ears."

Connanre smiled appreciatively at the exasperation in her voice. "You don't like Imry. And here I sent you to him because I thought you'd have fun."

Red grinned, a shifting of the slab planes of his face which rendered him stupider and uglier-looking. "It's hard not to dislike a know-it-all half one's age."

Elzhier laughed. "Especially when there's little opportunity for the redeeming 'I could have told you so.' Why did you call us? Are you going to provide your loyal minions with same?"

Red was attacking his food. Elzhier sipped her wine, and waited.

Connanre said, "If young Imry runs afoul of Ilerian and Svir, it will be his own doing. I help him when I can. Which is why I want to give him you two. I do like him."

"I don't like him, but I find him amusing. Unlike Efael," Red admitted unexpectedly. "Most of the time. He's an arrogant twit, but aren't they all. However, he makes me laugh. Efael is tedious in his predictability."

"Efael really is a shit. The thing is," Connanre spread his hands, "Yeres hates Imry."

"Ahhhhh," Elzhier drawled in pleasure.

Red gave a snort of rueful amusement, and returned his attention to his food.

Eight

TIRED, HIBERN LOOKED AROUND for somewhere to sit—and there, just ahead, was another gray bar.

Impulse made her run and jump up on top of it. She bunched her skirts in either hand and whirled around.

No wind, no variation in view.

"Selenseh Redian!" she shouted.

The words were faint, like the cry of a far-off sea bird.

This time the panic hit her like a tidal wave.

Belann Harbor - Imar

Marga Fer Eider, almost seventeen years old, carefully laid three firesticks inside the oven. Then she used both hands to shove the heavy stone door to and jammed the vent control for slow-bake.

She sprinted across the pastry shop and began scrubbing down the prep tables. She was halfway through the third table for the second time when her older brother poked his head in and sniffed.

"Smells clean. Done?"

Marga tossed her cloth over the bar with the air of one who

has earned her rest. "Done! let's go!"

They slipped out of the shop together, passing from warm, pastry-smelling air to cooler brine-tinged dusty breezes as they started down the alley toward the main street.

Milnat sighed, flexing his fingers. "Eighteen-dozen dragon-licks, and each one with initials." He made a face. "Intertwined," he added, the word midway between a drawl and a groan.

It was a bid for commiseration that Marga, as always, acceded to promptly and cheerfully. "I saw 'em. They were gorgeous! Did you get a chance to see how well Lesim did with the cake, or were you too busy?"

Milnat shook his head, still grimacing. "Half a moment of delay and everything would have been ruined."

"Oh. Thelem Elder was there?"

"Long nose poking over my shoulder, and jaw never still once. Cackle cackle cackle! No wonder I was so fast," he grumped. "Self-defense."

Marga's chuckle somehow managed to be both sympathetic and guilty, and it made Milnat grin. He thrust a hand through his fair hair and said abruptly, "Look, Marga. I'm glad Lesim finished early. I wanted to get you alone. Your birthday's next week."

"True," she said, with hesitant question.

"Seventeen," he said, as if that explained everything. "What would you like?"

She sighed—and empty of air, her lungs yanked in a sob. "Oh Milny . . Her eyes squeezed shut but tears came anyway.

They both stopped walking, neither of them seeing the village street, familiar for so long. Milnat gazed at Marga in blank surprise, his skinny neck knuckle working. "But— Marga—it's not like I'm going to buy you a house—" His honest perplexity gave her balance, and laughter again. "It's just— seventeen—my favorite year. Promoted to journeyman, won the civic ribbon for archery twice—" His brow darkened for a moment at that, and both sidled looks around to see if a Norsundrian might be lurking around the quiet streets, listening.

Marga realized with inner sadness that Milnat had sensed her inner tension and had interpreted it within his own view of the world. He loved being a pastry-maker in this tiny harbor town of Belann, Imar: he was genuinely sorry she would not make journey-worker in her seventeenth year.

The entire family was sorry. And because she never complained about anything important, none of them realized that they cared more about The Baker's Touch than she did.

She dashed her knuckles across her eyes and said, "Whew, I'm cold! I stupidly left my cloak behind. Don't wait up for me, you do so dislike cold dinners." She whirled around and ran.

A short time later she shut the heavy shutters of the oven-room and stood against them. A big, shaky sigh.

Then there was a light rap-rap on the other side of the wood, and she pulled the shutters open for her best friend, who had slipped down from the hill-end of the narrow, crowded alley. The window was at the level of her knees, as the pastry shop was set into the hill. Tolia scrambled in and the two girls slammed and latched the shutters together, then Marga moved to light a candle against the gloom.

They looked at one another from across the shop. Tolia's round moon-face and slanted pale eyes set in a speculative expression, her short body stiffened. Marga's cheeks flushed. The tears on them glittered. Her slight form was tight-wired as a harp string.

Tolia held a square hand up in the direction of the oven, from which slow heat emanated comfortingly. "You're really going to do it."

Marga said in a low voice, "Day after tomorrow, if the wind stays right. Eras'll let me know, when he brings the chart."

Tolia pursed her lips, working hard to hide the sick feeling that had become a familiar sensation ever since Marga had confided in her. "All right, then," she said, knowing that to hint at her own feelings would just hurt Marga the more. "Let's get started."

"I hid the stuff down here." Marga dashed light-footed into the adjoining room, returned with two bowls, one covered, and a baking pan.

Tolia pulled a little bag from beneath her apron. "I brought a few things of my own."

"I'm sure I thought of everything! What d'you have?"

"You'll find out when you bite into 'em. Now, out of my way. I don't want this to be a mess," Tolia added gruffly.

Marga sank obediently down onto a stool and laid her arms along the clean prep table as Tolia lit the work lamp, then turned to the bowls. Marga watched her friend's strong, deft hands rapidly working the half-prepared dough.

"You still going to tell your family?" Tolia addressed the shape in her fingers, and then she punched it.

"I have to." Marga shook her head. "Really. You shouldn't worry. Flighty some of them are, and angry most of them will probably be, but they'll close ranks every time against the enemy. And if I never come back, they have to know where I went, and why."

Tolia was quite aware of Marga's reasons. She turned her back to the prep table so only the bread dough could see her own pain. "I just hope if you find her, you tweak her nose for me."

Marga's breathy chuckle made Tolia scowl more fiercely. Tolia punched the dough with two hard fists as her insides twisted at the inevitability of never again hearing that sound.

"Auntie Liere hasn't forgotten us, Toli, you'll see. I'll find her up to her chin in adventures, her plans involving the saving of more places than just us in Imar. You have to remember she thinks of everyone in the world. Her family no more, but no less. I don't think she can help it—any more than I can, because I think of everyone, too."

Tolia agreed, desolately. Tenderly. Marga, she believed, was the light in all their lives, and if she vanished, the enemy would have truly won.

Punch. Smack. The dough flipped over.

"I just realized," Marga added, and Tolia risked a quick glance, to see the expressive blue eyes distant, and suspiciously bright. "Auntie Liere said once, during my last visit to Bereth Ferian, as the twins and I were pestering her about how grand the palace was. She said that it was merely a house, with walls and furniture, like any other. Then—when I was little—I thought she was just being tiresomely adult, after all why didn't she go live in a hot bake house, then? But it's come to me, now, she meant a home. She was never at home up in South End, when she was little. Cousin Lyren-Sartora flung that at us often enough when the boys would tease her. I don't think she was at home in Bereth Ferian either. No wonder she disappeared for years." Her face altered then, humor and self-mockery curving her thin dark brows. "Though maybe it's a little puffish for me to pretend to understand someone with all those powerful mental abilities—" Marga's fingers flickered round her head like butterflies.

Tolia snorted, and slapped the dough into the waiting pan

with a splat. "Human is human. She has to use the Waste Spell like anyone else. At least no one ever said she farts flowers. And—" Slap! "Family is family. If rumor is right and the blight in the west is indeed the commanders of Norsunder, then she should be here protecting you. After all, as she herself had said so often, none of you inherited those selfsame great mental powers—"

Tolia saw that the bright drops had become liquid tracks over Marga's cheeks, and she bit down viciously on her upper lip.

Rockhead, she scolded herself. Worse than a rock-head, to upset her so. Well, at least when she's out on that horrible ocean she'll eat real good.

All Tolia's pocket money for the last two months had gone secretly into making certain of *that*.

The travelers' loaf came out perfectly. Brown and smooth, the crust hard to protect the dense bread within, this loaf would surely last a good three weeks without rotting or drying out.

Tolia wrapped it in cotton and then oilcloth, not trusting anyone else to do it, before giving it to Marga to stow with her carefully accumulated gear.

Then the girls parted, Tolia glad to be away so she didn't have to hide her grief.

Late the next afternoon, while Marga was loading the delivery cart, a shadow appeared in the doorway behind her. She straightened up, enjoying the sea breeze cooling her sweaty brow, as she was joined by a familiar weedy, jug-eared boy— her friend Eras. He gave her a grin of triumph.

She had her boat.

A knot that she hadn't been aware of eased inside her chest, and so she did not see—as she would have another time—the pain constricting his eyes. She was only aware of that sense of greater purpose, that terrible restlessness that had made sleep so difficult for the past year, now calming.

"Told ya." Eras's smile was both triumphant and a little wistful. "Best I've seen."

She sighed, her gratitude adding a faint, high note. He couldn't meet her eyes—but few met her eyes these days. She didn't pause to consider why—as she would have another time—she was just relieved that her plans were moving toward completion.

"Come by t'night at midnight." He flipped up a hand, and he stalked down the alley and disappeared round the corner of the sail-maker's shop, unable to hide the tears.

Back in the pastry shop, she sat on a stool, wipe rag forgotten in her hand. The boat, ready. The supplies, ready. The weather...

As she moved out into the street, pulling the delivery cart behind her with both hands, she cast a newly-trained eye at what was visible of the sky beyond the crowded tile roofs. Wispy, white clouds, tranquil sky.

Likely the weather would be ready as well.

Leaving the last thing, the toughest thing.

Grandma Elen Fer Eider was setting the table when Marga, Milnat, and Lesim walked in. Milnat greeted her with the enthusiasm of the chronically hungry teenager, and Marga slid unobtrusively behind him into the hallway.

How would *Grandma* react?

Marga stood in the unlit hall and peered into the main room as Grandma laid spoons beside each bowl. Grandma was the primary reason Marga knew she had to tell her family before she left—and it was her reaction she most dreaded. Grandma never spoke much, but Marga knew she felt things very deeply. In the past she'd lost her home in South End and the family rug business. In the last year she had lost a son to the fighting; she had a daughter who was world famous and a granddaughter who refused to acknowledge the family relationship. And because of these two she had two more offspring living far away in Bereth Ferian and no one knew what had happened to them since the attack...

Marga knew she was Grandma's favorite grandchild, just as Aunt Marga (whom Marga so strongly resembled she'd been named for her) had been her mother's favorite child.

Aunt Marga. There was more tragedy, Marga realized, watching sorrowfully as Grandma lit the dinner tapers. Golden light warmed the thin old woman's face as Marga thought about her aunt's marriage two years before, when she was nearly thirty, to some land-rich lord. None of the family had seen Aunt Marga for years. The young lord's having died in the fighting last November scarcely touched the Belann Fer Eiders—except for Grandma Fer Eider.

Who kept silence.

Anxiety withered Marga's appetite. She was determined

not to spoil anyone else's dinner, so she sat and memorized each face, pushing her food around until desert was done.

Suddenly she could not wait another breath. Her gaze stayed on the collection of dirty dishes in her mother's hands as she said, "I wanted you all to know. I'm leaving tomorrow. To find Aunt Liere. To ask her to come back and help us against the Norsundrians..." Her voice quavered. She had to fill the shocked silence. "... she might not know they are here."

Now they exclaimed, gasped, questioned, or expostulated, exactly as she had foreseen. Grandma, whose face Marga watched rather desperately, looked down at her folded hands. When at last she looked up to speak, the storm of noise around her that neither she nor her granddaughter had heard died away. "Do you know where to look?"

Marga shook her head. "Not really. I figured I should begin at either Mearsies Heili or Marloven Hess, because Cousin Lyren-Sartora said that Aunt Liere is friends with the rulers of each. I thought whichever one I can reach first."

"How will you travel? Neither kingdom is on our continent," her father said.

"By sea," she whispered.

"But the patrols!"

"Not south. Or west up the strait. I would go east."

"By sea? The East-Beyond-Dawn Sea?"

Marga's mother sank down at her place, the dishes clanking onto the table, her eyes round in horror.

"I can do it," Marga spoke firmly, now looking into each face. "You all know I've been sailing with Eras and the harbor youths—"

"Ships don't cross that ocean, not without going south first and landing at East Arland and Geranda," her father said slowly, his face troubled.

"Yes they do," Marga said. "This time of year, there's often a belt of mild winds along the Fereledria line. The Norsundrians won't find that—but I will." She closed her eyes, bits of dream imagery flitting through her mind like jeweled moths. "I can do it. I—I have to do it. I have to go." She opened her eyes, and said desperately, "I have everything I need, the best of everything."

"Even a boat?" Her mother's voice was now kitten-faint.

"Yes. It's a long story, and involves someone else's secret, but I didn't pledge the family's credit, nor did I get it dishonestly."

Marga's parents sought one another's eyes, and her father rubbed his hand over his jaw in perplexity. He knew Marga had no turn for the art of pastry, but he'd hoped that she might find it in pairing off with Tolia, who was a baker. Or even with young Eras, who adored her equally, though he worked in the harbor—respectable enough before the enemy made it dangerous.

Marga had never been sick a day in her life, had never caused anyone pain—and now she wanted to leave?

Her father desperately tried to gather his wits. "What if you do not find her?"

Marga knew then that her family had accepted it—at least the immediate family. But if Grandma could not, then she would go down in defeat, because she could not exist if she caused her grandmother pain.

She spoke quickly, and everyone watched her clear, wide-set blue eyes, her rose-touched cheeks, and listened to the musical voice that was so intense. Her countenance was brilliant in its frame of curling dark hair. "Then I will find someone who will know. And I will be doing something I must do." Her smile crooked, tremulous. "I love you all, so dearly, but the truth is that I cannot spend the rest of my life in the shop—and I don't have the talent to make that a crime!"

It was an attempt at a joke, but no one smiled.

"I will come back. But it will be to visit. I have to make this journey not just to find help but to find my life. And so," she said to her brothers, "you two can have my share of the shop. Forever. But in return I beg you to take little Pirag on as prentice in my place."

"The little scrap I've seen shadowing young Eras?" Lesim said with rather shamefaced skepticism. "His sister, isn't she?"

"She's eight, small for her age, but she's got quick and clever fingers, and she wants so badly to prentice in. And they're hungry, with harbor business so bad. I think she'll prove better than I ever was."

"Oh dear," Grandma said. "Hungry?"

Marga gave her a misty smile.

Grandma, it seemed, needed only a cause.

All that remained were the details.

It was so very much a relief for Marga to let her face relax at last.

Either adventurers are hard-hearted, she thought, or they don't have families and friends. How else can they bear the good-byes?

Her crumpled mouth ached from smiling, and her eyes blurred with tears that she could no longer prevent from falling. But Marga knew the two figures standing on the quay couldn't see, because she couldn't see much beyond their shapes in the pre-dawn darkness.

The previous night's good-byes, one by one, had hurt worse than she'd thought they would. Then she'd had to meet dear friend Eras, and continue to be light-hearted as they loaded the boat, because she knew they would all ask him.

She had insisted on leaving alone, for reasons of safety. She was therefore attended only by Eras — who knew where the boat was — and faithful Toli, who had hidden outside Eras' house all night, not emerging until Marga was ready to cast off.

Marga put up a job sail, just enough to luff the boat into the outgoing tide, and sat up straight, waving brightly to the two motionless figures on the quay. The thin one had his hand up in an answering salute; the other was short and square with hunched shoulders with arms straight and stiff, fists buried in apron pockets.

Marga watched and waved until they were melted into the jumbled dark shapes that marked the harbor. When, in its turn, the outlines of the harbor had retreated into the outlines of the landscape, she turned around at last, even thought she was crying open-mouthed, and sent up her mainsail. The eastern horizon brightened with pearly light of sunrise, wide and limitless.

She made no effort to stem the tears, because this would be the last of her grief. She did love them all, forever, but she could not exist with her heart prisoned in the human-made confined spaces of Belann. Her dreams had been pulling her away for at least a year, ever stronger.

She faced eastward, gazing and gazing at all the glory of sky and sea.

As the day brightened the water and the sky, more beautiful than she remembered, she threw her arms wide to embrace it all, and began to sing.

Nine

ATAN EYED ARTHUR, WHO shrugged off the entirely empty title of King in Bereth Ferian that he had inherited, but was very proud of being chief archivist. They had known one another since they were teenagers, so she scowled at him; he stared back, recognizing that it was Atan scowling, not Queen Yustnesveas V of Sartor.

"Mildred vanished," Atan said. "The same day as Rel. But they are not together. I wrote to him. He was as surprised as I was."

"I know," Arthur said, and made a motion to return to his book. There were some very surprising discoveries in this small library here in Mearsies Heili.

"Is her sudden disappearance a bad thing or a good thing?" Atan asked, tapping her pen against the inkwell.

Arthur lifted a shoulder. "I would say that it's a thing."

"Yrtur Vithyavadnais."

When Atan used Arthur's real names, she was sliding over into her Queen Yustnesveas manner.

He sighed. "Detlev sent her, all right? And no, I don't think he's secretly on Norsunder's side. She went to Ama Hazanth. My guess is, Detlev thinks the Crow will listen to her. Maybe. I think he's right."

Atan said quietly, "I was going to ask about her background."

"Ah."

She'd also had some choice words about Detlev coming in and handing out secret orders right and left, but she preferred keeping her stance on the moral high ground; though she distrusted Detlev, she no longer believed he was an agent for Norsunder. She was certain he was working for his own ends, but what those might be, she could not discover.

"Is it her eyes you object to?" Arthur asked.

"I don't *object* to anything about her. I quite like her. But you are the one who brought her to our world, and now she seems to have been dispatched on this mission, without reference to the rest of us. I would just like to know something of her background."

Arthur set aside the book, then said, "I don't know everything, only what I was told by Dak. Mildred herself hasn't said anything other than that she wanted to learn magic."

Atan accepted that with a wave.

"She was born on one of the larger islands of their archipelago, in the weird, magical area known as the Marsh. Wild magic there. Very wild. Not at all like the jewel caves here, or the weird lakes. That's why her eyes are the way they are; Dak believes she has a cat's senses of smell and hearing, though it's normal for her, and there isn't really a vocabulary for it. One of the reasons she is here."

"I find I envy her for that. Go on."

"Her mother was a young queen who had finally tired of a bad king, and the people of that island glaring whenever she ventured out. She decided that even a crown and a palace was not worth birthing her child there, and ran—but felt the birth pangs when she blundered into the marsh. Which is wild with its own magic."

"Dangerous," Atan murmured. "From what Rel learned when he went to Geth."

"That's what I've heard," Arthur said. "The queen took one look at her cat-eyed baby, couldn't cope, and vanished, leaving the little princess to a nursemaid. Who, not knowing what else to do (for she had been abandoned by the queen as well, with the local inn unpaid) worked off the queen's debt and then took the princess home, to discover that the disgusted populace had risen up and swapped out the bad king for a council of guild representatives. The maid and the babe were tossed into the dungeon, mostly to protect their lives while the council debated what to do."

"You're saying she lived in a dungeon?"

"Yes. Dak says, though the new government had ridded themselves of the worst of the old king's corrupt followers, nobody wanted to kill an innocent baby princess. Hoping that someone else would come along and resolve their dilemma, they eventually freed the maid but left the princess in the lockup and pretty much forgot about her."

"Not everyone." Roy entered quietly.

Atan swung around. "You know her history?"

"A little. You'll understand why in a moment."

Arthur ducked his head in a nod. "She was raised by a former royal guard."

"Like me," Atan said inadvertently, thinking of Gehlei, in charge of the palace servants in a morvende geliath. It had been Atan's last command.

Arthur said, "In a way. She had no Tsauderei."

Roy spoke up. "But he was a superbly trained martial artist. It was all he knew. Mildred warned Rel the first day she came to our practices. Some paid her little heed, until, and in the cheeriest manner possible, she dumped pretty much everyone on their butts."

Arthur flashed a sudden smile as Roy came over to stand behind Arthur's chair, one hand resting on Arthur's shoulder.

Arthur laid his cheek against Roy's arm as he said, "The former king's guard taught her from the time she could walk. Her society was her fellow prisoners, where she was well liked, some teaching her things like picking locks and so forth, before their time was up." He looked away, then added, "The mages think that someone decided to do something about her, for her self-appointed guardian didn't turn up one day. He had been poisoned, by the former royal kitchen; apparently he had plans for restoring Mildred to her throne, whether she wanted to or not."

Roy said, "The prisoners urged her to run—they were sure that she was next. A baby, no one wanted to do anything about. But a girl almost in her teens, they had probably found an assassin who would do it for enough gold. She picked the lock and ran."

Arthur said, "She changed her name to Mildred, the name

of a hero in a tale of other worlds that was popular in her archipelago—lots of young Mildreds—and she eventually found her way to the island ruled only by underage wanderers."

"That's where we met her," Roy put in. "Though we didn't know her very long; she became a marine guard and left."

Atan had been listening as she studied her map. "Ama Hazanth," she said. "An island kingdom, but never conquered."

"They've been fighting off pirates for centuries." Arthur swept his hand over the eastern coast of Drael. "Except for a brief period long ago when they were ruled by pirates. When Ama Hazanth had treaties with old Everon, they protected the entire coast. But the current king, old and crabbed and cruel, jettisoned the treaty."

Atan sat back. "Now I have the context. If that treaty had been observed, Everon probably never would have fallen to Norsunder, and Tahra Delieth's family would still be alive." She eyed Arthur. "But it happened, and apparently this old king will not use that mysterious Ruby against Norsunder for us. Why did Detlev send Mildred there? To steal it?"

Roy opened his hands. So Detlev didn't even tell his followers everything, Atan was thinking—and Lyren-Sartora was also thinking, having listened outside the door.

But she knew whom to go to.

She went from room to room, greeting friends as she conducted a thorough search. Balked of her prey, she transferred to the forest below, a Destination that had paths leading to the weird pool with the bubbles, and above that the Selenseh Redian.

Lyren-Sartora suspected, correctly, that Sveneric would be somewhere nearby.

She was right.

She found him lying on the grass in a glade near a stream that fed the pool full of beings. He looked like he was asleep.

Staring at him from across the stream, Lyren-Sartora smiled in anticipation. If he indeed was asleep, one false move on her part and he would be up like lightning, knife (she was certain he carried one, even here in enchantment-bound Mearsies Heili) in hand. And if not, he'd say something.

She trod forward stealthily. Two steps, three, four—

Without opening his eyes, he said, "I'm away from the others because I'm fighting off the cold that's going around."

"Not fair." Lyren-Sartora sniffed. "Sense my presence you

may, but not my purpose. I take it Falinneh sneezed on you, too."

"Hasn't she sneezed on everyone?" Sveneric made his observation mildly, and with no malice whatever.

"The Mearsieans share everything." Lyren-Sartora held her pink robe hem above the rain-damp mossy grass, hopped over a jumble of gray stones, and sat on a rough-barked log near the grassy knoll where Sveneric had spread his cloak and was lying. "But not everyone is hiding." She breathed deeply, and looked around in appreciation.

Sveneric had stashed himself near a trickling fall. The sweet chuckling sound of the water melded with the breeze-stirred rustle of summer leaves in the dark green forest canopy overhead. Beyond that the air was soft, touched with silver in this glade, and smelled of loam and leaves and bark. "Oh, what a lovely spot."

He said nothing.

Lyren-Sartora eyed Sveneric. He lay there straight-limbed, his plain tunic and riding trousers clean and neat. There was no sign of illness in his lightly sun-browned face. His brown hair spread in a shiny fan behind his head. The dark eyelashes, unexpectedly long, lay on his cheeks without the tremble of effort. Neat, slim-square, he always reminded her of a properly organized pile of books. As she spoke again, a thought darted into a mind that never made such a choice, that Sveneric wanted to be alone.

But it was too late. "I can't believe you were much of a girl," she said, giving him a rueful shrug.

"Then you are a twit," he replied with complete and unheated indifference.

She sighed, for the moment setting aside her quest to find out what Detlev was really up to. She knew from experience that when Sveneric was in this mood he would be as informative as a stone. "I do wish you would tell me what's wrong."

"What's wrong?" he repeated. His eyes opened, looking silvery green in the soft light. "But then you got what you wanted, didn't you? What could be wrong, with all the potential out there for earning glory?"

Lyren-Sartora gasped as thought she'd been kicked. "How disgusting, Sveneric. Not even the deadliest mood can excuse your throwing into my teeth now my eight-year-old self's desire to lead an army against the Norsundrians."

"The name of the game has changed. How about the rules?"

Lyren-Sartora flushed angrily. "You still don't believe I take anything seriously, do you? Which makes you as omniscient as—as Liere's stiff-owl relatives, always accusing me of being spoilt for living above my born station in life, and 'I don't know the meaning of hard work.' Spoilt! The only time until Siamis came that I got anyone to notice me was when I threw a temper—" She gasped again and laughed, fists propped on her hips. "You were deflecting me!"

Sveneric closed his eyes.

"All right. I'll go." She got to her feet.

He said with unmuted resignation, "I'm tired of waiting."

"So is everyone." She flung up her hands. "We all want to strike back." She wrinkled her nose. "Sveneric, when you look just like your father I distrust you the most."

"If you're worried about what Rel and Atan and whoever else they are writing to will decide, I can tell you." He sat up. "Though my father was as general as possible, never giving even a hint of handing out orders, they will ignore all his suggestions and decide that everyone must go do what he or she wants, because too many have land responsibilities pulling them back. They'll coordinate through Atan."

"Then why don't you just—" She stopped, and sighed.

"Right. To tell them beforehand would make half of 'em mad, and would inspire the other half to hash it out even longer. Keep your lip buttoned. Two days, I'd give it."

"Then you do know what Detlev is planning! But...you're not a part of it, are you? So you're sulking here—" Her eyes rounded; Sveneric didn't sulk. He was either quiet, or active. "Sveneric. What are you planning to do?"

"I'm planning to wait for Jilo." He jumped to his feet, and smiled. "I need a snack. Coming?"

⸻

Sveneric silently admired the generosity of spirit that made an ordinary occurrence out of what for him was a celebrative act.

It had been Siamis who pointed out to him this gathering every few mornings. It wasn't that the Mearsiean girls kept it a secret, but for them it was such an old part of their routine they attended or not as the mood took them—without ever thinking to tell anyone else.

Sveneric could see the mild surprise on Seshe's face when she came out of her bedroom early one morning and found him as well as little Aurora waiting. Aurora had been hopping back and forth in the main room of the underground hideout when Sveneric arrived, playing a silent and invisibly-marked game of hopscotch.

Seshe ducked into the kitchen and reemerged carrying with two hands the basket had been declared full the night before. Quietly, together, the three left the hideout, walking up the tunnel.

Outside the air was cool, the wind carrying a hint of autumn-to-come, the light slanting. Leaves crunched underfoot, the sound pleasantly distinct in the sunrise silence.

Then came the whirring, the sound of many wings beating on the air.

The three trod up the smooth path to the clearing, the girls moving ahead as they talked. Sveneric followed behind, to watch. Aurora chortled something and flapped her arms once, hopping on one foot; her white curls bounced on her back. Next to her Seshe, tall and slim as a reed, walked more slowly with her heavy basket, her long blond locks swaying against her skirts.

The whir overhead swelled to a light-thundered rush, then the cries began. Trills, caws, peeps, and screeches circled overhead with birds in dizzying numbers. More than she'd ever seen before save last winter, Seshe had said. Not surprising.

Seshe set her basket down. She and Aurora bent to pick up handfuls of seeds carefully harvested, or picked from stale bread and biscuits, and fling them high overhead. It was part of the game for the birds and the humans: never diving at the basket, the majority of the birds circled, waiting to lunge at the arcing seeds, while on the grassy ground smaller birds (and more practical ones) waited for uncaught bits to fall. If the fall was deemed too scanty Seshe scattered bits for them, and the expectant heads bobbed and pecked.

Sveneric watched with deep pleasure. The tall girl, her long hair and turquoise gown and smiling face half-obscured by the wheeling, darting shapes; the small girl's hair gleaming in the new sun as she held her childish hands up high so the birds would feed from her fingers.

Aurora piped up suddenly in delight, "Here's one all the

way from Halvarian!"

Sveneric had no desire to communicate with the birds. He knew that the ones with Dena Yeresbeth were out in the world. These were ordinary creatures, congregated here for safety, with little or no desire or ability to converse with humans. Aurora's lingering emphasis on country names as she called them out identified her own yearning to be ranging as widely as did the birds.

Sveneric stepped forward, dipped his hand into the basket and held it up. Shapes whirled and flashed overhead, converging near his hand. There was a beating of wings, bright-eyed darting birds beaked and beaked at his palm. He laughed.

Then a prickle of warning brought his arm down and his back smoothly to a tree trunk. Never really relaxed, unable to abandon himself completely to pleasure, he was ready—

For—

Jilo and a boy with dark curly hair rushed down the narrow pathway that led down from the Selenseh Redian. Jilo was grinning all over his travel-tanned, homely face; his companion stared in silent wonder at the birds.

"Heyo," Seshe called, flapping a hand. "Welcome back. And to you, just welcome!"

"This is Retren," Jilo said, as his companion laid his palm over his heart in greeting.

"Heyo, Retren," Seshe said with her friendly smile. "Are we in for an exciting story?"

Sveneric noticed the swift look of amusement and shared-secret that passed between Jilo and Retren.

Jilo's got a friend at last, Seshe thought with happy surprise. Her mind was not blocked, and Sveneric heard the thought as if she'd spoken it.

"Some chases," Jilo said.

"You were in Marloven Hess, weren't you?"

"Yes."

"And—with David the poopsie? Sartora said a few weeks ago that you were heading for a meeting with him." When Jilo nodded, Seshe said, "I'd better get CJ right now! She's been anxious to know—"

"Just did!" Aurora chirped triumphantly, flinging seeds up into the tree branches overhead, causing a cacophony of chirps, squawks, and rustles in the foliage. None of the seeds came back down.

CJ popped into view then, still in her nightgown, her hair messy. "Pilo!" she exclaimed. "You're back!"

The birds scattered in twittering surprise.

Seshe silently emptied out the basket, and started back down the trail so the birds could feed undisturbed. The rest, except for Aurora, followed.

"Finally," CJ groaned. "What took you so long?"

"What?" Jilo mimed astonishment. "According to my count—which might be off—the first week of harvest season starts in three days—"

"Where's Boneribs? Didya see him? Why's he not here? Oh, hi, you! What's your name, and where'd you splat into ol' Pilo? And didya see David, and is he—Augh!" CJ windmilled her arms. "Tell me everything at once or I'll turn into a cactus from being patient too long!"

Jilo grinned. "Then someone's going to have to gag you, because—"

"Okay! Okay! I'm shutting up now!" She pressed her lips together, making a terrible face. Then a corner of her mouth opened just enough for her to say, "Talk!"

"I saw Senrid. He's staying in Marloven Hess, but he will keep in touch via his magic-paper. I saw David and travelled with him. He's fine."

CJ looked down, obviously remembering that she was in her nightdress, but just as obviously she dismissed the fact as irrelevant. "What happened?"

"We travelled. He—" Jilo saw disbelief and exasperation in CJ's face—she knew he was hedging. "He had a serious knife wound, if you remember. He wasn't able to do much. We took MV's boat and sailed while he recovered, and then went to Marloven Hess."

"What about Caris-Merian? What happened to her?"

Jilo shook his head. "No one knows. Or no one that I saw, anyway."

By then they'd reached the underground hideout, and tramped down the tunnel. CJ collapsed onto the braided rug in the middle of the hard packed dirt floor in the main room. "What a yucky business. I keep feeling like maybe I should go and try to find her, but then Detsie said the best thing for us would be to stay out of her life for a time." She looked up, her eyes blue and staring, and skewered Jilo again. "Why did David leave the cave early? Detsie also believed he hadn't recovered enough."

"He hadn't. He said he felt so good in the cave he thought he was stronger than he in fact was."

"Hee hee!" CJ cackled. "Was he acting like a drunk?" She rubbed her hands, loving the idea of a poopsie snockered, like in Earth cartoons.

"Almost, there at the end. Actually," Jilo said, determined to keep the topic on David's health, and not on his experiment, "it was the strangest thing. His mind was gone increasingly for a time. I thought it was the boredom of my company until he said once that the borders were insubstantial."

"What? Between Norsunder and here?" CJ made an expression of cosmic nausea.

"No. He never said, but I saw it once, just a glimpse, a memory image from him. I don't believe Norsunder incorporates any fields of flowers high above a sea. Sveneric, is that where Detlev lives?"

Sveneric had control of every nerve by then, from lips to hands. "In the general region, yes," he said. "It just occurred to me. When have you two eaten last?"

Retren's mighty sigh evoked centuries of primeval hunger.

CJ snickered. "Let's go up to the white palace. We've got a whole staff now that even more people have come than when you left, Jilo. There's always bread, and cheese, and fruit, and usually at least one cake. We'll start you on a chocolate malt, and then—"

Most of what she reeled off was unfamiliar to Retren, but that did not diminish his interest in the slightest.

Ten

THE BELL RANG ANNOUNCING dinner.

The weather being beautiful, most were eating out on the broad terrace, which boasted a spectacular view of the forestland far below.

Atan arrived to find most of the younger refugees gathered around Jilo and the Marloven boy he'd brought with him, who had yet to say a word in Atan's presence.

When they had their fish, rice, and snapbeans, they discovered that Jilo was in the middle of describing his journey, which would probably have been summed up in three sentences, except that the Mearsiean girls kept pestering him for details.

Out it came, making everyone laugh at his experiences with sunburn and bare feet, and intriguing them with descriptions of the famous hermit Igkai. David's spectacular rescue at Al Caba was another high point, and so was his painstaking recounting of the spell to free spy birds. That won applause from the listeners — and that made Jilo give a silly grin and blush.

Atan's attention strayed to Lyren-Sartora. Her dark, gold-highlighted curls were shining, her blue gauzy gown graceful, but her smile was more rueful than happy.

"What's wrong?" Atan asked in an undervoice, without disturbing the others.

Lyren-Sartora picked up a roll and an apple and sat down.

"I should know better," she said softly. "What's worse is, though I believe Liere when she says she doesn't know where he is, she wasn't surprised when I told her he's gone—"

"Who is gone?"

"Sveneric." Lyren-Sartora sighed, and delicately began to peel the apple.

Atan stirred honey into her steep. "No word to anyone?"

"Not that I can discover. And what makes me mad is, he as much as told me, but I didn't understand what he meant. I thought he was waiting for Jilo to arrive so we could plan, but I think he waited only to hear something from Jilo."

"About?" Atan said.

"I don't know. And I hate being left out, especially when I think they're making some sort of plan underneath, or beside, or outside of ours." She laughed, her gold eyes reflecting the morning light. "And they won't tell me because I'm just Liere's silly daughter who likes to dress up."

Atan could sense how upset Lyren-Sartora was. Hiding her own increasing exasperation, she said everything that was appropriate, and once the meal ended and people began dispersing, most to attend the playhouse not far from the white palace, Atan went in search of Jilo.

He was not in the palace. She cast a tracer spell, and found him with Retren below in the forest. She transferred.

Jilo and Retren looked at her in surprise. They were sitting under a tree near the Destination.

"Pardon my intrusion," she said evenly. "But I hoped to beg for an interview, when you are not otherwise occupied, before you too depart on secret missions that somehow fail to get mentioned."

Jilo's nose and cheeks glowed. "Haven't got any secret missions. We came here because there are no distractions. I'm working on a project, and teaching Retren here some magic." He clutched an old-looking, rather grubby book against him and turned to Retren. "Mind a postponement?"

Retren shook his head, his sea-gray eyes solemn. "I've got lots to practice."

"We will be upstairs in the library," Atan told him, forcing her voice to cordiality—which seemed to intimidate Retren the more—and they transferred.

The short transfer was not a hardship. Atan watched Jilo's eyes go to the big map on the main table before she said, "Did you know Sveneric was going to leave today?"

Jilo shook his head. "Didn't tell me. We've hardly spoken more than twice. My guess is, though—"

"Yes?"

He flushed again. "It's a guess. Really. No more. But I think he's gone off to join David."

Atan sighed. "What is going on in Marloven Hess that no one seems to feel able to share?"

"If there's a plan, it's still in Senrid's head." Jilo's brief, shy grin was lopsided, and the last of Atan's irritation melted away. "I did give Senrid his magic-paper."

"You did, did you?" she said grimly. "Well, either he's lost it, or he's not answering. I've tried—ah, no matter. Perhaps it's time to try again." She moved to the desk where lay her magic-paper and a quill pen.

Just after Atan began to write, CJ came in. On discovering from Jilo what was going on she clapped her hands and rubbed them as she looked down at the note Atan was in the middle of penning:

> *Dear Senrid. Jilo, who appeared safely with his friend*
> *Retren, has just informed me he did indeed give you one*
> *of these papers before he left Marloven Hess. Very*
> *shortly we will begin planning, which prompts me to try*
> *once more to —*

"No, no, Atan. That's much too polite. Here, give me the pen. I know what to say to old Boneribs when he's being a buckethead..."

Below Atan's scribe-trained hand, CJ added in her small, uneven letters:

> *Boneribs! Maybe you ARE as fatheaded as old Banana*
> *Brain Elsarion and leave your Siamis paper behind, in*
> *which case you are in for a BIG SURPRISE! Because, if*
> *we don't get an answer back by the count of a*
> *hundred—the next time I see you, your face will meet a*
> *giant avocado-and-fish pie, a week old one, with cooked*
> *cherry-squelch topping! Or maybe I'll put it in your bed,*
> *so you'll climb into it when you least expect it! And*
> *YOU KNOW I'd LOVE to do that, when you're being*

*such a groanboil! Okay, so you think your stupid
kingdom more important than the rest of the world. I
guess I feel that way about Mearsies Heili. But does that
mean you won't help us AT ALL?*

Ten...

nine...

eight...

seven...

Oh. Is David still there? Yours, CJ

Moments after CJ laid down the pen, the following words appeared, in a familiar neat handwriting.

*CJ. Sometimes I leave this thing behind when I go out
spying. If I've slowed you up any, I beg your pardon. Let
me know how I can help. David was here, but now he's
gone. M-A.*

CJ looked up in mingled triumph and satisfaction. "There. See? All you gotta do is get a little tough."
Atan laughed. "I will remember that."
"C'mon, Pilo," CJ said. "Have you eaten dessert? Where's Ret? There's a really funny play going to start soon, that I think he'd like..."

Darchelde Forest – Marloven Hess

Sveneric appeared in a forest glade blue-silver in moonlight.
When the malaise from the long transfer had diminished he looked around at the dark foliage, the twisted boughs, and said, "Darchelde."
David, who was waiting, smiled a welcome.
Sveneric looked around once more, brow slightly furrowed. "But it's changed. Was that you?"
David flashed a grin. "I thought the blight had been here long enough. And I needed the vitality."
They assessed the changes in one another, then David said, "Jilo and Retren?"

Sveneric spread his hands, palms up.

David laughed. "Don't give me all the credit. I merely accelerated a process that Jilo began on his own."

"Where's Senrid?"

"He's in the hideout. Shall we go down?"

David led the way to the dark path. Sveneric said, "I'm glad you finally contacted Detlev."

David shot him a look of irony. "He found me."

"He didn't tell me that."

"Does he ever gloat when one of us has made a fool of himself?"

Sveneric sighed. "Not the plan, then. What?"

"It's Imry. I think—I'm not sure—but I think I've found a way to get to him. At least I have to try, and soon. Now that I've recovered, I want to make my try. If all goes well, I should be back here before anything happens."

"Except you haven't gone," Sveneric observed. "You didn't know I was coming. Why?"

David stopped walking, and so did Sveneric. David concentrated, then he said quickly, quietly, "In a few days Senrid's daughter would have turned six. I want one of us to be here. He might disappear—he certainly won't say anything—but I think one of us should be in reach. The hideout is here." David showed Sveneric the trick entrance. "Jilo dreamed this up. Nifty, eh? Did you tell anyone about the Selenseh Redian transfer?"

"Detlev asked me not to." Sveneric spoke normally as well, knowing that the sound of their voices carried ahead. He grimaced. "It doesn't always work."

David looked over in surprise as they started down the glowglobe-lit tunnel. He smiled. "How many times have you snuck back to camp out above the house since you found out about the transfer?"

"Only last night. That's what I mean, it doesn't always work."

They emerged into a round underground chamber, where a group of teens looked up expectantly.

Sveneric sent a fast, expert glance about, taking in the tidy, barracks-plain room; dropping a step behind, David watched him do it. The military motif was emphasized by the swords, knives, mail-coats, barrels of arrows, and bows stacked neatly in varying numbers around the perimeter of the underground room. A vagabond fire burned smokeless on a little hearth; near it, on the ground, sat three youngsters clad in forest green, two playing cards and one reading a book by the firelight.

Sveneric's gaze flicked from face to face. He was startled to see an uncanny match for Retren in the reader. Match for features, but not expression. Sveneric gave no sign of any of his observations; he assessed the signals both sense and sensed, and decided any kind of reaction would wait upon consultation with Senrid.

Senrid.

He was seated at a table across the cavern, the candlelight making a golden nimbus of his hair as he worked steadily at drawing out the borders of his kingdom on a map.

Sveneric's fathomless gaze shifted from Senrid's face to David, who was still watching. They moved to the table.

David laid a hand on the back of the chair across from Senrid and sat down. For a moment Sveneric looked at them there, like bookends with their candle-gilt waving blond hair and the Montredaun-An bone structure thrown into high relief on the one's left side, the other's right. The differences sparked images of a different sort: Detlev's shared-memory, blended with experience. Indevan's son shorter, compact build, broad forehead. Kendred's son with long bones, mild wide-set eyes. The images flickered through Sveneric's mind: Kendred and Indevan, brothers who never met after babyhood; Tdanerend; Imry; Crystal Ingrid.

Then he smiled in response to Senrid's greeting, and dropped onto a stool. "Where's Cath?" he asked.

Senrid's gaze lifted to David, who said, "He was anxious to find Charis-Merian."

Sveneric smiled in relief. "I'm glad. He's exactly the right person."

Senrid cast his pen aside and sat back to contemplate his visitor. He'd had to be convinced of the wisdom of sending someone so newly straightened out on such a difficult quest into dangerous territory. Obviously Detlev's boy felt differently — and obviously he saw the world with the same sort of eternal patience as his father. Only the kid appeared to have attained it without having had to live in Norsunder for four thousand years.

David laughed and reached to ruffle a hand over Sveneric's head. "Here," he said. "Let's introduce you to the gang."

Eleven

WHEN IT SEEMED IMPOSSIBLE to go any longer without seeing someone, Hibern of Roth Drael spotted a human-shaped form in the middle distance. A few long strides through the gray dust brought her nigh.

Apprehension tightened inside Hibern. Fear—

The silhouette whirled around. Horror jolted through nerves and bones as a death's head fixed black pitted eyes on her. Yellow teeth parted and a cackling laugh issued forth.

Fighting the urge to back and away and run, Hibern said in her most business-like tone, "You appear to be at home here. Can you tell me my way about?"

More insane laughter.

I don't see a tongue, she thought grimly, squashing the ever-present panic. How can it talk?

She walked on with deliberate tread.

Now watch. Of course it will follow, just to menace me—

Somehow the gray dust allowed the nightmare figure thudding footsteps.

Hibern's pace quickened.

So did its.

Finally, desperately, she whirled around and said with mendacious delight, "Since you seem to desire company, I will admit that I do as well. And I have been aching to share my favorite memories of Roth Drael's loveliness in the springtime." She began to describe the city, using all the superlatives for beauty that she could think of. They fell on the air, tinny and dimensionless and curiously distant-seeming—

She almost forgot to notice:

She was alone again.

Eastern Sea, approaching Fereladria

Marga Fer Eider had secretly looked forward to passing her seventeenth birthday alone on the ocean under the endless sky. She had sailed often enough around the harbor and on short excursions beyond it to know how to handle her boat, and what to expect on the open ocean. Thus she assiduously tended her little water condenser (in fact had not yet broached her precious cedar keg, with its simple spell keeping the water fresh), tiresome as it was, and she enjoyed the early morning ritual of unrolling her crackling sky-chart to check the positions of the fading stars against the rising sun. The weather stayed fair and mild, and she tacked steadily, though at no great speed, northeastward.

There were other changes she had foreseen, for which she had prepared. Robes were an encumbrance on a boat. She had brought two pair of the twins' outgrown summer knee pants and three tunic shirts. Likewise, on a small boat with no cleaning frame and no cooking possibilities, bathing in fresh water would be a luxury too expensive to indulge. A dip over the side of the boat felt great on everything except long hair; the fourth day out she calmly and carefully took her one sharp knife to her braids, and the resulting sense of freedom still caused her to exult. She had deliberately held off from this as long as she had so that she would suffer no regrets, and Grandma would not know. Grandma had always been proud of her hair, saying it was like her own grandmother's, the one who had been famed throughout the region for her charm and beauty. But hair grew back. Meanwhile, slinging those salt-gritty, heavy braids away was a relief.

She was aware how slowly she was progressing. The current was against her, the playful fingers of south wind nearly so. And the mild weather, though fine to live in, made her careful with her moisture-gathering containers. All things considered, she was enjoying her trip past all expectations; the sense of rightness buoyed her in heart, in mind, and spirit.

And she hadn't had that dream once.

She lay across the bow of her little boat, her head propped against one rail and her feet on the other. One arm was hooked over the side, where her fingers caught the cool splash of the lapping waves. She glanced lazily at her elbow, thinking it almost unfamiliar with its deepening golden brown. So very odd that she, who had always been surrounded by people — and who had liked it so — felt so happy this way.

But. She closed her eyes, feeling the ocean beneath her boat. It seemed that life surrounded her here, too. The moving water, the smiling sky. There was a sense of belonging here, and no loneliness at all.

Not that she didn't think about people. Images of them drifted through her mind, distilling each individual.

Thelem Elder's nose. The way she wrinkled her upper lip and cheek on the right side whenever she was annoyed, which seemed most of the time. And the way she walked, like a goose, the nose the leader, and trailing behind the never-ending cackle. She doesn't like anyone, except why did she always favor me?

Colbora's nose is just as big, but his grin is bigger, and his laugh outsizes all else, rumbling up from that huge chest.

Hris's long curls, her fingers always in them, combing and patting, when she wants attention. Her hair ribbons.

Tolia.

Just another Baker Street playmate until the spring they turned nine, and Marga found her crying behind the north-side communal shed. Curled up in a ball in the dirt, crying so hard she was sick. How ignorant, how humble Marga felt when she realized yes, Tolia comprehended what it meant that as a bread maker she belonged to a different guild than the pastry makers. She wasn't ashamed that the bread makers were part of the craft guilds and the pastry makers the artists' — she said, "There's beauty in bread, but no one sees it. It's an art, it's a true art." Dear Tolia, seeing beauty in texture and taste rather than in mere forms, your loyalty and honesty staying true despite a bullying brother and a stingy-hearted father...

Family.

Lesim's delicate fingers, fashioning rosebuds for cake tops.

His quiet laugh, which sounds from another room like the lid dancing on the rice pot. So quiet and calm a person.

Milny's moods, and the way he swayed when working the pastry dough...

Ah, Tolia, it's really better for you that I left when I did. I am afraid you would have been puzzled, and hurt, both you and Eras, once you understood that I was happiest not making pastry but dreaming about the sea, and wondering what it would be like to talk to a centaur, or how birds stay on the high air without moving their wings. Or that I love you, but the way I love the world: I cannot seem to love just one person, when there are so many to love.

Rain came on during the night. Marga woke to it stippling the sea and the sky in all the subtle shades of gray. Marga huddled in her cloak and oilcloth, crouched in the tiny hold of her boat as it tossed jerkily over the restless waves. She looked out and grinned.

Today she would drink well—and as if every cell in her body had woken up thirsty, she realized how she needed it.

To celebrate, she cut into Tolia's loaf for the first time. Her fresh food had been gone for two days, but she had resolved to start on the loaf only when she was truly hungry. By sitting quietly the day before and just daydreaming, the day had passed quickly.

Ah, that fresh smell. Cinnamon! And—Marga opened her eyes to look at the bread—it seemed Tolia had laced it with all kinds of tasty tidbits. Marga cut off a small slice and carefully rewrapped the rest.

She sat back, watching the rain through the small hatch, and nibbled her bread. The dream was back, but no longer urgent, pulling her from the inside, as if invisible strings had hooked into her heart. Sometimes the dream came on during the day, her mind skimming over the water, and even through the air. She enjoyed the thrill of new vigor coursing through her body.

Magic surely could not feel any better.

This cinnamon...*cinnamon in my apron when I went with Grandma into her room to say goodbye. How the scent on my fingers now puts me back into that day! How gallant I thought her, and how dear, to think to bolster my courage with her story about her own grandmother... 'And you and Marga are her image, or very nearly,' she finished. 'She was a great lady, a very great lady.' I said, 'She could read minds?" And Grandma wrinkled her nose and brushed her fingers up like chasing away flies. 'No, she did not. She had no need to trespass into others' thoughts. What she understood was hearts.'*

Did you hear about her, Aunt Liere? How will I feel when we are face to face again? I remember thinking how lonely you and Lyren-Sartora and Prince Arthur were, in that big palace, with no real family about. Shall I tell you that? Will you let me talk about the family? Oh, I will probably be in awe of you once again, and I will sit at your feet to learn if you will teach, but I will not let you forget the family...

Twelve

Mearsies Heili

THE CRASH OF GLASS in Clair's room brought CJ at a run.

"Where is the Norsundrian?" She skidded to a stop and stared, bewildered, when she saw Clair standing alone before a shattered mirror, empty-handed. Her gaze went to the heavy silver candleholder on the floor lying among the glass shards.

CJ sighed, reaction making her shiver. "You saw him again," CJ said. "That ghost guy."

Clair sank down wearily into a chair. "I couldn't sleep. Somehow I knew I'd have a nightmare, and I still thought it was my imagination providing my ghosts for me."

CJ groaned. "Now I'm beginning to wish that Detsie hadn't told you as much as he did."

Clair shrugged. "I had to know." She gestured. "This time the man's face appeared in the mirror. Beautiful white-haired morvende face."

"Did it, like, say anything this time?" CJ asked, her expression pruning.

"Nothing. Only that feeling came, part challenge, part *jus-s-s-s-t wait.*"

CJ plumped down onto the edge of the bed, batting down her puffing nightgown, then pulled her feet up and tucked her knees tightly under her chin.

A quiet tap outside the door startled both girls.

"Who?" CJ's eyes rounded.

But Clair had an idea who it was. "Come in," she called.

Siamis entered only a step, taking in the room at a glance. The night air was cool, Clair's bedroom windows wide open. CJ was in night clothes, which was to be expected at three hours past midnight, but Clair still wore yesterday's clothes—a mute sign that she had meant to remain awake through the night. But nature had defeated her.

Clair looked the question she wouldn't ask, and Siamis said reassuringly, "I was walking on the terrace below and heard the crash." In other words, yes, her mind-shield was still tight.

"Walking this time of night?" Clair asked, as CJ's wide blue gaze flicked between them.

"Someone," he said, "has to listen for the enemy."

Clair's breath sighed out, a sudden release. "I didn't mean for anyone to have to..."

He repeated, as gently as possible, "Someone has to." And then, "What did you see in the mirror?"

Clair's gaze dropped, then, woodenly, she told him, ending, "That was one of the Host. Wasn't it?"

"My guess is that you saw an image of Ilerian."

A breeze made CJ hunch into a tighter ball, and sent the candles flickering then streaming. Then she said with a fair assumption of bravery, "Of course it's the Host creeps, but it's fake, right? They can't get in."

"Not physically," Siamis said. The point had been made; to remain any longer might make them even more skittish. "The safest place for you would be the Selenseh Redian. Good night."

He politely went out and transferred.

The two girls looked at each other, CJ rubbing her arms vigorously. "Mearsieanne didn't add magic protection against alien minds—she wasn't used to the idea of minds flapping around without bodies attached."

Clair said, "As long as my mind-shield is strong, and I keep it all the time now. I think—I thought—they couldn't get to me."

CJ considered that. "Do you think that thing in the mirror was real?"

"What's real in this situation?" Clair retorted, hugging her elbows against her. "Here's what I'm afraid of: that they might try to take over someone's body from a distance, someone without a mind-shield."

'But if that happens, you could still mentally smell their stench, right?" CJ's voice rose in anxiety. Then she scowled. "We keep hearing all these warnings about mind-shields, and not doing long distance contact lest they trap us on the mental plane—well, can't we do that to them?"

Clair shivered, knuckling her eyes with trembling fingers. "You mean trap them?" She rubbed her eyes again. "I think I'd better go down to the D. Ask Siamis."

The D had been the girls' name for one of the larger stones down in the Selenseh Redian, a great diamond so brilliant in its lucence it almost hurt the eyes. They had believed that this diamond was sentient in some form—it was the only way they could define how they felt when they were in the caves. They had not known the ancient name for the caves; now "the D" still served as a shorthand.

"Here's my worry," Clair said. "I might have to stay there, if the country is in danger."

CJ understood immediately that Clair was afraid she was abandoning her duties. "I think you have to if it keeps you safe. If you're safe, the kingdom is safe. As for trying to turn one of us into a zombie to attack you, I'll tell everybody to be extra careful about mind-shields. We'll manage." She thought of something, then grinned. "And if we do have problems that Siamis can't fix, or if he goes somewhere, well, I'll write a magic-note to Detsie-poopsie-potsie. Maybe he'll know some ancient spell to mess 'em up."

"Good idea," Clair said. "It's in your hands." She looked around the room, her mouth twisting sourly as she muttered, "And here I am, once again abandoning ship."

She disappeared on the last word.

CJ heaved a sigh, got to her feet, and doused the candles.

Knowing that sleep was gone for now, she headed down toward the kitchen in search of some consoling hot chocolate.

Eastern Sea – along the Fereladria

That very day, Marga reached the Fereledria line.

East-Beyond-Dawn-Sea—also known as the Eastern Sea— this was the blue, or white, space on maps below the mountainous land formation named Sky Island, or Skyhaven. The ocean was so broad here that three global weather-patterns intersected. Whether the ships that dared this crossing were drowned or driven so off-course they seldom found their way home again, people at home rarely found out, and an east-west crossing of this sea was rarely attempted. Trade routes between the framing continents wound the long way south, hopping from coast to coast during the spring and summer seasons.

Marga knew all this, of course. She, like all harbor folk and those who made a living from the sea, had a great respect for the ocean's might. Especially this ocean. She also knew the Fereledria was weird. Inimical to Norsunder, and to lighters strange—not always friendly.

Yet it had seemed right to her to attempt the crossing. She'd once tried to explain this sense to Tolia, who said fiercely, "If it's so right then why isn't it a trade route already instead of it being something everyone avoids?"

Marga couldn't answer, any more than she'd been able to explain why her attitude toward things that were important to other people—from crowns and laws to work and earnings—had been different. She'd learned early to hide it because people took as flippant her disregard for the importance of those things.

Was it because she'd stayed with her aunt Liere and her cousin Lyren, and had been surrounded by important people and awe-inspiring buildings? No, for those hadn't interested her nearly as much as the changing of the seasons, the patterns of birds against the sky, and the smell of the wind when the weather changed.

She'd decided that she was just weird, and it was this weird sense that had convinced her that sailing her little boat across this great, mysterious ocean along the Fereledria line was perfectly safe for her to try.

And now she was here. The sea and sky looked the same as always, except for a faint iridescence at odd times. Sunrise. Sunset. When she woke from a doze. When she'd been lost in a reverie too long and looked up. She was now so sensitive to the ever-changing minutiae of ocean patterns it was as if she lived on, or in, or with a vast living creature.

Alive, that's what it seemed, but how can water and air be alive? The word was too limiting! Because the ocean and sky need not be concerned with eating, changing clothes, sleeping. The pulse here was measured in tides and winds, but it was not ruled by the human measure of time, or prisoned between the frames of birth and death.

Alive. Alien. I see no living beings, yet I am never alone. I look east toward morning, and my boat moves steadily east, whether my sail is up or down, whether I feel a wind or not. I neither hunger nor thirst; the wind sustains me, the warm rain drenches me from within. Do I move because something wills it? Or because it must be? I guess those questions don't matter, it just is. Just the way I dreamed it would be.

Sartor

Before Sveneric vanished, Rel left for Sartor.

It was too long a distance for him to try vagabond magic on his own, and none of his circle was present. When he reached the Selenseh Redian, pack over his shoulder and sword in hand, Siamis said apologetically, "The Norsundrian transfer spell keeps changing. I wouldn't trust it currently, so I'm afraid it's either one of the other six Selenseh Redian or Shendoral Forest."

"Shendoral it is," Rel said, thanked him—and vanished on the last syllable.

He was grateful that transfers between places of indigenous magic didn't hurt. He arrived in the familiar forest, where it appeared to be early spring, though Sartor was located in the same half of the world that Mearsies Heili was in. But Shendoral had always had its own ideas about time and seasons.

The forest seemed to know him, or maybe that was the unseen eyes of the Loi, the caretakers. Shendoral could, and had, caused people to wander for days, their way blocked by hazards. But he had not walked far before he heard voices ringing through the trees. Either Siamis or the Loi had set him down near the little cluster of mostly stone cottages left from previous human inhabitants of the forest.

As Rel crunched over the duff, smelling pine and running water and clean soil, he reflected on Shendoral's nature. A life for a life, that was the rule in Shendoral: you kill, you die. Human or animals, you lived by scavenging, and the forest did provide: limbs of trees fell, as did showers of nuts of a hundred different types. Fruit, blossoms blown on the breezes. All there to be eaten, or broken down for the trees and plants. Abide by that rule, and the forest was benign.

It wasn't only Norsundrians who had tried to destroy it over the centuries. There had been kings whose plans did not include a vast woodland that could not be controlled, or tamed, by anyone but itself.

"Hai! Rel! You're back!"

Rel recognized one of the castle runners, usually impeccably dressed in Landis livery, but now barefoot, running about in old trousers and a long, shapeless shirt. "The mages will be glad to see you," he said, and, lowering his voice, "Do you smell it? Eidervaen is burning."

"What?"

Rel's easy mood vanished. He bolted into the clearing. Mages emerged from the various huts, along with a couple of nobles who found refuge in this forest a worthy trade for their former fine living.

"We sent two runners, both experienced," a gray-haired mage said, her face distraught. "Neither returned."

Rel peered northward, but of course nothing could be seen for the trees. "How long have you been smelling smoke?"

"Two days, maybe three? We were not certain, because there was rain," a young mage student said, an inky quill stuck behind his ear, which reminded Rel of Adam. Who he hadn't seen since their confrontation in the woodland at Wnelder Vee. Rel still regretted his ill will at that time, understandable though it was.

"Where's an extra bunk?" Rel asked.

He expected an answer from the servants or citizens, and to be shunned as usual by the nobles and ignored by the mages, who tended to stay with their own kind. To his surprise, a clamor of voices rose, "Here!" "You are welcome among us." And, "Yaneas, shift your things, and share with your brother. Let Rel have that room."

Rel nodded to one of his fellow city guards, a tough old codger called Old Helas, who had begun patrolling Eidervaen back in the days before the previous Norsunder attack. As Rel chucked his bag inside the cottage, he said, "I'll take a look," and loped toward the northern trail.

As soon as he was out of sight of the refuge, he looked up, assessing the magical currents. There were easily enough to shift himself; he chose for a destination a venerable old tree on a hillside overlooking the city. It was a famous spot, and he knew he risked running into a patrol, but he was fairly sure no

Norsundrian would be picnicking at that spot.

He sneezed violently moments after appearing. The city was not on fire, but the shimmer of heat rising, and drifts of dark smoke, surrounded the white tower central to the first district. Two or three smaller fires gouted fitfully here and there.

He set out at a run, taking a circuitous route through the older portions of the city, which were a snarl of twisting alleys and streets dead-ending at ancient walls. Those walls had long ago ceased to be functional as sentry walks. Lookouts had been posted on rooftops, but he spotted all those well in advance, and so made his way inward until the withering air that stank of burning metal halted him.

He splashed one arm in a fountain that was still running, and stuck his nose into his elbow to breathe as he moved cautiously through the service buildings beyond what had been the mages' end of the first district, now mostly deserted; early on, the Norsundrians had used the mage buildings as barracks until they discovered that the rooms were small and modestly furnished compared to the houses of the wealthy all up along the north end of the city at Parleas Terrace. The mage buildings were mostly storage now, and empty.

Rel flitted between those, catching sight of the white tower now and then. That stench was due to far too much dark magic being used; no magical currents were left in the area surrounding the Tower of Knowledge.

A tall Norsundrian supervised laborers throwing broken furniture and tapestries and other materials in a fire surrounding the white tower. As the Norsundrian watched, arms crossed, a mage wrung his hands, then called up magical fire, and threw it at the white stone wall, which remained unmarred.

Rel's first reaction was derision. That tower would never burn. Nor would Norsundrian mages get into it. But as a wave of hot-metal heat buffeted Rel from the mage's attempt, the mage readied another spell, and Rel understood what he was seeing: they were trying to build up enough heat to set fire to the treasures within the tower.

It would gain them nothing, and enormous amounts of magic had been expended. The motivation here could only be malice. And there was nothing Rel could do: too many to fight, and the way that mage was forcing his spells to draw magic from farther and farther away was already dangerously unstable. Judging by the reek of burning metal, there would be a violent reaction before long—but whether or not the heat reached the inside of the tower, and would torch its ancient contents or not, he could not guess.

Furious at them, and at his own impotence, he backed away again, turning toward the alley that would lead toward one of the two bolt holes he had arranged with his defenders before the invasion.

Last he'd checked, the dank, dripping tunnel beneath the ropemakers' home for the elderly was still intact. He took four long steps in that direction when a loud clap from behind knocked him staggering, and hot, metallic heat buffeted the air. Even lessened by the two stone corners he had turned, the blast of air made his eyes water, and he fell to one knee.

He picked himself up and ran, his ears ringing. When he reached the series of tiny courts that served those old guild buildings, he heard footsteps, and halted, swaying in the lee of an archway made of trained wisteria. He pulled his sword—and one of his own city guard ran in, toward the cellar doorway that led to the underground bolt hole. "Beak?"

The young man nicknamed Beak jolted to a stop. "Rel? You're back?"

Rel saw the question more in Beak's lips moving than he heard it, though his hearing was returning.

"I just arrived." He shook his head, trying to dislodge the ringing. "What was that at the Tower? Do you know?"

Beak's face spasmed in hatred. "New Norsundrian turd, Aldon. Fighting Bostian over Sartor. Keeps coming back, trying to burn out the Tower. That outburst did for a lot of them."

"Aldon one of them?"

"I don't know—I was sent to get help," Beak said, and urgency ratcheted up his voice. "I haven't slept in..."

"Who? Where?"

"Foreign boy."

"Boy?"

"If he's any older than sixteen I'll do your patrols and mine. Came looking for Sartora, he said. Name foreign, Lexan Gla, no, Glenara, Glenereth, that was it."

"Glenereth?" Rel repeated in amazement.

Beak's eyes widened. "You know him?"

Rel had not told any of his Sartoran friends and fellow guards anything about his background. "Where?"

"Aliana bridge."

Clear on the other side of the district—of course.

Rel ran, leaving Beak to rouse whoever was in the bolt hole.

The Apsos Way, running alongside the palace, was the shortest route. Rel hated using it, as it meant passing by Atan's beloved Purrad labyrinth, which had been kicked apart in the first days of occupation, the trees hacked at.

One glance, looking for enemies, then he averted his eyes as he ran past; it hurt, every time he came back to Eidervaen. Not just seeing the desecrated Purrad, but the wreckage of Eidervaen. Animals were tidier. But for calculated viciousness, there was nothing equal to humans.

His own mood was vicious as he reached the once-elegant Aliana neighborhood. He wove between buildings, until he heard the cracking echo of shouts and ringing clashes. He slowed, moving warily. If the Sartorans were outnumbered, he'd have to make his approach in the most effective way possible.

He squeezed between an ornamental shrub that had somehow survived being attacked and a date tree, and surveyed quickly. What he saw was bad enough. The bridge, which had once had a pretty little toll booth on top, had been turned into a sentry outpost. A lone figure sat atop it, sword in hand; as Norsundrians shot at him from below, he struck the arrows out of the air. Excellent form, but Rel could see he was tiring.

Before Rel could choose which Norsundrians to attack, the *z-z-z-z-ip!* of two arrows—three—five slashed the air, and the Norsundrian archers jerked and fell, two dead, one clawing at the arrow in his left shoulder.

Everyone's head snapped to the origin of the shots as a husky young man leaped from a rooftop five stories above the ground, to a balcony, then to a flagpole. He spun around that and landed running as he pulled from his shoulder harness two sticks and snapped them together into a staff. And though an entire squad of Norsundrians charged him, with several more shooting, he spun that staff until it hummed, cracking Norsundrians across heads, backs, knees.

Then he leaped up to the bridge, ran along the rail, using the staff for balance—except when he whapped a blur of arrows out of the air. A leap to the top of the sentry house, and he paused, the fading light full on his face from the west.

Rel knew that face, though he had last seen it in that woodland in Wnelder Vee: one of Detlev's boys. Who took hold of Lexan Glenereth. Rel caught a glimpse of deep-set eyes not unlike his own, and a shock of dark hair, before both vanished in a magic transfer.

Rel backed up. He caught Beak's gaze in the alley, and made the retreat sign.

Before long they were all in the bolt hole, which was so dank no one ever stayed for long.

They exchanged news, including reporting on who was still alive and who not. Then they dispersed, and Rel used sunset magic to return to Shendoral.

When he saw the mages, again there was little strategic talk. Everyone was tired and bewildered, fighting against a sense of defeat. Personal news was vital, no matter how high one's rank, or how silver one's hair: another reminder, Rel thought as he withdrew at last to Old Helas's cottage, that naked bodies were much the same under the silks and the woolens.

Rain began to fall, a steady drumbeat on the thatched roof, as Rel and Old Helas sat near the fire with cups of pear cider. They caught each other up, then Rel observed, "I have to admit I was surprised when not only the mages but that count offered to house me."

The firelight on Old Helas's profile deepened the grooves in his face. "Heh, I'm not surprised. King Rel."

Rel snorted a laugh. He would never get used to that. "I thought there'd be more resistance to Atan's edict. About my becoming her royal consort."

Old Helas grunted. "Would have been, before the attack. No doubt. But I don't think it's that so much as your being a big fellow who knows his way around a sword. What's more, when those old mages, and the duchases and counts and the like, start in with, *Oh what do we do now?* You usually have an answer."

They both reflected on the anxiety beneath the suave, or knowledgeable, exteriors in their high-ranking fellow refugees. Everything that had happened lay outside their experience. No one likes to be helpless.

Rel stared soberly into the fire. He tried to look competent for everyone's sake, as Atan had insisted. "Give them the comfort of believing you know what you are doing," she said. "Even if you don't."

Rel suppressed the urge to let out his own worries. He knew Old Helas did not have the answers. So he finished his cider and straightened. "I'll hit the rack, then. Tomorrow I start on the rounds. See how we are doing with the secret harvests."

Thirteen

Ama Hazanth

Mildred was angry.

No, she was furious.

Despite Detlev's and Arthur's warnings. Despite the conversations she'd carefully plotted out in order to intrigue a criminally deprived and desperately unhappy individual into changing perspective through wanting to experience all things good and beautiful in life, she got mad.

Getting mad meant all her plans—made during the extraordinarily difficult journey she had endured, always keeping in mind the importance of this task she'd agreed to undertake—smashed into glass-shards of rage.

Siamis had transferred her to the Selenseh Redian close to the shore across an expanse of ocean from Ama Hazanth. Coming from Geth-deles, a world of island archipelagos, she was very familiar with boats. She stole a one-person skimmer from a Norsundrian outpost, and sailed into a two-day journey without food, and only rainwater to drink.

She beached the boat on the west side of Ama Hazanth. From there things happened with gratifying speed. Arthur's signals worked so well that she was silently and efficiently passed from person to hideout. At the right moment, when some heavily armed and antagonistic lieutenant her own age asked her business, she gave the "crow" sign—and was thereafter treated with a kind of instantaneous respect that set her teeth on edge. Didn't take marsh madness to smell fear as motivator.

"I want to see the Crow as soon as possible," she said.

"Like today? Tonight?"

"Like now." Mildred looked around in distaste. She hated what she regarded as unnecessarily utilitarian surroundings; it was the arrogance of the military and their unspoken message that the point of life was the ascendance of power, if not the giving or the endurance of pain.

She glowered at the little shed that was so bare of any comfort. It further offended her by being scrupulously clean. The idea of a lookout in this lonely outpost cleaning floor and windows, and polishing weapons each day against some military inspection, irritated her. Those orders weren't necessary, they were somebody enjoying flaunting power.

Ah, she'd been told what to expect.

She smiled blandly at the wiry, dark-eyed young man standing before her, and watched wariness tighten his face at the vertical narrowing of her pupils. He swung around and pushed a little flap up on the side of his shed. "I'll send a message. It'll be a few hours."

"It is well. You track him down. Me, I'll wait."

She got little from the lookout, but didn't really try. Mostly she dozed in the sun. Late in the afternoon they both watched a high-soaring bird wheel overhead, then circle down to the perch on the shed. The message strapped to the bird's leg said cryptically: *There's an Assize tonight. Boat at Point Zill for crossing to camp.*

When he held it out to her, she only glanced at the illegible markings, having taken the gist from his mind. She said, "I'll be there."

As soon as she stepped down into the long, low rowboat, she sorted the scents of excitement, tension, and neck-tightening fear from the silent rowers. They were a boy and a girl, both younger than she. And both kept their minds on crossing as swiftly and as soundlessly as possible.

No easy task. They were rowing in darkness lit very weakly by stars. It was a doubly dangerous sort of trip—from nature and Norsundrians both—nevertheless their minds veered away from whatever was going on at the camp on the bare little island no bigger than an outthrust of rock. That they feared their own leader, and the mysterious appointment at the camp, greater than they feared the enemy, made the back of her neck tighten.

At length one of them murmured, "Nearly there."

Mildred surveyed the jagged, utterly black rock hump squatting on the ocean. "Why here?"

"It's central to all the islands," the girl replied. "And in the daylight harbors nothing but birds."

"Assize." She repeated the word that had yet to be spoken aloud by anyone, inner ear ready for associations that might flash into minds—

She saw a silent, tense group of dark-clad young people receiving orders and facing judgment—

She frowned into the darkness, and focused on the rocky island from which no sound could be heard. She sent her mind out.

And what she found smashed all her plans under that irresistible tidal wave of rage.

She did not wait for the rowers to ship their oars. Instead, startling them almost witless, she vaulted over the side into the choppy water. Both were left staring in amazement as her head disappeared and did not reappear.

She shot onto a beach and clambered up the treacherous rocks, not noticing the scratches scored on hands and feet. And, homing in on the misery and cruelty of deliberately meted out (and accepted) pain, she moved swiftly over the tumbled island to the entrance of the cave, her bare feet soundless on the soft dirt of the tunnel.

There was the briefest instant of tableau.

The crooked figure poised over the supine one, both lit in the fierce reddish glow of fires on either side. Ringing them, still and silent, were firelit faces with expressionless pits for eyes. Focus totally center-ward.

None of the Hazanshi saw Mildred until she descended among them with an inarticulate cry. Then shock smashed the stillness imposed by tension, obedience, and determination as her black-clad figure, with hair flying and hands outstretched, tackled their leader.

None of the watchers were able to move.

Marseth Ghandorjien, called Crow, and Mildred were eye to eye and just about matched in weight. Her martial skills were better than his, but his strength, honed by years of implacable hatred and single-minded focus, fueled by fury, was much greater. He flipped Mildred and flung her down into the dust with a bone-jarring slam. He dropped on her, pinning arms and body with deadly accuracy, and wordlessly jerked his arm back, knife poised for the strike.

Fire glittered and sparkled off the edge of the blade, but she never gave it a flick of attention; as he started to bring it down toward her heart she locked eyes with him, her pupils snapping to vertical lines.

Now her strength prevailed.

He stilled, knife upraised, point unwavering two feet from her sternum as fretful movement rustled among the watchers, and the person lying two hand-spans beyond Mildred's head moaned, unheeded. Nothing broke the blended gaze of the two combatants, then slowly, with sweat-beading and muscle-quivering reluctance, Crow lowered the knife, and dropped it harmlessly in the dirt.

He jerked backward and she swung to her feet. She kicked the knife into the fire, then pointed at their compatriot staked out for ritual punishment, and spoke distinctly, her accent strong. "If he recovers, you'll find me. And if he doesn't make it, you will as far as I am concerned deserve exactly what you are about to get."

She took off. Her pursuers, stunned for a heartbeat, were just in time to see her dive from the highest promontory straight into the night-black sea, and vanish.

⚓

Amfa Harbor - Chwahirsland

"A flasket, a casket, I've got my market basket..."

Andri Elsarion tried to smother his snickers as MV, singing nonsense rhymes in a high voice, shot the arrow (lit and handed him by Andri) with swift hands and sure aim.

"One! Two! And baby makes three — *don't* drop that torch, shitbird. We'd make a merry bonfire in all this oil you spilled. Now, there!" MV finished in a voice of satisfaction. "Isn't that a pretty sight?"

Andri managed to swallow his laughter, and squinted past the glare of his torch toward the Norsundrian camp below, made bright and glowing by the fires on the tops of the tents.

"Yes. Gorgeous. Whoops! Missed two."

"Ah. So I did. Would you care to try?"

Andri shook his head. "Told you I'm a donkey with a bow."

A long forefinger poked into Andri's chest. "Lax, boy. Lax."

"Shut up and finish those tents. Looks to me like we'll soon have company." Andri dipped the torch toward the Norsundrians boiling out of the tents like angry ants.

"Good. These'll give 'em a direction. In the mood for a run?"

Andri lit three oil-rag bound arrows, and made a grand gesture as he handed each to MV. Pang! Pang! Pang! Thud, thud, thud. Three hits (an extra to the main tent) and then, with a mighty heave, Andri sent the torch spinning after. They leaped from the wall, laughing and joking, and the chase was on.

What had begun as a routine rescue had, by the time MV unloaded Andri into the Selenseh Redian below Fereledriath and waited for Detlev to contact him for his next orders, developed into a promising friendship.

Andri recovered very rapidly in the cave's intense magic. MV was temporarily free. They talked, to pass time, and on discovering how very much they had in common, they ranged over nearly every subject under the sun. Several days trickled away unnoticed. When Detlev finally responded, sending MV on a fact-finding mission, Andri volunteered to go with him. ("It's on my way — the same continent!") and MV accepted gladly.

By the time the two had worked their way up the rugged coast at the eastern end of the Sartoran continent, counting Norsundrian maritime outposts, new shipyards being gouged into wooded shores, and ship arrivals and departures, the friendship had metamorphosed into a devastatingly effective partnership.

Attitudes, habits, and practice matched closely. Both would have liked to be doing something more active than totting numbers, but went into it with much the same matter-of-fact practicality; they were both tacticians, they both fiercely enjoyed action, and winning, and both possessed a stabilizing sense of the ridiculous.

MV was better trained, of course, but at the prospect of refining his skills Andri was like a dry sponge in water. Upon completing Detlev's work, they stood at sunset high on a bleak mountain and looked into the gloom of Chwahirsland — and all it took was an exchanged grin.

In a spirit of agreeable competition, they set forth on a campaign of destruction as they ranged back and forth, choosing randomly, from harbor to harbor. They never seemed able to stop laughing as they set up and carried out increasingly risky dares — and they made a shambles of Efael's command structure over Wan-Edhe's naval bases.

They set fire to every structure, but only attacked Norsundrians, who had been put in command over the Chwahir navy. Once Efael realized that the unknown assailants were avoiding the Chwahir, he was furious, but not enough to give up stalking Imry Llyenthur's organization and actions. He transferred back to Narad, where Yeres was still hiding to escape the pressure of time, and together they forced Wan-Edhe to investigate personally.

Wan-Edhe found nothing. His own people were strictly obedient; the Norsundrians, in contrast, regarded him insolently, knowing they were protected by Efael and Yeres.

Enraged at his impotence in his own kingdom, Wan-Edhe walked the smoldering remains of the outpost most recently attacked. MV and Andri watched, perched high on the adjacent stone tower, eating stolen food and discussing the basic principles of dark magic.

Their triumph latest two days. While camped in an abandoned hut as they argued whether their next target should be east or west, they heard a step that startled them into drawing weapons — and there stood Erol, wearing a Chwahir uniform, his arms crossed, head tilted to one side.

MV was the first to realize that Erol had let them hear that step. He cursed violently as he shoved the boot knives back. "All right, all right, we were asleep," he admitted — hating the necessity. "Where have you been?"

"Narad," Erol said, the old stammer barely a tremor now. He was a slim, slight young man, sallow-pale and round-faced; he had always had a knack for making himself unnoticed even among people where Chwahir were rare. Here, he would be next thing to invisible.

"Damn," MV said. "All right, hit me."

Erol quoted woodenly, "'When you have finished assing about the coast of Chwahirsland with Andri Elsarion, I want you stationed off The Fangs and maneuverable.'"

MV grimaced. "I take it you're still squatting here?"

"Monitoring Narad, and backup in case they get Jilo. Which I can't do riding out here," Erol said, with no inflection in his voice.

"Sorry, sorry," MV said, palms out. "Aw, shitfire, I just remembered, my boat's not at Jaro. David stashed it somewhere off Halia, on the wrong coast."

He glanced aside, but Erol had vanished even more quietly than he'd appeared.

Andri jerked a thumb at the place where Erol had stood. "Who was that? Besides a local?"

"Erol's only Chwahir-born," MV said. "Detlev picked him up off one of Wan-Edhe's battlefields. But he grew up with us."

"And he's hiding in that reeking city with all the bad magic?"

"Volunteered," MV said. "After we hopped the fence, he spent two or three years training with Siamis, while Siamis worked on his comms project. Erol was already good at stealth, almost as good as Ferret, but Siamis made him better. Also better with his hands." MV twirled a finger in the air, meaning sword and knife work. "He's been in Narad a couple of years. I thought they might pull him out when the invasion happened, but it seems Detlev's keeping him in place."

Andri whistled.

"Let's go."

<hr>

Torquende – Ama Hazanth

Torquende was a high stone city, built centuries ago to protect the inhabitants from fierce winter storms. The jumble of dwellings, bridges, and streets all built into and onto ancient palisades within the massive city walls was dauntingly confusing to a stranger.

Sitting high above most of it on a hilltop tavern's terrace, with one of the local cream-blended drinks before her, Mildred shook her head. What a place for a chase.

Chase. How long had it been? She counted up the days, guessing it was nearing harvest season on this world. The sun had begun to lower its daily arc, and the air at night carried a chill. Mildred sipped at the odd but pleasant and warm combination of dark coffee, cinnamon, cloves, honey, and cream in her mug. She relished warmth easing its way along her arms and down to her stomach as she sent her mind out to check the latest positions of Crow's toughs sneaking in to block off her lines of escape.

There... There... And there. One route, the best, still remained.

She smiled into the mug, and sipped again.

A sudden silence inside the tavern snapped her attention round. The voices resumed conversations in a lower, self-conscious business-as-usual tone.

Here goes, Mildred thought. Outwardly she gave no sign whatever — and when she heard a quiet step, and Prince Marseth Ghandorjien dropped into the adjacent seat she merely looked up with cool inquiry.

They studied one another in silence for a few moments. Mildred's smooth, rounded face was impassive, her glossy black braids shining against the dull thick-woven black of her tunic. Her hands remained motionless, relaxed, on either side of the ceramic mug.

Below the terrace wall, unseen, three knife-wielding teens moved like wraiths into the afternoon shadows and stared upward mutely.

Mildred shifted focus back to the prematurely lined triangular face before her. She saw unkempt dark hair, the eyes so narrowed by both genetics and experience it was impossible to see enough of the iris to distinguish their color.

He said, rusty-voiced from too many hours spent screaming alone in a cell as a child, "You've been picking at the minds of my people."

She smiled faintly. "Me, I wanted you to know I was doing it."

"That's how you got our access signals."

Her lips quirked in denial. "Got such from Arthur."

His gaze had been on his tense, twisted hands. Now his head lifted and he squinted at her in surprise.

She leaned back in her chair and pointed her forefinger at him. "What I got from your underlings was the progress of your victim. Eh, and also as much of the history of your gang of brutes as I could get. And I let 'em know I was in their minds to prove to you, ah, so stupid, you! That just because no one can pick your brain doesn't mean that piss-bucket wasn't messing with the lesser fry. You know the one I talk about?"

"Arthur?"

"No, no. I talk about this so-interesting twit who showed up a week or two after Arthur left. He knew all your stupid signals. Impressed you with so much power-talk on how he can take you at any time. Which is true. But won't, ah, that is fart noise. You should see it, how very much it isn't true. And how amazed and impressed he was with your, eh, your setup here. Which is even more fart noise that you just snuffed right up."

The prince called Crow said nothing.

Recent memory flashed, melded into an old and nasty one of her own, and she said with sudden, low-voiced intensity, "You seasick twit, don't you see you are being set up to do that Imry Llyenthur's work for him? Did you possibly think the fact that he hadn't taken you meant that he wouldn't? That such as he would so treat you as an equal?"

"Why did you come here?" Crow's voice sounded like a rusty hinge.

She gave a short, mirthless laugh, and looked out over the stone city. Then back, and shook her head slowly. "Ah, me! To try to save you."

Fourteen

Essla Harbor - Chwahirsland

ANDRI ELSARION CROUCHED SHIVERING behind some brine-stinking barrels and cursed to himself. His coat and hat—both stolen from an outpost—had recently gone into molding the phantom rider their pursuers had chased eastward so furiously.

At first Andri had been too relieved, and entertained, to notice the cold, but after stumbling about the harbor in a strengthening wind that promised an autumn colder than usual, and him only in a thin summer shirt, ragged pants, and waterlogged boots, he wished MV had been the one to sit there while Andri ran up and down the docks looking for gear to steal, and likely boats. Except Andri knew nothing of boats.

He grimaced. Boats. Well (he brightened) maybe MV wouldn't find whatever he was looking for. Boats. Hah. Clumsy, rickety damn tubs, no escape route. Despite the fact that he and MV were very nearly penned by Wan-Edhe's army, Andri still favored stealing a couple of fast horses, some gear, and taking their chances. The odds they faced (two against an army) were nothing new.

"Here, rattail," came a soft voice as a hand yanked the grimy yellow ponytail between Andri's shoulder blades.

Andri whipped around to find MV behind him, barefoot and grinning.

"Got one. But the tide's almost out. We'd better hustle."

Andri rose to his feet, and took a step. The rap of his rundown heel on the warped dock board was followed by the liquid squelch of his foot inside the battered boot.

MV laughed softly. "Soon's we're on board, over the side those go."

"Then you go with 'em."

MV smothered a snort. "First lesson in civilization: there are other means of travel besides the horse. You'll thank me for this someday. Here's our new home."

"Oh, dammit, I'm sick already," Andri mourned as they vaulted a fence, and ghosted down to the docks.

Narad - Chwahirsland

Wan-Edhe glared at the approaching courier until he saw the scarcely suppressed excitement in the fellow's stupid face.

"What?" he snapped, restraining the urge to hit him with one of the nastier spells he'd recently concocted in preparation for the capture of whoever was out there.

"We've found them, Sire! That is," the courier amended, his ferret-eyes flickering to Dungeonmaster Arech, who lounged expectantly near the throne, "we know where they are—where they aren't. They left the country!" he yelped as Wan-Edhe's frown of irritation changed to the urge to do something drastic. "They stole a cutter. Must have used some kind of invisibility spell—we checked reports from the Channel blockade, and nothing! Likewise the coast watch."

"So they went north." Dungeonmaster Arech looked disgusted.

"Unless this deflection illusion is still in use." Wan-Edhe frowned more, then suddenly laughed.

The laugh was horrible; the effect on the courier was amusing to behold.

Wan-Edhe rubbed his hands. "Shall we speed them on their way?"

Still cackling, he disappeared to his tower to put into effect some of the magic he'd nightmared up recently.

Torquende – Ama Hazanth

Neither Mildred nor the Crow had time to say a word. They sensed a patrol coming.

Mildred leaped expertly over the terrace wall.

The Crow paused long enough to watch her skip over two or three slated roofs, well out of reach of his erstwhile converging trackers, then he made his way silently down an adjacent hidden stairway.

Mildred dropped into a narrow street, and looked about. Quiet. Windows all shuttered. That interruption, she thought sourly, couldn't have been worse timed if it had been planned for a century.

She moved on, orienting herself swiftly.

It was hours later when she stopped on a narrow parapet and gazed out into wind-scoured darkness. She was cold, tired, tense and jumpy from playing hunt-and-prey with the intent, indefatigable stalkers who'd tracked her through their city.

She had to get to Crow and finish talking, finish trying, before her words about mind-shields sank in and he closed his gang's minds to her. Her one advantage, she thought, stamping and swinging her arms, and it was diminishing fast.

It was dangerous to lurk about this city much longer. Leaning against the cold, damp stone wall high above the unseen crashing sea, she expelled her breath sharply then breathed more slowly, trying to will exhaustion away and clear thought back. But she'd been on the move too long, with scant food. Her body knew it was after midnight, and she hadn't slept through an entire night for over a week.

Focus. She sniffed the wind.

No one around. A tunnel-visioned patrol making its way southward several levels below ... farther ... farther ... Mildred located one of the minds she'd learned to follow. Ah. Crow still hadn't shown up at his usual haunts. Which sometimes meant he'd go prowling the haunts he frequented when he wanted to be alone.

Like here. This wall, where he met Arthur.

She'd seen the incident in someone's mind some days ago. Now she looked down into the spray-tangy dark, and wondered what Arthur had been thinking about as he stood in this very spot—

Ah!

Her remarkable night-vision picked out the flicker of movement, black on black, on a lower stairway. A quick mental check: no one with him. Then he stepped out from the archway into the pale glow of the cold stairs overhead. His hands were in his pockets.

He said, his voice barely audible over the wind and the distant crashing waves, "Arthur sent you?"

She stepped closer in order to hear.

As she hesitated, trying to frame an answer, his bony head turned and he squinted directly into her face. He probably could barely see her in the faint light. She saw with some clarity someone who, in his exceedingly rare social encounters with equals, was painfully — excruciatingly — shy.

The insight took her so completely by surprise that again she abandoned her carefully constructed argument and this time she did what she rarely did, brought in her own past.

"No," she said. "Someone who thought I'd be the best. Because once I held a crown in my hands — after a lifetime locked in a dungeon —"

The insight, and the immediate reaction to cut through with a direct approach also, blinded her for a crucial few seconds to the inherent warning.

A faint sound, shoe against stone. The subtlest change in the no-longer empty breezeway.

She cut herself short, and whirled toward the parapet edge. Darkness hid the extent of the rocks below, but she was willing to try — then the Crow stepped sideways in front of her, his heels against the edge of the drop, in order to block her from diving.

She backed against the wall and yanked out her long knife and a short one, as five mind-blocked figures emerged from the breezeway upwind of her, with deadly efficiency and intent.

"Faked out. Ah, I am the seasick twit now, me!" she said — and attacked.

They were as good as she feared. And she was reluctant to kill anyone not a Norsundrian. Still, she won three or four feet of parapet against them before the world exploded —

She lay on the stone, seeing her knife inches from the Crow's foot. He never moved as from somewhere a heavy shoe thumped on her arm as she reached for the knife —

And something else thumped on her skull.

She opened her eyes to total darkness.

Overtired. Over-hungry ... and she fell for the most obvious of traps. If that wasn't a convincing reason to take up a life of luxurious living. But that didn't stop the headache from pounding.

She'd been out, what? Her inner clock said maybe two bells. Her mind spent the waking time in what she termed the 'mental marsh'. She didn't know if, when she was wiped out or feverish, she went to the Geth's marsh or if a little of it lived somehow in her, and she didn't really care. It was a relief, when her body was in rotten shape, that her mind for a time rested in the kaleidoscopic life of the marshland. It always helped her — even when, like now, she came out of it feeling a very long way from home.

Here. Well, she was definitely back in self, so to speak. Her entire right side was on fire in protest of her right arm, which — don't even think about it. Skull aching fit to split, left ankle twisted.

As for location, she didn't need to sniff to recognize the distinctive ambience of very old dungeon. The cold, soft, still air, suspended in dust and dampness, that has been without movement for so many centuries it should really (she'd always thought) have a name besides 'air'.

She was lying on something lumpy and coarse. Piles of old sacking? Nets, maybe? Her limbs were straight, including — ow! — her right arm, and her weapons were gone. All of them.

"Enough," she said out loud.

She had picked up from vivid memories that Crow's gang had little knowledge of, and no access to, medical care. They were expected to wrap up their own wounds, and those who were beyond that were made more or less comfortable and left to recover, or not, on their own. Just like their Fearless Leader — except he'd been denied care by a father who hadn't quite had the guts to kill him outright. Those who died were weaklings. Good riddance.

Willing pain and nausea from overwhelming her, she explored the break as well as she could. Then, moving by stitch-narrow degrees, she set it. When at long last her right arm was disposed carefully — properly — across her middle, she dropped her sweaty, trembling head back on the nets and slipped into sleep.

Nothing disturbed her. She slept for a long time. When she woke, the headache was manageable, and the pain in her arm, though it still hurt like crazy, had subsided to the extent she knew she had done right in bone-setting, and if left alone it would go about its business and heal.

Now what? One of their spiffy executions? Some kind of obnoxious bullying interrogation session? She'd toss herself off a cliff before she'd cooperate in their games.

She sniffed the currents in the air, her mind traveling along them. She sensed people near, all shielded. Crow. Asleep—now awake. Waiting.

With a heavy sigh of resignation, she eased herself into a sitting position against the nearby stone wall, her arm disposed across her middle, her knees up to protect it. A heavy door graunched open. Flaring orange light groped fitfully in, outlining two silhouettes. One turned away; steps diminished back down a stone hallway.

The crooked silhouette reached up to jam the torch into a socket on the wall next to the door.

Discomfort, the fact that there was no way out, made her belligerent. "I should've known you cannot handle a conversation face to face. You can't score points without knives, eh? So much for your brains."

"I didn't know what you'd do next," he said, sitting down on her pile of nets so he could see her face.

The light glowed uneasily on his left side, throwing his features into high relief. He was so bony and thin and twisted that from time to time he looked like a wizened old man.

She snorted. "If you believed anything I said, you should have seen that I do not harm. And if you disbelieved me, eh, then why didn't you shoot first?"

"When people appear and nose around here, we like to find out why."

The words were uninflected, nonetheless she felt the cold finger of danger poking at her mind from inside her skull.

Ignoring it, she snorted again, with even more emphasis. "Me, I have been trying to tell you!" Then she remembered their very first meeting, and knew from his sudden smile that he was as well. She grinned.

"Tell me now. Who sent you, and why?" he asked.

"Detlev is the name of the person."

The Crow's head lifted in surprise. "But he's with Norsunder, is he not?"

"Bah, you are so, so behind the times!"

"Llyenthur said his switch is just a pose."

"Wrong." Mildred figured she knew from Llyenthur's lie, and from the Crow's own exemplary life, what he thought about Detlev's mighty past. And she really didn't want to hear about it. "I do not know him. But I can assure you of this: he's fighting against Norsunder. Llyenthur and the rest of his rotting chum are wailing like sea-wolves, wanting to nail him. But they cannot get near him."

"So ... Detlev and his followers do not want to see me ally with Norsunder, and they know little enough about me not to understand when I told Arthur that I go my own way, that's what I mean."

"Hai-ya," Mildred said with derisive cheer. "You'll say that right up until Llyenthur carves a blood-ward on your throat. Despite his so-called promise."

The Crow fell silent, eyes on his hands, then he said, "And you came because you were once in a position similar to mine."

"Similar! Me, I came so, *so* close to being just like you." Her tone made it abundantly clear that she did not mean this as a compliment.

He said, "You said something about a crown."

She sighed. "There was a morning. I'd broken out of prison."

"Prison?"

"I was raised in one. Did I mention?"

"No. You didn't," he said, and there was enough respect in his tone to convince her that he really did come from as twisted a background as hers. A salute to you, Detlev, and I hope that comes with a broken arm.

She marshaled her straying wits. "I skipped out of prison, as I said. To practice. I was walking, alone, so. And for the first time instead of feeling dizzy from the variation and intensity of color surrounding me, I ... what is the word ... yes, I assimilated it. And then I thought to myself, instead of listening to one person's view of the world, why not to try listening to others? Because what if he is not right? Right or wrong, if there was a fight, then people will die. On both sides, who otherwise would live to see another morning like that one."

"You said you had the crown in your hands. That was figurative?"

"That's figurative. Though I knew how to do it. How to take the capital, as planned. Whom to kill. They'd been represented to me as targets, see?"

He jerked his sharp chin down.

"This is what no one knows. Me, I almost did it. I knew I could do it. But once I was out of the prison, the scents, the sounds, the colors ... nothing was simple. Not in the way I'd been taught. I told him, my guardian, that I was walking to understand trees, and to assimilate colors, and to accustom my eyes to light. This I had been doing."

"He believed it?"

"Why not? I'd never lied before. But I used all those lessons, and sneaked into one, then another of the guild council homes. Ah, the more I listened, the more they changed from targets to people."

"Targets to people," he repeated.

Mildred couldn't defend herself against a two-year-old right now, but she had passed the point of stifling her words—all Crow's scents, the sounds of his breathing, indicated his close attention.

"That night, you, between the fires. You were busy making that boy from a person into a target. Me, I do not care what your goal is. I do not think it is ever worth to make my people into targets."

He was silent.

She wondered if he'd ever heard even that much criticism, and went on with her story. "Eh, not much more to tell. I learned that though one was greedy, and another told everyone what they wanted to hear, between them all, they governed well enough. Then I began to understand why my trainer was truly training me. I wasn't just recovering 'my' crown. I was to conquer the archipelago. For him. When I saw that, I left. New name, new life. Never looked back."

She sighed, fighting thirst—she hadn't talked so much in ... she couldn't remember. "Fighting in the name of freedom? Bah, it was not only him. It happened again, not much later. Freedom is a word thrown around, a handy one to raise sentiment, yes? In both situations, they did not expect me, ignorant as I was about anything but revenge and tactics and strategy, to begin to understand that there are many kinds of freedom."

"My people come to me freely. They seek us out."

"And there ends their ability to choose for themselves, yes?" Her mind flashed vividly back to the wretch between the two fires, condemned for countermanding orders. Then saw his squinty gaze on hers. Expectant.

He knew what was coming. And suddenly she began to laugh. Despite everything—broken arm and aching head, empty gut and filthy clothes, despite the dangerous mindset of the people around her, and the Norsundrians loose on the world and she so far from home, she laughed.

He was *listening*.

"Me, I know this is so, so weak," she said, wiping her eyes with her good hand. "But I could use a square of cloth. For a sling. And I also would very much like to drink a little water?"

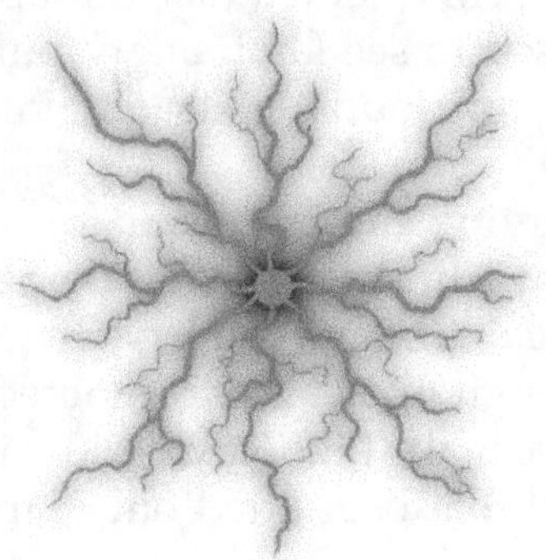

Fifteen

Elgar Strait – off The Fangs

ANDRI GRITTED HIS TEETH, carefully lifted one hand, slipped the rope noose MV had fashioned to help hold the helm, and slid it over the next spoke. Just that brief time strained his hands, arms, shoulders; this kind of storm usually required at least two, maybe four strong sailors at the helm, MV had said with cheery heartlessness as he knotted together the series of nooses to help ease the strain on the brine-soaked wooden wheel.

"Hold it steady!" MV had yelled to him before moving off in the howling, ink-black mass of flying water to do whatever needed to be done to the sails.

It was night, steely cold, with a knife-edge wind driving the rain, and waves that seemed to be growing with every swell. The wheel shuddered and creaked and hummed under Andri's hands, protesting its confinement, until he was using his whole body to maintain control. That, and willing his guts not to play carousel with last night's brief meal, took all his concentration.

When MV finally appeared next to him out of the wild darkness, black hair sticking wetly to his face as he grinned fiercely, Andri had half forgotten his existence.

"What are you laughing about?" he shouted. "I can use a joke!"

"You've got it," MV roared back. "Name is Wan-Edhe. Must be him! Don't know who else would be that crazy! This storm coming—"

"Coming? Seems we're in it!"

"It's coming." MV jerked his thumb westward, where Andri was surprised to see faint, angry purple glows through the uneven canopy of clouds. A steady glow as well as faint—the sun was trying to appear.

"And it's carrying enough magic for me to use vagabond magic all the way through the blockade. But I'll need to concentrate. Ram us through. You have the helm."

"Ram us through like..." Andri shouted.

MV's teeth flashed. "Like David did with my boat."

"You claimed that boat lifted out of the water! How do I man the helm for that?"

"Not when we lift. When we crash down again!"

The wind whipped away MV's laughter, leaving Andri alone at the wheel.

⁓

EASTERN SEA – ALONG THE FERELADRIA

Marga's dreams changed.

She woke up, poked her head out of her little hold, looked around, and frowned westward.

There was a hazy purple line on the horizon. She looked around again at the blue, sparkling sea, the bright sun just up in the cloudless eastern sky. And back to the west.

She shivered, which surprised her—and for the first time in days, she remembered Tolia's bread, and decided to eat some.

The storm pounded northward. The cold air merged with what would have been a more benign rainstorm, normal for this time of year as the cold northern current drifted south, and gathered strength.

Along the coast of Imar, and half a day later in Everon, shore folk took one look at the black line approaching out of the south and battened down everything.

Behind shuttered windows and thick walls some people drank, or socialized, or slept, or worked, trying by industry or by noise to shut out the fury smashing down on their land with torrential force. Their houses were strong, their docks sturdy. They'd make it through. As for anyone out there—better turn over, or pour another mug, or grab another card of wool, another nail to hammer.

Some stared at the greeny-black chinks between shutters. Their hearts were only half home, and half with some dear one caught out there in that tempest.

By nightfall Wnelder Vee's coastline was flooded, but word had zapped its way northward earlier and refugees from Norsunder, who had been planting in secret since spring, were huddled on higher land, waiting, and watching the terrible purple flashes striking through the sky, and wondering if their labors would be washed away before the enemy even discovered them.

MIDLANDS HAMLET – EVERON

So far inland, the storm was merely a heavy and sudden rain. Nonetheless Adam felt the evil intent driving it, and warning gripped his neck. He paused as if to study closer a feature on his model; actually he directed some of his attention to making sure his face did not change, or his hand falter.

Most of the five years since he and Detlev's group had left Norsunder Adan had spent doing anything but art, from building to working in a pleasure house. There were times, when he was a boy, he had felt old, and now that he was an adult he sometimes felt surges of childish heedlessness.

What did people see when he came into a room? In appearance he'd altered very little. He was still thin and slight, and no more than medium height. His brown hair still grew in a fine riot of curls, which tended to turn into extravagant waves when he forgot to cut it. Which was often, as he had no interest in his own appearance. He wore old clothes, and he tended to hide his long, sensitive, scarred hands in gloves. He had only recently taken up the chalks and paints again, always in short spurts, lest the once-torn muscles cramp.

His forehead was high, his brown gaze steady, and clear, though perhaps with less ready humor than before. His nose still freckled, but only when he was long in sunlight, and he had never lost his infectious grin, though it didn't break as often as it once had. He looked sixteen, except for the beginnings of fine lines around his eyes that pegged him closer to his true age, in his early twenties.

So close to Imar, the growing enchantment could be sensed by some, making sleep troubled and daylight hours haunted by the feeling that one was watched by unseen and evil eyes. His appearance here had not been hailed with immediate welcome. Fear, distrust, hope, interest had marked the faces who halted in their tasks until the elderly matriarch whose portrait was now shaping under his chalk had studied him, sniffed, and invited him in for a bite and a sup.

The homestead was a rambling one, and scuffed supports of the long battered table he sat at hinted at the many knees that had (until recently) been gathered there. Now the family barely filled half, and all but two were old people.

The two teens, a girl near his own age and a boy of thirteen, had worked silently all afternoon, first in the kitchen before and after the meal, and then with other household tasks as Adam entertained them with songs from far lands, a few funny stories, and now the portrait in payment for hospitality. They'd been watching him, listening for something beyond his words.

The girl came by him as she picked up another ball of yarn from the big basket near the hearth. Her guarded gaze was much darker than his own, taking in the drawing. The portrait was good enough, if lacking in fine detail that his hands, as yet, could not quite manage. No false flattering, but somehow he had invested in broad lines a dignity that the dumpy old woman only showed in her movements and in her conversation.

Adam met a glance of approval. Then the girl exchanged quick looks with the boy, who'd been sanding wood, and Adam thought, *here it comes.*

The rain increased. There were plenty of empty bedrooms in the house. When the family retired Adam set his candle near the window in the room he had chosen and he sat, looking out at the rainy darkness, and wondered what was going on out there.

His self-appointed task between errands for Detlev was traveling around in the areas where the Host's barrier lay heaviest, trying to give the people encouragement, laughter, hope. His songs and stories were carefully chosen. Triumph over great hardship, light magic's enduring strength, tales that made the Norsundrian villains look ridiculous. In order to give his message credence he'd sometimes had to hint at his own experience, and he knew that that was the focus of the two teens' attention.

A quiet knock. Invited in, they studied him with revealing eager wariness.

The boy said, "You must know where there's an army forming. We want to join it, and fight the Norsundrians."

"How do you know I'm not one, looking for people like you?"

Pause.

"Your stories," the boy said impatiently. "You don't need to test us."

Adam smiled a little sadly. "There's a member of the Host of Lords who specializes in pretty songs about Norsunder's defeats. He just betrayed and brought down an entire underground not too far north of us now."

"Granda likes you," the girl said softly. "She knows."

Adam turned to her, and held up a hand to stop the boy, who was about to launch into speech. "What will happen to Granda if you leave?"

The girl grimaced. "They'll manage. Though in truth it's hard."

"They're tough," the boy said stoutly. "They'll hang on until we're free again. You watch!"

"And if you don't come back?"

The two exchanged looks.

"You've been arguing with them about it?"

The boy grinned. "Haven't we just! You should hear their excuses. I'm too young. We don't know anything about fighting. You'll get killed. Over and over until I'm ready to—" He stopped, laughed sheepishly. "Well. They don't see I'm strong, and she's faster than I am. So far," he added in a challenging undervoice.

"Uncle Zoen is the only one who says *to do what we want*," the girl murmured, but her troubled expression indicated that this was somehow worse than the arguments with the others.

"There's something weird about him," the boy said. Hastily he added, "Not creepy. But strange. Ever since Mom went. Dad and our oldest brother and four cousins all died in the first battle, last year. Then Uncle Normath got caught in the winter. And then Aunt Halin. And in the spring," he finished with a sort of morose braggadocio, "they caught up with Mom in the courier relay. She pretended not to know, and poisoned them when they were trying to trick her into talking—"

"She prepared the food. And drank the first glass," the girl said in a tight voice.

"Which brings me to my original question," Adam said. "What will happen to the old folks if you don't come back?"

"They'll work." The boy shrugged, hands outflung.

"For what?" Adam asked. "If there's no one left? And when the Norsundrians are defeated, will it matter to them as they watch one another die off, one by one?"

The boy chewed his lip then rubbed his nose vigorously. Lightning flared outside.

The girl said, "Granda says we're not cowards to hide, but I thought that was twisted words for *You're too young.*"

Adam knew it was twisted words for *you're all we have.* But they were too young to react with anything but impatience at what they saw as the constraints of familial love.

He tilted his head, briefly smiling at her. "Why haven't you asked Granda what she means?"

The girl flushed a little, then smiled back.

Adam said to the boy, "You'll be a hero to your great-grandchildren because you survived. You did the work to rebuild your home. Because no one else is going to do it. They will be rebuilding their own homes. And finally because you took care of the old folks. If you die in one of the many battles, there won't be any grandchildren. You won't have anyone at all to sing the songs, once the old people are gone."

The boy sighed, and because he knew there was nothing more to be said, he slouched out.

Adam said quietly to the girl, "The queen is coming back. She will find and ride with the Knights. But her real strength—Everon's strength—is in people like you, here, at home, planting tool in one hand, building tool in the other. But you already knew that going hopeless into battle is a form of suicide. Of giving up, like Uncle Zoen."

Tears glistened in the averted eyes. "My mother—"

She stopped, then left noiselessly.

Sixteen

Torquende – Ama Hazanth

A SOUND.

Mildred's eyes flicked open.

Darkness, an hour before dawn. What?

The Crow whispered, "I've got to use the Ruby. Want to see?"

"Sure," Mildred said, though what she really wanted was a little more sleep. But as she sat up she sensed something wrong in the air. Even down here in the dungeon hideout, deep in the living rock palisades of the island. Her arm ached, from a peculiar premonition of wintry chill.

Instantly awake and alert, she followed Prince Marseth silently up a very long ink-black stairway. Occasional arrow slits let in a tiny bit of starlight, which gave her eyes enough light to guide her feet by. The Crow appeared to have the stairs memorized.

Presently he pushed open a stone slab, and abruptly they were in luxury. Stone walls still, but thick carpets under their quiet feet, tapestries on walls. Furniture. Glowglobes in beautiful gold holders. Obviously they were in the main part of the huge royal castle.

Crow knew when to pause, and when to move; he had the guard patterns down. Mildred matched his start-stop pace without complaint, until they halted after a long spiral-staircase climb. Long slit windows had been cut into the walls all the way around.

"We're in the highest tower on the island. "

"Is the Fire Ruby kept here?"

"This *is* the Fire Ruby." He cackled, a rusty sound.

Mildred glanced down—and noticed for the first time the mosaic in shades of red that covered the entire floor, in interlocking patterns that spiraled inward in ever smaller tesserae. When her eyes tried to follow the pattern, her inner ear shifted uneasily, and though her feet knew that the floor was flat, she could not but see the different shades of tesserae as three-dimensional patterns. It gave her vertigo until she lifted her gaze to the windows.

The numerous windows looked out on the blackness of night. But while far in the north stars still winked peacefully, the southern darkness seemed thick and brooding. As Mildred stared into it, a sudden flash of greeny-purple lightning stabbed out of the looming black. There was an answering glitter, the color of bright blood, deep in the mosaic floor beneath their feet.

Crow stook in the middle of the room, eyes closed. Mildred watched in silence. For a long time there was nothing else to see beyond the occasional distant flickers of lightning. Then, just as she noticed stars gleaming in the southern sky, he looked up, and let out a long breath, like a release.

"That's one big storm," she commented. "What did you do?"

"Drove it away." He indicated the mosaic. "Ever since the ruby was built into this tower, the bad storms that used to flood the lower islands and wipe everyone out are pushed eastward into the great ocean. Sometimes a really big storm, like this one, is too much for whatever magic is worked into the pattern, I guess. They'd hit anyway—until I figured how to look into it, see the storm's eye, and ward it away."

"What now?"

"Now we sneak back.

Eastern Sea

North of Geranda a fleet stood off, hoping to trap Jehan of

Khanerenth. Or, that had been their orders. The captain was watching northward through a scope when one of his underlings approached. "Dispatch," this individual announced.

"Let's hear it," the captain replied.

The underling was amused at the news he carried. At his expression some of the hands gathered round. "We've lost Tobin in that storm."

Raucous laughter went up at the unpopular Tobin's doom.

"Debris is washing up on the Decael shore."

"Storm's moved east," the captain interrupted. "Put the flags up. We'll move east, too. We're bound to snare whatever was up north of us, trying to outrun it."

"If they outrun it," commented the helmsman, laughing in anticipation as the signalman ran to flag the rest of the fleet.

Eastern Sea – along the Fereladria

When Wan-Edhe's storm hit the Fereledria, Efael, idle at the moment, played with it. He increased the force, watching as the impenetrable magic along the equator steadily resisted. He did not know, for he did not read minds, that someone was in the storm's midst; he sent a killing storm because killing in any form amused him.

For Marga, lost in the midst of the storm, the attack was shockingly sudden. And it was an attack; she had weathered storms, but this one was different. She sensed malevolence all through it.

She barely had time to tighten everything when it first came on. The rain was stinging cold, like hail, and the waves came fast and increasingly large. There was no time to get her coat—within five minutes she was so thoroughly soaked the coat would only have been more cold weight.

At first she was afraid. It wasn't just the storm, it was the sense that she, and the air and sea and sky, were under attack. Then she was too busy to think about anything beyond her immediate survival.

Her little sailboat began to look impossibly frail in the steadily building gale. Furious water above, before, and below warred with the sea she knew. No. It wasn't the water—

A wave crested, and rushed down the length of the boat,

drenching her again. Another loomed from behind as she struggled to keep the tiller pointed eastward, and the handle jerked against her with a blow she took in the ribs.

Gasping for breath, she braced herself. Held...

Lightning exploded around her and the wind screamed. Again, as if yanked by an immense and cruel hand, her tiller jerked, scoring a gash across her palm and almost dislocating her other arm. She fought for balance, and to keep control of the boat.

Another wave washed down, and her slender jib-beam snapped with a loud *crack!* She caught a glimpse of her neatly battened jib-sail spinning away in the terrible foam. She wrapped another loop around the tiller, bracing the one she'd already bound tightly to her mast. A plunge downward, a neck-snapping lurch up the next wave—and the rope wrenched tight, hummed, held. She wrung her bleeding left hand, shifted her feet—

And a green-black wave appeared, throwing the boat upward. She'd been holding on one-handed, and her weight easily ripped her stiff fingers free. The violent rise threw her backward, to smash into the mast. Turning, she got one arm around it to steady her, and held on tight.

The next wave poured down the boat.

As it rushed back into the boiling sea, she braced herself, preparing to leap for the tiller, and watched, helpless, as the rope stiffened and then went horribly slack. Under her feet she felt more than heard the splintering crack. Beside her the tiller swung loose, and banged against the taffrail.

She locked her fingers around the mast—to find her left hand was no longer capable of grasping. Shifting her grip to her left wrist, she hugged herself against the mast as the wood twisted beneath her, stressing deeply. Its groans were like a live thing wrenched beyond endurance.

Monster waves built with inexorable power, and smashed down unrelentingly. The murderous intent of the storm bore down from directly overhead. From below. Waves slammed down the length of the little craft, bow to wallowing stern.

She could do nothing.

She pressed her cheek against the streaming wood, and shut her eyes.

The boat tipped up again at an impossible angle. Scudding, tossing, the downward plunge...

It's still going east.

What did that remind her of?

A long, horrible dousing with chill seawater. The strength of it tore at her arms. Her head broke free of the cataract; she gasped and choked for breath, seeing the waves as armed towers —

War, that was it.

War means two are fighting.

I am still going east.

By rights the boat should have veered and been flung upside down into a one of the deep troughs between the towering waves, but something was keeping it upright, and pointed — rudderless — east.

But the storm was not moving on.

Howling, as if with fury thwarted, the wind ripped down at her. The rain hardened into barbs of ice, and water tossed and smashed and pounded from all directions. Against her body, the mast's groan increased, then with a rending crash the wood splintered down right near her head. The top, with sail, flew like a giant arrow into the foaming monster ahead, and vanished.

War.

It was important. Her instincts fought to surface in her numbed mind as her lungs labored for air. But it was impossible to think, to see — to right herself. The wind and rain clawed coldly at her arms and she no longer knew if she was holding on. Her sense of balance rocked violently until the invisible thread pulling her east snapped and the boat whirled away into the storm's vortex.

I am lost.

There was a sense of despair, the yearning that mourns separation, but within these feelings gleamed the briefest flash of wonder, of question, and a last lingering trace of laughter.

And, choosing freedom, instinct won free and she disassociated.

And ... *release.*

Like a single bead of oil poured from a slim-necked bottle to touch a still pool, then spread in an ever-widening circle. But the soothing, calming touch could not heal, not against that violent will striving to harm, to destroy the harmony of air and sky and sea.

The world lives.

And it is under attack by...?

Shooting upward, her awareness paused in the crystalline stillness of the stars' canopy, and looked below. There! Clear, a roiling of destructive magic, directed by a malicious will. It had been met by the glowing world-belt, and neither gave way, the thing because it wouldn't, the world because it couldn't.

As she turned in question to the world, it turned to her—

Midlands - Everon

Adam was just waking to a clear, dripping dawn. His dreams had been full of storm and warning. Ignoring the chill of the unwarmed room, he got up and moved to the window, but his mind reached far beyond the limit of his gaze, into the storm.

"Someone is out there," he whispered.

Sinking onto the bed, he covered his eyes with his hands and sent his mind far ... bending past otherwhere-focused danger ... Ah, relief!

: Detlev, I don't know what we can do, but there's someone in the heart of that storm over the Fereledria, and Efael is driving the storm to kill.

Dei Manor - Imar

Under a clear sky, Ilerian and Svirle Treloar of Yssel looked up, then at one another.

Ilerian opened the window and they walked out onto the terrace.

Ilerian smiled. "It's Efael." But his smile faded into question.

Svir stilled, watching beyond the horizon.

Eastern Sea – along the Fereladria

The effort came naturally, like swatting at an angry insect, and below—within—around—a wind swept out of the east and blasted through the thunder-wall of black clouds.

It was a joining of all things.

I am really a part, we are one.

Marga sang, celebrating freedom, the winging, rushing, soaring freedom. Faster and faster, wider. A little farther, a little longer, and the joy and song will be forever, without barrier, without wall, wider than the stars and into eternity —

But the world pulled her back, and soon she forgot regret and the nearly-met pure bright fire. There was contentment in being sky, and air, and sea. Contentment and oneness.

There was no space for mere identity.

By that time a number of minds used to long-distance observing were watching in their various ways. Marga's sudden unity within herself and without was felt by all, but understood by few. Her gesture, backed by the magic that never quite stayed barricaded along the equator, despite the Norsunder mages' efforts, appeared in the mental realm like a comet, arcing high and fast, then shimmering into invisibility. Efael's clouds were scattered into distant and harmless rainspouts, demonstrating ineffable power, but the act had been too quick and too unexpected to track.

No identity was discernable in the realm of the spirit to seekers of either side.

Presently everyone withdrew.

Only the Ancient Sartorans among them knew what they had seen.

PART TWO

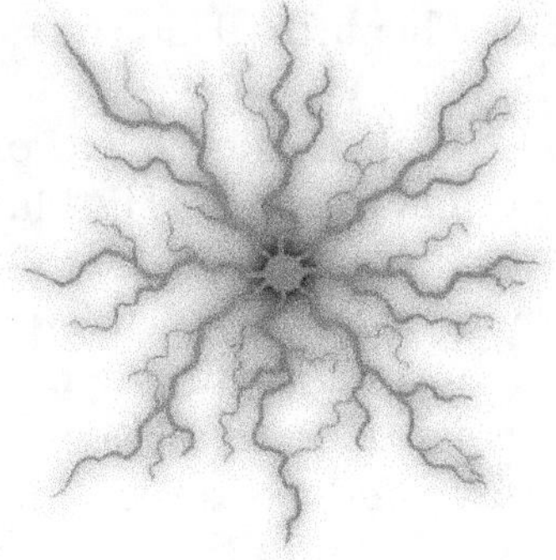

One

TEARS BURNED HIBERN'S EYES, or was that the dust? Or merely a sense of overwhelming weariness? She longed for real tears to fall. To slip down her cheeks, so that she would feel their warmth, and then she would taste a little salt.

She longed for something to be real.

She tried a deep and unrefreshing breath, but that too felt more like the dream of a deep breath, and not the rib-expanding satisfaction of a lung-busting whoop of air.

"Hibern Deheldegarthe!" she said aloud, and at the clatter of syllables on the dead air, she breathed a laugh. "Detlev was right! You are a coward."

Erai-Yanya—CJ—Roy had all been here, and got out. She had to remember what they said about this place. Then she would escape as well.

She began to walk.

As she tramped through the dust, she thought about her experiences so far. Wasn't there something about them—something significant—

A broad-chested military man appeared next to her. He wore armor—chest-plate, shoulder pauldrons, greaves, a chainmail battle tunic, and iron-shod boots—and a crested helm atop his head.

She looked up into a rugged face as brown as hers. The man's expression was one of agreeable humor. "You are?"

Her chin came up. "Hibern. Of Roth Drael."

Now she perceived other people around. Norsundrians, warriors all. She folded her arms. Had she found the threatened occupation force, then?

Her companion smiled. "Relax. No one will touch you. Haven't you realized that by now?" His bluff voice ended on a note of contempt.

"What is there to realize about this place?" she retorted. "Everything is false. Illusion." Including me.

"Norsunder has its rules, too. No one will interfere with you until Ilerian returns and desires it." His accent in Sartoran was very old-fashioned, akin to the oldest magically captured moments in the archives.

She heard this news without any pleasure. "And—what? We're waiting?"

"That's it. We're all waiting. These reinforcements—" He waved a hand, and her vision cleared, revealing a vast array of military encampment before the featureless gray winked back across her vision and blotted them. Another stab of horror hit behind her ribs when she recognized the strange raptorish fox head, gold against black, on the cavalry banners: the legendary First Lancers, elite warriors of Marloven Hess's bloodiest king.

No. She was not about to find herself face to face with the horrible Ivandred of whispered childhood warnings. That vast and distant encampment had to be illusion, therefore so too was the fox banner atop those spears. Perhaps a captured image, for it remained in the dim distance. A truth, perhaps, but not the truth. Concentrate!

She understood then that she was supposed to be shocked into terror. Perhaps into witlessness. She looked away. "Who are you?"

"Theronezhe."

"Do you know when it is on Sartorias-deles?"

He laughed. "Whenever you like."

She cut through his laughter without apology. "If we were to leave, this moment, by the shortest possible route through space and time, when and where would we arrive? Do you know?"

"Where would be a matter of choice—and the availability of rift through which to transfer. As for when—" He shut his eyes. "Late in the year 4759."

That did shock her, but she hid it. She had been walking in this poisonous atmosphere for months. More like a year. She looked around in revulsion and disgust.

Theronezhe seemed to find this entertaining. "Are you very much bored? Shall I give you something to do? Haven't you, in some measure, been studying us? How about an opportunity for experience?"

"To exchange one sort of boredom for another?" She heard the empty bravado in her voice, and tried more sarcasm. "How thrilling."

Theronezhe only laughed, and raised a hand.

Everything around, and above, shifted to impenetrable blackness. Under her feet, gray featureless flooring extended in a circle maybe three paces around her.

Since he was waiting for a reaction, she snorted.

His smile deepened at the corners. "For now, how about seeing some history?"

"When I want lies, I'll go to a play," she said with all the bravado she could muster.

Theronezhe looked amused. "All our archives were captured at the moment. And lies are tedious, useful only in the field. For the weak and credulous."

"The biggest liar is the one who claims never to lie," she said. "And even if I trusted your words, I don't want to be wearied with a lot of torture and destruction."

"The predictable is always tedious," he said. "Many say that about Efael—you always know he'll go for the knife. But Hibern of Roth Drael, I thought you Sartoran mages valued the days of early Sartor."

She was going to point out that she was not a Sartoran mage—that there were those among the Sartoran mages who would refute that claim—but decided against giving him any more information than she had to.

He went on with an indulgent laugh, "I find it amusing how your guild busies its members over the years, like rats burrowing in a midden, snuffing out the odd scrap left here and there, usually for its unimportance, from the conflagrations of four thousand years ago. But here we have hundreds of eyewitness records from that time and after."

Hibern eyed him with distrust. "What of any value would I get from the destroyers' points of view? I'm not all that interested in the Fall of Ancient Sartor anyway. I know the gist of it, that it began at the height of a ceremony at a time when government was conducted by ritual. Successful because they operated on trust."

What had Erai-Yanya quoted Lilith the Guardian in saying? *People could differ in details when arriving at consensus, but everyone had faith in the best of human endeavor, made music and art together, then departed in peace.*

Into this dance-like ritual Ilerian had supposedly walked, beautiful and graceful, and when the famous bard Connanre pointed out the best victims, Ilerian started randomly killing, hurling everything and everyone into chaos.

Senrid had once said, "I don't know that human nature back then was any improvement on now. Maybe it once was. But it seems to me that they had the savage in them just as we do, or they'd have bowed their necks to the blade."

The part that Hibern did not understand was how a morvende could appear two thousand years before their kind came into the world. But she was not going to gratify Theronezhe by asking that, either.

Hibern said to the man in warrior's armor, "I don't need your evidence that violent death rips apart the social concord. Engenders anger. And people reach for weapons to survive— then as now. I'm not enlightened by details of the struggle for survival. My interest is in how people find trust and faith. Harmony and concord. And beauty. Those things exist, they are real, but everyone must work together to make them."

"Then let us look at beauty, and how Detlev regarded it."

As she began to object, a late afternoon, springtime forest scene came to life around her. She stuttered to a stop and gazed in wonder—and then realized she was breathing the same stale, flat air of Norsunder. Then she looked down, and saw that the waving blades of grass and nodding dandelions grew right through her feet.

She resolved to close her eyes at the first sign of the inevitable Norsundrian blood and destruction as the blue shadows and gold light intensified directly before her. Through the dappled light, Hibern glimpsed the soft woven overtunic and pure white hair of a morvende.

Looks like I'm being pushed into seeing it anyway, she thought as the morvende youth walked in silence toward her, between one step and another moving between sun and shadow. He was taller than she, and looked about sixteen—though he might have been older. Or younger. His countenance was one of mind-dazzling beauty, so beautiful it was difficult to calculate his age. His amber gaze was down and inward, the tapered morvende hands peacefully clasped before him. No talons on those finger-ends; he was either from very early in the morvende years, or had one morvende and one sunsider parent.

Theronezhe's amused voice reached Hibern, though she could not see him: "Yours and Erai-Yanya's studies have probably testified to the fact that Dena Yeresbeth made its appearance once before on Sartorias-deles. Not understood, it went by another name. Before it disappeared again, it saw the beginning of your empire period, and it left an imprint on certain of your present, eh, versions of history."

The morvende was now a couple of paces from Hibern. She looked into his remarkable face, trying to find any sort of clue to his thoughts. The curves of childhood blended with the emerging adult to come; his thoughtful, high brow was as unmarked as First Snow. The shadow-lashed amber eyes glinted with golden depths in the summer sunlight. His mouth was straight-cut, its contours betraying no hint of the tightness of anger. A work of art envisioned by angels, she thought, yet where is any sign of life?

"He was regarded as a singularly promising vessel, holding the hopes of the morvende. About fifteen, but already well on the way to uniting them—making them world leaders in knowledge and magic—"

Two men appeared in the forest glade. Hibern drew back, startled, then remembered this was only illusion. But cold fear clenched her vitals as she perceived a tall man with black hair, a neatly kept, pointed beard, and an expression of anticipation that unsettled Hibern, though she could not define why. His form was hidden in a layered robe of tasteful ivory under pale yellow and peach, with fine green embroidery in the form of egrets.

"I'm supposed to know that man?"

"Svirle Treloar of Yssel is the architect of this place."

Next to him was Detlev, only it was not the Detlev she knew. He looked younger than he did now, barely her age. Younger than that, even, by a year or two. His skin showed the traces of old suntan under travel-dust, and his long brown hair lay dirty and unkempt on his shoulders. The distinctive silvery-gray robe she had seen only in a picture was almost unrecognizable; this one was shapeless at the elbows, dusty-hemmed, and here and there thin gaps that might have been made by a carelessly used sharp instrument. Such as a sword. Her stomach tightened as she recognized the brown splatters down one side as dried blood.

His face had hardened into an expression of either terrible anger or else deadly concentration as he cupped his hands.

"In his present guise," Theronezhe went on in his humorous, informative tone, "Detlev is unlikely to tell you much about those days. It was he who sniffed out the undesirable reappearance of Dena Yeresbeth—and it was he who rampaged through the world, burning all the records of Old Sartor he could find, which is why you and your fellow beetles crawl around probing for scraps. But that was another time. This, here, was his recruitment of Ilerian, finding the killer and consumer in that vessel of promise, the truth motivating every human being—"

Detlev stepped toward the morvende boy. Sunlight glistened on something in his hands. The morvende's gaze was caught by the light. He looked up in mild curiosity. His gaze met Detlev's, and he stilled.

"—and letting it free," Theronezhe finished, laughing.

Hibern clapped her hands over her eyes, willing herself away.

Two

Eastern Sea

OUT IN THE OCEAN past Geranda, an enterprising Norsundrian naval captain had spread his fleet into line-of-sight running east and west. For three days they monitored the south-moving current. Even so, they nearly missed the single product of the big storm. The boat was small, mastless, and it drifted south-eastward in a rudderless way.

Signal-flags fluttered between the ships. The fleet broke line and the flagship hauled its wind then slackened sail to investigate.

As the little boat bobbed nearer, anticipation hardened into wariness. Then puzzlement. The boat fetched up peacefully against the side of the flagship, revealing to the armed Norsundrians standing at the quarterdeck rail no crouched and waiting lighters. In fact, the sole occupant seemed to be beyond any kind of response.

The boat looked as if it had been scoured clean of gear either for sailing or living. Sprawled in the middle of the dried boards was what appeared to be a teenaged boy in the ragged remains of a summer-shirt and knee pants. His motionless arms and legs and the upturned side of his face were the color of ripe red apples.

"If not dead, near it," someone commented, disappointed.

Disgusted at the evident dissolving of what he'd looked on as a sure opportunity to gain loot, if not promotion, the captain said curtly, "You two. Make a search. If there's nothing, slit his throat and axe a hole in the bottom of the boat." He gestured to the nearest sailors.

A rope-ladder clattered down to the boat, and the appointed pair clambered down. Only one was armed. He'd thrust an axe through his belt, figuring this weapon would handily cover both orders.

The little boat bumped up against the side of the big three-master, and the two Norsundrians dropped in. They moved in a perfunctory fashion, one to the sunburnt figure and the other looking for storage openings in the clean-swept deck. The first Norsundrian patted pockets on the victim, found nothing, and reached for his partner's axe.

The second backed away, claiming he'd brought the axe so his was the privilege of execution, when at the sound of the voices the recumbent figure stirred, coughed, and spoke.

Both Norsundrians stared, then turned their faces up to their captain, who still stood at the rail.

"Well?"

The first Norsundrian said, "Only part I could make out was a name, Liere Fer Eider."

The captain frowned. The second Norsundrian said, "There's nothing here," and he hefted the axe as he waited for the signal.

The enterprising captain knew the capital list by heart. Liere Fer Eider was on it. He jerked a thumb sideways. "A courier, then. Better have the brat up. Sink the boat."

As the Norsundrians climbed back over the rail, one bearing their unconscious prisoner, the captain stepped close and frowned into the upside-down burned and swollen face, the sparse, gritty spikes of reddish sun-bleached hair, and he shook his head. "Bya-Var!"

The Norsundrian who served as ship's medic popped up from below, and thumbed his chin as he surveyed the victim's upside down face.

The captain said to the two searchers, "You sure he said Liere Fer Eider?"

"That part was clear."

"Must be carrying a message. Bya-Var, see if you can bring him around. Careful."

The medic ducked his head, his lack of enthusiasm clear. Everyone knew what happened to those who bungled inform-ation related to cap-list names.

There was an empty cabin below, with two narrow bunks, that they used as a makeshift sickbay. The courier was unload-ed onto the nearest bunk and the medic went about making him more or less comfortable, with rough and ready efficiency. During this process he made the discovery that the 'he' was a 'she,' a find met with complete indifference until he remem-bered what had (temporarily) saved the girl's life.

A girl? Liere Fer Eider? He looked doubtfully at the mess on the bunk, trying to remember what this Fer Eider girl was supposed to look like. Not that anyone would recognize that sunburned face and sun-bleached hair.

He went topside to report to the captain.

"A girl? What's that, he's a girl? You sure?" At the medic's third nod, the captain pursed his lips. "Never mind waking him up. Her. That might even be Liere Fer Eider. I think we'd best leave her to HQ. Get back down. Make sure she stays alive until someone comes for her."

The medic picked up from supply a pot of the greasy, strong-smelling salve the Norsundrians had concocted mostly for the Chwahir, whose pale skin had for centuries not seen much sun. Pots of it had been randomly distributed through the fleet. He began slathering some on the nearest red limb. The girl stiffened and went utterly limp.

He remembered that the stuff stung before it numbed. "Cure you or kill you," he informed her unconscious figure with grim cheer, splashing a viscous dollop across her face.

The galley bell rang as he finished, and he went out. When he returned with a tray so he could watch and not miss a meal, he noted that there was a visible improvement in the angry red flesh. He slapped on another load of salve and went up to report.

Just then the captain was surprised, gratified, and a little unnerved by the appearance of Llyenthur himself.

"I was in the area, and I've sent Colleron out of it," Llyenthur said, hands on his hips. "Where's your Liere Fer Eider?"

The captain hastened into speech. As they climbed below, he explained how his message had been worded so as not to convey the impression he claimed his prisoner was Liere Fer Eider, and perhaps someone on the dispatch desk at HQ passed it on incorrectly?

Llyenthur stepped into the sickbay and waved a hand to shut the captain up. He did not hide his skepticism. "All right. Understood. Since I'm here..." He bent and lifted the least swollen eyelid. Sighed. "Blue eyes. You didn't think to check?"

The captain, in the doorway, was having difficulty breathing. The little room was suddenly full of too much energy, and a sense of danger; his own fear, in trying to ward it, was choking him. "But we never tried to say..." he began.

Llyenthur ignored him and once again bent over the girl. This time he put three fingers lightly on her brow, above the grease and below the gritty hair. The captain recognized the gesture and shut up. Water plashed against the hull as the air simmered, and then Llyenthur looked up. "Identity gone. She won't last through a transfer—"

The girl stiffened. A badly scabbed hand shot up and grabbed Llyenthur's wrist with a grip remarkable for someone presumably so close to the threshold of death. Llyenthur broke off short and looked down into bloodshot eyes as the girl croaked, "Put me back on the sea. The wind and the water are mine now..." That was Imaran.

The danger stilled and sharpened. The captain's ears throbbed with his racing heartbeat as he said, "What was that? I didn't hear—"

"Just nonsense words. Meaningless." Llyenthur snapped his hand free of the girl's grip, and once again pressed fingers to her head. Her eyes stared upward, unfocussed as faint question quirked her brow.

Llyenthur straightened up and said briskly, "I might as well take her off your hands. If she dies, she dies."

He picked her up, then said to the captain with smiling irony, "I suggest you also review the wording of the signals."

He and the prisoner vanished.

The captain's considerable relief found vent in anger, and he stalked topside to ream his signalman, while a considerable distance away, Imry Llyenthur appeared on a narrow pine-shaded path that overlooked the harbor at Aloca.

To his left, the late afternoon sun slanted down, touching the water to pewter. To the right stretched the mountains marking the Khanerenth border.

A little way above him, the path opened onto a clearing at the top of a cliff. At one end a low-roofed shack squatted under the bowl of the sky. He walked toward it with measured pace. At the sound of his steps crunching pine needles and gravel, the door opened and a small, wiry old woman wiped her hands on her floury apron and smiled. "Khem! It's the young—oh, my! What have you there?"

Behind the woman appeared her brother. Old, and lame from a long-ago sea wreck, he spent each day spying over the bay through a powerful scope that Llyenthur had given him. With loyal and dedicated patience the man watched, and meticulously noted down, the appearance and movement of every Norsundrian ship within range.

Every so often Llyenthur dropped in. He had never given them a name—for safety reasons, of course. But between brother and sister he was referred to as the king's young aid. He'd pick up the sheets of paper that of course he never read. Then he would eat the sister's wonderful pie and talk over this and that, and during the course of the conversation he gleaned from the earnest old man most of the covert movement of Jehan of Khanerenth's fleet.

The increase in lighter defeats subsequently made old Khem more determined to keep closer watch. He was thinking of the latest disaster now as he said worriedly, "I fear I must have dozed off, or not gotten up early enough, for we've heard the worst news, something about a storm—what's this?"

Llyenthur laid his burden on their settle. She had passed out again from the jolt of a double-transfer. Even Llyenthur grimaced; he was not going to do that again any time soon. It was very dangerous to transfer two at once. The air smelled of tinged metal, which he coughed away.

Brother and sister forgot all else as they looked down at the sunburned girl with compassion and pity.

Llyenthur said, "I just now rescued her from the Norsundrians. She is bearing a message that is very important to the king. I was hoping you could restore her to some semblance of humanity. And—this is imperative—write down everything she says. It won't make any sense, but no matter. If she begins to make sense, in fact, please use that emergency sign I taught you. Will you do this for me?" He smiled.

Both nodded fervently. The sister said, "You couldn't do better than to bring her to us! Plenty of fresh air, my cooking, and sleep will do for the poor little soul. And as for her skin— what did they do, those cursed vultures? Why, Gora Lanyed's ointment will take care of that in no time. I'll walk down the path right away, and be back before dark. Good Gora'll make me up a jar soon's I ask—"

"But Good Gora will have to think it's for Khem. A boiling water accident? It is very important no one finds out she is here. In fact, I can safely say that, right now, her remaining a secret is far more important than the watching of ships."

Khem shook his head sadly.

His sister clucked and said, "It's a bad time when girls scarce out of childhood know anything of war."

"We all do what we can." Llyenthur smiled pleasantly. And he left.

Three

Darchelde Forest – Marloven Hess

SVENERIC LOOKED DOWN AS carefully written letters appeared on his magic-paper. It was from Erenlara Sofar, the single remaining member of the Land of the Venn's ruling family.

Sveneric: Yes, I am on my way home, and alone. I left Mearsies Heili on the morning of the eighth, just after they resolved everything. Even with their magic aids it's a very long way to the Land of the Venn.

Rel was divided between his shaping plans and going with me. I think he felt he owed it to my beloved brother, whom I shall forever mourn, but I also think he was seeing me with my brother's eyes. When therefore I refused his offer, I tried to indicate I do not question my own competence for the task ahead. Perhaps this made him aware of what he was doing. At any rate we were agreed without any further discussion.

The conversation with Rel was conducted out of CJ's hearing. We both knew she would have been annoyed at any imputation that I cannot address my own affairs. She would not have had any quarrel with the first reason.

CJ and I were still talking about her accompanying me. I could see that she wished to go, and Clair encouraged her to. I think it might have been, when the idea was summarily ended. There was another try at Clair, following which CJ was far too worried for me to persist. She would have lightened a grim road with her humor, and I had come to rely mentally on her advantage in perspective granted by her Dena Yeresbeth. But I salute her firm loyalty to her troubled friend, and acceded to necessity.

Winter's bite is in this mountain air, but I am warm and reminded of home. All those with land-ties are going back to those lands. Others go with friends. Have you yet an appointed task?   Erenlara

Sveneric wrote off a swift answer, folded away his magic-paper, and stood up to stretch. It was then that he heard the sound that he had been waiting for: the quiet shift of the upper door, the step in the tunnel that meant Senrid was back.

The two of them had arrived at the hideout in Darchelde earlier in the day, under cover of a rainstorm. A couple hours later a courier caught up with them, with the news that Senrid had been awaiting. He had promptly departed again, leaving Sveneric behind.

This was the first time they had been apart since Sveneric's arrival in Marloven Hess. Sveneric had made himself so useful that Senrid had shown no inclination to have him leave. Thus Sveneric had fulfilled David's request without ever having to commit the unpardonable affront of making allusion to its reason.

Senrid, who until last year had been particular about what he drank, if he drank at all, now demonstrated a proclivity for anything fast-acting. He got drunk just about every night for a week preceding the twelfth, and the day itself he drank so steadily he was glow-nosed and puff-eyed by mid-afternoon, and puking-drunk by sunset.

But he'd learned something from his public drunken binges last year: while he wasn't exactly clear-minded, there were no scenes or even harsh words. Those last three days were spent in the hideout, penned supposedly by an autumn squall. Even on the twelfth Senrid remained silent, but to any who had known him, his demeanor was a cold shock just by the contrast; Senrid, who had always been so fastidious, lounged back in his chair with his hair in his eyes and his tunic unbuttoned, drinking and smiling on the others with a sort of ironic amiability, though he never once spoke.

Sveneric was sick at heart to see it—and equally sick that the other Marlovens pretended not to notice anything amiss. Apparently drunkenness to the point of insensibility was Marloven adults' accepted method of dealing with grief for dead family members, and with the humiliation of military defeat. He had already seen it in local villages, on the anniversary of the slaughter at Aladas Pass. Once they woke, despite how wretched they probably felt, it was back to work.

By the night of the thirteenth they were halfway across the country, and Senrid was busy with his current project: organizing the Halian subcontinent's southern kingdoms' resistances for the counterattack that everyone longed for.

This called for a great deal of diplomatic conniving, as the Marlovens' ancient military rep (a plus) was far outweighed by the Marlovens' ancient foreign policy (a minus). David had made himself particularly useful in this regard, for as Senrid put it, he had knowledge, patience, tact, and humor. Any two of those was rare—and all four might even overcome the stigma of past Marloven foreign policy.

Except that Detlev had yanked David abruptly, leaving Sveneric to cover for him.

Senrid came down the tunnel, removed his rain-glittering hat and cloak, and hung them neatly on their peg near the fire's warmth. He looked at Sveneric. "What are you doing up so late?"

It was about three in the morning, and Sveneric was alone in the general room. Everyone else was asleep or out on night patrol. "Writing letters," he said.

"And?" Senrid bent to rub his hands at the fire, then cast an inquiring look over his shoulder at Sveneric. "David returning?"

Sveneric noted that Senrid didn't ask where he was. He knew what Senrid wanted to hear about, and what he did not care about. "David will return as soon as he can. We'll have suitable reinforcement soon: MV has a boat, and will fetch and bring them. You?"

"I'm on my way." Senrid's hands went up. "I guess it's me alone, though I have no patients or tact. And others will add knowledge and humor to that."

Sveneric looked at the two flat palms, and laughed. "I gather it took a few hundred assurances?"

"More. I am to go alone, no weapons. I guess any more than two of us would conquer all surrounding lands as we rode, and if I had a knife I'd slit every throat that I passed. Either that or I'd offend their noble sensibilities by eating with it. No—don't say anything—there's worse to come. Valta seems to think he wants to play around being a warrior."

"Can you dissuade him?" Sveneric did not hide his dismay.

"His father apparently thinks that Valta will be able to ensure that I and my people are not secretly fomenting any conquering plans. Not that he'd recognize 'em if he saw any. I think he's hot to play warrior for a time. I will do my best to deflect him, but if I have to give in, I'm counting on you, and the teens, to keep him happy—and out of trouble."

Everyone had heard the temperamental, spoiled Prince Valta of Perideth.

Sveneric sighed. "Very well."

There had been some trouble between the Darchelde teens and Sveneric when he first arrived—always when Senrid was otherwise occupied. His gang of young Marlovens, who considered themselves privileged persons, at first had resented the apparent swap of David for a short, thin, quiet boy who liked to draw pictures from nature. There was only one person smaller than Sveneric, and Marend had taken Sveneric into a sort of puzzled dislike almost immediately. Sveneric had figured out the why of that fairly quickly.

He said nothing to Senrid about the various jabs he endured, the water poured into his shoes, the destroyed drawings. One afternoon, when it became clear that the challenges would not end until he ended them, he arranged to be strolling through the woods at a time when the four oldest and toughest teens were leaving for a patrol. Betraying no more than a faint air of regret during, and decided sympathy after, the resulting martial arts encounter, he helped them all back to the hideout and volunteered himself for replacement duty while they recovered. Their attitude had changed markedly—and his toward them remained the same friendly politeness beyond which none of them could see.

"We will be fine here," Sveneric said.

Mearsies Heili to the Elgar Strait

Dawn was still a watch away in Mearsies Heili.

Liere had finally fallen into an exhausted sleep. The dream came again. She was trying to will it away when it changed. Worsened. Danger!

She sat up, hands striking at the cool night air. The dream dissolved, but not the terrible grief, or the exhaustion. Pressing fingers on her eyelids, she concentrated on regaining control of her breathing. When she had calmed her breathing, she rose, put on her dressing gown, and drifted noiselessly downstairs to fix a cup of steep.

On a bright ocean morning, Andri had been thinking about Liere, and caught a hint of her distress.

He was high in the air, clinging to the yard as he shifted the outer jib sail. Help and support were still too novel—luxuries—for him to think of calling for them, but why did she not? Ah, he knew, or thought he knew, but if he was right, there was nothing that he could do to amend. He sensed the zap of danger, and a surge of the terrible wordless grief that had been haunting Liere off and on for weeks, intensely for the past three days.

The sense of danger was new.

He selected a long rope—a *stay*, he muttered to himself—and lowered himself rapidly hand over hand to the deck. Dropping down full length, he closed his eyes and focused on Liere. Found her, and she expertly enfolded them somehow so they could not be detected on the mental plane.

: *You heard me?* Came her thought.

: *Because I was trying to reach you. What was that about fire?*

: *The nightmares are worse. This time the lost one walked into flames. And the sense that this has something to do with my mother was stronger. That doesn't make sense, it has to be unresolved guilt for neglecting them since my return from Geth. Once we're safe again I will go back to Imar and see them. Explain why I was gone those five years, if they are angry with me.*

Andri felt her desire to go now conflict with her determination to stick to her part in their plan. Presently they both broke contact, and he lay where he was, thinking hard but to little purpose. He was too ignorant, too new to what he privately termed Detlev maneuvering.

Meanwhile the sun pressed warmly on his eyelids, and the strengthening breeze ruffled along his skin and through his hair. Crossing his hands behind his head, he sighed, prepared to nap right there in the sun —

And a foot nudged his bare ribs.

"What's that for?" He glared up at MV. "I finished changing out your ripped sails."

MV crouched down beside Andri, his yellow-flecked eyes holding then losing the strong light as he glanced about the sturdy, un-ornamental Chwahir coastal cutter. With a flicker of a smile he said, "If this were my craft, your chores'd be just beginning."

"Even with the wind finally normal?"

MV's crazy plan had worked.

Andri still couldn't believe that. Not that he'd been able to see anything, but he'd felt them ride the howling wind — a wind so fierce it would probably affect currents all down the strait, MV said when the storm abated, leaving them still alive. But the sails were in tatters.

MV's desperate experiment had probably saved them. He'd certainly shot them along the wind up the strait at an impossible speed, to emerge at the other end of Drael. Then they'd just had to ride out the end of the storm — bad enough under normal circumstances.

But MV had said (when they could hear one another again), "It had to be far worse going north. I guess Efael had to play with it, too."

Andri shook his head. "And you think boats are fun. What's fun is a fast gallop over ground that doesn't move. What's going on?"

"Time for you to make a decision." MV crossed his arms, his face serious, so rare an expression that Andri's danger sense flared. "If you want to go home, I can put you ashore in Martan or thereabouts."

"Otherwise?" Andri stifled a yawn and propped himself on his elbow.

MV's eyes flicked northwards. "Going to make a pickup or two."

"Who? What's going on?"

"Sveneric, just now. Rolfin. That Geth martial artist, what's her name? Mildred. Apparently she's with another wild talent, much like you." MV tapped his head. "Detlev's put the word out, time to gather up some searchers who've skill with their hands and with Dena Yeresbeth skills."

"Why? Going back to Mearsies Heili again?" Andri sat up. "Liere said a day or two ago that nearly all of 'em have left."

"Nah." As the sails began to snap in the rising wind MV squinted upward, then down. "First, there's a massive search going on; David got yanked. Rest of us are to carry on the search up here."

"For?"

MV shrugged. "Right now? Whatever was in that storm. Something's got the Host hopping around like their asses are on fire. Whatever it was, was on the sea. So we're to spread out among harbors both sides of the strait. Listen around, with regular ears and in the mental realm. There should be some talk, at least, even if we don't find what it was."

"And second?"

MV squinted at the horizon, then back at Andri. "Take the war to the Host. Ilerian, specifically."

Andri choked on a laugh. "What? Me? I'm as trained as a two-year-old in this Dena Yeresbeth stuff."

"Won't be, by the time Adam is done with you."

"But there have to be far better people."

"You'd think. But the fact is, there aren't. Part is the timing. Another ten years, it would be different. Of course, if this war had happened ten years ago, we'd have lost outright. Detlev said to talk to you, so here I am, talking."

Andri grimaced. "What about David?"

"He'll be part of it."

"So he's no longer chasing Imry Llyenthur?"

"He'll be back at that, is my guess, soon's they find out whatever's got the Host on the run."

Andri scratched his ribs thoughtfully, then gave a low whistle. "Vengeance David's leitmotif?"

MV snorted. "David's the only one thinks Imry's salvageable."

"Salv—huh! I take it you don't agree."

MV shrugged one brown shoulder. "No opinion. Haven't seen Imry since he left us."

"His ally Efael's also hunting his chitlins. Now that sounds characteristic." Andri grinned. "Yeres too?"

MV shrugged again. "Who knows, with her?"

"Mmm. I almost feel sorry for him, shit that he is."

"Imry?" MV ghosted a laugh.

Andri's grin widened. "I have to admit, I kind of liked him. Though our interview only lasted about ten heartbeats before Efael blundered in."

MV's lips quirked at the mention of Efael. His gaze lifted to the horizon and the sun touched them with an orange glow. "Ah, Imry was always a snot. I used to think he had about as much chance of making it as a snake in an armory."

"Meaning?"

One shoulder lifted again. "Meaning in some ways he was a mess. Despite Detlev's efforts. We all saw it. When Detlev began preparing us for hopping the wall, Imry resisted. Can't help regrets about that."

Andri's brow furrowed in perplexity. "I thought Detlev handpicked you lot?"

"Eh, some think it was happenstance. More like rescues. Including Imry." Seeing that Andri wanted to pursue the subject, MV swung to his feet and tipped his head toward the wheel.

Andri joined him on the bench behind the wheel. MV untied the restraining rope, settled back, and propped one foot on the wheel to hold it steady. The sea had been lake-calm; now water plashed playfully against the ship's sides.

MV cast an idle look over at Andri. "What's on your mind?"

Andri looked up. "Is your Imry a spectacular disaster, then?"

MV laughed, and finished the implied question. "Or would any of us have followed the same path if we'd split off, and rustled up a world-wide war to prove our independence?" He laughed again. "Imry was different from the start. Weird. Abilities—" The short shrug. "He'd had training. I'd just had size."

"Weird?"

MV's eyes narrowed reminiscently. "He and I were the oldest, see. Four, going on five. Rest were babies, or near. Boring to us. When we first arrived, Detlev introduced us to one another right off. Saved the others for later. Anyway, he outlined the plan. Lots of exciting stuff about martial arts and espionage and so on, but in it were the rules governing the group. First names, all equal—and as if he hadn't heard, ol' Imry spouts out with *He shall address me as Prince Imry*. Voice like the squeak of a bat. He was small, too, stick arms, dressed like an emperor. Of course I started in on his prissy clothes to show I wasn't going to put up with any Prince Imry horseshit. He started mouthing right back, and Detlev intervened before I could sit on him and give him an uninterrupted airing of my views on the proper deportment of pipsqueaks. Truce, for a while. Rest of the day."

MV paused, noting Andri's grin of interest. He took sightings, adjusted course, and went on. "That first night. We were told to share a room. Imry was aghast, and refused. I figured he was afraid of the dark—"

"What?"

"Yep." MV jabbed a finger toward Andri. "And what's more, he never got over it. Bet you he hides out even now, when he has to go to cover."

"Not fear of monsters. But of safety?"

"No such thing as safety," MV amended.

"Go on."

"Detlev said 'Try it' so Imry gave in. We shucked our clothes. Both got another surprise. Me to see a kid all black and blue and green, scars under the bruises. Him to see someone not. I climbed into the sack, hit the pillow. I was out. Then he jumped me. Woke up with him trying to strangle me."

Andri whistled. "What did Detlev do?"

"Pulled him off. Said he'd watch him, by mind, the rest of the night. Did. Imry sat there on his bunk all night, back to the corner, watching me snore. Couple nights of that, Detlev gave him his own room. Slept then."

"Ah."

"He shed a lot of the bad habits he'd gotten in those first four years, but not all. He already knew something of weapons, as I said. He had to be searched pretty much every night before bedtime, for a couple of years. Never trusted any of us. He'd charm one or two of the others only to practice divide and conquer. Life was a state of war. Grudges. And he always had to have his own room, unlike the rest of us. Which he barred, every night. Eh, surprisingly the grudge he had against me ended the day he managed to thrash me. But he never stopped ragging David and Adam. Adam being the smallest. David because he was his brother. Oh yes! And there was the one against Senrid."

"Senrid? Montredaun-An?"

"Kept yammering about how our first plans should be against him and Marloven Hess — it was clear enough, in retrospect, he was blathering what he'd been told by that old shit Kedran Llyenthur. Detlev kept the two of 'em — Imry and David — on Geth or Five exclusively, our early runs. His approach being, showing how limiting the desire for one country was. Guess he finally prevailed with that one," MV added with some irony, though to himself he amended, *With everyone except Laban.*

Andri said, "I remember the talk last winter, some of you thought Llyenthur'd set up his HQ in Senrid's country. And the surprise when it turned out he hadn't."

"Yep. Still can't figure out the connection between him and Larkadhe, but then thirteen years ought to have produced some new quirks. Question?"

"Why Detlev couldn't see he was failing, and what was likely to be the result."

"And why he kept training him? You'd have to ask Detlev."

"You haven't?"

MV's shrug was faint. "What is, is. And Detlev seldom gives a straight answer to questions like that."

"He lies?"

"Nah. Straight —" MV gestured, a horizontal slash. "Linear. Dyranarya types don't think linear. And Detlev has a habit of answering certain kinds of questions by reflecting on your motive for asking."

"David thinks he can, in effect, right a mistake of Detlev's?"

MV snorted a laugh. "Got it."

Andri whistled again. "Damn. Back to you and me. Detlev really said to pick *me* for an attack on Ilerian of the Host — ?"

"Orders now are to corral you if I can. If not, let you off on some coast. Make those pickups I mentioned. Rolfin and Adam'll be waiting. And Dirk."

"Dirk?"

"Yanli's found him. Told you, Detlev wants people with skills. Can move fast, and listen in the mental realm."

"I'm fine with the first, rotten at the last. You'd need Liere for that."

"Detlev says different."

Andri had to admit that the Selenseh Redian seemed to have done something to his reach in the mental realm. But he had no training. Liere insisted she had no training in Dena Yeresbeth either. He always thought her skills far superior, but he was gradually coming to understand that Dena Yeresbeth could manifest differently for different people.

And if he returned to Enaeran? He knew that any hint of his presence now would cause Adon Marsael to harass people again in hard target searches. Or worse. Whereas Adon Marsael wouldn't be looking for Liere.

"What happens if the sea mystery's already found?"

MV lifted a shoulder. "Adam wants us to decoy Norsunder away from places where refugees and the like have been planting in secret, usually in tough terrain. I think it's a waste of time."

"Why are secret harvests a waste of time?" Andri retorted. "We were getting that organized in Enaeran before I got nabbed by Llyenthur."

MV's brows canted at a steeper angle. "Did you really think there's any secret harvest that Imry doesn't know about?"

That hit Andri like a blow to the chest, and he stared out over the sea. "You think he's merely letting them keep busy all spring and summer, eh? I should have seen that possibility."

MV shifted his foot and lazily pushed Andri off the bench. "Why d'ya think we're making our own plans, shitbird? Whatever Imry's got going, eventually we'll have some fun mucking it up everywhere we can. But first we've got to uncover this sea mystery. Don't remember the old man being so serious for, eh..." His mind reached back, and remembered Detlev's grimness after Efael had nearly killed Adam. But no one talked about that. "Put a shirt on. Looks like we've finally got enough wind to move, and it's coming in cold."

Andri went below, and stared at the deck planking, which was nearly dried out. The smell of brine still suffused the air. Secret harvest not a secret? They'd been so sure that the Norsundrians were spread too thin, and they were unfamiliar with the terrain ... but then there were those damned spy birds.

There was also Adon Marsael, willing to torture anyone if he thought that person might know where Andri was. He was obsessed about Andri, which is why everyone thought it best if he kept a distance. Liere had been spreading the word, one person at a time, encouraging them to hold on, and promising Andri's return when he had gathered allies.

If you looked at it that way, he was gathering allies right now. Not running. Except he knew he was running.

When Andri hopped back up on deck, MV said, "Well?" He had no interest whatever in being yoked to any form of government, but he understood the pressures on those who did.

Andri looked up. "I figure I owe Detlev a couple."

MV grinned. "Search it is, then," and threw the wheel into a spin.

Four

Norsunder-Beyond

HIBERN FOUND HERSELF IN what appeared to be a circular room, utterly dark above, with no identifiable source of light around her, yet she could see that shelves and shelves of books encircled her, a featureless gray floor beneath her feet.

They tell the truth — part of the game — but only what they want you to know.

Theronezhe had obviously wanted to shock her with that magic-captured scene, which had a whiff of immediacy about it, mostly in Detlev's messy appearance. As if he'd just come from a fight. She knew from her experience so far that that appearance meant nothing: if, no, when she escaped, she would be wearing the same clothes she had been wearing when Ilerian forced that transfer on her, right down to her uncombed hair and summer sandals, however much time outside passed between then and now.

So, though that scene seemed immediate, she didn't trust it. She considered it carefully, and identified the anomaly: it was the young morvende's lack of startle. A peace-loving, gentle individual suddenly beset by those two, especially Detlev, who'd probably smelled of smoke and steel and blood, would have caused a stronger reaction, wouldn't it? Or would it?

She knew she was guessing. What she could not guess was

the purpose, except for a sense that if Detlev was trapped almost five thousand years ago, and told that he would make his first foray two thousand years later—with proof—would that sense of inevitability be a weapon to use against him?

More guesswork. Time to deal with what she could actually see around her. Even if it was more fakery. She also had to remember that, whether or not she was being watched, she must behave as if she were. The question now was, had she been sent, or had she somehow blundered into this space?

Libraries had always been her solace. Her retreat. And, most importantly, her source for investigation. She forced herself to examine that experience, unpleasant as it was, and yes, she was fairly convinced that Theronezhe had been startled mid-laugh. He had not sent her here; she had willed herself away from him, and long habit as well as instinct brought her to books.

But she could not trust any library in Norsunder. And he still could be watching.

She looked around. What will you wager these are all about Norsunder and their rotten deeds? Ought she to leaf through them and mime suitable horror? She pulled down a book at random. Or what she assumed was random: she would not believe even that.

The Norsundrian script was unfamiliar at first glance, but scrutiny revealed familiar Sartoran lettering here and there. This was like a puzzle, and she had always been good at puzzles. She blinked at the page, thinking about the nature of time. She had yet to eat or drink; if she pinched herself, it hurt, but she had discovered that this was the memory of sensation, and when she forced herself to pinch hard enough to bruise, there was no bruise on her skin.

She would make this semblance of time work for her—since she had nothing else to do, why not learn Norsundrian?

Royal Castle - Larkadhe

Duin cast a sour glance up at the tower battlement, where Llyenthur and the hawk master gazed out at the western peaks.

Damn forsaken place, nothing but mountains in all four directions. Hunching his shoulders forward, Duin let loose with a huge yawn. Relief made his eyes water. The aches in the sides of his jaw from long hours of yawn-repressing eased.

"I like to sleep," he thought morosely, glancing upward again. His eyes stung. Squeezing them hard to get rid of the blur, he then studied the two figures on the battlement. Llyenthur was standing with his hands clasped behind him, his head bent to catch the words of the short, stocky hawk master. One of the master's bulky gauntlets gestured northward toward the strait, creating a martial silhouette against the cloudy afternoon sky. The distant Ghildraith peaks were cloaked in a heavy gray mist.

Duin shifted his elbows on the wall, and yawned again. No telling how long they'd be at it. The minor aides yakked about their rec-time drunken binges, or trips to the pleasure houses, but Duin thought longingly about sleep. His eyes drifted closed. And dreams. In his dreams, he was never tired. Won all the fights...

Snorted. Damnit! His head jerked up and his eyes opened. Close one!

He sent an angry glare up at the unheeding figures. The hawk master's gloved fist now pointed to the west, and both heads turned profiles to Duin.

He yawned again, gratefully, but as his mouth closed, anger at his eternal exhaustion tightened round his skull. All a matter of control, he thought sourly. Sure. I notice you're never around to be kicked out of the sack for goldbricking.

He sent the thought nastily at Llyenthur's back, not caring — now — if it might be heard.

Nearly forty-eight hours on my feet, tell me that's not control. Meanwhile who's to say half your incommunicado spy trips aren't really just sack-outs in some warm, luxurious castle somewhere?

Duin yawned again and stretched his stiff neck. He detested the swarming, screeching spy birds and preferred to be out of range when the hawk master called them in; Yeres's spy birds had been bad enough, with their disturbingly fixed gazes, like the mindless soul-bound warriors Efael seemed to like so much, until he saw how easily they got cut down. These birds were worse than soul-bound, they were obnoxious, fractious, and clearly thought themselves kings of the sky. Four of them appeared now, swiftly-growing gray specks. With shrill, ear-rending shrieks they flapped and circled around the high tower.

Duin made a swipe at his watery eyes and watched with

slightly warmer interest. The gray birds did not settle, but continued to circle and squawk, and then the hawk master's body stilled. He punched a fist toward the north.

Duin shifted his stance, gaining a better view toward the north. Maybe the big one would come, which would make this less of a waste of time — time that could be spent sleeping — than had been the case for the last three watches.

The only reason Duin was along was because Llyenthur disliked being weighed down by extraneous objects. Like notecases. When he was what he called 'focused' and wouldn't hear one of his mental emergency signals, he made Duin come along merely to listen. A duty Duin had at first thought exciting until he came to hate the inner tug of the signal, like someone plucking at a nerve in his brain, and the long watches of sitting and waiting. And when a call came, he seldom got any explanation before Llyenthur abruptly transferred.

Duin thought over the signal words for which he waited. Names of the Host, of course. Detlev, several of those brats he used to run — David, MV, one called Laban. Various lighter leaders on the cap-list. Some other obvious ones — capital cities. Eidervaen. Ferdrian. Choreid Dhelerei. Mearsies Heili. Then there the words and names. Those were the obscure ones — blade, for instance. That could mean anything. Same with moon. The latest was a name, Khem. No idea if it was a person, place, or thing.

A loud *Kek-kek-kek!* from above brought everyone's gazes skyward. A dark shape arrowed down from the clouds, then slowed with long wings spread in a shallow V. Finding a current, the peregrine falcon hovered in savage grandeur above the tower. The smaller hawks shrieked and retreated to a safe distance, wheeling like excited sparrows about the lower towers.

Duin's sourness lightened to a kind of parochial pride as he watched the hawk master back away a few prudent steps. The falcon dropped closer, the wind from the great wings blowing Llyenthur's hair and sending ripples through his shirt.

Duin smirked, remembering with undiminished pleasure the discomfiture of the local commander's aide after he'd pompously proclaimed the experiment as impossible. Llyenthur had said earlier to Duin — and Duin had repeated smugly and loftily into the glowering face of the aide before the entire mess — that it was simple. The mistake has been in insisting on the usual enchantment, which the birds fought even after the magic was laid over them. "They need their freedom. We need merely focus on the hunt instinct and the bird will do the rest itself."

This falcon flew tirelessly over the higher peaks that the smaller birds did not attempt, and it permitted Llyenthur to ride along by Dena Yeresbeth when he had the inclination.

Now it screeched at the human, and dropped still closer. It was three or four arms' lengths over Llyenthur's head, the terrible yellow taloned claws outstretched.

Llyenthur flung up one arm, elbow out, bracing as the talons closed round his forearm and the wings folded down. You forget the size of these birds, especially the females, seen up close. They were so much smaller at cloud height in the sky. Duin could see the yellow eyes from where he stood, as the head darted back and forth. Then the falcon again gave its hunting cry. Llyenthur's shoulders tensed as the bird flung out its wings and shot upward. Llyenthur staggered back a step, and Duin heard him laugh in surprise.

The hawk master came forward and a short exchange followed. Duin straightened up as Llyenthur waved a casual salute and ran down the steps to the lower battlement.

He joined Duin, flexing and wringing his hand. Thin runnels of blood marked the white sleeve, and through one ripped gap, torn flesh oozed. "What was that for?" Duin pointed at Llyenthur's bleeding arm.

Llyenthur grinned. "Who knows? Coquetry, perhaps." Still wringing his hand, he said, "We didn't hear from Laban? Or about him?"

"Nothing," Duin said, straightening up. Had he missed something when he nearly fell asleep? No. He would have felt that horrible twang. "Nothing."

"Ah, as well. I need to catch up on far too many fronts. Let's let him marinate a little longer," Llyenthur said. "He's right where I want him." He transferred back to his office.

Five

Border Mountains – Southwestern Everon

THE SAME NIGHT, ADAM sat forward, gloved fingers laced loosely around the heavy ceramic mug so popular in this part of the world, and stared down into the fire.

He'd already glanced once toward the door. The innkeeper knew he was waiting for someone. Any more looks would raise curiosity in the other idlers on the perimeter of the celebration.

Presently the door opened. A swirl of cold, rainy air blew in and chilled the back of his neck. The clean scent of wet hay cooled his lungs briefly, then was closed out again by the heavy warm air redolent of roasted food, spiced wine, and cool-weather clothes that had been laid away in last spring's blossoms and now were worn for the first time this season. From the far room, rhythmic stamping of a dance set the floor to vibrating. Over the rumble lilted merry melodies from a tiranthe and a flute. Glad cries of greeting gusted from else-where in the tavern's great room. A jovial voice exclaimed with determined cheer against the weather.

In the opposite corner, two reedy pipes added their harmonics to the tiranthe that had been plied steadily over the last couple of hours. Bright, happy tunes, always. Adam had counted three variations on one familiar theme so far.

He let his breath out slowly, careful to keep his expression appropriate to the occasion. He had already earned his keep. The sketches of the newly wedded pair and their relations and friends had been carefully taken charge of by an aunt. Now he was merely a guest, part of the background of the celebration.

The door opened again, to the leisurely rap of riding-boot heels on the wood floor. No greetings called.

Adam turned in his chair and lifted his hand.

Laban slid his cloak from his shoulders, shook the rain off, and slung it over one of the few remaining empty pegs. His wavy hair had darkened to black by the wet. His summer-sky blue gaze swept the room, found Adam, and held there.

Inevitable was the flurry of interest at Laban's appearance, for the loud, brash young Laban had grown into a rather dashing young man. His vivid coloring was now heightened and highlighted by the rain-washing and by the golden glow of the firelit inn.

But Laban's attention was wholly on Adam, his expression abstract. And his clothes were nothing to draw further interest: an old, coarse-woven vest over a heavy linen shirt. Threadbare cuffs. Dun woolen trousers bag-kneed from long hours in the saddle. What could be seen of his blackweave boots was scuffed and worn, as was the heavy belt he wore over the vest. A careful observer might have noticed that the sides of the belt were suspiciously smooth-rubbed (as if the weapons that usually hung there had been recently removed) but there was little else in Laban's manner or appearance to warrant careful observation.

At least, not from the revelers.

"Hungry?" Adam greeted him as Laban dropped into the adjacent seat.

An outburst of laughter followed by a skirling of music as a new song began almost drowned the word. Laban flung a look over his shoulder, then nodded, assessing Adam—who, he decided, had not changed essentially at all.

Adam seemed to be waiting until the hovering innkeeper brought food and drink. When the innkeeper had set down plate, silver and cup of hot wine, and Adam still had not yet spoken, Laban paused in his attack on the food and said, "How long have you been waiting?"

"Just today."

"Then you knew where I was."

"I had a good idea." Adam smiled apologetically.

"Wherever there's ruin?" Laban's response was bitter. "Why did you invade my dreams?"

Adam did not immediately answer, but shifted his gaze to the fire.

Laban picked up his fork again. When he was done eating, Adam said mildly, "Detlev has called us together. MV is waiting on the coast of Eleyad."

Thin flushes of anger ridged Laban's cheekbones. "And so?"

Adam's fingers lifted away from the sides of his cup. "Come with me," he invited.

Laughter from behind. A woman's voice, high and not very tuneful, began a song. Stamp! Stamp! Stamp! The dishes rattled on the table to the thunder of feet in the far room.

Laban threw them a distracted glance as he said, "I thought I made myself clear enough last year."

"Not to me."

Laban paused, eyeing Adam. There was no sign of irony or even of disbelief or skepticism in Adam's face, so Laban opted for the literal.

"Then I will tell you what I told Rolfin. I'm solo now. And I am not on this world by choice."

Adam said, "There were several weeks between the appearance of Norsunder and Kessler's spell."

As Laban looked up in irritation, his head was jostled by the elbow of an unheeding soul pushing to join the wedding guests, who were forming into a circle around the wedded couple.

Laban's brows quirked at Adam. "If you picked this place deliberately for a talk, your sense of timing has changed for the worse." And, as Adam responded only with a slightly rueful shrug, Laban said, "You don't believe what I told Rolfin."

"I believe you."

"Then why are we having this conversation?"

"Because of the reason why you stayed."

"I stayed out of interest. To see what would happen. If I'd known about Kessler's trap I'd have left at once."

"You stayed because it was Imry who led the attack."

Laban's lips curled sardonically. "Is that why this bleating and twitching? Imry was right. You always were a rabbit, Adam."

"He did catch up with you, then."

"Caught up with me indeed. After smashing my third resistance ring the other night. We had an interesting chat before I went through a window. After he chided me, enumerating all my errors, and ending..."

Laban paused, but instead of betraying shock or astonishment, Adam just winced and shook his head slowly. Laban fell silent.

Adam said, "With an invitation to come join him? Because you 'aren't worth his time yet'? What did he offer you, a special spell for when you do decide to go to him?"

"You too?"

"No." Adam turned to stare into the fire, his face troubled. "I haven't seen him at all."

"And you've managed to avoid a second personal invitation from Efael. Imry told me that, too. Thought it was a rare joke." Laban rubbed his hands up his face and through his long wet hair. "I'm sorry, Adam."

Adam grinned, looking suddenly very young. "Even a rabbit can run."

Laban smiled. The anger was gone, but not the bitterness. "You've been hanging around this continent, dodging Efael and watching my failures from afar, and what, hoping to clean up the mess? It's heroically admirable of you, but why?"

"Because we always look out for one another."

"Was it altruism that brought David to Geth-deles to hunt me down?" The anger was back.

Adam turned to watch the dancers. More couples joined the wedding pair. Adam seemed to be finding pleasure in the shabby group, many of them oddly matched — very young with very old, tall with short and round. And all awkwardly trying to maneuver in too small a space.

Adam said, gaze still on the celebrants, "He didn't take over your pirate empire, did he?'

"He dismantled my eighteen months of work — and fun — in two months, and walked away saying the episode was unworthy of me. Unworthy! Was it worthy of Detlev to have killed off half the Delieths before deciding he liked the lighter side after all? I am answerable to no one. I sided with neither of the corrupted midden-heaps there on Geth-deles. Worked for my own enjoyment, for what else is there?"

Adam said, "You know that was Henerek. Then Kessler."

"He could have stopped them. Why didn't he? Whim?"

And when Adam didn't answer, Laban repeated slowly, "I am not answerable to Detlev. Just as he has never been answerable to me. I suppose he stationed you here to spy on me?"

"No. I was stationed here to monitor what the Host is doing to the Eid in Imar. Finding you was my own doing."

The fire leaped and crackled. Adam watched the dancers, and the musicians, without moving.

"Well?" Laban said in a goading voice.

Adam turned his head to meet Laban's gaze at last. "Would you object if I stayed with you?"

Laban did not hide his annoyance. "Why?"

"Anything more, young fellows?" The innkeeper appeared at their elbows.

"Sure." Laban handed over his cup. And again, as soon as they were alone, "Why? I told you I'm solo now. Ah! You're afraid I'll go over to Imry? If so, do you really believe you could stop me?"

"He would like nothing better than to have you come to him out of self-loathing rather than out of conviction. Then you'd make the perfect perpetual lieutenant."

Laban sat back, not hiding his derision. The innkeeper put down fresh drinks then left. Adam's sat untouched. With an extravagant and defiant gesture Laban drank off half his spiced wine in one go.

Adam said, "You were his shadow when we were small. Do you remember how you felt when he walked away and didn't look back?"

Laban's derision did not change.

"After thirteen years you still have some of his mannerisms, and some of his attitudes. Shall I go on?"

"I'm not the only one. But say whatever you have to say."

"You stayed here to fight perhaps out of a sense of competition with Imry, and he'd know that. He'd also know why you chose this area. He's not omniscient—he knows you. What you don't see is that in trying to fight him here you are setting up your own defeat by accepting and playing by his rules."

"Back to Detlev and his 'we exist to serve'?"

"Whatever his reasons, past and present, you know better than to call them convenient." Adam was watching the dancers again.

Laban looked up at the red-faced bride, verging on middle

age, her pale blond hair damp from heat. Her husband, a tall, homely man in his late forties watched her with dark-eyed passion. They danced breathlessly, heavy-footed, bumping accidentally against guests. One of the bride's pinned-up braids slipped and she snatched at it and lost her balance. His hand reached, and gripped her plump arm. There was a convulsive squeeze; firelight glow-etched muscles and tendons. Not just passion, but tenderness.

Laban's gaze moved to the faces. Laughter edged with hysteria in some of the young. Celebration smoothing sorrow-lines in the old. The border between sadness and joy was nearly insubstantial: the little common room, just this once, comprised for them all the world.

No matter which side in the fight got the upper hand, these were the people who too often died.

Laban spun the liquid in his cup, shifting his gaze to the ruby glow.

Derision still marked his face, but the hostility was gone as he remembered Detlev facing Efael in order to rescue Adam, nearly dead. No, whatever his reasons, they were not convenient.

"Who are you fighting for? For them?" Adam's gloved thumb indicated the Everoneth dancers. "Or for yourself?"

Laban shook his head, then dropped his cup down with a decisive clunk. "I'm fighting because I've been taught how to fight." He stood up. "Wish 'em long and happy lives, will you?"

Adam rose with him, slowly, the acknowledgement of defeat. They walked together to the entryway and Laban was reaching for his cloak before Adam said, "Will you stay blocked against us?"

"I can't, can I?" One of Laban's expressive brows quirked as he smiled down at Adam.

"I will stay out of your dreams if you ask me to," Adam replied. "I had to try."

Laban slung on his cloak, then smiled briefly. "Right." He opened the door, and vanished into the rainy darkness.

Instead of heading back to the ruins of his camp in the hills to marshal his hot-heads for another, desperate try, he turned his face northward, and vanished into the night.

Six

Off the Gerandian coast

WHEN IMRY LLYENTHUR FOUND it necessary to do his own spying, he preferred the oblique approach. In some circumstances a spider-web can be a more effective barrier than steel cables—at least when one wishes to mark, unobserved, someone's crossing.

One of the sailors on board the ship that had found the unidentified courier served unknowing as his flag, and also as his eyes and ears. The tracer was a minor one, unlikely to set off any alarms: if the sailor set eyes on, or heard the voices of, any of the Host, the spell zapped an alarm to Llyenthur, then vanished. There was always the chance that the sailor would be asleep or on shore leave and miss them altogether, but Llyenthur gambled on the speed with which word usually gets around in a fleet. Everyone would be wanting to get a glimpse of the feared upper command, or to put it more correctly, try to grab an opportunity to ear in on Great Business.

However, when Efael did turn up, Llyenthur's man was right at his post behind the wheel, near the captain scanning the Gerandan coast with his spyglass. Two continents away, in the middle of a rainy night, Llyenthur felt the alarm. He dropped his pen, held the man's mind while carefully dissolving the spell, and sat back to enjoy the show.

Ilerian stood in the background, against the rail.

Seeing him, Llyenthur sat upright, his habitual mind-shield now tightened down to a thread. He watched Ilerian watching as Efael lamped the captain. Ilerian seemed to be just standing and looking at the ocean; Llyenthur knew he was checking the ship and its surroundings for interfering magic, and finding nothing.

Now the sailors. The white head turned and the amber eyes scanned each individual. Llyenthur shielded himself completely, then sensed the man whose mind he'd invaded shuddering as if a cold wind scoured through his brain. When Llyenthur looked through the man's eyes again, Efael was listening to the captain talk. The captain's manner was nervous but his big smile indicated he expected credit for the earlier action.

"... and so when she said 'Liere Fer Eider' I thought it best to invoke cap-list commands, and sent word to HQ. Llyenthur himself came a couple hours later, and looked at her —"

"What did he say?" Efael interrupted.

"What? When?"

"When he arrived." Efael's tone softened with threat. Llyenthur noted he looked bitterly tired, almost drunk.

The captain was plainly terrified. He spoke faster, defensive now. "He said Colleron wasn't around. Said he was near, so he came. He said, where's your Liere Fer Eider? The signalman had either garbled the message or the receiver at HQ did. He went below. I did too. He looked at her eyes. Said, blue, didn't you check? Something of the sort. The girl woke up and gabbled something. He said it was nonsense, and he hoped she would survive transfer — and they disappeared."

Ilerian's eyes were on the Gerandan coast, his manner absorbed. To the sailors he appeared divorced from the proceedings. Llyenthur knew he wasn't.

Efael raised a hand to form the transfer sign. He stilled when Ilerian left the rail and joined them. Llyenthur's man watched in horror and fascination; when Ilerian's attention was otherwhere he appeared a tall, slender, striking white-haired morvende who seldom noticed (or reacted to) anything around him. The light everyone shared seemed somehow different around him, as if he were physically more at a distance, or more separated from events. Even in bright daylight there was a wintry lack of highlight to the blue-white hair, or the fine, pale features, or the light-colored unremarkable clothes. But when he drew near it seemed all of a sudden, and when he looked you in the face it was difficult to perceive features or an expression, even. To a sensitive it was as if a little of Norsunder-Beyond moved always with him. To Llyenthur's man, seeing Ilerian however briefly face to face was like being exposed to the kind of deep-winter ice that, dead-white and light-strange, numbs, and burns, and then when you try to pull free tears your flesh.

"I want to see that," Ilerian said.

Llyenthur knew it immediately as a rebuke to Efael but the captain stepped backward and cried, "I reported the truth!"

Ilerian locked gazes with the captain, and ripped the memory from him. Llyenthur knew that his own appearance, voice, words, and manner were the focus of Ilerian's attention.

When he had finished, Ilerian glanced up at Efael and they disappeared. The captain sagged to the deck with the mind-crippling headache inevitable after that kind of contact with Ilerian, blood running from his nose.

Llyenthur abandoned his stunned receiver, and laughed. The hunt was on.

Several days later, Llyenthur topped the path high on a mountain overlooking Aloca Harbor in Khanerenth. He paused in the shadow of the pines, looking at his prize.

A more unprepossessing object of an intensive world-wide search by the greatest powers of both sides would be difficult to find. She sat on a bench in the waning sunlight, hands lying motionless and loose in her lap, expression as empty as a doll's.

The doll resemblance ended there. The girl's face and arms and hands were a dismal patchwork of brown scabs and mottled, peeling skin. A good portion of the hair on top of her head had fallen out, leaving the healing scabs clearly visible on her scalp. She was dressed in a coarse, ill-fitting gown of a particularly unsuccessful shade of mustard. Semeh had never claimed to be much of a seamstress, and because she was poor it was to be expected she would sacrifice the least favorite of her few gowns.

Semeh and Khem's goodwill had manifested itself in other ways. The new skin on the girl showed the pink of returning health. Her remaining hair was clean and had been carefully trimmed of the sunburned bits, and there was a small, fresh bandage on the top of her left hand.

Llyenthur walked toward her, passing from shadow into slanting sunlight. His own shadow slid over her face before the girl looked up. Her wide eyes were blue and clear and utterly incurious.

He said nothing as he passed by and walked noiselessly inside the little house, which was warm and smelled invitingly of paprika, braised onion, and roasting potato. Semeh hummed to herself as she bent over her tiny brick oven to check on some biscuits.

Llyenthur glanced at the back window. Khem's shadow outlined against one wall: the old man sat loyally at his usual post, attention on the bay below.

He could kill them, but that would engender exactly the sort of talk he needed to avoid.

Two swift, silent strides and Llyenthur came up behind Semeh without her being aware. He touched the crown of her head above the braided bun. She stiffened into immobility. With delicate care he murmured the spell he had prepared, blocking the girl's presence from Semeh's conscious memory. Anyone with Dena Yeresbeth, searching her mind, would know the spell was there—the idea was to insure that never happened.

When he was done, Semeh sighed and straightened up slowly, as if she felt slightly ill, and she shuffled into her bedroom to lie down. Llyenthur then systematically removed all signs of the girl's presence, not that there was much.

On the scrubbed round table lay a sheet of paper with each date scrupulously listed in Khem's paper-saving minuscule hand. Below each date random series of syllables had been laboriously copied out. Most of it was recognizable as Imaran words, and little of it beyond the name Liere Fer Eider (spelt phonetically in Khani) made much sense. Llyenthur picked the paper up and laid it on the fire, then went silently out to memory-bind Khem.

When he was done he walked around the side of the house to where the girl still sat. Touching the mustard-yellow shoulder, he transferred them both away—

—And to a small island.

An expression of dismay at the wrenching jolt of a double transfer residue transformed the girl from a life-sized doll to a human. She fell, dazed. He blinked away the darkness billowing at the edges of his vision, wiped his suddenly runny nose on his sleeve—damn, it was bleeding. Ignoring that, he bent over the girl and laid fingers on her forehead. She did not resist, or react—and her mind was as accessible as sunlight on seawater, her lack of identity as fluid.

Llyenthur regarded her in amused perplexity until his thundering heart slowed to a gallop. Then — bracing — he transferred out.

She stood, motionless, watching the light change over the vast ocean. When the day had cooled to a purply-indigo star-glittered darkness and the sea was little discernable beyond its restless hissing and whispers, she shivered suddenly, then peered up and around as though startled.

Directly behind her on the narrow cliff someone had long ago built a small stone cottage.

It looked, and was, ancient. She walked inside the open doorway to discover a small room, each wall with a window that allowed free passage of air. The only furniture was a narrow bed set under one window. She moved to it. Picked up the blanket crumpled at the foot, stretched out under the blanket, and went peacefully to sleep.

Back in Khanerenth, Semeh had started up from her own bed in alarm when she smelled the burning biscuits. Bustling into the kitchen, she was further amazed to discover how many biscuits she'd made, as if they expected company. But they had invited no one.

Calling to Khem, who had dozed off at his job, she wakened him. They discussed the mystery thoroughly. When they parted for bed they had settled it that the latest rainstorm had brought in some kind of malaise. It did seem like there was going to be a hard winter, didn't it?

Royal Palace – Yaldar Northern Goerael

Connanre of the Host sat in a deep window-embrasure, idly watching the storm's fury through the streaming windows. In an equally idle manner he strummed a new notes on his mandolin, then reached to dip the pen and write a few notes down.

The hot-metal singe of transfer-magic caused him to still — and Yeres appeared. The disturbance of the air caused by her transfer made the windows bang open. Bitter wind flung a wash of stinging rain into the room, accompanied by loud thunder.

Anyone else doing something that risky, transferring

directly to him, would have earned a rebuke at least, but Connanre only set his instrument aside and reached to close the windows.

Yeres recoiled from the sudden cold wetness. When the air was still again, Yeres delicately flicked rain from her gown and hair. Connanre planted fists on hips and glared in disgust at the collage his composition made decorating the perimeter of the room.

With a soft mutter and an imperious wave of her hand Yeres reversed the dispersal, causing the stink of expended magic to burn their noses. That was a very wasteful spell. After the papers had neatly gathered themselves and come to rest in their original order, Connanre leafed through the top two.

He smiled. "Thank you."

She shrugged, already bored. A flicker of her brother's impatience sharpened her features — then, as Connanre was not disposed to question or scold her, she laughed and whirled around, draperies fluttering, before perching on the hassock near Connanre's window seat. "Was that you, by chance, a couple weeks ago? The seventeenth? The storm?" She reached up and began to play with the laces of his tunic.

He knew better than to respond.

Instead, he picked up his mandolin again, his smile slight. "You greatly overestimate my abilities — and even if I had the skill, I would never rile Ilerian. That's why I thought it prudent to occupy myself here, as far away as I could get."

Yeres sighed in disappointment. "Then you've given up your plot?"

"By no means!" A plaintive chord sounded from the instrument, hummed on the air, then was absorbed by the rumbling thunder of the storm. "Whatever that was — far too quick, and too powerful for me to be certain — it surprised me as much as anyone. I have been contemplating how to use it."

"It's a perfect diversion," she said.

"It does seem so, doesn't it?" Connanre's fingers moved up the frets and a high, parodic chord tinkled; he knew she enjoyed pitting people against each other. Especially Efael. Playing with her was playing with fire. He knew it, and relished it. "I said patience and events would provide us with a cover. And here it is."

Yeres studied him. "You are boring when you're smug."

"Then think ahead to the result!" he countered with a

rueful smile.

She tossed her hair back, and watched his gaze on her copper-highlighted curls. "I'm sick of waiting for you to tell me what Detlev's two great blunders are, Connanre. One of them his having been born at all?"

"He will certainly think so when we're through," Connanre promised with easy humor. And, as she laughed, sudden passion at the promise of anguish made her lick her lips—watching, as always, the effect in his eyes.

"It's your proximity to Ilerian," he admitted. "Really, do you want to be guarding your mind all the time? I'll tell you this much. Detlev has forgotten that, while the rest of you were sitting around in the Garden of the Twelve debating truth and beauty, I was usually out doing field work."

Yeres sighed, flung back her hair again. "Field work! While Efael's been tramping all over two continents, terrorizing the populace for Ilerian, I've been stuck—alone—with both our games. And I have been so *bored*. Until," she shook with silent delight, "I found out that Detlev is busily searching for Ilerian's mysterious storm-rider as well, while Ilerian is hunting him."

Connanre grinned. "He is? I thought he might, though I would have expected a measure of secrecy."

"Quite reckless." Yeres gestured extravagantly. "I just returned from dear Imry's HQ—a sober and legitimate visit, helpfully turning in that troublesome old man." She gestured eastward. "What a lovely chase! Efael will be tiresome about missing his chance to tear poor old Begherian apart but I wasn't about to sit and wait."

"You took him to Imry and—?"

"Oh, Imry wasn't there. He's been playing with spy birds, I'm quite sure to show me up when my lattice-bindings didn't hold. He's also busy chasing down would-be rebellions in Everon. I asked that nice young Chwahir fellow for the latest reports. The delicious part is, what with all this busy searching, the relay desk keeps such scrupulously correct records of all communications, and there, for all to see, was the message from the ship captain who first found the courier. About Liere Fer Eider. And noted and dated next to it 'D.I.T.' Imry's minions are always charmingly helpful, I will say that for him. He's taught them those nice manners of Detlev's."

"I'd say it's a healthy regard for their own skins," Connanre returned with considerable amusement. "Died in transit! Then why is Ilerian running around? Efael as well? Is it related to the dead courier?"

"Not certain." Her hands fluttered wide. "All that matters is that it has nothing to do with me."

"Help me consider how we can use it," he invited.

Intrigue! Danger, but not aimed at her. Her mood improved, and she let him come back to Narad, where time wouldn't drag, and their passions would infuriate that disgusting Wan-Edhe.

Seven

LLYENTHUR TRANSFERRED TO EVERON; to his surprise, there was no trace of Laban whatsoever. Irritating, but he had a much bigger game running. He just had to find out why Ilerian had halted laying the lattice ward over Imar in favor of hunting ... what? It couldn't possibly be that girl. Could it?

Why?

He waved at his plant in Everon to carry on, transferred, and walked into his map room in Larkadhe. He knew immediately from Duin's face that one of the Host had recently graced the place with a personal visit. "Who was it this time?"

Duin blinked, swallowed, and rather obviously suppressed the *How did you know?* "Yeres."

Llyenthur turned to the pile of messages on the desk. "Did she leave word?"

"No. Brought in Begherian from Hier Alverian."

"Mmmmm. Lucid?" Llyenthur bent over the dispatches.

Duin grinned. Yeres never got tired of bullying prisoners. "In a day or two he will be."

"Excellent," Llyenthur said, grateful for the reprieve.

Duin then saw the familiar bright smile that indicated annoyance. "Eh?" he asked.

"Aldon," Llyenthur said in a chiding tone, reading one

paper closely.

Duin smirked. "I checked on that. Dispatch has it straight. And—"

"Yes, I saw." Llyenthur gestured toward one paper that he had set aside. "Choreid Dhelerei. Forges, this time. I don't want Aldon in Marloven Hess. The Marlovens will never understand his variety of good theatre." He was speaking absently as he read further, so a laugh was surprised out of him, and he looked quickly up at the map. "Nearly missed that. Detlev flags—"

Duin got up. They looked at the marks dotting the eastern coast of the Ar Jaran peninsula.

Llyenthur said, "Are you sure these aren't failures of quite an ordinary sort?"

Duin shook his head stolidly. "Had 'em looked into. All the Detlev-signs you yourself gave out—mind-frozen guards. Vision and memory tampering. Prisoners freed. No other traces. We can't explain how he's getting around so fast."

"We'll have to change the transfer wards again. Yeres saw this, didn't she?"

"Yes."

"Then she'll see to the magic, no doubt." Llyenthur flicked a hand in dismissal, not giving any sign how much he was enjoying this new information. "Breis ... Jara ... Khanerenth ... Devrea...Seems quite desperate, doesn't he?"

"Yes, and if Wan-Edhe of the Chwahir is to be believed— that last one, on the bottom there—it was Detlev who raided his palace yesterday, trying to assassinate him. On, and Dungeonmaster Arech was apparently trashed as well. Not dead, but near. Wan-Edhe is demanding the return of all his armies to protect them both."

"If Wan-Edhe's mind was less on the entertainment provided by protracted pain and more on work I wouldn't have to waste so much time there. Perhaps I'll finish Detlev's job. If it was Detlev. These Detlev flags—" He gestured. "If there weren't quite so many..."

"Shall I go myself?"

"No. I will. If they are lying I'll want to end the trend summarily. And if Detlev had learned to replicate himself by fission—" Llyenthur transferred out mid-grimace.

Duin guffawed.

Knowing he was being watched, Llyenthur let a few days go by as he transferred to various fronts: stalemate in the seas off Khanerenth, thanks to Efael yanking the remaining Chwahir to blockade Toar and Mearsies Heili; Sartor, where Bostian glowered, resenting the leash; Goerael, and the coverts at Ralanor Veleth still eluding the Fhlerians. Everon—where Laban, unaccountably, had not taken his bait after all.

In the midst of this busy round of inspections, Llyenthur appeared on the island, and looked into the little stone house. It was empty. He walked around the side, and picked his way up the rocky hill in back. Hardy wildflowers and blooming shrubs clung to what soil there was. He did not remember seeing any such growth before.

At the top he found his mysterious prisoner crouched over a little burbling stream that sparkled steadily up from a crack in a great slab of stone.

She drank from cupped purple-stained hands. Then, seeing that she had company, she dropped her fingers to her skirt and wiped them in an absent gesture. Her gaze was friendly yet incurious; her eyes were drawn away to the white, gliding wings of a pelican. She watched the bird hover, and dive suddenly into the deep blue water far below.

A reminder. Llyenthur never bothered himself with the day-to-day care and maintenance of prisoners—he'd forgotten that she might have gotten hungry since he'd left her.

He said, in Imaran, "Are you hungry?"

"No," she said, tranquilly. Eyes still blank.

He spied the tangle of vines lower on the far slope, and guessed correctly that the purple stains on her fingers and skirt were from wild grapes. Grapes? Here?

A poke—gentle, but inquisitive—on his forearm. His shirtsleeves were rolled to his elbows. The girl tentatively touched the healing scabs from the spy-falcon's friendly challenge.

The girl shoved one of her grubby yellow sleeves back, and she held out own small, thin forearm with its bright pink scar-blotches next to his arm. She studied the two arms intently, then turned away, dropped to her knees, and pressed her hands against the huge rock that produced the fountain. A new fountain, he noted. Grass grew in cracks in the water's path but as yet the stream tumbled freely. There was no sign of carving.

The girl was silent, intent on the stone. Then she looked up and said in Imaran, "There was a terrible wrong here."

Llyenthur came near, and sat down on a rock close by. "Yes?" he said encouragingly.

"But 'tis coming right again."

He kept his voice neutral. "The islands were sunk many, many years ago."

A crease troubled her brow for a moment. "Someone with white hair. The shadow is still here." And she lifted her palms from the stone.

He took a careful breath, and — nothing in her mind beyond sea and sky and light. If it was a defense, it was the best he'd ever seen.

Experimentally, he said, "What is your name?"

"Name?" she repeated, the word clearly meaningless.

Her head turned, her gaze tracking a large speckled brown bird that approached rapidly from one of the islands that lay directly northward. It carried something large and green in its beak.

The bird hovered above. The thing dropped down, squarely into the girl's lap: a fully ripened pear.

Llyenthur walked around to the other side of the rocks, then eased back to watch, keeping himself hidden.

The girl never turned her head. After slowly munching her pear, her eyes wide and unblinking on the distant horizon, she flung the core out into the air.

A young gray gull flapped up, squawking, and caught and ate it.

Her hand dropped to her lap and lay limply cradled in the other. She smiled, a gentle and vacant smile, at the blue and sparkling sea.

He left.

⁂

Torquende – Ama Hazanth

Mildred shifted, trying to ease her shoulders as she leaned against the rough dungeon wall.

She'd deliberately — reluctantly — provoked this argument with Crow. Deliberately because she was running out of time and a challenge was the fastest way to get action with such people; reluctantly because she didn't want to win, and she knew she was likely to.

She knew it because Crow thought so much like she once had. Curse that Detlev anyway! She'd worked hard to leave that life, and that way of thinking, behind. But after watching Crow use that ruby so effectively — something few could do, and none purely by mind — she had to admit that Crow was a wild, untrained talent in the mental realm. Which could be as dangerous as his forming his martial group around the endurance of pain.

Yup, he needed another path, and it looked like she was the one to point the way.

Mildred grimaced at the mossy dungeon walls around her, and was momentarily diverted when she noticed the pale blue eyes of Crow's second-in-command flick to her face.

A strange one, that Chashan. As hard as a steel blade, and about as forthcoming. But Mildred — when she had to be — was reasonably adept at probing certain kinds of natures. Though half the convictions that Chashan held to were worthy of a Norsundrian, there was utter loyalty in her heart. To those benighted principles, and to Crow.

Chashan's blue gaze took in Mildred's expression, then shifted back to Crow. He was, as usual, watching his hands as he mulled what to say. Frustrated anger deepened the lines on his broad forehead.

Mildred leaned back and flexed the fingers of her healing arm. It had passed out of the pain stage into ache. A couple more weeks and she could start using it again.

Faces altered, observing her. She gave them a challenging grin. The tension did not ease.

All Crow's lieutenants were there, sitting around in his dungeon room. Mildred had chosen the time and the subject and now they hotly debated the superiority of force over freely given loyalty.

She hardly listened. She'd heard it all before — had once argued just as hotly on one side, and then on the other. She sat back, daydreamed, and at the point at which Crow was about to invoke force to underscore his argument, Mildred leaned forward and said, "You will not leave your own followers, yes? You have no trust?"

The shift from the theoretical to the personal electrified them all.

They waited for his answer.

"I trust them," he said.

"But they do not have freedom of movement—"

"Of course they do."

"Not of speech. Not if you must bide, to hear every word."

"Freedom of speech." His hands flexed.

Mildred knew he wanted, so very badly, to close those iron-strong hands around her neck.

She smiled. "Prove it."

His eyes narrowed. He leaned against the wall. Either she provoked him and earned another broken bone—if not a broken skull—or she shifted the focus for the third time, restoring his prestige with the promise of the highest danger.

"Prove it," she said, more gently. "Come with me. Get some training—we both will—and carry the fight to the enemy."

Eight

Mearsies Heili

THE SOUND OF THE wind in the trees below her open window woke CJ early.

She jumped out of bed and ran to the window to look out at the tossing autumn-colored foliage. She loved windy weather. She flung off her nightgown and wrestled impatiently into some clothes.

She paused in her headlong gallop downstairs when she reached the courtyard and saw Atan exiting one of the spire archways, her color high. Sartor's queen wore a long-sleeved robe over loose, floaty trousers—cool weather clothes. CJ instantly squashed the urge to run around yelling, which was one of the ways she enjoyed the return of cool weather. Eyeing the odd expression on Atan's face, she said cautiously, "Um, is everything all right?"

How to answer that?

Atan had turned to gaze back up at the spire. She had begun from the earliest days of her stay in this strange palace to walk random spirals for exercise. But gradually she found a pattern emerging: if she began at the far west, with the fading night, and worked around eastward and back, the colors in the arched windows, and the slants of sunlight falling, brought the meditative serenity of the Purrad to mind. Except the effect of this place was actually stronger, as she walked not in two dimensions, but three. Or more. Her thoughts lifted and expanded as she climbed, awareness intensifying—and as she descended, it was like, oh, it was like snow falling softly on dried, autumnal land. And when she finished, the sense of body, mind, and spirit in balance enabled her to go tranquilly to face the day's challenges.

Further, she was pretty sure that someone regularly walked that same pattern as well. Someone she never saw.

She said, "Have you—all of you who live here—ever noticed certain patterns to the spirals and the levels of the landings?"

CJ blinked. "Patterns? Besides..." She motioned up and down with her hand.

"Loops ... in a circular pattern?"

CJ's smile was polite. "You can go in any pattern you like, here. Even zigzags. We used to try to deliberately get lost, just because it was so much fun to suddenly figure out where you were. And there always seemed to be new rooms you'd never seen before." CJ stopped there, perceiving disappointment in Atan's expression—no, it was more puzzlement. Maybe even confusion?

"Has something creepy happened?" CJ's mouth pruned in apprehension.

Atan's smile was quick. "Now, how shall I answer that? No, and yes."

CJ plopped onto a stone bench and drew her legs up inside her skirt. "What is it?"

"I finally heard this morning from the Sky Island Council. It seems they had to deliberate for two days before returning a negative answer to my inquiry. No, no reports from their southernmost reaches of anything unusual happening on the seventeenth. Merely a short, fierce rainstorm. I wonder if that is the truth? I suppose I'd have a better idea how to find out if I knew what it was that Detlev wants to know about that day. But I'm doing my best to be exceedingly cooperative with him because he is doing the same with me." The sad smile again.

"More names for the blue map," CJ said—not a question.

Atan nodded.

"What's the blue map?" a voice interrupted from behind.

They turned to see Lyren-Sartora, gorgeous in yellow silk and ivory lace, trip lightly up the broad steps toward them.

"Where have you been?" CJ exclaimed. "We thought you'd gone after Liere without telling us!"

"No. She wanted to go alone." Lyren-Sartora's brilliant smile dimpled her cheeks on either side.

Atan saw at once that Lyren-Sartora was in a dangerous mood, but CJ—so straightforward—saw only the smile.

Lyren-Sartora went on, "I was out experimenting alone. With no success." A disarming shrug. "What is the blue map?"

"Come up to the library and I will show you," Atan said.

Atan spoke to both, conscientiously including CJ, which the latter misinterpreted as a not-quite-order. Flinging a mental promise to the wind for later, CJ followed the other two to the library, which was beginning to take on the ambience of a military command post. Two world-maps were pinned to one wall, and a map of Sartor lay over a table. More maps were stacked up in rolls in a corner. Atan's customary vases of fresh flowers, and other resident decorative objects, had been set on a side table out of the way. On the table that everyone regarded as Atan's desk lay a third world-map, with colored markers laid on it: ship movements, and resistance groups. Even CJ could see that it was woefully incomplete.

One of the wall world maps had a haze of blue in clusters over it. Lyren-Sartora stepped close, studied the neat blue lettering, then turned around, her eyes wide. "Rulers' names. These can't all be—"

Atan nodded. For a moment silence gripped them all as they stared at the blue patches. There were too many kingdoms who shared with their neighbors a blue listing of dead rulers. Rarer were the red listings, which created a tentative warming in a great icy sea.

Atan said, "Blue, either taken or killed by Norsunder. We do not yet know how many of these have been enchanted. We have to assume a percentage were. Red are heirs—family members—prominent citizens of one sort or another, who are alive and safe elsewhere. Note there are a few red rulers as well."

"Lyren-Sartora said, "The blank ones?"

"As yet unknown."

"Where are you getting your information? This is very widespread."

"From everyone who travels and keeps in communication, but most of it comes from Detlev."

"From Detlev?" Lyren-Sartora repeated with distaste. She spun around, glossy curls and embroidered hem flaring and falling.

CJ spoke up. "Turns out Detsie and some of the poopsies were helping those friends of Senrid's in saving rulers and heirs and people on the Host grab list. Sometimes," she gave a grim laugh, "they have to bag 'em and make 'em hide out."

Lyren-Sartora turned her questioning gaze to Atan, who said, "It's true. And their action is so necessary I don't find it within me to question the arbitrariness of their decision on whom they save and when." She flicked her long brown braid back with an absent gesture, and sat down. "Look at the number of names! It's worse than I had imagined. All these countries. After — if — we get rid of Llyenthur's hordes anyone could walk in and take them."

CJ frowned. "And don't think they won't! Just like that grunge-buzzard Wan-Edhe tried to do *right here* after we squelched Siamis's first enchantment."

"Even knowing this, there's little we can do beyond what Detlev has already done."

"I'm not questioning your looking ahead," Lyren-Sartora stated. "We should do that. If it turns out we don't win, nothing we do will matter." Her eyelashes narrowed over her golden eyes. In the morning light her gaze seemed to glow with smoldering ire. "But. If he is giving you these names, why didn't he do so before?"

"I never asked."

"Oh, yes you did. I remember quite well how effectively he snubbed you before."

"But I wasn't asking him what he was doing for us, I was — really — demanding some kind of miracle plan by which we could destroy the Host. And I was implying that he owed — well, it doesn't matter. My perspective has changed a little since then. And it was that conversation, really, that started me thinking about afterward."

"Yes. I see that distinction." Lyren-Sartora's mouth thinned, and she added with a dramatic toss of her curls, "I hate Detlev." She turned to face Atan. "And you can't tell me you don't agree."

Amusement brightened Atan's face. "But there's something so very ... congenial, you'll have to admit, in having him so ready to hand. Relatively speaking."

CJ said, "He always answers magic-notes."

Lyren-Sartora swung about and studied her.

CJ added, stoutly, "And he's been asking *us* for help."

Lyren-Sartora said, "I know. Liere told me. This whatever-it-was that seems to have broken up a Host-propelled storm over uninhabited ocean on the seventeenth." Her tone was scornful.

CJ said, "You don't believe it was anything?"

Lyren-Sartora's shrug was both elaborate and graceful. "Oh, I'm sure *some*thing happened. But as for its real importance, it seems to me if it were *truly* vital, he'd keep it to himself. As it is, it would be very like him to get us lesser mortals scurrying busily about working on errands he's too exalted for."

Atan gestured toward her map. "That occurred to me as well. But as long as he's so cooperative with me, I will give him whatever aid I can." Her smile faded as she studied the blue map. "We all need it."

Lyren-Sartora flounced out, leaving behind a sense of summer thunder in the air amid a drifting scent of starliss.

CJ forgot her when she spotted Clair through the kitchen windows. She ran downstairs and across the terrace, and burst into the kitchen as Clair was getting her breakfast. "How'd you sleep?" she asked—as she did every day.

Clair said, "I slept well," as she invariably did.

CJ'd had to accept that Siamis waited up all night, vigilant so that Clair, and the kingdom, could slumber in peace without the dread of invading minds. But he didn't act at all like he was taking over as king—he mostly stayed in the Selenseh Redian, reading and writing, so you could even forget he was around. The caves, so large, had all kinds of alcoves. Clair had picked one from which she could look out at the waterfall. She and CJ had fitted it up with some of Clair's familiar furnishings to make it as homey as possible. Siamis's was down another corridor, gradually taking on the characteristics of a library.

Atan entered, and when Clair turned to her, CJ knew they were going to talk ruling stuff. She slid out, then transferred to the forest floor for a good, long run.

A day or two later, on a cloudy, mizzly morning—unpleasant for bare toes, but not horrible enough for shoes—CJ's wayward steps led her through the kitchen.

She hunted, found, and pinched a piece of pie, and then

wandered in the direction of the throne room. Today was the day that Clair had appointed for non-citizen audiences, and she had asked Atan to back her up on these.

Angry adult voices echoed out, making CJ pause in the doorway uneasily.

Clair had put on a dress, and shoes. Atan sat on her hassock beside the throne, sewing. Atan's face was calm and her occasional glances up were direct, but CJ knew by now that when the Queen of Sartor was withdrawn or disturbed, she busied her hands with the exact requirements of exceptionally fine embroidery.

Who were those men? One was wearing silver velvet. The other was a purple-velveted, nasty-voiced beardo who was now ranting at the two queens.

CJ did not want to know what the dispute was. They both looked like trouble, and if she went in she might get mad at them for ranting at Clair, and make things worse.

She noiselessly backed away, and sank her teeth into the pie.

Why was she bored and restless? Here's the kingdom crawling with a zillion people and animals from all over the continent—even farther—and she's bored and lonely.

She passed a window, and glimpsed Keritar's bright green hair in the garden below as she romped with the youngest Delieths. CJ thought of Jessan and Carl—and knew without looking that the two little kids were ensconced in the room set up for them as a library, studying. This quiet and unrelenting determination on their part to acquire an education as soon as possible was unnerving to the Mearsiean girls. It was usually Keritar who, after a long stretch of hours, bustled in and shut their books and ordered them outside into the fresh air. Grateful for refuge, Keritar, who had blue skin and green hair, came from a kingdom up north on Goerael where mages long ago had experimented with coloring skin, and managed to mess things up so that people were born with rainbow combinations. Completely random, Keritar had said cheerfully, when Falinneh asked. If she had kids, they might turn out to be orange and yellow, or all purple. CJ was fairly sure Keritar was somebody important; she had once looked at the blue map, turned away quickly, then never looked again. She had volunteered to be the Delieth kids' nanny.

Maybe it was time to try to study magic again. CJ had loved

it in the early days, but the farther you got, the more it felt like the drudgery of math. "Groanboils!" she muttered as she opened the library door—and found Lyren-Sartora bent intently over Atan' big map.

Lyren-Sartora was leaning on her left hand, the knuckles of her right rapping with nervous energy on the edge of the map as her gaze roamed the colored pins.

CJ hesitated in the doorway, as Lyren-Sartora pinioned her with that bright golden gaze. "It looks," she said without preamble, "as if the exodus is over for so many. They're all going home."

CJ's guts churned. She hated sensing anger, and she sensed it now. It lay like a hidden pool beneath Lyren-Sartora's pleasing voice and equable tone. Lyren-Sartora's shoulders under their graceful lace drapery lifted a little, but she did not immediately speak.

CJ's gaze roamed down the familiar map. Once her idea of geography had been hazy in the extreme.

Lyren-Sartora said, "The morvende offered to help?" Nothing could be read from her tone, and her focus was on the map, her eyes hidden by a thick fringe of dark curling lashes.

CJ nodded, adding, "Leander was in one of their geliaths, hiding from Norsunder. He talked to them a lot."

"Who is this 'D' with Troy?" Lyren-Sartora's hand flashed over to the west of Wnelder Vee.

CJ made another pickle-face. "Diana. You were here when they left." As the gold eyes flashed up, CJ wished she hadn't spoken. "On their way to Dthel Rendm," she muttered.

Lyren-Sartora's gaze lowered again, and moved slowly over the markers as she considered what she saw. Morgeh Troiad going home to Wnelder Vee. Darian Selenna, Bren, and Innon were going home to Sarendan. Rel was on his way to Sartor. Terry on his way to Erdrael Danara. The smart and beautiful Erenlara Sofar, embarked upon a very long journey home to the Land of the Venn. Senrid—already home.

Liere—also home. New home. *Her* home.

Lyren-Sartora's mouth tightened, then curved a little with subdued amusement. "Randon went back to Vandary with quite a vanguard, I see."

CJ cackled, relieved. She was beginning to feel slightly giddy before the force of Lyren-Sartora's simmering moods, as if she'd been in the sunshine too long. "All the wanderers, sailing on Puddlenose's *Lheit*. They broke through the blockade in one of the storms that came after the really big one."

Lyren-Sartora's answering smile brought dimples flashing in her cheeks. CJ regarded her in bemusement. These past few days around the white palace had seemed curiously full of Lyren-Sartora's presence: playing with Keritar and the Delieth kids; sitting decoratively on the steps of the throne room dais and listening; walking in the forest down below. And once, surprising nearly everyone, breezing into the upper ballroom, which was now the designated martial arts salle, practice and stunning the succeeding row of fallen opponents with the focused, cool strength and stylish speed Siamis had drilled into her. That night she elected to go out with Roy's border irregulars, to sail with Captain Hereford through a fierce storm as they broke the blockade so that *Lheit* could get through.

Lyren-Sartora had done well—and had been heard to say in disgust to Atan that same night, "Who was it who said fighting never resolved anything?"

Something was going on, all right.

Lyren-Sartora's gaze had shifted to the gently billowing curtains in the window, a slightly derisive smile curling her lips.

Feeling a little like she was putting her hand too near a brightly twirling diamond pinwheel, CJ said, "Something wrong?"

Lyren-Sartora's smile was brilliant and decidedly self-deprecatory. "I asked Sveneric that very question several weeks ago, and nearly got my head ripped off for my pains."

CJ rolled her eyes. "Sveneric?" she repeated doubtfully. "Whaja do, boot him into a pond first?"

Lyren-Sartora laughed. "Even Sveneric has his moods. Have mine been disturbing you? If so, I beg your pardon."

Confused and daunted by the intense golden eyes, lovely smile and smooth-walled politesse, CJ beat a hasty retreat.

The rest of the day she brooded, disgusted with herself for her reaction to Lyren-Sartora and genuinely bothered by all the strains in the air. The only thing she was sure of after that interview was, whatever was on Lyren-Sartora's mind was private. So she said nothing to anyone.

Which is probably one of the reasons why just after midnight, having been woken by the moon edging past the side of her open window and gleaming with a mystic silver glow directly onto her face, CJ was startled by a ghostly figure gliding soundlessly into her room.

"Clair?" she croaked.

But she knew immediately it wasn't Clair. The trailing white gown, the gliding walk, the long dark hair belonged to someone else.

"Cherenneh." It was Sartora's pronunciation, but Lyren-Sartora's soft and musical voice.

CJ sighed. "I know we're safe, but! I nearly had ten heart-attacks! What is it?"

"I think I had better tell someone," Lyren-Sartora said. "Before I leave."

CJ wished she could see Lyren-Sartora's face—and then thought, Why? I'm a worse face reader than I am a mind-reader! "Where are you going?"

"To Imar."

CJ jerked upright in her bed. "What?"

Lyren-Sartora's light laugh was acid. "No, the Host can sleep easy—I'm not going anywhere near them." She moved to the window, and looked out.

CJ saw sadness in Lyren-Sartora's profile. "Why?" she asked cautiously.

"Did you know Liere had another of those nightmares recently?"

CJ shrugged. "Atan said something to Clair at breakfast, after reading a note—" She faltered, and stopped.

Lyren-Sartora's lips parted on a laugh no louder than a breath. "Right. I wasn't there. And no one thought to mention it to me. Including Liere, of course."

"Then how did you know?" CJ asked more bluntly.

"Because Liere can't always block me off when she's real tired. For my own peace of mind, of course."

CJ said, "The dreams have mostly been about her mom, Clair said. Liere told Atan it's because she feels guilty about not going back to see any of them after she got back from Geth. On account of going to Enaeran, and meeting Andri, and all that stuff. But she feels it's her duty to go to Enaeran and protect the refugees planting secretly in the mountains by using her Dena Yeresbeth to scan for enemies, since Andri is helping Senrid."

"I know. And she's spared me because I never liked the Fer Eider clan any more than they liked me. They were rotten to Liere when she was little, and they reveled in their cloddish mediocrity like it was some kind of virtue—" Lyren-Sartora laughed, an unsteady-sounding laugh. veering between sounding like a kid and like a grownup, and again CJ felt dizzy. "Well. I can continue to blame them for everything, can't I, and won't that make Liere feel better! She's doing what she feels is her duty, as usual, but I know she has to be torn by guilt, or why the nightmares? So *I* will go. I'm useless at everything else, but at least I am capable of making my way to a tiny harbor town of no importance, where nothing ever happens, to see how the Fer Eiders are. And at least I can set Liere's mind to rest on this one thing."

CJ's guts writhed at the self-loathing she heard, but she kept her mouth shut. "Take a magic-paper, please?"

"Oh, yes, I will."

CJ sighed in relief. "Meanwhile, who can I tell?"

"Anyone." Lyren-Sartora gestured with careless grace. "Who cares to hear. Those who think me unable to perform a simple task such as that will assure one another that I'll soon need rescuing—and everyone else is too busy." She sighed. "CJ, there's something else I must tell you before I leave."

"Okay." CJ hugged her arms tight.

"I picked this out of Liere's mind as well. Detlev asked her to keep it secret, but since I don't care about him or his secrets, again, tell whom you like. That is: the caves will transfer people to other caves. Sometimes."

CJ nodded slowly, not admitting that she'd known that before. But the Mearsiean girls had long ago learned not to talk about the Selenseh Redian so near them.

"I wonder who it is who decides? No matter. It's your secret now. Do what you like with it. I expect your judgment is better than Detlev's is, anyway."

Yeah, and Wan-Edhe loves to wear pink pajamas, CJ thought, but aloud she said only, "When are you going?"

"Now—while Clair is talking to Siamis."

CJ didn't ask how Lyren-Sartora knew that. "Be careful."

And as Lyren-Sartora drifted out, CJ collapsed back onto her pillows, knowing that another night of sleep had just been zapped.

Lyren-Sartora wore her sword-fighting practice clothes for her trip to Imar. She hoped that a plain gray tunic-shirt over riding trousers would not earn her the scorn of her family for being "too ostentatious." She braided her hair into one long tail, then went downstairs to pack a basket of foods from the buffet, things that would last a few days.

The Selenseh Redian transferred her to the cave above Wnelder Vee. Now came the challenge: to use all the skills Siamis and Van had taught her to find and ride a succession of horses south through Wnelder Vee and Everon to Imar, and Belann.

Nine

Aloca Harbor - Khanerenth

DETLEV AND DAVID HAD walked silently a ways down the path before David stopped and struck his fist against the trunk of a tall pine tree. "We were so close."

Detlev smiled sympathetically. "It was a memorable chase."

David shook his head.

"Let's get out of here." Detlev gestured.

David cast a look back up the trail. "Those people. Damn! What do you want to do about Imry using the old man to follow lighter ships' movements?"

"It's a deft move. I think we can effectively counter it with a word to Jehan Zhavalieshin. No need to disturb Khem and Semeh again."

They descended the long path to the village where they'd left their horses, and galloped southwards along the coast of Khanerenth. They rode in silence for a time. Presently the sun began to set. When night fell, they found a small inn built on a hill at a trade crossroads, overlooking Aloca Harbor.

The inn was warm and, as is usual with such places, full of the welcoming aromas of strong drink and spiced food. A fast check and they knew the clientele would not bother them. They sat at a corner table halfway between the fire and a convenient window, with the door well in view.

David's tacit acknowledgement of defeat — of a dead end — was the dark ale he ordered and drank deeply of while they waited for their food. Detlev had asked for steep, but he sat with it between his fingers, his gaze abstracted.

David waited until the ale's pleasant buzz had spread warmly through his insides, then he sat back, sighed, and said, "All right. What next?"

Detlev looked up. "We know our target is a girl, we know she's alive, and we know Imry's got her. We're ahead that much; at least. I don't believe Ilerian has any of those three, which would explain his movements. Though we cannot trust that for long; he will be following another trajectory entirely."

David made a little gesture of impatience. "Are you going to call the others off?" He still didn't understand why Detlev had dropped all his plans, and yanked David away from his, for a search that turned out to be for a teenage girl.

"Partly." Detlev saw his impatience, of course. "Yanli should be monitoring Kessler. And Carlian has a sick boy — she should go home. Our search will be different now. We must find out — fast — where Imry'd be likely to keep a prisoner he wants safe from us as well as from Ilerian."

"Ilerian." David's brows contracted and he began absently to make wet-circles on the wooden table with his ale cup. "Ilerian in the field, and us running over the world, hunting down some kid. If this is a new plan, you might have told me in the Selenseh Redian a couple months ago."

Detlev's eyes narrowed humorously. "If I'd had any idea what to expect, our conversations would have had a very different shape. But I had not. Nor had Ilerian."

The ale was having its inevitable effect. David yawned, then flexed his right hand with its bruised knuckles, and grinned.

Detlev interpreted the gesture and the grin without difficulty. "Though you did not understand the gravity of this chase, I take it you found consolation in breaking your hand on Asiarch's teeth?"

David's grin widened. "What could I do? He jumped me first. From behind, too." He fought a second yawn and stretched his legs toward the fire. "Been a long time since I've seen so much action at once. Must be getting sedentary — "

" — in old age." Detlev's irony was reassuring.

David said, "In fact, between us, we must have made a splendid ants-nest of Imry's eastern garrisons." He looked up. "Well, if Imry's got her, and he doesn't want the Host to know, then we can rule out any more garrisons. Leaving, I suppose, everywhere else in the world?"

"Nearly," Detlev said.

"And the questions left behind! Why those two old people in the first place?"

Detlev contemplated the fire. Marks of tiredness shadowed his eyes, though his manner did not show it. As usual; David fought another yawn as Detlev said, "Adding together all we've seen, I suspect that the girl was in bad physical shape when Imry got her. I don't know how Imry figured out who she was from among the various prisoners taken that day, but her being so badly off might have been a clue. He put her on that mountain out of everyone's reach so she could recover enough to be questioned, and so that he could consider his next step."

"Does he know why Ilerian is on the hunt?"

"I'd be very surprised if he did. I suspect he acted out of curiosity, and now he's playing a waiting game. My guess is to try to determine what it is he's got."

"A missing dress ... and extra biscuits," David murmured. "And one minor flunky's greed."

"A remarkably tenuous chain of connections," Detlev agreed.

David's mind ranged backward through the past few days. Lived at desperate speed, slamming from one location to another, dodging Ilerian's and Efael's spies as well as Imry's, breaking into prisons and scanning the jumbled, emotion-turbid memories of the poor wretches they found, all in search of someone — male? female? — who might or might not be alive and who might or might not have ended a killer storm near the Fereledria on the 17th.

Then, last night, just as he was beginning to relax over a two-day-overdue meal in the popular port city of Aloca, David overheard a smug regular regaling his cronies with his views on life. No indeed, no living on the mountains for *him*. Bad air up there, too high and thin. That was his theory. "Why, here's a prime example, just one of so many. My cousin Gora from Neshvit up the mountain recently told us about a siege of illness in that village..."

Gora must have been nearly as big a gossip as her cousin.

The man had retailed how "poor Semeh" on the mountaintop had gotten so sick she had given away a gown without remembering to whom, and one day she'd fixed biscuits for company and no one expected! Poor Semeh being so poor she could hardly afford such fog-headedness...

David might not have investigated had he not sensed from behind a hard flash of mental triumph, instantly suppressed. The dress and biscuits were facts, but the secret pleasure was a vector. When the spy greased out a little later, David was out there waiting for him, to discover that the man had stumbled on something suspicious, and though he was under Efael's orders, he was considering who would pay more for the information.

Which he no longer knew, along with his name. Greasy, venal memories, a sickening amalgam of equally petty triumphs and hates. But no actual murders, so David hadn't killed him. Instead, he left him on a distant island, as ignorant as a two-year-old, crouched down watching a crab hunting among the barnacles on a submerged pier. David had learned the theory of mind-wipe, but he had never before done it. It left him feeling at least as greasy and venal. But at least Efael would not find out, and tear that village apart, or kill those old people, who were completely innocent.

What was done was done.

David shifted his overtired mind back to the subject. "Is there time now to tell me why this hurry?"

"Here you go, gents," came the waiter's cheery voice. "That'll be six, which includes the drinks. We have to collect right away, times being what they are, you'll understand."

Detlev responded with bland politeness as he paid up—having thoughtfully provided himself with local coinage—and when the innkeeper moved away, David eyed Detlev, who assessed the room.

And though the people around them were involved with one another, and with the three musicians busy tuning their instruments in the corner, he switched to Ancient Sartoran. "You know why," David observed. He picked up the mug, then set it back down. The ale, though excellent, wasn't helping him think. Clearly this search had to do with that storm over the ocean—the one that had caused Adam to invade all their dreams, looking for Detlev, in spite of the risk, while the two most dangerous of the Host had been focused along the Fereledria.

David said, incredulously, "It has to do with the plateau?"

Detlev, satisfied that there was no listener within range, murmured in the language of his birth, "The word was sirei-atanrial."

David assumed a long-suffering air as he attacked his food. Between bites he said, "All right. Let's see. 'Atanial' means shining sun. 'Atanrial' was, oh, blessed sun. 'Sirei' a person-prefix to a thing-noun. Back to the root for the symbol, 'atan', sun. Which could be—considering that you Ancient Sartorans never seem to have done anything simply—'One-step-short-of-creation,' light, life, and so forth. How am I doing? When is this going to make any sense?"

Detlev gave in. "Stripped of our old poetic forms—which sometimes were more direct than you realize, but we can debate that some other day—you could translate the term as 'shaper' or 'maker'."

"And so—?"

"Want the long explanation or the short?"

"Meaning this isn't the long one? Fine. Let's have the short."

"For our purposes now, consider this person as potentially the opposite number to Ilerian."

The mug slipped from David's fingers and crashed to the slate floor.

The waiter was apologetic but firm. "Sorry, gents, but times are rough. Breakages cost us terrible. Prices for replacements being what they are, you know. That'll be one and three, sir, for the mug. Thank you, and may I bring you another ale?"

"Yes," David said, with feeling.

Detlev laughed softly.

⸺⸺⸺

A remote island off Narieth

Llyenthur had seen nothing of Efael or Ilerian. From Svir there was silence.

It was early morning on the island, and already the air was hot. The girl stood on the extreme edge of a rocky overhand above the ocean breakers. Below, a wave surged in a greenish mass and boomed against the rocks. The girl flung up her hands and stood poised; white spray shot up into the air and hung there for a long moment. Sunlight transformed the drops to the brightness of crystal, and then a playful breeze pushed the cooling spray over the girl's waiting form.

No spells spoken. Llyenthur knew the Old Magic when he saw it; he also saw that, unlike his own limited experiments, this girl required no particular effort. But—as yet—she did no magic that would catch the notice of the seekers; it was akin to illusion, evanescent.

She gave a sigh of pleasure as the water splashed over her in a fine, cooling spray, drenching the hideous yellow thing she still wore, her feet bare below it.

"Don't do that."

She jumped, startled by Llyenthur's voice. She blinked stupidly in mute question.

He said slowly, "The man with the white hair is looking for you. If you do too much magic, even foolery like that, he will be able to find you."

"Magic," she repeated. The word was as empty of meaning as 'name' had been on the earlier occasion.

He looked at her in exasperation, aware that he was running out of time.

By walking off with Ilerian's quarry and then lying to cover his tracks he was making this gamble an all or nothing affair. He'd sensed at the start that there was something important about the storm episode. Ilerian's interest and reactions had corroborated his guess. And now the fact that Ilerian had abandoned the geographical search and instead was silently and seamlessly weaving a trap around Imry proved that this girl was of vital—perhaps fundamental—importance. This particular tactic on Ilerian's part indicated expectation of retaliation of equal, or even superior, force, once he was certain who was at the center of the trap. As yet Ilerian was not certain, or Imry would sure as damnation not have this freedom.

But he could do nothing until he knew the nature of the weapon with which he was trapped.

Weapon.

The girl was now staring blankly down at the water, looking again like a mindless doll. Yet she did have the Old Magic at her command, and she called on it without any visible effort—while having no mind to speak of.

"How are we to restore your brains?" he addressed her.

As he stared into that vacant face, he thought that maybe it was just as well.

He said sharply, "Listen!" And in a voice of command, as he pointed to a jagged boulder emerging from the rocky jumble halfway up the hill behind the stone house, "Move that. Into the sea."

She looked obediently enough to where he pointed, her expression slightly puzzled but mostly blank. Finally she said, "It cannot be moved."

It cannot, not *I cannot*. Llyenthur's voice changed to threat. "Do it."

He raised a hand, and when she looked blankly back at him he dealt her a blow across the face. Not hard enough to knock her down, but certainly hard enough to sting. "Now."

She pressed fingers to her cheek, her mouth open. Then she made a move toward him. With both hands she grabbed his, and studied the palm intently as though seeking something.

With increasing irritation he snapped his fingers free of her grip. He'd already stayed too long. He'd have to contrive a few hours together. Next time he'd take control of her mind, and experiment with forcing her to use that magic. She looked strong enough for that now — but if she wasn't, well, she could hardly be less useless dead. And she'd certainly be less dangerous.

Ten

Belann - Imar

LYREN-SARTORA STOOD IN THE lee of a bakery and stared across the narrow alleyway at the closed-up pastry shop with the Fer Eider name in modest lettering swinging in the slashing rain. Did it always rain in Imar?

It had been a dreary journey, caused not only by the weather, but the oppressive atmosphere of threat hanging over the country, nearly as palpable as the clouds. Something had roused the local Norsundrians. Impossible they should be so ever-present and tirelessly hunting back and forth across this otherwise backward section of a second-rate kingdom. Or maybe this was the outer reach of protection for the Host, who had taken a manor far inland. But why would they rely on warriors and horses when their magic was so much more deadly? No, something else had to be going on.

Despite the searches, and the weather, and tiredness, she'd made it. Oh, and one chase. That had been carelessness on her part, a mistake she did not repeat.

Standing in her wet clothes with mud splashes up to her knees, she thought with amusement of her first, grandiose conception of this altogether charming undertaking. She'd envisioned herself sweeping in, sorting out the Fer Eiders with suitable speed, and then speaking her piece about reverse snobbery and using guilt as a weapon, before shepherding them all to safety. Somewhere.

And then the letter to Liere informing her of what she ought to have done, before sorting out those Enaeraneth.

Now, facing the boarded-up shop—so many she'd seen in every single town and village—it didn't look as if there was going to be an audience to hear her speak her piece. Nobody was in that shop, and what's more it looked like it had been closed up for days.

She had no idea where they lived. The idea of traipsing that widespread jumble of narrow, twisting streets, staring at old, weatherworn houses through all those hills behind the harbor and market area was dismal indeed. And even then, how would she find them? No one talked to anyone anymore. The mere sight of a stranger sent everyone to locking doors and slamming shutters. She was sure if she managed to corner someone, what she'd hear would be lies. And they were so mind-blocked out of sheer terror, she'd never get the slightest glimpse of the truth.

She leaned against a wooden support, and stared at the tightly shuttered shop for inspiration. How awful, how humiliating to have to give up now.

A voice said from behind, "Looking for something?"

Though little showed outwardly beyond a ripple in her cloak as her head turned, Lyren-Sartora tensed for action.

She shifted her balance to use the wooden support as a shield and her hand slid over her knife-handle as she looked into the face of a stolidly built girl a little taller and older than she was. A lot older? Or maybe that was the effect of her closed expression, and the jutting jaw under her moon-face. Tilted blue eyes studied Lyren-Sartora with unblinking, and wary, scrutiny.

Lyren-Sartora slid the knife back into its sheath under the panel of her tunic, and she smiled slightly. "Someone would be more correct."

"Who might that be?" The girl spoke so curtly her tone bordered on rudeness. And her expression did nothing to mitigate the effect.

Lyren-Sartora's brows went up. She was tired and cold and depressed or she would have called on the friendliness which she habitually armored herself. But she didn't feel friendly. Not a bit. "Did I indicate that my business is yours?"

The girl snorted, a loud, very rude sound. "If you want to find someone here, you will have to ask someone, and there are few who will talk to strangers. I know everyone in Baker Street."

"All right," Lyren-Sartora said. "I am looking for Elder Elen Fer Eider."

"Elder Elen." The small mouth pressed together and the girl breathed hard, once. Then as Lyren-Sartora began to speak, the girl spun around abruptly. "Come in."

It was not an invitation so much as an order.

Lyren-Sartora followed the squared shoulders and swinging braid into the bakery. It smelled wonderful inside.

"You can sit down there." The girl stabbed a finger at a low stool which already held a half-full water bucket. "First put that down."

The stool was damp, but then so was Lyren-Sartora. She set the bucket down and settled onto the stool, looking up at her hostess, who began thumping and kneading a big white wad of dough with an aggressive vigor that seemed hostile to Lyren-Sartora's eyes.

Lyren-Sartora sighed. "I suppose you won't believe this, but I am not a Norsundrian. All I want is to talk to Elder Elen. With handy sword-bearing witnesses, if need be."

The girl glanced at her, then back at her dough. Finally she said, reluctantly, "They've had bereavement."

"Hasn't everyone?" Lyren-Sartora pitched her voice to be sympathetic, but the girl's shoulders jerked and her cheeks reddened as if she'd been struck, and she made a vicious jab at the dough. Lyren-Sartora fancied that was meant for her, and rose to her feet. "Look, I can see I'm taking up your time for nothing."

"Why do you want her?"

Lyren-Sartora suppressed her words about her own business and strove for politeness, because at least this person was speaking to her. Unlike anyone else. "As it happens, I am related to her. And I've come from far away —"

"Yes." The word came out like an arrow. "I have eyes."

The idea that she resembled any of those cloddish, judgmental Fer Eiders took Lyren-Sartora aback.

The girl issued a short bark of a laugh. "In fact, if I was to guess, I'd say you were the famous Princess Lyren." Her tone indicated she did not expect any prize.

"I am not a princess," Lyren-Sartora said, moving to the opposite side of the table so she could confront the girl directly. Her golden gaze was narrowed to pinpoints of reflective light, and her cheeks glowed with splendid color. "So their delightful opinion of my younger self has leavened the stodge of general town gossip, I take it."

"Where is Queen Liere?" the girl stated, so curt her question came out a flat statement as she slapped the dough over with a thump.

Surprised at this subject-change, Lyren-Sartora was ready to verbally whittle this offensive lump of righteous virtue down to size—until she perceived the tears on the flat moon cheeks. The girl dashed them angrily against her shoulder.

Lyren-Sartora said in a quiet voice, "Fighting the Norsundrians in her husband's kingdom, which is now her home."

The pale eyes flickered up. "Husband?"

"A few months ago. Right after she escaped from the Norsundrians."

The girl's ribs tightened on a deep breath, but it sounded shaky anyway.

Lyren-Sartora continued, "She's been having nightmares about her mother. But so many people depend on her that she's felt torn between duty to them and worries about the Fer Eiders here. So I thought I'd come instead."

"It's too late." The girl's voice thinned with grief.

"What?" Lyren-Sartora gasped. "All of them?"

"No, no. But they may as well. No, that's not true. It's bad. They'll all live, except I don't think Elder Elen will. She's faced the wall and won't take food." The girl struggled with her trembling voice, which got incrementally steadier.

"Why? Did these searching Norsundrians kill them?"

"No—they can't find them. Or they don't care. I don't know. What I can tell you is, Mistress Elen has given up life because Marga is gone." A little of her anger came back. "Do you even remember Marga?"

"I remember Cousin Marga," Lyren-Sartora said, and added with her own return of annoyance, "though she was your age, not mine. She might have told you that the horrible Sartoras count among their few positive attributes perfectly good memories. By the way, may I ask who you are?"

"Tolia. Marga was—is—was my best friend." The girl slammed the bread into a baking tin and glared at her unwanted visitor.

The resemblance was there, all right, Tolia though

desolately. Yet this creature's golden eyes and perfection of feature and form, the elegant riding clothes, the mannered grace of her movements were so very alien to Marga's reckless, laughing joy, and her love of bright colors that had never had the remotest connection to fashion.

"So," this princess, or non-princess, said in her musical voice, "let me understand. It's Marga whose nasty end has upset Grandmother Elen?"

Tolia clenched her teeth on more tears and continued to glare. To answer seemed to open the wounds again, and for what? *They'll have their reasons*, Marga had said. *You'll see.*

Tolia sucked in a hard breath. If it was the last thing she could ever do for Marga, being fair seemed an appropriate effort. "Yes," she said. "And if you remember her true, you'd see why. Everyone—everyone misses her. It's just like the light has gone out of the world." Her voice trembled again, and she shook her head hard, hating to be so weak in front of this intimidating young girl. She scowled at Lyren-Sartora in helpless dislike and added, "You'd never understand."

"But I want to. And so will Liere," Lyren-Sartora said patiently. "Did the Norsundrians kill her, is that it?"

"We don't *know*. We haven't seen her since Eighth-month. A week before her birthday."

"Did they take her away?"

"No. We all gave out she went to Bereth Ferian to look for work, but the truth is, and only the family and Eras and me know it, and Eras signed on to a ship right after. And she went out to sea."

"Went to sea?" Lyren-Sartora repeated, her eyes so acute it almost hurt to look at them, though Tolia could not have told you why, because they were pretty eyes, all in all.

Tolia scrubbed her own eyes on her apron, and sniffed. "Alone. In a boat. That way."

A floury forefinger stabbed at the east wall of the bakery.

Lyren-Sartora had grown up knowing her geography. "That makes no sense! That ocean is dangerous. Why?"

"T-to find you," was the angry accusation—and then a numb amendment, "that is, not you, but Q-Queen Liere. To ask for help. For them, for us here in Imar."

"Across the sea? But didn't she know that that would take months—if the Norsundrians or a deep-ocean storm didn't get her first?"

"She said she has a way. On the — the world-belt. What's it called?"

"The Fereledria," Lyren-Sartora whispered as icy question squeezed her heart.

"And it was fine, for a time. Mistress Elen said, each night, she'd have these dreams. Marga would be laughing and waving to her. To us all. And all around her the sparkling water and the rising sun. Mistress Elen said she was never one for those mental things that the rest of you make so much of, but she knew in her heart those dreams were right. That Marga really did think about her every night."

Lyren-Sartora nodded. "Go on."

"That's it. The dreams stopped one day. The next she had a bad nightmare, and then took sick from worry and no sleep. It was just a cold, but like I said, just took her bed and is waiting to die."

Lyren-Sartora forced her thoughts away from her grandmother. "Marga left Eighth-month?"

Tolia's head bobbed once. "Yes."

Lyren-Sartora shut her eyes as painful realization exploded behind them, leaving an empty, cinder-strewn pit inside her skull. Or so it felt. She opened her eyes again. "The day the dreams ended. It was the seventeenth of this month. Wasn't it."

She had no idea how strange her voice sounded.

Tolia gazed at her, now confused, and took another swipe at her eyes with her apron. "Yes. How did you know?"

But Lyren-Sartora had turned and stepped outside, into the rain, looking like a sleepwalker. Tolia watched, sniffed, then shrugged and reached for the next batch of dough.

Lyren-Sartora's first reaction was that weird, cold explosion of connection, of pain. Then hot fury coursed through her as she sorted through memory, and put together Liere's dreams, and the images Detlev had sent to Liere, and what Atan had told her.

And she saw again the image of the heart-numbing beauty, the power, of that arc of white light striking through Efael's black clouds and smashing them into impotence.

It should have been me. It should have been me.

Eleven

DAVID HAD, IN HIS haste, neglected to discover whether Efael's spy had reported in to Efael before he'd obliterated the spy's memories, but at least he'd lifted the current transfer spell being used by Norsunder. The spell was altered frequently, any time either Efael or Imry suspected an enemy might have access to it.

Using it, Detlev and David shifted themselves to the Searn Selenseh-Redian, which was central to the Sartoran continent. Beyond exhausted, David plopped down and dropped into a dead sleep.

He woke up from his short nap to see Detlev standing in the entrance to the cave, leaning on one hand and staring out. He hadn't rested, then. Though nothing showed in his face or bearing, David knew he was running dangerously close to the limits of his endurance. The abstract eyes, the disinterest in food despite long hours without; when Detlev was this intensely focused, the cumbersome distractions of the physical plane took an effort of will.

David got up and stepped out to join him. A small stirring of wind bathed his grimy face, as high clouds paraded northward. The smell of late-blooming herbs and pine and autumn loam was, for once, not reassuring.

Now that he knew the why of this quest, he said only,

"What next?"

Detlev smiled slightly. "I'm trying to think of a way around it, but I believe it's time to find Imry. Before Ilerian closes in on our target. He's close—very close. That much I know. I am going to have to act before he does find her."

'Act' in this situation meant 'surrender.'

David sighed. "All right. If there's no other way to let Imry know. But not you. Both of them are eager to destroy you. Whereas I—" He forced a grin, though his heart yammered in panic. "Well, Imry did promise to restore to me the black sword."

A voice echoed out from inside the cave; Siamis joined them, having transferred from Mearsies Heili—his fingers still ink-stained, which meant he had checked on them mentally while in the midst of writing. "We'll draw straws, shall we?"

While the three debated who was to sacrifice himself by transferring to Larkadhe, unknown to anyone on either side, even Tolia the baker, Lyren-Sartora stood in Belann Harbor locked in debate with herself.

She was fairly certain now what she had seen. She also knew that she was the only one who had put it all together. Oh, how it would pay back Detlev for everything he'd done if she kept this secret! It would also spite Liere, who had so loftily decided to hug her misery to herself.

It would serve...

It would spite...

Well, that was it, wasn't it? In the end, keeping the secret would only amount to spite, forever. And even if she were the only one to know it, that would be the sum of her life.

Sometimes, Lyren-Sartora thought, trite as it is to say it, the truth hurts.

But it was still the truth.

Scalding tears mixed with the cold rain and washed down her face. She turned and reentered the bakery.

Tolia looked up. "What?"

But Lyren-Sartora did not even hear her.

She knelt down at the stool, and pulled from her pocket a beige sheet of paper and a drawing chalk. Tolia glanced curiously, then back to her dough, as Lyren-Sartora wrote:

Detlev: Liere said all you needed was an identity, and I rather think I've found it for you. Surprise! Yet another

Fer Eider, this one called Marga. I have details if you desire them. Lyren-Sartora.

Tolia glanced down again, and her breath hissed in as the words vanished on the paper, to be replaced by words in a different hand.

Lyren-Sartora: Thank you. Detlev.

Twelve

DETLEV SILENTLY HANDED THE magic-paper to David, who saw Lyren-Sartora's message before the lettering vanished. "Marga?" he repeated.

Detlev sat down on the stony ground in the cave entrance, cross-legged, elbows on knees. "This might take a while," He dropped his head into his hands, and stilled.

"A name is enough for him," Siamis said. "Dyranarya training. Since neither of us has had that, why not ask for details?"

David pulled over Detlev's magic-note and wrote to Lyren-Sartora requesting details. A short time later, the paper filled, and Siamis read over his shoulder. It was a long screed in Lyren-Sartora's beautiful slanting hand that had begun to lose the childishly rounded letters, full of humor and threaded with self-deprecating irony. In some ways it seemed very much the sort of note you'd get from a thirteen-year-old — and in others, not at all.

"I don't really know Lyren-Sartora," David said to Siamis. "She was always a small brat who liked fussy clothes romping around with Liere and Senrid in the early days, and with Sveneric and Ian Selenna and the rest of the second generation, more recently. How could she have figured it out, alone of anyone? I can't get my mind around it."

"Accident, of course," Siamis said. "She left Mearsies Heili in pique, I learned that after she left. The rest is clear enough." He pointed at the note. "What she learned from the Fer Eiders about her cousin enabled her to put together the person, the place, and the time."

David shook his head at the close call. A very close call—they had still been arguing over who was to throw away his life when Detlev felt Lyren-Sartora's message arrive.

"Lyren-Sartora's at a bad age," Siamis continued. "Rootless—and wants a home. Good at everything she tries, but doesn't know what to do with herself. Was born with her ancestors' taste for the fine life, and all her relatives and most of her friends deplore it. On the threshold between childhood and teenage, with all its attendant questions and assumptions about the world. and everyone still sees her as the little mascot trotting at their heels. Meanwhile it is a bad age for accepting anyone's authority but her own."

"Nothing a dose of self-discipline won't cure."

Siamis sat back against the cool stone walls of the cave, his eyes on the cloudy westering light past Detlev's bowed head. "How much of this do you want to hear?"

David's attention shifted to Siamis himself as he hesitated. He and the boys had known Siamis their entire lives, but did any of them really know him? Yanked at an age younger than Lyren-Sartora from a happy life into the dirtiest of wars—tormented by the filthiest of the war-mongers—the stakes an entire world. Imprisoned in a place beyond time-measure for what elsewhere was centuries, and then raised by the blood relation against whose surrender Siamis's life had been held forfeit, only that relative had become one of the enemy.

Until Siamis hopped the fence in '48, the Host had, according to all accounts, found endless amusement in watching the two squabble. What was the real story behind all that?

Neither of them talked about it. Siamis's mild demeanor suited a scribe or bard or steward. He was tall, slender, fair-haired—in fact, David had thought when he was small that Siamis was a blood relative of his own and Imry's, and had been considerably surprised to find out they weren't even remotely related, that Siamis had been born, like Detlev, back before the Fall. Though he had done a good deal of their martial arts training, he moved without any hint of swagger, and even MV admitted that he was still faster and stronger than any of them.

Not long before Detlev left Norsunder, Siamis had adopted a daughter, another mystery, though Adam had murmured once that Siamis had located her in Halia, specifically down there where the Cassadas family had originated, and Adamas Dei had settled.

Siamis and Yanli seemed to enjoy one another's company, but she was an independent spirit; there was little evidence of the extraordinary rapport that existed between Sveneric and Detlev. Siamis seemed to be content to let her study with the northern magic school and help in the archive. He'd confined himself to teaching her martial arts.

She and Lyren-Sartora had been a lot like sisters, until Yanli got too serious about magic studies, which Lyren-Sartora resisted in favor of socializing in half the royal palaces of the world.

David said, "Sveneric and Lyren-Sartora seem to be fond of one another. All that group is. But he also seems to think she's unfocused."

Siamis said, "Those two are opposites. They won't understand one another until they have finished changing, and in effect, trade positions."

"Trade?" David repeated.

Siamis looked out at the misting rain. His voice, which David had always found pleasant to listen to, now sounded meditative. "Sveneric inherited his father's global paradigm. Lyren-Sartora sees people as individuals. Sveneric chooses solitude for contemplation; she is happiest surrounded by people, and she finds them all interesting. Sveneric had to learn much too early his father's self-discipline, and the combination of that with his other qualities tends to make people regard him somewhat warily. Lyren-Sartora was everyone's little sister, and they got in the habit of correcting her for her own good, a habit that has not desisted. She is as adept as Sveneric in a number of ways that would surprise you, but to Lyren-Sartora everyone—especially her nearest—says, *Find something! Focus on it!* Didn't you read that line about the Fer Eiders keeping the secret about Marga's true intent? Lyren-Sartora's aware of the responsibility of family without quite feeling its benefits."

David repeated the words to himself: Responsibility without benefits. Was it that, then, behind his conviction that Imry could be brought back? Was it behind his sense of guardianship over the independent Senrid?

No sense in pondering that now. "What's this about Sveneric and Lyren-Sartora trading places?"

"Not places. Paradigms. And I don't know if it will ever happen, but if it does—if her gifts enable her to see globally, and his to connect with individuals the way she does so effortlessly that no one notices it—they will probably understand one another. And incidentally become people of some influence."

"Sveneric thinks about people all the time."

"As an observer. Wary, even sympathetic. But without connection," Siamis said, his voice too gentle to be contradictory. "It was his shield back in the Norsunder Base days. But it's holding him back now. He has more to learn than he thinks he does. Which is to be expected in the young."

David reflected that he didn't even know what that meant. Where did that put *him*? Amused at how callow he felt, he glanced over at Detlev, who was still sitting motionless in the cave entrance.

Siamis said, "It also sums up why Ilerian failed to find Marga Fer Eider."

"The family connection?" David guessed.

Siamis gestured toward the purple-hazed, distant hills. "His focus appears to have been on powerful individuals. It seems to have never occurred to him to look right there in Imar, at this family of pastry-makers of no political or magical import."

"Right," David said. "The Host adopting that manor that once belonged to a branch of the Deis was meant to be a slap at Detlev."

"Ah, that was Yeres, but yes. She had the Eid province pegged. It's widespread tradition that manors descend in families, but Yeres, obsessed with hiding from the march of time, missed the changes that dispersed that branch of the Deis five or six generations ago. No, I don't think she missed the circumstances so much as misunderstood the significance."

"Ah. The line of descendants who had become commoners rather than fighting their way up to noble rank again?"

"Exactly. Which is a real thing, whether or not you scorn it. It was certainly something that Liere's father resented his entire life, and his attitude has shaped a lot of the dynamics we see now, from Liere's fundamental sense of unworthiness to Lyren-Sartora's thorough distrust of that family, though her grandfather has been dead for some years."

"But his poison lingers, and each requires a different antidote. I see it. How can his training really help Detlev find Marga?" David tried to imagine sorting through the uncounted human beings of the world, and failed.

"He knows the Deis. The way dyranarya see the world. Listen, I'd better return to Mearsies Heili, at least to check on things." Siamis pointed back inside the cave, where David perceived a basket full of carefully wrapped items. "Help yourself. Just leave enough for him."

David sat back, still feeling a strong sense of relief that the search was over, even if the danger was not. Living with danger was a constant. Detlev might have been able to force himself to surrender—he'd had to once before—but David had been so horrified at the prospect, he was still feeling the reaction. Not on Imry's account. His brother's ambivalence he'd perceived in spring, when David was Imry's prisoner. But if Imry handed Detlev off to the Host...

To rid himself of that path of speculative horror, he reached into the basket and pulled out the first thing his fingers encountered, which turned out to be a biscuit stuffed with cheese and greens.

He ate slowly, but still, half an hour went by with the speed of half a year. Detlev's 'while' might be a long time indeed. David left the rest of the food for Detlev, who would need it, and wished that he'd provided himself with a good piece of wood for carving.

Norsunder Beyond

Imagining herself in a bubble, Hibern bent over the book once again, and worked at teasing out the familiar elements until she perceived that Norsundrian was a simplified Sartoran. One could almost say simple-minded. Almost. She would not want to debate, say, societal syntonics in it.

But at least she could read the title of the top book: *An Account of the Adoption of Detlef Reverael ne-Hindraeldrei, spoken by Ereis Mironcolere to —*

Hibern slammed the book shut in disgust, thinking that

she'd rather sit and twiddle her thumbs forever than read Yeres's version of how they'd tricked Detlev. But she'd learned something, to trust her instincts a bit more, for she was very certain that her random choice had not been random at all. Theronezhe, for whatever reason, had put that "random" choice of a book to hand.

She stared at the book, considering another instinctive reaction that had occurred midway in her puzzle-solving: that feeling of being on a stage had lessened. As if the audience had turned away from watching her, attention elsewhere. She still had to be wary, and to maintain her mind-shield—but that was second nature.

She tried an experiment: sending the book to its place. Nothing happened. Magic spells she did not know? Except that she did know the laborious chain of spells to move a thing to a place. It was the sort of trick advanced students learned, to show off. Easier to get up and replace the book.

Maybe she was going about it wrong.

She scanned the shelves, then envisioned the book among them.

She didn't see it happen, but the book was gone from her hands—and only then did she realize it had had no weight. So, that was ... a new thing. Perhaps these books were semblances of books, much as she seemed to be a semblance of herself.

This time she focused her eyes on a specific book—bound in green—and imagined it in her hands.

It turned out to be written by some Norsundrian with an unfamiliar name about the events centering around Ilerian in his time. She did not want to read it. There'd be no point, as she didn't know enough to distinguish lies from truth. Anyway, she was fairly sure now that Theronezhe had willed her to find that last book, and then for some reason—possibly boredom—went away, and she really had chosen the second one.

Therefore, instead of walking along the shelves, could she test the method of selection? What to read here in the archive of the enemy? And then there was Detlev, who was no longer an enemy. What might he have written?

She opened her hands and reached in her mind for books written by Detlev.

Two books lay across her palms.

They had no weight, no smell. The handwriting, even the paper, were both so smooth and even that she was sure that this, too, was a semblance, though the hand was distinctive. A copy of real paper and ink somewhere, or was the entire thing a fabrication?

Immaterial right now. She turned her attention to the content.

The first book was a description of the foremost kingdoms a thousand years ago, followed by an outline of a plan. A quick, stomach-shrinking perusal of this portion was enough. She already knew plenty about the outcome of the main actions of that particular plan. She leafed past, seeing status reports on the world at various times during the last millennium.

She slowed, ready to slam the book if she spotted anything horrific. Curious, she looked for mention of famous names, beginning with Sartor, because its history was the best known. She found pretty much what she expected, though stated briefly in unvarnished terms that might once had made her laugh. The famously beautiful and winsome Mathias Lirendi of Colend fared little better. It seemed Detlev, for one, was not impressed.

Hibern turned to her own country, known as Iasca Leror in those olden days. Senrid's ancestor, Indevan Algara-Vayir, rated scarcely a mention, with a strong intimation that he was merely present at important turning points.

Hibern had to laugh at that. So much for Leander's theory that there had never been an Inda—no one that famous would neglect to leave behind some sort of written records.

Hibern read on. According to Detlev, Inda was an effective enough tactician, but had no concept whatsoever of strategy. His chief claim to fame, according to Detlev, was that he managed to attract excellent captains, mainly through the promise of steady loot. Interesting. Well, maybe it was true, that the stories about him grew after he died.

She paged back to the segment describing Sartor, this time to follow Detlev's reports of those fascinating, sometimes troublesome Deis. She skimmed through these, slowing when she reached more modern times. The prose was succinct, and dispassionate, giving no clue to the writer's thought.

She was not surprised to discover that two different Norsundrians had tried to recruit Harold Dei, to be turned down because he would not take orders from anyone.

The second book had printed in a neat hand across the top of the page: *General report, year 4720.* This was the decade of Hibern's birth. It began with the recent disasters suffered by various Norsundrians; among the lighter names, Tsauderei and Evend were most evident. The implication behind the list of defeats was that while Detlev was not involved in the action, events went downhill for Norsunder, largely due to an incompetent named Dzydes.

There followed a kingdom-by-kingdom assessment. At the end of each segment was a recommended course of action.

She leafed ahead, discovering that he'd updated the general report in '730, and again in '740. And at the end, she found an update in '750—not long before he switched sides.

Had he known he was going to leave Norsunder by 750, three years before he did?

She looked away, keeping her face neutral by dropping her jaw slightly, with her lips closed. It had been her shield when her father was berating her, and she'd used it ever since—most recently when the previous Sartoran Mage Guild Chief dropped hints like boulders that no Marloven, ever, could be trusted.

Ah, but that poor woman was dead now.

Hibern shrugged that memory away, and looked down at that neat handwriting. Instinct insisted she was on the verge of an important insight. Could she stomach whatever she was going to find?

He tells the truth.

Thirteen

THE SAND FLOWED SOFTLY from June's fingers into the cup, the colors of the grains blending into a warm milky flow. Flakes of metallic stone among the grains winked and glittered, reflecting the bright afternoon sun behind June' shoulders.

She'd decided to stay in Mearsies Heili lest she trigger off dark magic alarms elsewhere by her experimenting. The problem was, the kingdom was so crowded with people almost the only place she could count on being alone for any length of time was the middle of the desert. She was not far, right now, from the western border of the Senyavin Desert; she could see the smog-haze of a nasty ward that some Norsundrian sought fit to set up to catch anyone leaving Mearsies Heili through the desert.

The hot desert. June pushed her damp hair away from her neck and with a quick gesture flung the sand out of the cup, watching it scatter over the nearby dune. Then, sitting back, she watched absently as her fingers scraped up more sand and funneled it thin-streamed into the cup again.

She was very tired. She was tired from running with the Border Irregulars at night, rescuing desperate refugees from the sport-seeking Norsundrians. She was tired from spending daylight hours researching and experimenting. And she was tired of the burden of a responsibility she had not asked for.

After Detlev had identified the cup, she had quietly gone about checking every reference available in Clair's library. There was very little about Old Sartor, and less about other worlds of that time. The total gleanings being several mentions of Elesh Orom-Alsh (all spelled differently), one going to the miraculous length of describing it as a world on which humans were a minority. Nothing about a blue-green-eyed Guardian from a far world four thousand and more years before, six or eight years older than June, who had felt through her magic that teenage Earth-born June was enough of a kindred spirit to be the right recipient for the object she Guarded. Nothing about Alshi. Nothing about their magic.

Nothing, in short, of the slightest help.

Detlev had called it the fifth of five Protections, with a capital P. Which suggested that each had one job, as the saying goes. Was this one's job defensive or offensive? June already knew from her own experience with it that its magic kicked into active mode—ready for use—in the presence of dark magic.

Right. Ready for use.

She'd already learned how to use it in a limited way, through intense concentration. But she knew, in the same way it intruded into her thoughts and dreams while granting others only headaches and dizziness, that she was only skimming the surface of its potential.

Ethe—silver. No help there.

Defensive... Best defense sometimes is offense...

June's fingers scooped up more sand, and poured it into the cup. The blurred whitish flow with the occasional flashes looked silver. Like water—silver—

Her tired mind seemed to sink into the cup, pouring in like—

Her head snapped up. Rising to her feet, she began to run west, toward that smog border.

Despite toiling straight into the broiling sun, June covered the distance quickly. Then, standing with the cup before her and staring over its rim into the black magic haze beyond the border, June swiftly shifted her focus into the mental realm of the cup's magic. And, delicately, she reached—

Drew some of the evil magic down into the cup—

It was like the sudden opening of a window onto a limitless sea.

June sensed danger. She threw down the cup and slapped her hands over her eyes—as if that would do anything. She opened her eyes and cautiously surveyed the heat-simmering dust around her.

That was it, then. Was it meant to siphon off dark magic attacks while the other Protections focused on light magic? Except, hadn't someone said there was no "light" and "dark" magic back then? And why had the thing been thrust into Now instead of being used back Then?

Questions crowded out other questions. For answer there was only the silence of the desert.

June picked up the cup again and began the long trudge back, glad she was alone so she could have a good laugh at herself for her secret hopes that she had stumbled onto the thing that would save them all. But scorn, she had learned, was a trying companion, including scorn for yourself. She had this long walk to do anyway. Why not let herself imagine freeing the world? What a payoff it would be, after years of being the clumsiest, the last one picked, the unwanted, to be hailed from every side as a World Saver?

But what would that actually get her? The work would have been done by the cup, not by her, which meant inevitably someone would insist on her giving it back. If they didn't outright take it.

When she reached the white palace again, she went to find Clair, as this was her world, and her country, and June liked her. Clair came up to share dinner with the rest, and June sat down next to her. "The cup holds water," she said, bringing it out. "It also holds dark magic. Sucks it right in."

"Why didn't we try that?" Clair said, her eyes widening.

"It would not have made any difference," Siamis said, coming up behind them.

June and Clair looked up in surprise—no one had seen him enter. But they were used to his presence by now, never demanding, always easy-going. "These old artifacts are part of bigger systems. Without those systems they're more like magic tricks."

June was very glad she'd not shared her vision of herself as World Saver. "It's useless?"

"No, no, I'm sure it'll be useful, in its way, but as a kind of cleanup. Think of the drying cloth after the scrubbing has been done. No, perhaps a dust rag might be closer. And limited at that. Remember, Detlev said there were five of them. That means you have there one-fifth effectiveness."

June nodded, and as more people came in, the subject changed. Siamis wandered out again, talking to Atan.

Later, when June went upstairs to the row of guest rooms where she was staying, she was surprised to find Siamis waiting, a tall figure almost in silhouette, looking out one of the arched windows.

June was going to pass by when Siamis put out a hand, and she stopped. He said, "I did not lie earlier, but I did exaggerate, for effect."

"Why?" June asked.

"I'll only say this. Try, if you can, not to discuss any more magical protections or artifacts around Clair."

June scowled in resentment. "You think she's a spy for the other side?"

Siamis said, "I think that everything she learns, and has to protect, becomes another burden, and she already is laboring under more stress than anyone is aware."

That hit June like an invisible blow. "Oh. Didn't think of that. Okay. Cup goes in the closet, then."

"Before you stash it, may I borrow it?" Siamis asked. "I'd like to test something in the Selenseh Redian. You'll have it back by morning."

June shrugged, inclined to just chuck the damn thing and forget about it. But all she said was, "Sure. I'm not going anywhere. Take your time."

⸺⸺⸺

Selenseh Redian to a small island off Narieth in western Goaerael

Sunset.

Detlev had not moved.

Siamis reappeared with hot drinks and more food. He and David ate a silent meal, both considering recent events; they were startled when at last Detlev stirred, and lifted his head.

"She's alone." He got to his feet and stretched. "On an island west of Narieth."

"There are islands off Narieth?" David asked.

Siamis got to his feet. "There were once. And, apparently,

are again." He dusted himself off.

Detlev said, "I'll return presently."

"Wait," David said. "Don't you want backup? In case Imry's arranged a magic trap?"

"I don't think he has." Detlev's voice was softer than usual—the only sign that he was running perilously close to his limits. "Elaborate magic would draw Ilerian's attention, and an alarm would by its nature bring Imry too late. Perhaps he could make it in time to confront me, or Ilerian, but I do not think he'd like those odds."

David lifted his hands. "Then I'll wait here. Guarding your supper. Or would that be breakfast—yesterday's breakfast?"

Detlev smiled briefly, and transferred out.

It was early on the island when he appeared there, just before dawn.

Weak purple light glowed in the windows of the little house, and did not yet touch the corners of the small room. Detlev looked around without moving. Took in the openness of the cottage with its sea-worn stones on the outside and the dry, rough stone inside having been protected over the centuries by very old magic. He looked at the four glassless windows, at the austere and pillowless narrow bed on which Marga Fer Eider lay peacefully asleep, and he knew the place immediately for Imry Llyenthur's secret hideaway. Here Imry came when magic and will could no longer postpone sleep. Here Imry had come to sit and think, until the acceleration of events made sitting and thinking a prohibitively rare luxury.

Detlev stepped to the bed, leaned down, and touched Marga's shoulder. She woke and sat up. Her eyes were dark in the weak dawn light, their expression confused. As she stared wordlessly up into Detlev's face, the confusion swiftly began to give way to shock, and to a lingering trace of remembered fear as she raised one hand to her cheek; he touched her forehead, and she slid resistlessly back into sleep.

Detlev looked round the cool, silent room again, and listened to the sound of the ocean and the seabirds. A small table had been tucked into a corner. Paper and pen sat there; perhaps Imry had hoped the girl would find her mind again in doodling, or writing.

He wrote a sentence quickly, dropped the paper and pencil onto the bed, then mentally he gave Siamis the transfer signal. He saw Marga transfer first, then himself, and looked down at where Marga lay on the cave floor, an awkward tangle of gray blanket, filthy yellow dress, and pink-scarred adolescent limbs.

Siamis and David stared in dismay down at her mottled, half-healed profile.

David gave a long, soft whistle. "I'm surprised she survived."

Detlev smiled. "The magic kept her alive."

"Imry?"

"Not there. She was alone, and there was no magic on the place."

"Too bad," Siamis murmured, smiling.

Detlev said, "Imry and I will eventually have to meet and exchange views, but not yet."

David thought, just let me get to him first.

Detlev said to them, "This girl will, I believe, wish to wake up under the open sky. I will take her up to the lower plateau. She will also need a familiar person—perhaps not male, for choice. David, will you find Liere and request her assistance? Siamis, will you remain here as monitor?"

The two separated to carry out their orders.

Fourteen

Between Selenseh Redian at Ghildraith and Sartor

LIERE WAS ACTUALLY ON her way to Ghildraith Selenseh Redian, for the third time.

After far too many disturbed dreams about her family in Imar, whom she had not gone to see since her return from Geth, it was Lyren-Sartora refusing to write back to her that forced her to leave Enaeran's resistance, and guarding the secret harvest on remote mountain slopes, to take the by-now familiar road north.

Liere found this sudden about-face on her daughter's part bewildering and upsetting. Before the invasion, she would have done her duty to visit her mother and brothers and their children, but it had been Lyren-Sartora who had refused, and as Liere was trying to repair her relationship with her daughter before the war broke out, she had suppressed the impulse.

Well, she was going now.

Imry Llyenthur had patrols out ranging the Ghildraith mountains around the Selenseh Redian again, though only two that she sensed a distance off. She did not even have to slacken her pace to avoid them; it was a band of rain that caused her to hole up under a very thick, gnarled cedar. She pulled her knees in tight, seeing her breath, the first harbinger of the winter to come. Yanking her cloak around her, she put her head on her knees to rest her eyes, and slid into sleep.

Her dreams jumbled Lyren-Sartora, Bereth Ferian, and Eidervaen together, then through the nonsense trotted a plume-tailed dog that barked, "Contact."

She knew that voice. Didn't she? Recognizing David of Detlev's gang woke her. She couldn't remember him saying a single word to her during that arduous journey from Halarialgre west, and before that, when she had gone to Detlev's house right after her return from Geth, he had made it clear she was an interruption they did not need.

Except now, it appeared, they did need her. Surely he would not be dream-walking just to be snotty. With practiced ease, she closed her eyes, recovered the shreds of the dream—and found him waiting. Wordlessly he furnished a Destination, a Selenseh Redian. With it came a variation on the transfer spell, but in dark magic, a sense of urgency, and Detlev's image.

: Coming. She opened her eyes, shook out her cloak, and did the transfer.

The dark magic transfer slammed her into the outer case at the Selenseh Redian, where she leaned against the stone to recover. At least the transfer had been relatively short. As soon as she was certain she wouldn't retch, she went inside and used the cave's safe boundary to transfer to the Destination David had given her. It took a few moments to recover, but not as long.

This Selenseh Redian was new to her. Somehow there was a sense of blue to the air, though the stones were, as always, all shades of the rainbow.

When she exited the inner cave, she found David leaning against the smooth stone wall of the outer cave, hands in trouser pockets. His lounging posture, the baggy and rumpled half-laced tunic, called Imry Llyenthur forcibly and unpleasantly to mind.

Instinct was faster than manners. She looked into his face, and was reassured at the sight of the familiar brown eyes framed by light blond hair. At his expression of amusement she made a face.

"Imry's not such an ugly fellow, is he?" David teased.

Liere refused to smile. "If you mean ugly like Wan-Edhe of the Chwahir, no, he's not. If you mean repellant and disgusting, yes he most certainly is." She assessed his features again, trying to find the reason for a resemblance that had escaped her hitherto, but now was pronounced. David appeared to be both taller and thinner than he'd been the winter before, then there was the unusual carelessness about his appearance. Not that he'd ever dressed in silk and lace, but he'd always been so fastidious. Like Senrid.

"Have I altered so much?" he asked.

"Yes. Where are we, and why am I here?"

David's smile vanished. "We have Lyren-Sartora to thank," he began. "We are in the Sartoran Selenseh Redian, and there's a bit of a walk ahead of us."

Wasn't this summons an urgent one? She bit down on the question and followed. Outside, she looked up at the patterns of stars in the Sartoran night sky, so different from the stars above Bereth Ferian. While her eyes adjusted to the fading darkness she stepped with care, David's long strides matching to her pace.

The air was clear and cold and windy, the eastern horizon bluing toward a new day. Of course they were in the mountains, but perhaps not as high; the air didn't seem as thin and there deciduous trees around them. A pair of brightly colored birds chased one another, trilling excitedly at the unexpected sight of humans, and dove into a purple-blossomed tree.

"Where are we going?" Liere asked, breathing deeply. The air smelled of a distinctive blend of pine, and wildflowers. One would never know that Norsunder was anywhere on the same continent.

"I'll tell you presently—we don't transfer here right now. There must be no trace of magic. Up this path."

He led the way. The path was barely that—uneven, grown over, at times seemingly nonexistent. But David moved unerringly around such barriers as an ancient, deeply tangled hedgerow and a moss-touched rock fall, and here and there Liere saw signs that a path indeed existed. As the sun rose to its zenith, they paralleled an escarpment, eventually entering a short tunnel that breached a granite outcropping. That opened to an ancient lane of yew trees that had been planted by long-ago hands.

When they stopped for a drink at a little waterfall trickling into a pool, she glanced his way. "You said we had Lyren-Sartora to thank." Then she slurped again. The water was quite cold.

As she dried her hands on her robe, she surveyed David, who seemed lost in thought. She wondered when he'd slept last.

He glanced over. The expected impatience bordering on

contempt was completely missing from his expression. "She was the one who found your niece Marga Fer Eider," he said, as though continuing a conversation. "Marga was the one lost in the storm. You might say that she ended it."

They started walking again.

"Ended it? If that's the storm I think it is, unless things have changed more than I knew since the last time I checked on the family, little Marga could not possibly have learned enough magic to disperse a regular rainstorm, much less one propelled by one of the Host."

"Your little Marga is sixteen or seventeen, and she hasn't learned magic. According to Detlev, the magic has come to her. It is now a part of her."

"Marga?"

"She's the right type of person, apparently. He said there are usually a few potential ones in any given generation, scattered round the world."

"Characteristics being Dena Yeresbeth, and—?"

"—and instinctive attunement to nature as well as to people, no ambitions in the usual sense—political, social, material. Ambitions as most of us understand the word. If Efael hadn't interfered she would have made a peaceful and unremarked unity through the Fereledria magic."

"You mean, become one of the Geres?"

"No. More formidable even than that."

"I'm still lost."

"Put simply, she's in symbiosis with the world. Or will be, when she's conscious again, and sorts it all out. Detlev says it'll take her some time."

"Symbiosis," Liere breathed. "I have never heard of the like."

"Partly because there hasn't been one for several millennia. For which we can blame Ilerian. Who is, incidentally, the mirror-opposite of this particular phenomenon. Hunting for her hard."

"Ilerian..."

"Catches them, consumes their souls at his leisure, and his power grows. And he makes the anguish last for centuries."

His voice, usually so mild, reminded Liere of Imry again. She shivered as she followed him around an old spill of rock. "I know so little about Ilerian other than the fact that he was the architect of Norsunder. I also know he is behind the increasing land-malaise gripping Imar."

"He wasn't the architect. That honor is shared between Svirle and an individual named Sfenaraec. Ilerian merely brought the power into focus—as it happens, by making Sfenaraec his first victim."

They approached another lane of tall yew standing like black sentinels. Liere shivered, and shook away the subject of Norsunder, for now. She said, "And Lyren-Sartora found Marga?"

"No. Lyren-Sartora made the connection. Detlev found her, and don't ask me how, especially as she's apparently lost her identity. But I expect we'll both be learning that," his voice warmed with amusement, "when Detlev ropes us into his academy."

"His what?"

"I'll leave describing that to him."

Her thoughts raced along two different paths. With deliberate effort she set aside the personal one, and concentrated on Marga. "She lost her identity. And nearly her life. And yet she managed to break that storm."

"A fortuitous happenstance—we can say now." A soft laugh escaped David. "Because Detlev said, had she made this discovery and started experimenting on her own, Ilerian would have been drawn right to her."

"How did Detlev know that it even happened, then?"

"Adam niffed her. Contacted Detlev. He was in time to see it on the mental plane. Along with the Host," he added. "They only saw the, oh, call it the after-flash. Not enough to get location or identity. Or even to be absolutely certain what they saw. Though Ilerian is taking it very seriously."

"That's frightening."

"Yes," he said baldly.

They were at the end of the lane. "Symbiosis with the world," she murmured. "I am still not certain I get what it means."

"It means, once she figures it out, she'll be able to do just about anything," was the jaunty reply.

Liere drew in a deep breath.

They then emerged from the line of trees. They had reached a sort of plateau with a profusion of wildflowers waving gently in the wind like a sea all across it. It formed a gentle bowl with a stream winding through the middle. On the far side of this sea of wildflowers a rocky escarpment led to what appeared to be another plateau, shadowed by a grove of spreading trees.

"Where is she? Oh. There."

A blanket-wrapped figure lay surrounded by wildflowers. Liere took a step toward her, then halted, reaching with her mind. Marga was physically in no danger, but clearly unconscious; time to gather what information she could.

David slowed as Liere gazed wandered in a slow circle, looking at clusters of verbena, goldenrod, timothy, buckeyes and begonias among many other wildflowers, and breathing in their scents — sweet, acerbic, spicy. Detlev appeared at the top of the escarpment and seated himself on a huge block of bleached rock.

Liere gave him a nod, then turned again in a circle, more slowly. What was it that saturated the colors, and permeated the scents on the air?

"I love mountains," Liere said, mostly to herself; her senses brimmed with a joy that bordered on giddiness.

Aware that that probably sounded inane, she looked up at Detlev, saying earnestly, "There's something splendidly untouched by humans here, though perhaps my reaction is partly from those weeks of watching every word, and every shadow in a window, in Sles Adran."

Detlev smiled, amused. That smile vanished when she said, "Because I feel something..." She looked around again, this time with the focus of careful scrutiny. "Something was here... Ancient. Right?" Her mood changed, from delight to wonder. "That stone — that's part of a wall. Isn't it?"

"Yes." He brushed his fingers over the glistening white not-quite-stone on which he sat. "This is the outlying portion, actually. Do you want to see the rest?" He nodded toward the higher plateau. "It's a treacherous climb, I'm afraid."

"What is it?" she asked, covering the last of the flower-sea in a few running steps. "More signs of ruin? What was it?"

"4800 years ago, the Dyranarya Academy was here. Its remains are what you see scattered about." His eyes narrowed with amusement at her sharp intake of breath. "You can make out the Sartoran Sea from the higher plateau, to give you an idea of location."

He started up a narrow, rocky path alongside a little waterfall that fed the stream below.

"So this is — was — the place you ... well!" She paused halfway up the slippery path to drink from cold, clear water, then, looked around with renewed interest. Of course she saw nothing different, but increasingly she sensed—something. A deep breath. Something good, no, what an inadequate word, when it stood so sturdily for food or clothes or behavior or even an example of the fine arts. What she sensed was not syntonic but numinous.

"Watch your step up here," Detlev said, pointing to the steepest part of the trail, right below the top.

She picked her way up, David behind her in case she slipped, until they emerged on the upper plateau.

The thick trees she'd seen from below grew only on the eastern and northern perimeter. The rest was a stretch of tall grasses and myriad shades of daisy punctuated with canna lilies bare, except for tall grasses, and rainbow-hued clusters of heady alyssum, sweet loethe, astringent lister, and aromatic flossflower amid piles of worn white stone. The western edge proved to be another cliff, this one a sheer drop down half the mountain. In the distance westward gleamed a strip of ocean, the sky bright blue above.

She took it all in, then faced Detlev. "There is something else here."

He looked an inquiry.

She said slowly, "It reminds me of that night—in Roth Drael—when I was ten years old, and I freed Erai-Yanya's dyr. Is there a connection? Why did are we here? I thought this had something to do with my brother's daughter Marga?"

"It is all related," Detlev said, gesturing back at the sea of blossoms, indicating Marga, lying so still among the nodding wildflowers, not far from the stream. "As for what you sense, and few would even if they were here, is the presence of the disirad."

"Disirad?" she repeated. "I've ... heard that term before."

"It was what the dyra were made out of."

"The only books I remember mentioning it stated that it was all destroyed in the Fall."

"Norsunder believed it was." He smiled. "Though its reappearance is fairly recent."

"Can we use it to defeat Norsunder?"

"Alas, no. Though Ilerian would tear apart the world if he suspected it was here. There is little value in this place for our present difficulties, but once Norsunder is defeated, I have put forward plans to reform the academy."

"Really! Like your old one?" She looked around, imagining light, high-arched Sartoran buildings, flowering gardens, with larger-than-life robed figures drifting about looking Awesome and Advanced.

"Not quite," Detlev said. "There will be some fundamental improvements."

"Improvements?" she repeated. Then she thought, if they'd been so very perfect they never would have lost their battle, would they? "Like what?" she asked as she stooped to pick up a small, smooth white stone.

"What's the difference between what Erai-Yanya is trying to do at Roth Drael, and the Ones' establishment on Geth?"

Liere tossed the stone gently on her palm and watched the subtly glittering surface, then she looked up. "Both places of learning, but Roth Drael is a retreat, and the Ones go out into the field. Is that it?"

"Close enough."

"I thought the old dyr-holders—oh, I see, I think. People had to come to them, is that it?"

"Yes, and there were certain restrictions as well."

She gazed at him in surprise. "Whom will you pick first? What are you going to teach them? I mean, how does one make a real dyr-wielder—not just someone running around with one trying to use it in our magic, as I once did?"

Detlev stepped to the very edge of the sheer western cliff, and faced the strengthening wind. The tang of salt mixed with cedar was stronger now, but between the drafts swept straight up from the sea the scent of the wildflowers sweetened the last of the summer heat rising from below. Liere moved to stand next to Detlev so she could hear what he'd say, for the wind blurred all sounds but what it made itself. She willed her innards to stay still and her eyes not to focus dizzily on the canyon below, and turned her gaze firmly to the fiery sun sinking westward as the cool wind fingered through her braided hair.

Detlev seemed lost in thought. She went on more slowly, "I would be using a dyr, if I can. Really using it."

"Not yet," he answered, smiling a little. "You didn't even finish your Ones training. Mine would start where theirs ended."

Remembering that she had quit while believing she had little more to learn, Liere winced. "How long before you produce actual dyr-wielders? And who besides me—or," she amended, "did you have me in mind as a scout and not as a prospect?"

"Get used to the term dyranarya. You will probably decide to become one someday."

"Look, the sun is setting," David pointed out. "Unless you know the path, it's dangerous in the dark."

Liere looked back, understanding then that he was very familiar with this place. Though she was very certain that no one knew, or surely she would have heard about it.

They recrossed the higher plateau as Detlev said, "Among the people you know, only David and Adam are ready for the last part of the training, David having reached this point fairly recently. Adam, some time ago. I believe he has the potential to surpass my long-departed colleagues. At various preliminary levels are individuals you'd likely guess. Sveneric. Yanli. Hibern Askan would advance very quickly if she peeked out of her Marloven shell long enough to recognize coinherence, though I suspect she would prefer the magic end of studies."

Liere's mind was still back at David's easy familiarity with the place. "You've been planning this for a long time?" She waved a hand at the plateau around them, thinking five years back—maybe even ten.

Then she looked up quickly, and said a little stiffly, "In any case, this would not be for me. My life is in Enaeran, or will be soon—"

"Did you plan to lock yourself in a tower in Shiovhan with only Andri as a visitor?" Detlev retorted, but without bite. "Someday you might decide you have the free time to learn something new. In the meantime, I need people to scout likely prospects for me."

"That, I am most willing to do."

"To answer your first question," he said, "Yes, I've been planning this for a very long time."

PART THREE

One

DAVID HAD ALREADY VANISHED, reappearing on the lower plateau, where he went to check on the still figure lying peacefully in the grass.

Liere hesitated at the top of the steep path and looked back again, this time seeing the purples and roses of sunset intensifying the wildflower hues. The presence of the disirad was strong, like a continually sung or played chord too deep and too vast to be heard, but she felt it in her bones, in her spirit. And in the fading day, the prospect of leaving, the inward joy of that ineffable presence faded into a sense of separation, of yearning. Liere stopped on the rock to which she was clinging, and shivered in the wind, which now seemed cold. "Detlev," she called.

He was already halfway down. He paused and looked back.

"You know the trail at night, do you not? I think I'd like to wait out the sunset."

He smiled. "You'll be back."

"Yes, but still. Just until we finish talking about this stuff?"

He rejoined her in a few swift steps.

The sun's rim had vanished, and she could no longer see the expression on Detlev's face. Not that it had ever told her much. She glanced at his silhouette, wondering how long he would consider "a long time." Five years? *Ten?* She had come to believe he couldn't have begun turning his back on Norsunder until well after '48, when Siamis made his truce with Tsauderei, and vanished into a Selenseh Redian for nearly a year. Detlev and his boys had definitely been Norsundrians then. So, less than ten years. Well, that was easy to figure out; no mystery after all.

He'd moved off toward the edge again, and stood watching the fading light on the western horizon. His ponytail had come loose and his hair waved and tossed in the wind.

In silhouette he must look much like they did all those years ago. And her perspective shifted, one of those inner quakes that leaves one's vision forever changed; instead of imagining a dyranarya of the lost times standing in the academy garden she saw a man standing on the four-thousand-year-old ruins of his old home.

What must *that* feel like? Had he once had family, besides Siamis?

A lover?

From there it was easy to fancy herself standing on the ruins of Choreid Dhelerei or Bereth Ferian, and Lyren-Sartora, Andri, Senrid—all her friends dead. Every place she knew changed beyond recognition.

It was like standing on the edge of a bottomless well. She turned away, and scolded herself inwardly. Silly. Drowning in self-pity over hypotheticals, and the Host had not yet destroyed the world a second time—that's what she and her allies were striving to prevent! As for Detlev and the ruins here, if he ever had any such feelings, surely they vanished centuries ago.

Her emotions settled back under control, but her thoughts continued to spiral out, making a lacework of connections; meanwhile, he made no answer to this indirect question. "Yes I know the path at night but we will still have to go to the lower level. This path is slippery, too dangerous in the dark."

He turned away, and this time she followed, scrambling down after him in the twilight dimness as quickly as she could. At the bottom she said, "It's less strong here, but I can still feel the disirad. And I don't want to leave."

Detlev's amusement sounded in his voice. "Before the invasion, Sveneric used to camp up here for so long I usually had to come pluck him off."

"I understand not wanting Norsunder to find out, but why didn't you tell anyone on our side about this place?"

"Because the time was not yet right."

She opened her mouth to question him, then, looking around at the shadow-blended colors now going diffuse, she sighed. "Eventually I'll want to know why, but before that, why did you tell me just now? You could have kept Marga in a Selenseh Redian, yes?"

"Marga is here because I believe the disirad's proximity will aid her in recovering her identity. As for why I told you, because you will be traveling extensively, most likely, before we are rid of the Host and you settle into your Shiovhan tower. I want to take advantage of your eyes while you're seeing all kinds of people, as I said before."

"Scouting. I'd be glad to—if I understand what it is I'm looking for. Surely, the first requirement is strong Dena Yeresbeth—"

"And an interest in nosing into others' affairs," Detlev said with matter-of-fact humor. "And a lack of ambition in regard to taking advantage of one's ability to do something about those affairs. Think about it."

A mist had begun to rise, blurring the stars overhead. The plateau seemed empty until they reached Marga. Detlev bent, touched a couple fingers to her forehead, then straightened up, saying, "She will probably sleep until morning."

He moved a short distance away and with deliberate steps pressed down a patch of long grass. Liere watched in silence, trying to divine the significance of these mysterious movements.

David gave a sudden, soft laugh of surprise. "You aren't planning to take a snooze?"

"I am," Detlev replied with tranquil humor.

David looked over at Marga, then back. "And if Svir appears with an invitation to breakfast?"

"I like my bread toasted. A little fresh berry compote, for preference," Detlev replied, wrapped himself in his cloak, and lay down.

Making it clear to the two would-be dyranarya that they were now on their own—and in charge.

David tipped his head toward the cliff. Liere followed.

The mist was slowly thickening to cloud, making the darkness very nearly complete. She walked with care, dreading coming suddenly on the edge of the cliff.

Directly before her was David's pale head, his hair bleached of all color and his face a mere blob in the dim light.

She shuffled forward, testing the solidity of the ground before shifting her weight, and when he sat down, she sat down as well, then butt-scooted forward. A sharp scent of damp autumn-aged grass tickled her nose. The cold breeze carried a piney tang.

She drew her knees up and tucked her cape around her legs, even though she knew that the chill was mostly from within.

David said, "It's early here, you know. You want to sleep? I'll take the first watch."

"No." Her gaze probed the darkness, trying to resolve the abyss into the valley she'd seen the time before. "That is, I suppose I ought."

"But?"

"Well, the last time I saw Marga she was a small child, and I did not really know her."

"I never knew her at all."

Reminding Liere that Detlev expected both to be on hand when the girl woke. Liere understood the words, and then the tone; chill prickled through her when she realized that David was, obliquely, referring to what troubled her.

When had David the poopsie learned insight? Was it characteristic—

No. It was foolish to attribute everything to his family background, just because she had found it out. She said, "I failed Marga, and my own mother. I ought to have understood what those dreams meant. If Lyren-Sartora hadn't been so angry with what I see now as my misplaced sense of duty, she would not have gone off to make a grand gesture. And if she hadn't made her gesture—"

David's voice came, quiet and neutral, "Siamis calls this kind of thing the responsibility of family without the benefits. You're not the only one who feels it," he added.

Liere bit her lip. Far off to the west the silver glow of moonlight touched distant contours of coastland and cliffs. She closed her eyes, feeling how her emotions intensified and accelerated through unconscious resonance with the hidden disirad.

I will say nothing about the Montredaun-Ans, she vowed. She glanced David's way, barely making out his form stretched out on the grass with his hands behind his head.

He was waiting for an answer.

She said, "A few years ago, when I was blathering stupidly

to Detlev about learning control—which in those days meant trying to force myself into some kind of automaton—he told me about what he calls the inner eye."

David's unseen smile warmed his voice. "You'll have to forgive him the galloping poesy. They really used to talk that way."

"Maybe those old words, with their images and symbols, were more precise after all. He defined it for me as 'the separation of self from circumstance,' which sounds simple enough."

The words "separation of self" seemed to linger on the cool, pine-scented air, but David did not answer. The low moon briefly emerged from the slow-moving clouds, and etched his profile with blue-white light. His eyes were wide and unblinking, focused on the emergent stars. Her senses, almost painfully acute, recognized him listening with concentrated focus.

She said, "I have learned how that works for physical control. One sees what might be done, what can be done, and what has to be done. And if a few meals are skipped, and a few nights blend into days without rest, one adjusts, and goes on without significant danger or damage. But to turn that process outward—" She gritted her teeth.

"Go on."

She said, her words coming almost too quick to consider, "When does that stop? I see where I should have applied it in this situation. If I had looked past my own—well, concerns, I would have perceived the connection between all those people and events. But does one kindle it and then snuff it like a lamp? That suggests that all compassion, joy, even grief are unnecessary—illogical—or else are to be consciously permitted only where convenient?"

"Go on."

The compulsion to express the headlong thoughts seemed to seep up through her feet. "If logic dictates that one at last, in the longest vision, acknowledges which side is strongest and then rationally adapts to circumstances, is that not immoral?" She shivered, and then glanced back at Detlev, lying scarcely a dozen long paces behind her.

"He's out like a rug," David said. "If he wanted to listen to us he'd be sitting here now."

"I'm sorry." She sighed. "I have no right to pose as judge."

He sat up on one elbow. "I might point out that a judge has power of decree granted by both petitioners and executors, right? I don't invest your opinion with the weight of law, so you can safely say whatever you want to me. And here's my answer to you: looking on the world through the inner eye does not sever one from emotion any more than it severs one from moral or ethical awareness, and action."

Liere sat in silence, pressing her cheeks against her knees.

The disirad propelled mind, emotion, memory and spirit like shooting stars. How could she speak the conclusion that seemed so inevitable?

Despite Detlev's possessing all the strengths that she had come to acknowledge, and even to value, and despite the ways in which he had guided her own racketing attempts at making sense of the world — and her place in it — she could not, at the last, overcome the fact that he had been one of Them. Had been their servant, had used all those talents and that impenetrable mind to do deeds for them, perhaps using that selfsame inner eye.

And so, what was to stop him from using Marga to his own purposes now — and what were his purposes?

She turned her head, her eyes stinging, her heart full of turmoil. She reached no resolution as she sent a questing tendril to check on the sleeping girl. At least no resolution that she had the strength or the wit to perceive and to alter in need. Inner eye notwithstanding.

A flash of sky-bright dream color arced through Liere's dark thoughts, not from her, but from Marga, who still slept peacefully.

Liere realized that again silence had gone on too long, and she tried to think of something to say, but David forestalled her; he sensed her turmoil, but there was no accusation with it, much less any moral superiority. Or her old self-abnegation. She had been straightforward, and he found his old prejudice melting away. "I take it," he said conversationally, "you met my brother. What did you think?"

"Our meetings were brief," she said, and was relieved at the subject change, and at how normal her voice sounded.

"Brief?"

"For which I'm grateful! Not long after I blundered into him the first time, he — without a shred of decent animosity — broke my arm. Then he sent someone in to wrap it up."

David laughed. "Sounds like he was brandishing you as bait."

Yes—for Senrid. And Andri happened to be there as well. She flinched away from the memories of those days, and said, "Our subsequent encounters were equally brief, and not designed to boost my self-esteem. Quite horrid, in short."

"I gather it was he who gave you the family news."

"Well, I half-recognized him." She hesitated, then said firmly, "It was Detlev who told me about the Montredaun-Ans. Poor Senrid!"

"Poor Senrid indeed." David's laugh was almost soundless, but she felt the irony. "If this is any comfort, remember he was bred up amid problematical relatives. I do believe his fervent desire to get his hands round Imry's neck is neither lessened nor enhanced by shared cousinly blood."

"I must say, I wish him all speed."

"You know, it's still early," David went on. "I won't be able to sit up all night. It's been a busy week. What do you say to a split watch? I'll take the first. What's more, when I wake you I promise no pails of cold water. Instead, I'll get Siamis to transfer something to the Selenseh Redian—I think the Norsundrian transfer spell is still good. We can test it with food. Which she'll need when she wakens."

"The ultimate persuasion," she said, backing away from the cliff.

She found a flat, grassy spot near Marga, surrounded by ghost-white, delicately fragrant alyssum. She wrapped herself her cloak, lay back, was pleasantly aware of the complexity of autumnal scents on the cool breeze—

—And the welcome aroma of hot coffee seemed to bring her, with savory promise, out of a deep sleep. She recognized at once a masterly touch in contact-wakings, and appreciated it.

Opening her eyes and sitting up, she perceived David, holding out a mug. She took it, nodding her thanks. Then he moved away and lay down, melting into the dark landscape.

She sipped, looking upward. The stars had shifted half a watch's worth. Warmth spread slowly and deliciously through her body.

She looked about. Utter quiet. No night creatures—at least, no sounds other than the rustling brush of the wind through the grass. Overhead, clouds silently sailed, playing hide and seek with the sinking moon.

Her mind reached along a familiar route, and found Andri deep in sleep.

All the world seemed asleep.

She smiled a little, her gaze seeking the still figure in the quilts. *The world sleeps indeed. And if I must, how shall I act to protect her?*

Her eyes moved past Marga westward—and away.

She would not think about Imry again—Imry or the Montredaun-Ans. It seemed intrusive, and it wasn't as if any of them would ever ask her opinion. And why would they? She had chosen another life.

Two

Liere's coffee was gone when she became aware of the first indistinct lifting of the darkness silhouetting the stand of trees. She turned herself around so she could watch the gradual spread of pearl-soft blue light, and the restoration of color to this rim of the world. The scent of pine seemed to intensify, which somehow sparked anticipation.

She got to her feet and stretched, then walked about, careful to keep from making noise as she warmed up her body. Her gaze lifted to the upper plateau. A clump of wide white-blossomed shrubs threw back the new light.

Day was near.

She turned back, wishing Marga would waken now. But the slight figure was as still as she had been all night. So too were the two cloak-shrouded ones, some paces distant.

She ventured a few steps nearer to David, and paused, looking down. He lay very still in the tall grass, his cape covering everything but his face. As the growing light touched his features, she was reminded of her initial surprise the night before. Right now there was nothing of Imry Llyenthur's extravagantly drawn features in the refined ones before her. The resemblance had, after all, been superficial.

What had happened to David to make so drastic an alteration? There was more to it than his thinness of person or carelessness of dress, all of which were easily explained in his one brief reference to a "busy" week. Instead, she sensed a qualitative change that had nothing whatever to do with his brother.

A step nearer. In repose, it was a remarkably young face, and — she found her answer. She remembered the David of the past, the sense that violence lay directly behind the mild manner and the tidily civilized appearance. After he'd left Norsunder, he'd still been sarcastic and impatient, the single time she'd seen him, and most of all he'd simmered with that perpetual readiness for action — but now it was gone.

It was so gone that it invested his carelessness with an odd, other-worldly quality, as if his mind walked frequently in realms far from this one wherein his body resided. Yet that greenish bruise on his forehead — -and she vaguely remembered from that brief time in the cave that one of his hands had been stiff and discolored — were both indications that he had seen action, and recently.

His eyes opened. Startled, she stepped back. He seemed not to notice, but sat up, and yawned.

"I'm sorry," she whispered, her neck heating, because she knew she'd been caught staring. "I was debating whether or not to waken you."

He smothered another yawn, and blinked his eyes. "Set myself to wake at sunrise." He looked around. "Detlev still lolling about? Look at that." He grinned, waving a hand in the direction of the black-cloaked figure. "I won't say he hasn't earned it, but the sight of him being lazy is a hoot."

Liere smiled, then walked over to Marga, and stared down in surprise, and shock, at the scarred skin, and the bald patches on her head. So much at stake here... She looked up.

David was right there, his brown eyes awake and aware. "Your turn."

<hr>

: Marga?

Awareness. Some currents sparkled with light, with promising flickers of color just ahead, just beyond —

Swimming...gliding...pursuing...what?

Drifting. Long and long and long.

Some currents were dark. Cold. Close-reaching fingers. She dove lower, hiding.

When the light returned again, beckoning with enticing color, she reached —

Drifted —

: *Marga Fer Eider.*

The softest of whispers. Marga? Familiar.

Was that a light thing? It brought so many images!

Reach! Drift...

The voice repeated the words. A friendly voice. Inviting. Familiar.

Flashes of color came slower — faces. Ohhhhhh, she knew those things, faces, trees, water, sky.

She swam upwards, toward crystal-light. Images — memories. Memories! With increasing delight, she floated among them. Icing-flowers shaping under her father's patient hands. Real flowers in her mother's hair. Music. Faces, all smiling in welcome, in love, and in joy. She looked at each one, their names coming to her like new gifts —

A touch.

She opened her eyes, and looked into the light of peace and stillness. Eyes — in a man's face — in a room —

Who? Where?

Where is my boat? I must find —

The boat was sinking! Her hand hurt!

Memory surged back in a terrible wave, washing through her heart, cold, cold. The water closed overhead, and she dove down swiftly to hide among the good dreams.

: *Marga Fer Eider. Waken. Stay with us now.*

The name caught her and she rose upward again, looking about for the happy images. And they came! Tolia, dancing at Spring festival. Milny. Grandma Elen. Mama's red gown, whirling and twirling, and her singing a new song for Lesim's birthday —

Iridescent water, sparkling endlessly eastward into the sunrise.

Sunrise.

She opened her eyes again. Deep pleasure at a wide sky bright with silver clouds, a new day.

Her eyes travelled down, touched nodding yellow blossoms, and near them the intent gaze of golden eyes in a face of beauty and kindness.

Marga stared, remembering those eyes. Recognizing the brows so like her father's, the mouth shaped like Grandma

Elen's —

"Liere?" she asked in surprise. And laughter streamed through her — because her voice sounded like a frog's croak!

"Marga." Liere smiled. "Welcome."

Marga sat up. Looked down at the quilt over her lap. "But how did I find you?" Her voice thinned when she saw her own hand lying on the grass, with its half-healed scars and pink new flesh.

Horror spiraled into memory of fierce green waves —

Strong, slender hands closed around hers and squeezed. "Marga!" Liere leaned close. "It's all right. You're here, with us. You are safe. Now. Here. With me. Look at me."

Marga scanned Liere's face, and memory crowded back. But with memory came the glimmer of sunlight over Liere's shoulder. Her gaze shifted eastward and her mind shot toward that sun, reaching for the familiar bright path —

Spreading outward and outward —

And another mind was running with her. Calling, Marga. Marga!

She slowed, coalesced back inside her body-self. Found her body-self sitting in a field, the other mind a boundary — and then another face. This one a young man. Brown eyes. Brown eyes, green eyes, no, a stinging slap, no — gold eyes!

"Liere," Marga said, gazing earnestly at Liere as she held onto her body-self. She blinked, and rubbed her own eyes. "I don't remember — how I got here. I came to find you."

Liere said, "There was an accident with your boat. A storm."

"Yes, I remember that."

"And you were rescued," the young man said. Marga liked his voice. But it wasn't the same voice — "And brought here," the young man finished, and she lost the thought.

She rubbed her eyes again. "So that's why I —" She lowered her hands to look again at the scars. "I feel so weird. But it's so nice to find you! Is everyone at home — no, you wouldn't —"

"But I do know," Liere said. "Lyren-Sartora is there, now, in Belann. Everyone is quite safe, and happy to know that you are as well."

Marga sighed, and looked around the field with evident pleasure. "How beautiful this is. But I don't remember coming here."

Liere, watching, saw Marga's expression haze into

abstraction again, and again David swiftly caught her attention, and brought it back. The way Marga's mind disassociated and her identity disintegrated gave Liere a disquieting sense of vertigo.

Marga looked up at them again, her smile wavering.

Liere hastened into speech. "Are you hungry? Would you like something to eat?"

The sweet smile brightened Marga's scarred face again. "Oh, yes, I would! Who are you?"

"My name is David," he said.

Marga turned to Liere. "There was another—a man. Wasn't there? When I was remembering. A man, in a stone room. No. Two men. One with green eyes. Another..."

"His name is Detlev," Liere said briskly. "He's the one who found you. He's sleeping, right over there."

She pointed—and at that moment Detlev sat up, and put back his hood.

The kind eyes, yes. Not the curious green ones. Marga's gaze dropped to her hands again, and moved up her arms. She raised her hands to her head.

"Good morning, sunshine," David addressed Detlev. "You're up bright and early!"

Marga's gaze flicked from David to his arm. His sleeves were rolled back to his elbows. She looked puzzled, reached tentatively toward his forearm—

"Marga?" Liere asked.

David set down the basket he had fetched during his watch. He lifted the cloth covering the food, and scents rose. "Oh! Those rolls smell good! I am so very hungry." She reached for one, then stared down at the golden roll and her fingers began to turn it over and over in her hands. And her gaze diffused again.

Liere dropped the roll she'd just picked up. "Marga?"

But Marga turned once again eastward, toward the sun, and then back. She searched each of their faces in turn as she said uncertainly, "We're not near the Fereledria. We are in Sartor. I—I know it. How did I know it? I—" Memory returned again, flooding her mind.

This time Detlev intervened. It was too swift for Liere to follow; Marga finally was enabled to hold onto her own identity.

And her face puckered.

She was beginning at last to comprehend the vast change

she had undergone. But it was overwhelming. In the spiraling rush of sensation, memory, image and emotion, Marga held her identity—and her mind reached, grabbed hold of one concrete fact, and clung to it.

And she cast herself suddenly into Liere's lap, laughing wildly. "I'm bald! As an egg! Egg-bald!"

Unseen by her, David collapsed back into the grass, his shoulders shaking with soundless, helpless mirth.

Detlev glanced briefly skyward, then he reached for a buttered roll.

Liere breathed in relief: Marga was indeed going to be fine.

The sun rested on the horizon when Imry Llyenthur appeared on that remote island.

He knew within a heartbeat that the girl was gone, but he walked around the little island anyway, as if looking for any kind of a clue.

Finally he entered the house. His gaze slanted to the pencil and paper lying on the empty bed. He stared down, recognizing Detlev's hand in the familiar Norsundrian script.

Once again you had the world in your hands, and you lost it.

Llyenthur backed away a step. He looked around once, then disappeared.

Three

Norsunder-Beyond

HIBERN STARED DOWN AT the Norsundrian lettering, reviewing again the facts.

Fact one: she was Ilerian's prisoner, which—ironically—apparently meant some kind of freedom, within the confines of Norsunder. Until he turned up again. Then she would face a different set of problems. But until then she appeared to be on her own. The way a player is alone on a stage. Except that her audience was also an enemy.

Fact two: Norsunder was not a place, not in the sense of east/west and north/south. Nor was it a time.

Fact three: For whatever reason, its leaders told the truth. Their version of the truth. And for their own reasons, none of which were for her benefit.

Why not read Detlev's old reports, and regard it all as an exercise in point-of-view? It wasn't as if she hadn't read plenty of old records by Marloven ancestors, some of which had been grim indeed. How could this be worse?

She leafed through the '730 report until she found the entry on Marloven Hess. It was after Tdanerend had murdered his elder brother, Indevan-Harvaldar, and had taken the throne as "regent" for Senrid. She prevented herself from betraying her rich inner enjoyment as she saw Tdanerend's manifold shortcomings described in Detlev's prose. Scorn seemed to seep up, a faint whiff, between the objective phrasings. The recommendation at the end of the report was that Tdanerend's vast and fairly well-trained army be used for any local plans, but commanded by someone else.

She wondered if Tdanerend ever saw this. Who did see these reports? Any Norsundrians who wanted? Or only the Host?

She looked for mention of Senrid. *The boy is backward, whether untrained or unable to learn remains to be seen.* Odd, that. But yes, Senrid's horrible uncle had refused to let Senrid train with the academy when he was old enough. Odd that Detlev believed Tdanerend's lies and assumed that Senrid was stupid, considering his opinion of Tsauderei. Though Senrid had acted stupid in those days. Self-protection. Hibern had certainly heard no good of him, even when he was supposed to be betrothed to her. She'd thought Detlev would somehow be more penetrating—ah, but he had been warded from entering Choreid Dhelerei. So all his observations were from a distance, except of course when Tdanerend came to him.

Hibern looked for her own father's name, and found a brief note to the effect that Latvian Askan was knowledgeable in dark magic but inclined to sit over his books, or correspond about theory with his friend Kwenz of the Chwahir, rather than act. The entry on Latvian ended with the note that he was as close to an ally as Tdanerend had.

She paged ahead to '740, and found here a much longer description of Senrid, as suited a ruler, after mention of Tdanerend's having been deposed in the middle of the previous decade. The description of Senrid's character appeared fairly accurate, though hardly flattering. She didn't like to remember those days very much. Though admittedly by '740 he had changed a great deal—for the worse, of course, according to the report.

But right below the section on Senrid she caught sight of her own name. She hadn't been prepared for that. Holding her breath, she read:

Interests light magic and history. Fostered by various lighter mages; given by a great mage a library of current records and of magic books. Considerable knowledge in limited areas, without any idea how to apply any of it. Allegiance shifting toward Erai-Yanya of Roth Drael.

And then her eyes widened as she read:

One of the multitude whose aversion to Liere Fer Eider's style of bleating heroics keeps her from Bereth Ferian's "Alliance of light magicians."

What?

Now *that* was a lie.

She shut her eyes. Neutral, neutral, neutral.

Though—she reflected back through memory. It was possible, from a very narrow view, to interpret her actions that way. But it was so untrue! She'd made friends with Erai-Yanya by then, and had begun studying the broad magics, which she really liked. Hibern had also liked Liere, and had been glad that Senrid had found a friend in her, since Kyale Marlonen was too jealous to permit Leander to visit Senrid much.

And Bereth Ferian's alliance? It had always been "the alliance" without any geographic reference. Arthur had been a part of it, but not even remotely a leader. The closest to a leader had been the Keperi brother and sister, Thad and Karhin. Did Norsunder discount them because they were scribes, with no military knowledge?

Ugh. Even though it was just a Norsundrian report, and an old one at that, she felt like something loathsome had crawled over her.

Skipping on, her attention was caught by Erai-Yanya's name. She skimmed through the summary, her inclination being to close this stupid book when her attention was speared by a shocker. Just a sentence, buried in the general description: it referred to Arthur as the child she'd produced on a whim and promptly abandoned to Evend of Bereth Ferian when he did not prove to be a daughter.

What trash! Yet—here again—she was obliged to admit that, from a distance, to a petty observer, Erai-Yanya's actions might have looked that way. But Detlev was supposedly so discerning. Had his switch to Norsunder made him stupid?

She remembered the sinister little smile, the villainous scowl, neither of which Hibern had seen in their encounters after he left Norsunder. Her curiosity sharpened to intent as she languidly paged back to Sartor in '740. And there, in the midst of a fairly accurate—and again subtly scornful—assessment of Atan was a calm, poisonous, and untrue statement that the perpetual sixteen-year-old's adolescent lethargy had been stirred recently to sixteen-year-old competition, and she was endeavoring to establish Eidervaen as a rival "center of light magic and learning in order to spite the northern school."

It could have appeared that way. But only if you didn't know the personalities involved, like Tsauderei, whose old age kept him reluctantly from long transfers to Bereth Ferian. There was no rivalry. Arthur and Erai-Yanya transferred to him regularly.

She read on. There were so many factors left out, twisting what Hibern knew as the real truth.

Twists. One thorn in the middle of all this dry grass—

She turned back to '740, and Senrid's description. She read it more carefully, and pinpointed the thorn: *He is currying lighter favor by patronizing the gullible new "Queen in Bereth Ferian."* Senrid? Currying favor? To anyone who knew Senrid in those days, it was funny!

The weird thing here was, all these thorns seemed somehow related. Sartora? No. The common connection was Bereth Ferian.

Slow, unhurried, she paged back and this time sought Leander Tlennen-Hess. No mention—Vasande Leror was just not important enough. She paged back farther, to 730. And yes, there again, in Tsauderei's segment, another hidden thorn, this time a reference to the jealous rivalry between Evend and Tsauderei. That rivalry, going back to when they were boys, had been fun for them—both had admitted it. They had been steadfast allies, choosing to live at opposite ends of the world for protection of Sartorias-deles, not out of dislike.

But you could have misconstrued...

She paged onward, stopping to read about kingdoms or people she knew, or had at least an acquaintance with. Sometimes with an inward wince, like at the cold assessment of Carlyle Lirendi of Colend's son Shontande in '750 as immersed in sexual and alcoholic excess...*within the next five or six years his brains will be sufficiently pickled to send someone in, supposedly from Bereth Ferian, or one of its rivals, as an 'advisor.' Lirendi will never know his kingdom was taken away from him, so long as we send someone handsome, young, and good at dancing.*

Ugh. And another, worse one about the Delieths in Everon; Morgeh Troiad, the reluctant king of Wnelder Vee, was unworthy of mention, like Leander. Their worst faults, she thought ironically, was their dislike of kingship, the one a superlative bard, the other a respected scholar. Apparently Norsunder only regarded those concerned with power as worthy of being spied on.

She paged through the rest of the reports during '750, so recently. Poison thorns existed here, too, among those she knew, only this time the references seemed to point to Eidervaen, and not to Bereth Ferian.

She closed her eyes. Her thoughts writhed like snakes, wriggling between Detlev, and the book, and herself as represented in this report, to memory again.

Herself fastidiously declaring once that she would as soon not hear about the geography of Norsunder.

But there wasn't any geography.

No geography. She had wandered and wandered—

No. Concentrate.

She remembered the strange distortions Dhana had begun to describe, and then she thought about her long, pointless walk in the featureless gray. Then the encounter with Theronezhe, and the images of the waiting warriors.

Then this library. Same one as Roy had described when he and Dhana came to Norsunder-Beyond?

The difference was, she had put herself in this library, instead of being—

A vast, black cloud of mental rage knocked her spinning.

Four

Plateau above the Sartoran Selenseh Redian

THE FOUR OF THEM had a picnic, there on the site of the ancient dyranarya academy.

For a time the pressure of myriad other problems, threats, and dangers seemed to recede, but as Liere looked at her niece, she wondered what was going to happen next.

David watched them all. His nighttime reevaluation of Liere held in the light of day. Her sensing of the disirad—faster than he had on his first visit—and her honesty during their conversation on the cliff suggested that he had underestimated her; none of them had been at their best the winter before. Though he'd found her absurd for forcing Andri Elsarion into marriage in the middle of a war, MV had commented that she couldn't have picked a better person. Not that he (or MV) posed as any sort of expert in matters of the heart. They'd been far too busy in recent years for much more than the sport they called "come and go."

Marga ate, and laughed, and looked from face to face, her identity holding, shaping, and reshaping as awareness after awareness evolved in endlessly fascinating felicity.

It was she who ended the picnic, not on purpose. She had been breathing in the cherished scents, and listening, not just with her ears, but with all her new senses, tender and sensitive as this blotchy skin on her arms.

She broke off from talking about how bread is made in different lands, for that had been the subject, and glanced at the odd milky stones that lay half-hidden in the wildflowers. "The other will be seen soon," she commented. "It's even prettier than these." She touched one of the white stones, and turned her gaze to the upper plateau, then turned her questioning gaze to Detlev. "But you are hiding it. I can feel a wall made of ... of ... of air, and time."

David stared at her, and Liere's eyes rounded.

"What do you remember now, Marga?" Detlev asked.

Marga's gaze diffused to remoteness. But she did not lose identity again. "It is hard to explain," she said. "If I think too hard about it I slide back into wind and water."

Liere sent an apprehensive look Detlev's way, as he said, "The disirad's emergence is a manifestation. Not a growth in the sense of a tree, or the erosion of soil that exposes rock. The wall you perceive was a ward I rushed to make when we first discovered the attack was imminent, in case the Host emerged. Which they did."

"*He* does not see it," Marga stated, but not with assurance.

"He did not. Probably cannot, but he suspects now, as he suspects what you might be. Your identity dissolving was the best protection you could give yourself."

"I don't remember any of it," Marga said in a small voice, more uncertain by the moment.

Liere would have tried to reassure her without furnishing details, but Detlev outlined to Marga what had occurred. She seemed amazed and a little frightened that she had been in the hands of the Norsundrians, however briefly. She did not remember Imry Llyenthur, or Khem and Semeh, or the ship that first plucked her off the sea. But once she had it all, she rubbed her hands up her arms, saying, "I think there are physical memories. Like, oh, like how I remember the smell of bread fresh out of the oven at my friend Tolia's bakery. And that brings Tolia to mind."

In other words, the plain truth steadied her better than vague reassurances could have.

Detlev continued, "The search for you will not end now. You must realize that, and also this: your magic will draw them if you are not circumspect. Strong magic that effects changes. The 'he' you referenced wears the form of a morvende, named

Ilerian—"

She flinched. "That is the one. I know his shadow."

"You will have to guard awake and asleep against him finding you."

Marga ducked her head in a nod.

Detlev went on. "When the time comes for you to experiment, I suggest you try shape-changing. No one else can do this without great expenditure of magic, but you will set off no alarms with magic limited strictly to your physical self. But do not assume that that a change of your outer form will shield you from Ilerian, because he will know you despite whatever form you take if you don't maintain your shield. Early in the previous attack, Ejhir Sunchild, the last sireatanrial, tried to hide by becoming a tree in a great woodland, but your mind alters as a tree and you cannot maintain a sufficient shield. Ilerian found him. And changing to a tree and back is a much slower process; he could not escape."

Liere shivered, and Marga ducked her head again, her joy vanishing. "I hear the enemy as well," she whispered. "I ... see his searching gaze when I am awake, and when I sleep. But I always stay in my pearl, my bubble."

Liere said, "Detlev, ought you to help her to hide?"

"No."

Detlev and Marga said it together—and Marga chuckled, winning from Detlev an answering smile.

He said, surprising Liere yet again, "Much of my time now will be spent in the shadow of those who are searching most assiduously for Marga."

"And I want to be with you." Marga turned her sunny smile onto Liere.

Liere looked back, feeling helpless. "Well—of course—but it's not really safe—"

"They don't know her by sight," David reminded her. He frowned a little. "Though the scars might alert someone who's seen a cap-list description."

Detlev said, "Marga, how often have you been sick in your life?"

"Never." She seemed mildly bewildered.

Detlev said reassuringly, "Her scars will be gone within a month."

"This will probably take much longer," Marga said, wrinkling her nose as she felt the denuded portions of her scalp.

"You could probably augment that within the safety of the Selenseh Redian," Detlev said.

"Sel—oh, you mean the bright jewel cave?" Marga's hand pointed unerringly behind and below her. "Shall we go into it, then? I have seen it here," she tapped her head, "since I woke, and I would like to see it here." She tapped her eyelids.

Liere drew a deep breath as she scanned Marga's form, which was very slender, much like her own. Marga was slightly taller, and her willowy body only had, as yet, the most subtle of female contours at breast and hip. "Well. Then I guess it's settled. If the report mentioned a girl, maybe you ought to go as a boy for a time. But we will need clothes. I only have one change." Liere touched her knapsack. "And it is the sort of robe that a married person would wear in Sles Adran."

"Siamis can help once we reach the cave," David said.

"Oh, that sounds like fun!" Marga scrambled to her feet then, and stood poised. "Shall we go soon?"

"I think we ought." Liere was uncertain.

"Then may I look—there—very quick?" Marga waved her hand to the upper plateau.

Liere spread her hands, and Marga was off at once, hideous yellow fabric bunched in her fists, pink and brown bare feet flashing among the grasses.

Detlev said, "Where she goes she will see allies where we might perhaps only see obstructions."

It sounded like an observation, but David knew that he seldom made random comments.

Liere turned her head, and resolve set her features. "Atan does not claim to have a spy network that even remotely compares to yours. But she does hear some things independent of your helpful snippets of information. And I, too, hear things. In fact I happen to know someone who witnessed—a few weeks ago, with his own eyes, one of your boys grabbing a young man named Lexan Glenereth, after fighting off a company of the enemy. And then making him vanish. I hope to safety."

"Whoops!" David shook with silent laughter. "Cork's popped on that one, eh? Who blabbed?"

"Rel saw him." Liere admitted. "He wrote to Atan, and she wrote to me, feeling that I ought to know, since he was seeking me. Is he safe?"

"He is," Detlev said.

Liere looked down, saw her tense fingers, and consciously

laid them in her lap. "I hate that he was seeking me. The impossible myth, not the person."

"As people do when desperate," Detlev soothed. "Don't fret about that. He was desperate enough to be throwing away his life on a false trail. We need his like in future too much to permit him that luxury."

"Luxury," Liere repeated, waving aside the jocular tone. "What decides your intervention?"

"Leef happened to be in Sartor," David said.

"Doing what?" Liere asked.

"Counting ships in the Sartoran Sea," Detlev said readily. "And at that particular time, riverboat transport."

Liere did not know if that was true or not, and there was no way to tell. That is, it was probably true enough—the ship counting—but that didn't address whether or not Detlev required those numbers for some bigger plan. Truth to tell, she both hoped he did—and she was apprehensive, too.

Aware of her own inconsistency, she said, "I know it's absurd, and that Sartora the World Saver is nothing but the worst sort of lie, but I still feel responsible." She regretted the words as soon as they were out, but at least the two before her did not scoff, nor try false reassurances, which would have been worse.

David said, "Look at it this way. Aldon was down there at the time, either mixing it up with Bostian, or trying to recruit him for his feud with Imry. If Aldon had caught Lexan Glenereth, he'd surely hand him off to Efael in order to get something he wants. Lexan is Efael's ideal target. Young. Strong. Smart. Handsome. Still innocent of adult experience. Leef recognized that at a glance."

Liere's skin crawled, and she raised a hand. "Don't go on. I feel dirtied by that much."

"Efael is the embodiment of filth," David said, his voice hard. Then he looked away, embarrassed at revealing that much.

Liere decided to approach the bigger question after all. But obliquely. "I'm sure you saw Atan's map with the blue and red pins, representing killed or captured leaders. She's marking them, but won't do anything beyond that. She says that she can't interfere with other lands. I guess I'm hoping that *some*one is making sure, as much as possible, that Norsundrian puppets don't step up to various thrones when we do get rid of their masters—" She caught a glance from David to Detlev and stopped. "What is it?"

"The question of thrones," Detlev said easily. "There has been little enough time for reflection on the aftermath of our present difficulties, but perhaps now is suitable for a reminder that when the clash between good and avowed evil is resolved, there are going to be clashes between self-perceived visions of what is good."

Liere gazed toward the upper plateau. Then she said, "I've been thinking a lot about that, as I talk to people in Enaeran and Sles Adran. The oldest contract, in so many lands since the Fall, between monarch and people: you support me and I protect you. So many people feel betrayed by their kings and by the mages. They are learning to think—to compromise—to adapt—to fight for themselves, and then what?"

David said, "Govern themselves?"

"How is that possible?"

"Decisions made in assemblies. Probably mostly guilds, to start with, as there is tradition there. Decisions made by majority acclaim," David said, stretching out on the grass, and propping his chin on his fists. "Smaller polities send representatives to a central assembly to speak for them."

"Listen in taverns," Detlev added. "You will hear plenty on the subject. Though probably not in Enaeran, as you have a popular young king and a recent history of far too much chaos. It's always going to be a messy process, arriving at consensus, but sustained good will can make it work. And education will eventually produce a process that the most can comfortably live with."

"The years of civil war and the lack of leadership makes the Enaeraneth all want a strong leader, that much I hear over and over." Liere said. "And Andri will be strong. But in general, I sense that the old order is gone. And the emerging one is different from the old. How to replace it? I do know something about public rule, from watching town politics in South End, when I was small. Most everyone looked to the loudest and most forceful, not the wisest, to speak for them—ones such as my father. How I despised the wrangling, and the lies, and the false flattery."

Detlev said, "No one makes wise decisions without education. And people naturally look to leaders for guidance."

David put in, "If people learn along with their lessons that self-governing is a part of daily life, it can happen. Already does.

More or less. Where guilds are strong."

Liere said slowly, "I'm afraid that those who most actively seek to lead are usually the ones who shouldn't. Who will stop them if people wait for someone else to do the deed?"

David said, "Don't forget the surviving nobles who, hardened by war, and yearning for their days of influence, will be eager to join the chase."

"The chase being the pursuit of power?" Liere sighed.

"Sport royal," David said with a laugh.

Detlev observed mildly, "The kingdoms likely to have the most success in our lifetimes will be those with the strongest guilds, and those with trade cities of long-established independence."

Liere said in a low voice, "What I'm hearing is to expect revolution. And I had looked forward only to peace."

Detlev smiled. "Everyone will look forward to peace. Those who wish to protect it will be watchful when the various visions of peace conflict. Regard it as more of a process, and less of a, ah, call it a single-action solution."

Liere's expression changed. "I see." She didn't say that what she saw was, Detlev was definitely not going to offer a solution after all. Ironic: everyone had been looking to Detlev, either overtly or covertly, for a grand plan for war, to beat Norsunder. She, too. Very inconsistent! Which was not the same thing as ambivalence.

She was distracted by an ant working its way along a long blade of grass toward a withering blossom with seeds still clinging to it, then looked up at the rapid tattoo of running footsteps. Marga sprinted toward them, her cheeks crimson. "It's so beautiful," she cried. "And the evil ones do not perceive that it is there!" She made a face. "But nowhere close to bathe. That stream is too shallow, and I itch!"

Liere rose to her feet. "Let's go back to the Selenseh Redian. I know the spell to get you clean, though it won't feel as nice as a bath."

"New clothes, too? I could not figure that out. This yellow thing is so hot, and its color makes me think of Thelem Elder in a temper."

"Thelem Elder?"

"In Belann. Oh, there is so much to tell you!"

"Why don't you start right now? It's a longish walk to the cave."

"Sure, but I nearly forgot!" Marga stopped, and whirled around. With her sudden, sunlit smile she swooped on Detlev, who was sitting with a knife in one hand and a last piece of bread in the other, and kissed him on the forehead. "I remembered your kindly eyes in the stone house. What shall I call you? I have a da, and so very many uncles."

"How about Grandpa Detlev?" David cackled.

"You do not look old enough for a grandpa. Thank you for saving me, Benefactor Detlev. Good bye, Brother David. Thank you, too!"

David saved his whoop of laughter until the two Fer Eiders disappeared down the yew-canopied path. "I'm sticking with Grandpa. MV'll love that."

Detlev said, "I've decided that these cracks about my old age are a sign that you two have far too much free time."

David rolled over in the grass, arms flung wide. "Imry doesn't know how much work he escaped."

That made Detlev laugh.

David lay there gazing upward, thinking over the conversation. He had begun to suspect that Liere was on the verge of voicing the very question he and the boys had debated since they first began to perceive a sense of history: what was Detlev's goal, and when did he form it? But then Detlev had deflected Liere with the question about thrones.

Detlev said, "Do you still wish to pursue Imry? If not, I could use your aid."

David sat up again. "Just give me until Efael strikes at him. We all know he will, probably soon. Then I'm yours."

"As you will," Detlev said.

Five

DUIN OPENED THE DOOR to the map room and looked around.

The only one there was Colleron, sitting at the relay desk, waiting to be relieved.

Duin said, "They just scalded more coffee. Want some?"

Colleron yawned, scrubbing his hands over his face and up through his thinning wheat-colored thatch of hair. "Naw. I'm for the rack." He looked up, his blue eyes watery. "Unless—"

"Haven't heard nothing."

They snapped fast checks at the door.

They were still alone.

And since they were alone—no Llyenthur, no Bergan, nor any of the other staffers who were less of a threat—Colleron said, "What happened yesterday? Nobody came in last night. At all."

Duin thought back to the previous day. A normal day— everyone around in the map room, busy sorting dispatches and updating the map-markers and relaying messages—when Llyenthur appeared, without warning, and without telling anyone where he had been. Of course that was normal, too.

Duin, who'd had day-duty, had been seated at the relay desk. "He came in. You weren't here, but I tell you, there was nothin' to see. No cause. He fingered through some o' the relays.

Then, sudden as lightning, he lit into us."

"Why?"

Duin flinched, thumbing his temples. What had occasioned that sudden, white-hot mind-invasion? It had been quick, too quick, and hurt too much to figure out what Llyenthur had been after. "I dunno, maybe he wants to know if someone has been hiding that mind-stuff?"

Colleron snorted. "More like hiding prisoners."

"Oh, that too. After he reamed our minds out—two days' memories, that's all I can recall—he went off downstairs, and then he transferred out, and then—"

Duin pointed at the relay desk. Where Llyenthur had gone was soon enough evident, as reports began transferring in—complete reports, listing capital prisoners that hadn't been reported yet for some reason, and also listing sudden changes in hierarchy. He'd obviously gone round all the upper ranks and reamed 'em. Without exception. Just the idea of that many transfers in one day made Duin's guts gripe.

"Who was he looking for?" Colleron asked. "I've seen nothing about rescues or escapes of cap-list prisoners."

Duin shrugged. "No one knows. I suggest we look busy."

For an hour or two, they did. Even Bergan, the world's worst slacker, Duin thought sourly, actually got everything sorted and reported, right down to the stacks they'd all regarded as non-essential. Bergan was an expert at finding excuses to leave tedious lists of requisitions and supplies to the next shift to sort, log, and copy. Colleron stayed to help since he'd had nothing to do during the night, and the relay desk was soon the cleanest Duin remembered seeing it.

That would have its repercussions too, Duin knew. No one liked trying to juggle the decreasing supplies, risking making the wrong decision—not until the head snakes punched back through to Norsunder, to get the magical keys to the stashes waiting beyond time and space. Until the lighters pulled in their harvests, everyone on both sides tightened their belts.

Duin didn't understand how or why magic worked. He didn't care. He was a Chwahir, and traditionally Chwahir got themselves killed if they asked too many questions. That kind of protective habit stayed with a person. All he knew was, the high command wasn't doing its job on the magic end, Norsunder was still cut off, and the big plan was stalled.

And the Host were watching. At least, for now.

No one knew when they would act. Or where.

Colleron got up, yawning. "Well, it's all yours." He jerked a thumb at the supply desk. "I'd as soon not be sitting this desk when Aldon bangs his way in and finds that override on his requisitions."

"Aldon," Duin repeated with loathing. Efael's current pet had been making trouble in Sartor, and in Khanerenth—everywhere that Llyenthur was overseeing, of course. Somehow he avoided Efael's claims. Talk was, Efael was behind Aldon's pushing for command of a kingdom, and others insisted he wanted Llyenthur's command. Duin was used to gassy talk. But Aldon was likely to act.

Duin hoped he'd be around to see it when it happened. He dropped into the chair that Colleron had just vacated, and glanced at the wooden tray where the incoming relays were transferred. Nothing, and none of that teeth-tingling sense of impending magic. Good. Trouble was only fun if it happened to someone else, and you got to watch. It was nasty if it happened to you. And after yesterday, anything coming into that box was as likely to be trouble as not.

Colleron stretched and sauntered to the door. "No weather?" he said, looking out. He had that grin that Duin had gotten used to seeing in those who were intending to make a visit to the pleasure house down in Rainbird Street.

"Naw."

Sure enough. "Think I'll drop by Rainbird Street for some fun," Colleron said. "Sleep better."

Duin waved the stack of finished reports, and Colleron let himself out the door. Duin looked down at the reports, aware that he ought to go through the pile and look for what Aldon had been up to. Llyenthur was definitely going to ask whenever he turned up after his world-wide temper tantrum. But Duin's brain hurt too much; he glanced after Colleron, and began thinking about sex.

Duin had never been around any women since he'd been taken from his home when small, because there were so few in Chwahirsland's huge army. In fact, just thinking about life in Chwahirsland made him think in Chwahir, because there weren't any words for common terms in Chwahirsland—for instance for the girls who were raised as boys, and lived as men their entire lives, to escape being killed. Even in the army. Chwahir had terms for them, but no other language seemed to.

Chwahir had terms for all kinds of things that no one else seemed to have to bother with, almost all of them having to do with secrets or disguises. That was one of the main reasons why he'd volunteered when Llyenthur came around. Anything had to be better than life under Wan-Edhe.

As for those men-women in the army, weird thing was, the ones he'd known about mostly hadn't paired off with men (if they paired off at all) they'd paired off with one another.

Sex, now. That was different. That was something you did in the dark, quick, so you didn't get caught, for Wan-Edhe believed men fought better without any sex. And the Chwahir's entire purpose for living was to carry out his will. So certain dark corridors down in the prison wing had been favored for encounters, and ancient alleys.

Duin had preferred drink. Drink enough, that urge went away. And you didn't get into trouble for it if Wan-Edhe's toadies caught you.

Life was sure different now. Llyenthur was a total shit, but at least your free time was your own.

———————

Duin woke with a snort.

Light flared, red and smoky. He closed his eyes, bracing for the knout—then realized he was not back in Chwahirsland, and his sleep had been legitimate, however brief.

"Hey." The whisper was familiar, but Duin was still too groggy to place the name. "You said you wanted to see Aldon in action, didn't you?"

Duin's attention snapped to the here-and-now. "Eh?"

"In the assembly. Right now. Get some clothes on! One sight of a bare-assed Chwahir'll—"

"Shut up." Duin was sick of hearing about Chwahir and slugs.

A snicker was his answer—and the torch and silhouette vanished through the door. Duin was going to snap the glowglobe on, then decided against it. What if all the windows lit? Would that make trouble somehow?

Everything made trouble, if Imry Shithead was in a bad mood.

After enduring a long day of his distinctive sarcasm, Duin had speculated, during the shift's end gossip out on the landing, how entertaining it would be to see their commander get a little taste of what he'd been dishing out.

So Aldon had chosen tonight for his challenge, eh?

Duin thrashed his way into his clothes, and was still lacing up his tunic when he ran downstairs. Not to the door of the hall they'd adopted as their assembly hall, it being a convenient size for holding all the staff for those times when everyone had to hear orders.

The room was long, narrow, and high, and both sides had this thing high up on each side called a gallery. Supposedly the lighters played music on it. Duin couldn't imagine why, but then again in Chwahirsland there had been no music, because Wan-Edhe hated that, too. He even hated the Chwahir hum, though that had been done in secret. But these musical noise-makers? What you didn't know, you didn't miss.

Whatever its true purpose, the gallery had been a prime spot for the staffers to do a little earing in when they'd a mind to.

Duin eeled to the entry to the gallery, and found three others there, all silent. They made space for him along the back wall—none of them daring to go near the railing, and risk being seen.

Aldon's parade-ground voice echoed up.

"You what? You what?"

The echo blurred his voice. His back was turned; Duin stepped, peeked, drew back. Aldon had taken the center, and three of his fastest personal guard covered all the lower entrances.

Llyenthur was alone with them, but he was walking around, like he often did, that restless, annoying pacing that made you dizzy if you felt you had to watch, but if you didn't watch it you felt the threat of an attack catching you by surprise.

Aldon went on, loud and angry, demanding the truth behind the blunders of the past few days. As the harsh voice outlined commands that hadn't come through the relays—no surprise there!—Duin reflected on how much he loathed Aldon. You forgot how nasty the ones were that you didn't have to see every day. He'd said earlier he'd like to see Aldon string Imry Llyenthur's guts up as wall decorations—but now, he thought, peeking again, he'd be just as satisfied if they gutted one another.

Glance. Aldon, dressed as usual entirely in black, was

armed to the teeth, big, strong, taller and broader than Detlev's ex-brat, but that wasn't hard. Everyone in the strike forces was picked for size.

Llyenthur, as usual, didn't have any weapons, at least not in sight. Definitely not the black-steel sword he'd taken off his brother during spring, but Duin wouldn't swear to no knives in those rumpled slept-in-looking clothes.

Duin rubbed his eyes, and almost missed the moment.

He heard it first; the scrape of steel, the hiss of boots on the stone floor. No threats. When Aldon went into action he didn't waste time on speech.

A laugh—that was Llyenthur.

Now Duin and the other three were all at the rail, caution forgotten, in time to see Llyenthur whirl, hair flying, the cold blue glint of steel in his hand. Yep, Duin thought with sour triumph. Wrist-sheath.

Blood splashed over the wall as the first guard got his throat slit. A kick took out the second one; his neck snapped, and the knife imbedded into the chest of the third, all three quicker than it took to draw a single breath, and all three kept between Aldon and Llyenthur. Aldon obviously saw his mistake in having his three close in, with him outside the perimeter.

Now the two leaders were face to face, Aldon with sword and knife, Llyenthur barehanded. Duin sighed without making a sound, and rubbed his blurry eyes. The wildly flickering torchlight hurt his head; the smell of sweat and blood lay thick and cloying in the still air.

Duin missed the initial move, but that didn't matter. He'd known the outcome when he saw the three die. It was that Detlev training. You heard about it, but you didn't believe it until you saw it, that's what Starith had told him before he was transferred up north.

A sword clanged on the floor. Broken wrist. What, kick? Aldon still had the knife in the other hand, but he only had time for one strike, and Llyenthur took the hit on the arm, deflecting it just enough, before he got inside Aldon's guard.

Three hits, face, gut, face again. The big one was down, still clutching his knife. Llyenthur bent slightly in front of him, hands on his knees, and said, "When I was fourteen, you gave me a lesson in the verity of politics. Here it is back again, student to master." With a palm-heel strike he smashed Aldon for the third time across the face, breaking his nose, and sending a spray of blood out like dark fog.

Some of it got on Llyenthur's tunic.

"Dammit," he said, looking down in disgust. He flexed his right hand and shook it, hopped over the one whose neck he'd broken, and paused at the door. "Duin!" he said, without looking up, and then he was gone.

The others on the gallery gave Duin looks of mendacious pity. Down below Aldon was ringed by his remaining toadies until he transferred out.

Bergan, who'd lurked on the edge, narrowed his eyes, and ducked out the door. Gone to report to Efael, no doubt, before finding Aldon to bootlick.

Duin followed, but not to the stairway down. He hurried up to the map room, which was next door to Llyenthur's study. What now? He was off-shift, and he wanted to watch the boys on maintenance force the lighter prisoners to clean up the assembly room. That was always good for some laughs, watching lighters clean up after action, especially if they puked or fainted.

He plunged into the map room, and found Colleron at the desk, his half-dome forehead gleaming with sweat as he watched Llyenthur. Who stood at the window flexing and wringing his right hand as his arm bled.

Then he turned around. Smiling. That nasty smile that was about as close to a laugh as a jab with a poker. "Colleron. You will be going to Marloven Hess. I am very much afraid—"

The flicker of transfer-magic startled them all. Duin saw the glowglobes make round pale moons in the middle of Llyenthur's black pupils.

Then Duin's brain froze in terror.

That white-haired figure was Ilerian. He looked around with what appeared to be mild interest, and then said to Llyenthur, "She has regained her awareness."

She? Duin exchanged looks with Colleron, but neither dared speak; the air in the map room had altered to the charge before a midwinter blizzard.

"Too late for me," Llyenthur said. He held out his hand toward the door—

And Ilerian followed him out.

Colleron and Duin heard the study door close.

Eban, on the supply desk, rubbed her eyes, then whispered, "What was all that about?"

Duin wasn't about to speak. He shrugged, and realized his armpits were soggy.

The two were back very soon, and both stood before the big map, looking up at September's Detlev flags, which were still there.

Then, with no further word spoken, Ilerian transferred out.

Llyenthur smiled. "Colleron. To resume..."

Duin looked at the empty desk, and groaned. So much for sleep.

Six

WAN-EDHE'S GIFT, THE CHWAHIR cutter that MV and Andri had stolen and renamed, had hauled its wind. The ship rode on the water, sail brailed up, anchor dropped, rain washing at a slant down the deck.

Sea, sky, and air were a uniform gray as a massive storm circled all the way out beyond the Nob, and clear up the west coast of Drael, the result of the magic-driven storm in the previous month.

Below decks, MV's small crew sat shoulder to shoulder on the bunks and the pull-down seats; they had all just boomed up the boat that Rolfin had sailed from Trad Valbidhe under cover of night. Everyone was wet, cold, and irritable; the weather had mostly been violent all up the strait as a result of that magic-driven storm. Add to that a useless quest, in extreme danger. Mutters died when MV glared around at them. "New orders," he said. "Shut up and listen."

MV's own mood was little better than theirs. He longed for his own boat, which was faster, tighter, and better organized below. He jutted his chin at Adam, who stood in the galley looking out at them, gloved hands braced against the bulkhead.

"Contacts are especially dangerous right now," Adam said. "So what I got was short. I might get more later. Right now, we only know two things: the search is over, and we're to proceed to Marloven Hess." His gaze met MV's.

"Marloven Hess?" Andri repeated, then thought, over the mountains from Enaeran. All right, he could do that.

"Is it far?" Mildred asked.

"Nope." MV jerked his thumb southwards. "Other side of the peninsula, down a ways."

Crow shifted his glance between them all, but he didn't speak.

"That's it, then," MV said, and jerked his thumb upward, sending them all aloft to set sail.

No one argued with MV acting as captain. Within a few days, he got them working not only as crew, but doing some martial arts on the foredeck while he watched and issued the occasional pungent criticism.

He was actually pleased with what he saw of their martial skills. Dirk was very well trained indeed — better than he and the boys had been at eleven or twelve — but of course he had no size or strength. Mildred was the best surprise, and in a different sense, Crow: he had some fundamentals, but what he brought to each match was that furious strength. On his first scrap, he actually decked Rolfin, who was the strongest of any of them. Rolfin was being sloppy, his expectation that this weed would be easy. As for Mildred, so far, she'd decked Rolfin three times, which — added to an unexpected love of practical jokes on both their parts — fired up a rivalry. All right by MV. Keep 'em on their toes. MV knew exactly what to do for martial training, and they'd begin on it soon. It was the rest of the news that seriously discomposed him.

His mood stayed bad as *Wan-Edhe's Gift* picked up the wind and began racing out to sea, preparatory to giving the Nob wide berth.

None of them were strangers to the sea now, though of them Andri was the newest, and Crow had hitherto only been in small one-person craft. Until he and Mildred escaped the king's guard, he had never been permitted to go to sea.

Andri assumed MV's clipped utterances and his silence was caused by the necessity to avoid Norsundrian ships on patrol. The Nob, they had learned, was very busy, one of the supply points for the massive blockade cruising straight west, to keep anyone from landing in Mearsies Heili. But they rounded the Nob and started south without spotting enemy rigging nicking the horizon.

A couple days passed, and Andri was finishing a turn at the wheel as MV peered at the horizon through a glass. Andri observed MV's scowl, which had persisted for two days. "Did you want a fight?"

MV slanted a derisive lip-curl his way. "Sure, I want to take on a Norsundrian warship with six of us in a cutter, two not ready yet." MV put his hand to the wheel and stood with his eyes shut, testing tension of wind and water through the wood.

At that moment, Mildred, who had been tending the tack of the flying jib according to MV's exacting requirements, gave a yodeling cry and launched herself off the masthead. She caught a rope, swung down—and her foot missed Rolfin's head by a hand's span.

Andri noted MV watching her expert swing through the air, the wind molding her flapping black clothes to a very taut body. But then he looked away again, out over the sea.

Andri mentally shrugged, and said, "A tough and dedicated crew."

MV grunted, then imparted his philosophy of command: "Get deadbeats, toss 'em over the side."

"What's griping you?"

Rolfin lounged casually a step or two from where Mildred had paused to admire her handiwork. Rolfin stretched—and then swung a haymaker fist that could have decked a draft-horse.

Mildred easily ducked, and came up chortling. "Slug," she taunted, and flung herself onto the bench along the stern rail.

Rolfin's rare, white-toothed grin slashed across his dark face. His soft voice did not carry, but presumably he made suitable retort as he sank down onto the bench on the other side of Crow. All four heads gleamed blue-black in the slanting afternoon sun, Mildred's glossy braids, Dirk's messy tight curls, Crow's hair straight and lank—there had to be Chwahir blood in the people of Ama Hazanth—and Rolfin's wavy and thick. Rolfin's mahogany-skinned, powerful build in summer shorts made a startling contrast to Crow's taut, twisted wiry form shrouded in heavy, dark tunic and long pants, his skin pale.

MV adjusted the wheel, and gave Andri a narrow-eyed glance. "Want to hear it?"

That was surprisingly serious from someone who usually hid behind breezy sarcasm.

"Yep."

"Keep it to yourself, because nothing was said, but I smell endgame planning."

"In Marloven Hess?"

"Naw. That is, we'll be there and we'll act if someone puts Aldon in charge of the kingdom." He drew his finger across his neck. "But really, it'll be training. Hard. Not just here." He gestured a knife-hand strike. "But here." His palm hit his head.

"What? Using Dena Yeresbeth? *Us*?"

MV's expression was grim, with no humor. "Us. You. Me. Kessler's brat. Crow. Mildred. Maybe not Rolfin—he might be sent out where his skills are strongest."

"But I'm terrible with Dena Yeresbeth. Liere's the one for that."

"Oh, she'll probably be roped in, too. Others. As for Dena Yeresbeth skills, I'm no better than you are. But the grim truth is, this invasion happened too early for us. The old man and Siamis tried every ruse they could to win time, until time ran out. We work with what we've got."

"Are you training us?" Andri asked.

"Only on the ground. Adam will run the mental drills. This, here, is the beginning of the end. I can smell it in the wind."

Andri leaned against the binnacle; he'd done a night watch, but he wasn't sleepy now. He shivered, wishing he hadn't asked. Then he rallied. Eh, so no one was ready. He'd never been ready for what had happened to him, but he was still alive and fighting. "Tell me more about Aldon."

"Aldon." MV hawked and spat over the rail.

Rolfin looked up at that, as the others talked in low voices, occasionally punctuating their remarks with snickers.

"Why go after him in particular?" Andri asked. "And don't tell me he's a shit. They're all shits."

MV's grin flared briefly. "That doesn't make him less of one." He squinted at the sea, and the sky, and the sails, then said, "You know what Senrid fears most."

"That's an easy one." Andri lifted a shoulder. "Getting nabbed and his brains ripped out by some kind of Dena Yeresbeth enchantment, forcing him to mouth out Norsunder's commands to his army."

MV grunted. "True enough. But there's something else, something he doesn't talk about. It's what Aldon would do if he succeeds in taking command in Marloven Hess."

"Making a further mess of it? All the rumors say it's bad enough now."

Rolfin spoke up, "He'll form another army. Like he did in Fhleria."

"Right," MV said. "He spent years building up an elite army in Fhleria. He wanted to run it against the Venn, but Imry got in first with the blood magic, and so Efael took that army, split it up over Goerael, and now it's being ground down to bones and ash against whoever it is commanding the resistance up there in Ralanor Veleth. Aldon can't do anything about it."

Andri said, "After what Norsunder did to the Marlovens, I don't see them signing up to follow this Aldon."

MV shot him a derisive glance. "He'll start with an execution. He doesn't even have to be in charge—he'd probably pretend to be a resistor. Watches to see who's enjoying it. Maybe even who is angriest, because he's good at twisting anger, given time. He courts those. Binds them together in a secret elite, extra training, maybe a badge only they can wear—anyone else gets killed. Goes from there."

Andri shook his head slowly. "Ah, I see what you're saying. Brings out the bloodlust, and gives them an excuse."

MV turned his way. "Senrid knows very well that the Marlovens are already halfway there. Aldon will make their worst impulses a heroic cause. David had a chance to take him out a few weeks back. I know he's annoyed with himself—only nicked him."

Andri grunted acknowledgment, then said, "If Detlev knows all this, why didn't he take him out a long time ago? Yes, I know you'll say to ask him, but he's not here."

MV grinned. "My guess is, because Aldon is predictable. And letting him prey on Norsundrians was pretty good sport. But now." He made a short motion at his throat. "Detlev's not in Norsunder. He no longer has to balance the shits against the worst shits. If he and Aldon end up in the same place, he won't hesitate."

"... no, you lost, you have to cook," Dirk said to Crow. They'd been playing Stick, Stone, Splash with their fingers.

"I'll help," Mildred said. "Since I have to eat it, too."

"So will I," Dirk said. "I'm starving!" He and Mildred took off and vanished below deck, Crow limping at their heels. Andri and MV watched him; with grim boyhood experience, they had spotted at first glance in Crow's warped body the small boy whose broken bones had knit while he curled into an infancy-ball for warmth and self-protection. An ingrown habit that extended mind-ward. The others would be good for him, even Mildred's enthusiastic "feud" with Rolfin.

Andri lifted his chin in the direction of the hatch to the galley. "He going to be a problem?"

MV grunted a laugh. "Nah. Give Adam a whack. He's still just sizing him up."

Mearsies Heili

Morning Court that day was crowded.

Roy seldom interfered there. He was usually going to bed after a long night of border-running, or helping Siamis to monitor the mental realm. Atan generally got everyone sorted before Clair appeared, but she was still up in the spires somewhere. Clair—who only came out of the caves during the day, and always in sight of at least one of the Mearsiean girls—spoke to her steward, then those at the front of the crowd. She was moving slowly, her eyes narrowed as if she had woken with a bad headache. Roy was not the only one who noticed; he spotted Gwen whispering to red-haired Falinneh, who muttered, "I'll fetch some listerblossom steep," and pelted off.

Roy squirmed his way through the waiting people in search of a few of the Irregulars. A good rainstorm was on the way, and he wanted to penetrate deep into Teldenor, on the south border, under its cover.

These various observations would probably have registered as random in most minds, but Roy was so attuned to building strategies on just such a scattering that the thought *This would be an idea time for an attack on Clair* coincided with his shifting attention from scanning faces for friends, to scanning faces.

Ordinary faces. Frowning, absorbed, admiring, annoyed, wondering. Heads together, gossiping to while away the long wait. Among them all he spotted a small, middle-aged woman he'd seen once previous. Clair did have some recurrent trouble-makers, but weren't those usually shuttled along to the regional governors to handle as soon as they were identified?

The woman stared at the floor, her face somber. Roy

moved a few steps closer as a large party of people surged forward to fill an empty space, and he saw a sheen of sweat across the woman's furrowed brow. Her cheeks were the pale, drained non-color one associated with intense and unpleasant emotion.

Her eyes lifted. Her hands clutched to her forearms inside her wide sleeves. They stiffened—

The crowd surged again, like a tide, and a gap opened between the woman and Clair up on the dais.

The woman's right hand emerged with a dagger.

Roy was still ten paces from her. He grabbed one of the embroidered pillows from the floor and snapped it high into the air. The flying knife pierced the pillow squarely, and the two fell to the floor amid a pretty snow of features.

Screams, feathers, shoving people all conspired to clear the floor for a considerable space. The woman stood alone, still as a carving, staring down at the knife piercing the pillow as though she, and not the inoffensive embroidered silk, ought to be lying on the floor.

Clair ran down the steps. Her green gaze took in Roy, the knife, and the woman. "Watch things, Roy?" she asked.

Without waiting for an answer she touched the woman's arm and they vanished, one after the other.

CJ raced in, looking around wildly, her black hair flying. She vaulted up the dais steps, then whirled around. "What happened?" she squawked.

Roy explained in two sentences. CJ's face paled, but she gave vent to one low exclamation—Roy heard reference to Norsundrian maggot-pies—then she raised her voice to get everyone's attention.

Within an admirable time she got all the petitioners sorted into groups. And, rather bluntly, sent several of them to rout with a flat command to "Take piddle like that to the governors, and if you don't like what they say, try another province!"

Order restored, Roy went about his business.

At dinner there was a conference in the library. Roy was there, having just returned from the border. He saw Atan (who had sought him out) in addition to CJ and Dhana and Clair.

This latter looked up tiredly from poking at her dinner to say, "She got around our spell, Atan, because this time there wasn't a compulsion caused by enchantment. I took her to the cave. She's a mess. She said, if she killed the white-haired queen, the white-haired man would cease tormenting her dreams at night."

Atan exchanged glances with CJ, and then put down her fork. "There is more, I am afraid, Clair. That knife was enchanted."

CJ said, "Probably to send you straight to Imar as soon as it touched your flesh. That snackle-nosed stench-weed must have coerced her into doing the enchantment right here in Mearsies Heili, or it wouldn't have gotten over the border. It was probably an ordinary knife from her kitchen or job."

Dhana muttered, "What's that, the fifth this month? Sixth?"

Clair sighed. "There have been more. Since the beginning, of course, and always at night. But nothing I would consider a close one, until today. What I hate most is, they are doing this stuff to people's minds. She's a perfectly ordinary person, not at all a Norsundrian sympathizer. She brought her little grandchildren here from down south. I hope she will survive."

Nobody pointed out that the woman was far more likely to survive than Clair if these attempts persisted.

Dhana burst out, "Mearsieanne was a blockhead."

"She didn't know," Seshe whispered.

Clair shrugged, and picked up her fork. "I will just have to be more careful."

No one said anything, but once she went to her room to lie down, CJ called the girls together. "I know that Siamis and Roy are doing their best, but they have other stuff they are doing. And even Siamis has to sleep sometimes. The creeps must somehow know when he does. The way I see it, we've got to stick closer to Clair."

"I agree," Sherry said, her fists pressed together under her chin.

"I do as well," Seshe murmured. "But we cannot tell her. She'll feel more burdened than she does already."

"And that's why we're going to split into shifts," CJ said. "Two of us at any time. Different ones, so she doesn't catch on." She saw fervent agreement in their faces. Even Falinneh was serious for once — or as serious as someone can look who is wearing a bright green tunic with exaggerated, comical pairs of orange eyeballs embroidered over it, over purple pants.

CJ looked them over, aware that none of them were all that good at defense, even if they did catch another zombie-ized would-be assassin. "I wish Diana was here," she muttered, not for the first time.

Seshe shook her head. "Clair specifically told us not to tell Diana what's going on, or she'll end up pulled by two loyalties."

CJ wanted to snark that it wasn't loyalty keeping her with Troy, the king who wanted to be a bard, but duty. Someone else's idea of duty. But she managed to bite it back; she liked ol' Troy. He was a terrific singer, and fun to have at any campsite or party. It's just that he was so absent-minded that nobody trusted him on his own now that Norsunder was on the loose.

Falinneh, who had been writing to Diana most, said, "Troy promised to stay in Dthel Rendm. One thing we know about Dtheldevor's hideout is, it's got magic protections. Norsunder will never find it. Once she gets him there, he'll be safe. Then she's coming home."

Seven

Off the Halian coast

SEVERAL DAYS LATER, WHEN Adam appeared in the hatchway of *Wan Edhe's Gift*, arms laden, MV raised his voice. "All set?"

The other four looked from him to the boat swinging from the cutter's booms.

"Let's go," Adam called, then loaded the last of their food supplies into the longboat.

Mildred went around to all the half-knotted ropes and pulled, letting the sails snap and bell open. The cutter seemed to come to life, lifting in the water as it pulled against the anchor. Andri jammed the wheel into a set position as Rolfin and Adam smoothly lowered the packed lifeboat to the water below.

Crow and Dirk finished a last sweep. Finding nothing that had accidentally been dropped, they descended the rope-ladder to the boat. Adam and Rolfin went next. Andri and Mildred followed. MV finished tying the wheel in place then gave one last look around the cutter. It was in no wise a handsome vessel, but it was well made, sturdy, and it had been home for all these weeks.

Evincing a faint air of regret, MV pulled his knife, and hacked at the rope that had been bound as a temporary link in the anchor chain. He pulled up the rope ladder and stashed it neatly from long habit.

The ship heaved on a swell, the light airs belling then loosing the great sail. MV climbed over the rail and dropped neatly into the boat. They all watched the crewless ship rock in a vague westward direction, pushed by current and fickle breeze.

"Wonder if it'll make it to Mearsies Heili," Mildred commented.

"Still too much easting in the winds. Current'll carry it southwest," MV said as he leaned back on the sacks of supplies and propped his long legs on one of the benches. Crossing his hands behind his head, he gazed at the hazy late-afternoon sky, then glanced down again with spurious surprise lifting his black brows. "No wind, no mast. Why don't I see them oars heaving?"

"No mast, no ship," Rolfin said. "Means no captain."

Andri kicked an oar-end over so it landed on MV's stomach. "Don't think we didn't notice while toiling half the day that you were lazing around with your charts."

"That's true." Adam yawned, lowering a disreputable wide-brimmed black hat he'd rescued from somewhere in order to keep the sun off his eyes. "Over the side with him." His gloved palm gestured thoughtfully to the gunwale.

"Right!" Mildred gave a bloodthirsty shout, then added with a jerk of her thumb in Rolfin's direction, "Him too."

"Nah. He's too good with the oars. Can't drown him." MV opened one eye lazily. "And me? There aren't enough of you." He shut his eyes again.

An expectant pause ensued, during which the only sound was the lap-lap of water against the longboat. Andri's eyes met Dirk's and Rolfin's, and the latter gave a tiny nod.

Moving in unison, the three pounced.

MV, of course, was ready. A mighty struggle set the boat to rocking, and some of their neatly stowed supplies slid about until Mildred gave an exasperated laugh. "Ay! Why do we not at least try to let the ship get out of sight before we capsize!"

Without speaking, Crow slid to the bottom of the boat, half under one of the benches, and insinuated himself under MV's writhing form. And while Andri wrestled with MV's arms and Rolfin with his legs, Crow raised his feet to MV's back, lifted—and MV went over with a magnificent splash.

"Good work!" Mildred cackled as Crow scrambled up.

He shot her a wry, twisted grin. Adam's reflective brown gaze touched one, then the other, before he turned to extend a hand to the curse-sputtering MV.

"Cold?" Andri addressed the erstwhile tyrant in a solicitous voice.

MV's streaming form landed in the rowboat, and he shook his head, splattering them all as he cursed fluently.

"You'll warm up fast with some exercise," Andri added, offering him an oar.

MV snarled a pungent reply, but his response in deed, matched with Rolfin's powerful strokes, soon had them skimming eastward toward the as-yet unseen Rualese shore. He had calculated that two to four days, if they got enough steady wind to step the mast lying at their feet, would see them in sight of the coast.

The nights stayed hazy and still. The major stars were visible as pale and colorless flecks, but they were fine to row by. Mornings usually brought enough breeze to use with a constantly tended sail. Four times they spotted patrol-craft hull down on the horizon, so they either sailed away or went dead in the water, and were not seen.

On midweek morning midway through Tenthmonth, in hot, still, summery weather, Adam and Mildred finally pulled in the oars, giving loud exclamations of relief. Inevitably the weather changed by noon, a coming cloud front bringing cool breezes from the southwest. But they did not step the mast again; land had formed an uneven line on the eastern horizon. If they could see it, they could be seen through an assiduously plied glass.

"Let the shrimp know we're here," MV addressed Mildred.

She flexed her fingers, rubbed them into warmth, then pulled out her magic-paper and propped it on a thick-folded cloak on her knees. Crow watched as she produced a scrubby quill, dipped it into some berry-juice ink, and carefully wrote a few words.

Andri leaned his lead back on the edge of the boat and studied the others through half-shut eyes. First, Rolfin's tranquilly stolid face, his brown body shirtless as usual. He was the only one who found the weak sun and nippy breeze comfortable. MV, lean as one of his weapons, motionless. Appeared to be asleep. Adam, hat low on his forehead, contemplating the whitecaps chopping away northward. Dirk glanced up at the sun's position, then reached into one of the bags and pulled out the last of their rations. With meticulous care he divided the dried way-bread and two small oranges into equal portions, then passed them out.

Andri just as silently took his share, and popped an orange wedge into his mouth. Tart and sticky, mostly. Not enough juice to be refreshing. But who knew what they'd eat next. Or when.

His worries winged away home, a familiar worry that he no longer tried to prevent. If MV was right about the secret harvest not being secret, it would be a rough winter. At least Liere was there.

Liere. He looked out over the water so the others couldn't see his face. They'd had so very short a time to be married. So far, he liked being married. He was even going to try to be monogamous, though Liere had not asked him to. She had already accepted his chaotic life, including his various lovers, with sunny good will—she'd liked them all—as she had accepted Enaeran, in spite of all its problems. "They are a part of your life," she'd said. "I'll share your life, the good and the difficult, and you'll share mine, beginning with my very, very teenage daughter."

Liere had no lovers other than him—she had said that so far in her life she was a one at a time person—but he had come to suspect that she was very new to matters of the heart, and also probably monogamous by nature. For certain there was one very complicated person whose passion she seemed oblivious to: Senrid.

Andri's mind turned toward Senrid. He liked Senrid. They were even related, way back somewhere on the family tree. Now, the winds were bringing Andri to Senrid's kingdom, which he'd never thought to see. A mistake? He had told Liere they ought to leave Senrid Montredaun-An alone, and he believed it. Problem was, he couldn't contrive it without calling attention to the fact that he was doing so, and his sense of honor—and of empathy—insisted on not bringing unwanted attention to Senrid's unspoken passion.

Two things were reassuring: this was Senrid's turf, not Andri's. Also, Liere wasn't along. He suspected Senrid would have no problem with Andri as a single entity. As for that passion, hopefully it would fade.

As he considered his complicated life, he chewed his way through the stale way-bread, and having finished that, took a healthy slug of the keg-flavored water that Dirk passed around next. Then an elbow nudged his ribs.

"Why the sour face? Planning your introduction speech to the Host in case the wards do bounce us straight to Imar?" MV asked.

"Of course," Andri said. "Also composing my menu requests. Unless they go in for the moldy bread and muddy water routine?"

Mildred's eyes rounded—which made her pupils contract. "Hai." She stabbed her pencil at Dirk. "You were a prisoner there, eh, last summer?"

Crow tensed up, studying Dirk.

"Yes." Dirk shrugged. "So?"

"Ah! What did they serve you? Swamp water and chum?"

Dirk snorted. "It's not like that at all, with them."

MV cut in, "Svir has no interest whatever in enduring, or witnessing, physical privation."

Dirk added, "They treat you like a guest. Said I could have any room—and there were about fifty nice ones, and no dungeon. Said I could eat with the company, or alone, whenever I wanted. I don't know where they got their fresh food, especially now that Ilerian has ruined everything with a few days' ride, but it was all right. If you have an appetite, which I didn't."

Crow looked so astonished they could almost see the color of his eyes.

"They wait to catch his father," Mildred said to him, low-voiced. "Then things go very, very bad. Ah!" her gaze returned to her paper, her pupils going from round to vertical slits. "Sveneric's answering."

Andri remembered very well what Efael and Yeres, who were considered the minor Host members, could do, and on Andri's home ground. To Crow's silent confusion, he said, "They make up for it in other ways."

Dirk's upper lip lifted, showing a pointy canine.

"Great!" Mildred scanned down her paper. "They have things ready. Meet us at the border."

"Senrid?" Dirk asked.

"No." Mildred lifted the paper in order to see better. "He's not even in the country. He's off doing something at his secret forge. Sveneric says he doesn't take his magic-paper into action so they don't know any more than that. But his people are ready for us."

A day of rowing and writing later, Mildred and Sveneric

guided the two parties together. Long habit caused MV to insist they hide the boat under sea wrack rather than ditch it. After some swift work on the empty Rualese shore, they swarmed up the palisade, Crow wincing at every step, but glad to be once again on steady ground. Andri was even happier.

They halted at the low stone wall that marked the border of Marloven Hess.

Mildred lifted her head, her cat hearing sharp. "They come."

MV and Andri scanned the scrubby Rualese hills. Still no one around.

They felt the riders' approach before they heard them, then the two riders topped the eastern rise, both horses plunging to a stop and turning. The riders swayed upright with natural grace.

For a heartbeat they were silhouetted against the cold, streaky gray sky, both straight-backed and slender. The smaller figure with braids brushing her shoulders and a wide skirt spread over the horse's bare back, the taller one's pale blond hair touched with silver by the wintry sun. Then one of the horses turned his head, and both mounts began jolting down the shale-strewn incline.

The others stood in a ragged line, watching. The horses disappeared briefly into the intervening gulley, then reappeared on the other side of the low, ancient stone wall. The riders resolved into Sveneric in girl's clothing, and the off-world assassin prince Zairna Raadi, who, with his diamond earrings hidden and his tunic high-necked, hiding his rank ink, looked like a Marloven.

Sveneric lifted his voice: "Step over in unison."

A murmur of snorts and snickers from MV and Andri's gang answered him. The seven held hands and stepped close to the wall.

"Makes a prettier girl than I do." Mildred squinted up at Sveneric just before MV rapped out, "Leap, shitbirds!"

With varying styles they vaulted the wall, landing at the same moment.

Sveneric and Zairna Raadi wheeled their dancing horses. Dirk and Sveneric exchanged looks; as the newcomers began scrambling down into the gulley, Dirk ran toward the horses. Sveneric held down a hand. Dirk vaulted up behind him, then the horses sprang into gallop. As expected, ahead a patrol of armed and mounted Norsundrians appeared where the border had been breached—by one person, they assumed.

The Norsundrians didn't even glance into the gulley as they kicked their horses into making chase. Still, the six lay flat until the reverberation of horse hooves had died away into the distance, then MV looked up from the mossy patch into which he'd thrown himself, and gave the rest a brief grin.

"Now we cross Marloven Hess all the way to Darchelde," he drawled. "Fun!"

Eight

Border mountains between Sarendan and Sartor

WEAK MOONLIGHT, AUGMENTED SOFTLY by those stars visible between the silent moving clouds, glowed blue as the morvende removed the last obstacle from the tunnel door.

Darian Selenna, Bren, and Innon looked out at the tall mountain peaks that they knew formed the border between Sartor and Sarendan.

They were almost home.

The morvende girl who had brought them the last leg of this tunnel said to Darian, "Harnan said you know the border trail."

"I do," Darian answered, and for a moment the shadows shifted on his narrow fox-face as he glanced at the other two boys. Stepping back inside the tunnel, he went on, "I smell approaching rain, which will hide the guide-stars. May I go over a few of the landmarks with you?"

Bren's jaw had jutted as the tunnel opened to the air, and he had silently surveyed the mountain peaks. Most of those mountains were black silhouettes against the sky, except for faintly glowing snowy slopes here and there. Innon was in the midst of a joking exchange with the two morvende teens who'd helped their guide with the tunnel opening. Bren heard him groaning about having to trek through mountains. Not that

Innon was any slouch. In fact, of the three of them, he was the sturdiest in build and had the strength of steady endurance. But he'd clung to his image of laziness for many years.

That image got shaken during this long journey. Not once but several times Bren had noted after long climbs, when he'd been puffing for breath, and Ian red-faced with effort, Innon had just looked around like he was on a picnic.

Bren had said—once—"Lazy, eh?" with a meaning tone.

Innon replied, "Ah, it's the thought that counts!"

How Lilah would have laughed—

Innon, who had sensed weird moods in the other two, broke off his attempts at polite chatter with their hosts when Bren plunged through the tunnel entrance and vanished among the trees. Was Bren mad about something?

Darian's voice rose as he spoke words of gratitude to the morvende for their guidance and hospitality. Ian was never rude, even when he was in a temper. It wasn't his being a prince so much as his being Peitar Selenna's son, Innon thought; while Ian thanked their guides, Innon followed Bren.

He hadn't gone far. On the other side of the trees there was a kind of clearing, from which the path led downward. Bren stood along the edge of the clearing, leaning against a jumble of boulders.

As Innon stepped up beside him, Bren said, "See the Dragon's Teeth?" Bren jerked his thumb southward. His voice sounded normal. Accustomed for years to the cousins' mood-changes, Innon stared in relief at the darkness, just able to make out the distant peaks with their familiar outlines.

A deep sigh filled his lungs. "We're home," he offered, suspecting that Bren had been mourning Deon again. "Though really, seven or eight weeks isn't snail speed considering how far we've come." No response, so Innon blabbed on, saying anything that came to him. "Fancy finding the Sartoran mountains so well-tunneled? And fancy ol' Ian knowing, and never told us—"

Air turned to ice in Innon's middle when he heard a muffled snort. He hadn't heard that particular sound since the night Siamis killed Derek.

Innon's head snapped around as Bren flung himself back through the trees. Floundering after, Innon remembered the day—nearly a year ago—they'd found out that the invading Norsundrians had killed Lilah and Darian Irad. He himself had turned into a wet sock but Deon had scorned him out of weeping with a truthful, *C'mon! Lilah would hate being splatted over! The Brothers are going to rise again — and fight! That's what she'd want! The Sharadan Brothers ride again!*

Though that's the last time we ever used the name, Innon thought, ducking a low branch. Leafless twigs scratched over one of his ears as he tried to spot Bren's dark head. And now Deon was gone, according to Sveneric and Darian. Dtheldevor and her crew had died out at sea.

Another branch, this time unseen, whipped him in the face. "Bren," he gasped. "Please stop."

To the right and just below, Innon heard a crackling of leaves, the clatter of rubble, and a very human gulp. Innon dropped next to Bren, who sat with his knees up and his arms wrapped round his legs. Innon wiped his sleeve over his stinging cheeks. "I wish you wouldn't just run off like that."

Bren ground his face into his knees, sucked in a breath, and held it.

Innon added, "I don't care if you blub. I did after Lilah and Darian Irad were killed. And I did after I found out about Deon."

"They'd hate it," Bren muttered in a grief-strangled voice. "The girls, I mean. I was holding it all right until I saw the Dragon's Teeth. I didn't think." Whoop! "It would feel so bad. Coming home. And. Seeing all the old stuff again."

Sick to the heart, Innon cracked his knuckles. Truth was, he'd dreaded coming home ever since they'd left, feelings he'd lived with for a year.

Bren laughed—or tried to, anyway. "How Deon would scorn me. Soon's I'm mad at the Norsundrians again I'll be fine."

"I'll tell your family about Deon," Innon offered. "You don't have to."

Bren gave a mighty sniff. "I'd better, and it'll be all right. You know how they were always predicting a bad end for her."

Innon said, with a hint of left-over grievance, "I heard your grandmother often enough. 'You'll either be hanged, girl, or titled. Or both!' And they'd all laugh, like all nobles were still as bad as the old days."

"Oh, that's just leftover family joke talk. Gran also told Deon she'd make a fine pirate if she had a sea to sail on, but Deon never thought that one a joke. That's what she wanted. And she did get it, there, for a time. Way back when we were little, before we even knew that Dtheldevor really lived, Deon loved the stories, and wanted to join her gang. And she got to." Bren sighed again, but his voice firmed. "There. Squall over. But I've decided." His voice was a low, fierce mutter now, defensive attack. "After this war I am getting rid of the Child Spell. It was always the girls who wanted us to have it. But they're gone. Bernal said I could come live with him whenever I wanted, and he'd sponsor me to some artist, or whatever I want. And I'm going to do it."

Innon said, "I'll release the spell with you, if you want company. I never minded the thought of being an adult. Though it was fun, the four of us!"

"All right," Bren said. "As for Ian, he really doesn't really need us, does he? He's got Sveneric and Jessan and Carl and Dirk."

The boys thought about Darian, who had known all these unexpected secret routes. Who sat up all night talking to tunnel-hidden refugees and foreign couriers aided by the morvende, long after Bren and Innon had been driven to sleep by unwardable fatigue. Who despite his puny size, and his lack of sleep, had saved the three of them in the two violent encounters they'd had with unexpected Norsundrians roaming around looking for trouble.

This latter Darian had shrugged off, saying that he knew how to trip the enemy up so he could run, which was nothing compared to the skills of Dirk and Sveneric. That might be true, but those two fought better than most adults without advanced martial training.

"Dirk and Sveneric are his real best friends," Bren muttered. And as if someone had questioned his own loyalty, he added in a stout voice, "He will be a great king. Better even than ol' Peitar. Rel even says so."

"Yup." Innon agreed. "But he doesn't need us to do it."

Bren dug at a rock with his big toe, then said, "What'll you do, then? Gonna take back heirship to your parents' property from your cousin?"

Innon grinned, knowing that Bren thought that this was as easy a matter as just walking in and announcing, *Well, I changed my mind. I think I'll inherit after all.* "Nope," he said. "Gave it up with a legal deed and everything. Peitar even signed it, and anyway, my cousin's been learning governing, so who needs it?"

Bren said, "Bernal did say you could come, too."

Innon was quiet, remembering Bernal's hasty and embarrassed, *Oh, and you're always welcome too, Innon*. The differences in birth status had ceased early on to mean anything between the four of them, but to Derek and Bernal it had never stopped meaning something. He said out loud, "I'll visit. Of course. But what I'd really like, for a while, is what Rel used to do. You know, be a guide for travelers. I sure like traveling, and foreign coins are so easy for me to figure value on. Meet interesting people, see things you wouldn't see." He sighed. "Yep, that's what I'd like. For a while."

"Sounds good. And on a vacation, if artists give vacations, I could come with you!" Bren now sounded more like his usual self.

They sat in silence, contemplating the future without the threat of Norsunder—even if it felt a lot like wishing.

Small town in eastern Sartor

Elzhier shifted position from one foot to the other, as if to obtain a better view of the entire display of hair ornaments. Yes. A familiar face was reflected there in a polished copper pot.

The woman was tall, maybe late twenties, dark, mole on her left cheek near her ears. Elzhier had seen that face twice in four days. Both just glimpses, but both glimpses had been in different villages.

That was enough.

Elzhier cast a fast gaze down the street—her assigned quarry, Rel of Sartor, still moved at a slow pace, deep in talk with a couple old men.

Meanwhile, the woman had turned when Elzhier did. She now wandered by a fruit-dealer, her thin, blue-cloaked back toward Elzhier, who slipped between two booths. When the woman turned again to look, Elzhier had vanished from sight.

She had always disdained the sort of contest that nature had not designed her to win. She seldom got mixed into brawls—the quick stab was her preferred method of violence—but she enjoyed causing fights and watching the outcome. Second best was the stealth kill.

She started walking along the busy, dusty street crowded

with folks either buying or selling or just looking, then eased into a crowd of village shoppers behind the woman, all too intent on complaining about the climbing prices of rice and bran to notice anyone else. A carthorse clopped near from the opposite direction, dragging a mountainous burden, and the crowd squeezed up to make room.

Elzhier's soundless feet were quick. A heel on an old lady's hem—a palm upsetting the heavy bundle bending a kid's back—a hard elbow into the skinny ribs of a rickety old man. Spilled baskets and confusion were the result.

The woman heard the cries, and looked back. Her mouth opened as Elzhier stepped directly in front of her, the gray shawl billowing like moth wings. Obscured from sight by its folds, the knife came up, and jabbed upward into the heart. Once. Then out.

Soundlessly the woman crumpled, and Elzhier slipped into another street, not far behind Rel—whose dark head was easy to spot above the crowd—before anyone figured out that the woman in the blue dress hadn't stumbled or lost her balance like those others still sorting themselves out.

Norsundrian or lighter? Elzhier didn't know, or care. Orders were, no one to know her mission, which was to follow Rel, undiscovered.

This was just the way she liked to work.

Not the longest but certainly the toughest hunt of her entire career. Two shadows eliminated so far in a week, but that was the easy part. For a huge man with such a distinctive face, Rel could move with respectable stealth—for a lighter. She'd lost the scent three times, two of them in the past two days. And she'd only picked it up again by watching the whisperings of gossips, like wake-eddies spreading out behind a ship.

Little Shit Imry had been right about that. She was tired and hungry. Gritting her teeth, she thought with pleasure of the humiliation awaiting Rel of Sartor as soon as he got back to Eidervaen. When he ever got back. Wasn't he supposed to be so fast?

Well, that had obviously been before he'd managed to snake himself into kingship.

Border mountains between Sarendan and Sartor

The gray light of a cloudy sunset slowly shrouded the bare trees dripping from the recent rain. Bren was in the lead, sniffing in the scent of wet leaves and hay that lay heavily on the still air. His jaw creaked as he yawned, and he hopped as he walked, trying to warm himself.

They'd been forced to walk most of the previous night, resting only through the morning storm and then resuming their journey as the clouds departed eastward. Once the sun set they had promised themselves a stop at the first promising spot they came to. Innon looked a lot more cheerful in the weak light as he stumped along in the rear. By now it was habit for him to go last, or else slightly behind, when Ian was overtired. Peitar's son tended to trip over the smallest obstacles; even with his eyes wide open he seemed to see nothing.

Bren swung his arms in vigorous windmills as he hopped from rock to rock down the narrow trail. To the right, runoff rainwater crashed and splashed in a deep gulley.

"Wish we were south, eh?" he said. "Wouldn't it be great to be flying? I just hope the Norsundrians haven't managed to get at the Delfina Spell."

"I think we've managed all right," Innon said.

Bren and Innon looked at Darian, whose eyes were wide and focused beyond time and place.

Innon sighed. He couldn't walk that way—he'd trip over some root, and smash himself up. "Don't you think we've done well, Ian?"

"Hurray!" Bren yelped. "Then watch out Bostian! I'll just betcha we were faster'n ol' Rel, I just bet. And we had farther to go."

"Well, that wouldn't be too hard," Innon pointed out—as usual being the fair one.

"What?" Bren looked back, eyes goggling. "Rel? D'you think we are faster than he is?"

"No, we're faster because he had to stop so much," Innon reminded him, patient as always.

"Did he?" Darian's eyes focused on them at last. "How do you know that? Have you been writing to him?"

"No. I'd tell you if I were." Innon looked surprised. "Anyway, wouldn't he be? Everywhere we've been, people of all kinds, even the morvende, talked about Rel Coming Home. You didn't notice?"

"Notice?" Ian repeated, his gaze going blank again.

Innon sighed. Even he could reach the end of his patience. "I told you that once before, and you looked right *at* me when I spoke."

Darian's thin, freckled face reddened. "I'm sorry to be such a fog-head. I guess you did. But no refugees mentioned it to me, not quite that way."

Innon shrugged. "Well, probably because you were always surrounded by Sarendan's refugees, not the Sartoran ones. Or by morvende, who didn't mention it as much. Or you didn't hear the talk when we were at those inns, before we reached the morvende."

"Go on. I'm listening now," Ian said.

Innon was surprised at his tone, which he couldn't quite interpret. "It was in those big caves that I heard it most. You know, the ones where the Sartoran refugees all gathered. We played with the smalls, you see, while you were talking to those couriers and the like, and they all knew Rel was Coming Home. They said it just like that, with a funny sort of emphasis, like everything was going to be right. Coming. Home." He shrugged, and hopped over a little stream.

"So anyway." Bren chortled. "I bet we beat him. That's why I haven't written to him, because I want it to be a surprise, when we reach Miraleste before he reaches Eidervaen. Rub it in. He'll get a laugh!"

"Everyone ... knowing," Darian repeated, then he stumbled over a half-buried rock in the muddy trail.

Innon's square brown hand clapped onto Ian's skinny arm; usually unfailingly courteous, Darian never even noticed. He frowned back up the mountain trail, as if enlightenment—clear thought—lay hidden on the heights. "Why does that bother me?"

"Eh, it's not as if anyone will tell the Norsundrians." Bren shrugged. "And ol' Rel is better than the best at sneakiness when he wants to."

Darian stopped, forcing the other two to stop as well. He rubbed his eyes. "Yes. I guess you're right."

"Come on," Innon said, nudging him with big-brotherly care. "Sun's gonna set. Let's find a good cave and sack out. We're all tired."

He was the first one to curl up when they found a good resting place, and as usual he dropped straight to sleep.

Bren curled up in a knobby-kneed ball, and he'd soon be

off ... hoped he'd soon be off ... but his nearly closed eyes registered Darian sitting upright near the cave entrance, staring out into the misting gloom of early evening.

Ian's slanting features were sharpened by the weak, reflected light of their fire, and by the wearing hours and habits they'd been keeping. He looked to Bren's gritty vision less than ever like Peitar's boy, and more like some wild, woodland being. "C'mon, Ian," he begged. "Make like a rug. Yer keepin' me awake."

Darian's head turned. "I can't get that out of my mind. Everyone knew about Rel coming? A rumor? Recent? A *recent* rumor?"

"The Sartorans, anyway. Yeah, most of ours as well. So what? No one is going to tell the Norsundrians, Ian, and even if they did, Innon is right. Not once did we ever hear exactly where he was. I know 'cause I was tryin' to figure, hoping we'd be able to beat him home, now that the harvests are mostly in, and hidden."

"Hidden," Darian repeated, barely audible. Bren could see his dark-circled eyes, and his mouth pressed into a thin line. "Bren. Supposing one person talks about Rel Coming Home. Not to the Norsundrians, but so that a single Norsundrian overhears."

"Unlikely—"

"Supposing."

Bren shrugged. He was thick-headed from lack of sleep. "So they do? They won't hear where Rel is. Not even where he was."

"But they'd—hear..." Darian's voice drifted, the odd tone sending warning through Bren's tired brain.

"Oh, c'mon, Ian. Rel's better'n than any of us at taking care of himself."

"But they must know that Home means Eidervaen. And if they know that, they don't have to chase him."

"What?" Bren snapped the word out, sounding sulky. He knew it, and regretted it, but oh, he was so tired and why was Ian acting so crazy?

Innon snorted and rolled over.

Darian got to his knees. "Most people think they are safe for winter. Because nothing has happened to the harvests..." Darian shuddered. "Here I've considered it miraculous that Norsunder hasn't acted yet, and maybe Sveneric is wrong. My abiding thought to get home before they do strike, if they do. And I have forgotten who is doing the attacking."

"Well, if you've forgotten that, Ian, you'd better lie down and get some shuteye," Bren stated.

But Darian whipped his damp magic-paper from his pocket — and then hesitated. "What can Sveneric do? He's in Marloven Hess. It's up to me. I'm the closest." And to Bren's annoyance, he got to his feet. "I've got to get there first. If I can."

"Where? What?"

"Bren. I need you to go ahead with our plans." Now he was Peitar's boy again, vision far beyond anyone else's. "Just as we've discussed. After they take the harvest—destroy it, I'm beginning to think—keep the people quiet! No fighting back! Yet. Promise them, soon."

"Wait! What? destroy what? Ian! Where are you going?"

"Eidervaen." He stared out of their cave.

"Why?" Bren's voice squeaked.

Darian's head poked back round the rocky entrance. "To intercept the symbol—if I can."

"Ian? Symbol? Wait!"

"Huh?" Innon sat up, his voice bleary. "Whazzat?"

Bren ignored him as he scrambled over the uneven rock to the mouth of the cave. He looked out into the darkness, but there was no sign of Darian.

He slumped back and groaned.

Nine

Sindan An – Vasande Leror

SENRID MONTREDAUN-AN RODE INTO the forest shortly after dawn, and found it empty of humans, which meant it was empty of Norsundrians. The multi-hued autumn leaves had mostly fallen, making a crunchy carpet beneath his horse's hooves. Birds twittered. Once he saw a shadow shift. He turned, hands going to his wrist knives, and a fox emerged from a hedgerow and raced up a hillock to vanish in the undergrowth.

It had been many years since Senrid had visited this pleasant vale bounded by a bend in one of the Ktan River's tributaries, but though it had been spring then, a world of green, and now the trees were autumn-colored, many bare, he still remembered the way. He and Leander had been enemies, that very first time, when Senrid had so carefully memorized the path. He wondered why Leander wished to meet him here now.

The bend—the bridge. It still existed, which wasn't surprising, because it had been built by meticulous craftsmen, and it was rarely used except by animals as it connected to no road. It had been the master's project of a forester hoping soon to go home.

Leander sat on the arched rail of the bridge, as if he hadn't a thing in the world to do but listen to the musical chatter of some distant birds. The intent angle of his head changed as

Senrid's horse neared. He looked up, and raised his hand in greeting.

They had not seen one another since Senrid had walked out of Mearsies Heili without a word to anyone, half a year ago. Nor had there been any communication. Looking at Leander's face now, for the first time it occurred to Senrid what a big mistake he had made to stay so silent.

Leander had asked to meet, but Senrid began. "Look. I'm sorry—"

Leander's dark brows quirked above the bright green eyes, their expression now mocking. "Miss my mighty generalship?"

Senrid tied the reins loosely to a bridge support and joined Leander in a few quick steps. "I wasn't excluding you," he said, his breath clouding in the cold. "I thought you were wrapped up in the artifact chasing. With the others." He was still studying Leander, without—for the first time—being able to define the change, or the problem that had brought them together. Had six months' silence made such a difference? Leander still looked much the same, except taller, his face bonier. And he was leaner, but everyone was these days. Tired. Everyone was that, too.

And his thoughts were hidden.

He smiled. Those green eyes narrowed with amusement. Senrid tried to smooth his expression, but Leander knew him too well. His smile twisted. "How long've you known about that? Years, no doubt."

"You mean, about Cousin Imry? David told me when they came over—oh, shit. Don't tell me—"

Leander laughed. "It was Kyale—almost a year ago this week—who said after seeing him that she was sure she'd met him before. But we both knew she hadn't. And later, she'd mention green eyes—"

"You mean, fling the similar color in your teeth," Senrid said. "You suspected that he might be a rat in the Tlennen-Hess pantry, when logic—habit—ought to have suggested his being yet another unsuccessful Montredaun-An byproduct."

"My family's only contribution being the green eyes, through Great-great Aunt Kyale, and her hankering for Marloven queenship."

Senrid turned up a hand. "Among other, farther back tangles. You no long claim this segment of our shared history as your private burden, I trust? And you never spoke up because…?"

"Because I saw, and misread, the problems last winter."

Senrid winced. "Pure self-pity. I suppose I'll spend the rest of my life apologizing for my behavior."

Leander said, "David tried to mend things, but I misread him as well. I guess..." He gave a slight shrug. "What I needed most was the opportunity to look into things, and to think things over, alone. I got that, late this summer. I also got an informative message from Roy. Take all those things together and I sent that message to you through Collet. It seemed appropriate to meet here, so I could give you this." He drew a slim packet of heavy, sealed paper from his coat-pocket, and held it out. "It's a formal abdication of the throne of Vasande Leror. Ceding it back to you. By our laws and yours it must be done in person. And in writing."

Senrid's fingers took the paper but he was hardly aware of so doing. He looked. Listened carefully on the mental plane. Realized with cautious relief that Leander's manner, though better guarded than ever before, was not that of one who winds up his affairs before taking a walk out of the world.

Senrid slid the crackling paper into a pocket of his grandfather's military coat and said, diplomatically, "Kyale?"

Leander said, "Roy kept track of her after she left the group going north hunting magic artifacts."

"I heard she flounced off after the others erred by taking her at her word — in the middle of a war — and didn't make a fuss over her Name Day." Leander's expression remained sad, and Senrid regretted his sarcasm. "What happened?"

"They'd passed through some city where players were still holding on. She asked to join them. Was accepted for her abilities with illusion, and they said they would train her to be on the stage. Then she discovered her family."

"She can't be a long-lost princess. Royal families don't take lightly to their children going missing."

"She's not. But Roy said she seems content in spite of that. I always hoped she'd grow out of her assumption that a crown — that is, attention — would always be good attention. On stage, you can control that. I think she finally began to perceive that in life, you can't. Oh. Your Uncle Tdanerend was right about her not being Mara Jinea's child, incidentally, if about little else."

"I never believed she was, right from the start. How did she find her family?"

"Roy didn't really say, but I suspect it was one of the things

Siamis discovered, during his time among the scribes. Her actual family is from that part of Goerael. Kyale is rather distinctive-looking, and Roy seems to have seen to it that Kyale and the family met, and they took it from there. As for me, the morvende invited me back."

And then enlightenment hit Senrid like the sun breaking the cloudbank overhead. Leander had—finally—made his unity in Dena Yeresbeth, and despite a disintegrating world, he was, for the first time in their association, truly happy.

Senrid laughed. "And what, you're expecting me to harangue you out of it, and force you back onto what never ought to have been a throne in the first place?"

Leander's smile was genuine now. "Some Lerorans tried to talk me out of giving it up. I've been going around telling friends. Helps when they realize it's not good-bye forever. Just, when I return, it won't be as a king." His expression changed. "But they don't..." He stopped.

"What?" Senrid prompted.

Leander shook his head. "I realized. It's all yours now."

"But?"

"They don't want to be forced to speak Marloven," Leander finished. "Though they realize they are a very small minority—"

"I won't force Marloven onto them. Iascan—their version—is older anyway." Senrid laughed. "It was you who told me, not long after we first met, that language is a stream. It moves on as it evolves, even when someone tries to force a hierarchy on it. That was like a door opening, for me. I'd been raised to regard Marloven as the language of rulers, and the various Iascan dialects as the language of the ruled. Except there was so much more of it, and then there was all that Sartoran in its roots."

Leander's relief was clearer than any emotion he'd yet shown. "There's no eradicating past mistakes, but at least they don't have to be repeated." His head turned. A crashing in the underbrush heralded the sudden appearance of a sleek dark dog. "There's Rori," Leander said.

Senrid then met the other change in Leander's life. During his time living with Kyale and all her cats, Leander had denied himself a dog companion. Or maybe potential dogs had been wary of a castle that smelled of big cat.

With a quivering leap Rori left the bank and landed on the

bridge. He gave one excited bark and sat down, panting gently as he watched Leander.

Leander looked back at Senrid. "That's it, then! I want to reach the mountains by tonight."

"By any chance in the mysterious and legendary Ghildraith geliath?"

Leander grinned. "That's right, but at this point I'd appreciate your keeping that to yourself. When the time is right I will contact Atan, and I hope to offer something for the defense effort. As yet I'd rather the others think I am still traveling."

"Sure. But that wouldn't be the mountains Nelkereth-ward to which you are going? Because the Norsundrians are swarming there."

Leander shook his head. "Dolossen. Then north." He looked a query, and observed belatedly that Senrid was fully armed: not only the usual knife handles glinting at his wrists, but knives in his boot tops, one in his coat sash, and a sword sheath attached to the saddle on the Nelkereth charger, who was peaceably nosing the grasses on the bank.

Leander faced Senrid. "I heard about the Norsundrians finding your forge. I'm sorry."

Senrid's teeth showed in the old, familiar nasty grin. "So were they."

⁕

Norsundrian outpost in Telyerhas

"Want the window shut?" Imry Llyenthur addressed the stiff, shivering man on the bed.

The clenched teeth didn't open. The barest fraction of a nod, and Llyenthur reached up to close the narrow, thick-paned casement. He paused to look down into the lower court, where the clatter of newly-shod horse hooves echoed up the stone walls. Ah. Arrival of a scouting party.

He studied the steep, rocky mountain peaks, noting fog drifting over the higher Southern Ghildraith snowcaps. Impossible-to-climb skyscrapers that hid, if rumor was correct, the biggest morvende stronghold outside of Sartor.

If they were there, he'd find them.

The latch clacked into place. He turned away from the window and met the watchful glance of the hovering medic. The fellow hardly merited the title; like so many others, he'd been thrust into service repairing his fellow men-at-arms because he either wouldn't speak up, or because he'd wanted a transfer and different duty was his way out, or because he'd known something about horse injuries. Or maybe he set a partner's broken bone once, and found himself the next week with new orders.

Llyenthur could see from across the room that at least two of Colleron's shoulder-bones were badly splintered, yet this so-called medic thought the problem was a cracked collarbone and a knife-wound. It seemed obvious to Llyenthur (who, granted, had seen many such) that the knife-wound, though long, was superficial. The real damage had been done by a heavy blow.

The medic sidled a nervous glance at Llyenthur. All of 'em felt their incompetence most keenly when their superiors were around—when there might be consequences. Otherwise they didn't care. They didn't join Norsunder motivated by the wish to help people.

The medic transferred his attention to the man on the bed. "Want some kinthus?"

Colleron swallowed, then managed a whispered "Yes."

Llyenthur said, "Where'd you get kinthus?"

The medic's reply was quick—so quick he was obviously on the defensive. "Eastern sector general supply. Uh, I brought it when I was transferred back from Vadnais."

More of the politics of supply. How many more Aldons would Llyenthur have to bruise his knuckles on in order to keep them under control? He dismissed that for later. "You know anything about dosages and dilution?" At the medic's blank look, he said, trying for patience, "The herb masks pain by interposing an artificial barrier between mind and body. Too much—easily done—and your victim will go out of his mind and stay there until his body dies."

The medic hesitated, then admitted, "I don't make up the drinks. Halvig does."

"Questioning," came Colleron's weak voice. "From..."

But Llyenthur recognized the name. And the more familiar use of the herb, which lowered inhibitions. Administered to prisoners, it was an effective way to produce cascades of information quickly and quite painlessly, therefore it was usually the truth—as the person saw it. But most interrogators found that method boring. Even if tortured victims mostly blurted out whatever they thought the questioners wanted to hear, there was the fun of getting them to that point.

Llyenthur raised a dismissive hand and the medic retreated with a prompt readiness that was expressive of profound relief.

Colleron was still conscious. He wouldn't be for long. Difficult to say how extensive the damage was, but it really didn't seem he was going to make it. Irritation burned Llyenthur at this waste of a competent man, a quality increasingly short in supply. And he was going to have to risk losing him by questioning him now.

He spotted a stool over in the corner. Fetching it and sitting down, he said, "Can you show me the sequence of events?"

Colleron's mind was pain-fuzzed, a jumble of non-sequential incidents as his mouth worked.

"Answer in thought. Don't speak. What I need to know primarily is if Senrid Montredaun-An was there. Do you know what he looks like?"

He could see that Colleron didn't. Oh, he'd read the cap-list description, but Llyenthur knew that that description—young man, medium height, gray-blue eyes, blond hair—would fit half the male population of Marloven Hess.

So he tried again. "Did you see the leader of the lighter defense party?"

Brief flash of memory—

"Again."

But it was pain-blurred, even more disjointed.

Llyenthur sighed. Colleron's right hand twitched in a weak gesture.

The medic reappeared, carrying a cup of warm listerblossom steep laced with kinthus. Colleron swallowed some, wincing with pain. Almost immediately his breathing became less labored. Llyenthur would have to talk fast now because awareness would drift soon, but for a time communication would be easier.

"Show me the lighter leaders, Colleron."

He saw, through Colleron's eyes, the Norsundrian assault squad breaking in the forge gate. At once a swarm of lighters emerged from tunnels and caves. Hard fighting, conducted in very little space. Smoke soon obscuring things... There. The back of Senrid's head as he ducked a blade and then turned to point with a sword down an adjacent tunnel.

Colleron gasped, "Marloven ... uniforms..."

"Of course." Llyenthur nodded, reestablishing contact. Again he saw Colleron directing the destruction team, then being set upon.

Colleron's whisper was very faint now. "Expecting us."

"Yes. I'd wondered about that. Interesting, eh? Too bad you didn't manage to waylay any prisoners."

Colleron tried to talk. A spasm of pain distorted his features, then he went limp, his breath rasping.

The medic said with nervous reluctance, "He wouldn't permit me to wrap his arm. All I could do is get the shirt off, then he sent me away."

Colleron had almost not made it this far. He would not live through the wrench of another transfer. There was no use in pointing out the medic's ignorance. Llyenthur said, "No tame lighter healers at hand?"

"He won't have 'em. Not since that lighter healer was killing our wounded over here in Choreid Dhelerei, after bandaging 'em."

"I've got one in Larkadhe. He won't kill Colleron."

The medic chewed an already chapped lip, then said, "They all want kinthus." Gesturing toward the door.

"How many are in serious case?"

"Eight. Including Colleron."

"Eight." Llyenthur raised his hand to make the transfer sign. "I'll be back when I can."

The medic promptly effaced himself.

Llyenthur's hand stilled as he glanced down at Colleron, whose breath had slowed.

It had not entirely been a botched exercise. No prisoners, but an acceptable number of troublesome lighters dead, and the forge completely destroyed. Llyenthur blamed himself more than Colleron. The rumors were true, then, Senrid was back. He should have guessed that, in spite of the number of captured Senrids who turned out to be harness-makers or glaziers or farmers, one at least forty, another no older than fifteen. Arrested by overeager would-be spies wanting promotion. Llyenthur had begun adding the overeager spies to the salutary beatings of the would-be Senrids before turning them all loose.

In hindsight, Llyenthur knew he ought to have put someone more effective than Colleron in charge of this particular investigation—but who? The balance in the southern hemisphere was already too close to jeopardy, waiting on that dilatory fool Rel, wandering around somewhere in Sartor. At a desk, Colleron was very effective, and in any case, he was going to be difficult to replace.

Two levels of thought, as he watched Colleron struggle for breath.

Senrid putting his civilians into Marloven uniform. Senrid knew that his Marlovens lived from day to day hoping for reprisals so they could launch into war again, and either erase the humiliation of their defeat a year ago by winning, or by sacrificing themselves right down to the last ten-year-old brat who could lift a sword.

Senrid also knew that Llyenthur had no use for a snuffed population. The forge had been a three days' ride from any civilization, so no one else could be held to blame. To go into a randomly chosen Telyerhas town and murder people who had never heard of the forge, and who already hated Marlovens like as not, would be pointless.

That stalemate was old news.

What Llyenthur had come to uncover was the possibility — now the certainty — that Senrid's people had known beforehand about the attack.

But all that could wait.

Impatient with himself for hesitation. Get out and leave the man to die, or...Or act.

Now.

No one around. Colleron was unconscious. No one would know.

Sinking onto the stool again, Llyenthur slid his palms down his thighs, then — slowly — stretched one hand out over Colleron's shoulder, a finger's length above the mangled flesh.

He shut his eyes, aware of torn muscle. Bone shards. One long splinter in the lung, causing great seeps of air-choking blood, another rubbing against a main artery at every breath.

Two main bones — there. And there. Their component pieces — that's the worst problem. Finite. To envision them back in place —

Sense, gather a finite amount of magic. Draw it...

Focus.

Snap! The sound was audible, as well as felt in the realm of the spirit. Colleron jumped as if he'd been slugged. He moaned once, as color slowly reentered his still-unconscious face.

Done. Two bones—whole! The rest, Colleron could manage on his own.

Llyenthur braced for the strong wash of vertigo and nausea inevitable after these experiments. He fought the dizziness, the urge to puke, and forced his stuttering breathing to slow, and his eyes to orient on the here-and-now. Waste averted, at least.

He transferred away the moment he was able, and turned his mind to his next task.

Ten

HIBERN CAUGHT HERSELF SHORT, and tried to imagine herself in a walled room containing nothing but a comfortable bed. No, a hammock. The magic formed around her and she lay back, trying to find rest, but there was no real rest.

Her foremost emotion was embarrassment. Was that blast of magic supposed to terrorize her into surrender?

She considered Theronezhe's purported memory spell. She knew what those were. Had seen them, aware that only the likes of kings could afford to pay mages to capture a limited time in a spell, within a limited boundary. Then the spell had to be in-fused with magic to make it last — and it had to be renewed every so often. There were archivists whose entire job was just that.

She wondered how that worked in Norsunder, whether the spells had to be renewed at all in this timelessness. Tremen-dous power sustained this construct. She knew that much of it had come from the life forces Ilerian had ripped from his victims; she hoped there was another source. The entire subject made her feel unclean. But contemplating that was a subject for later; she was stuck here, and had to figure out how to get out.

She concentrated on Detlev's face in the vision, narrow-eyed with intense focus. She considered her (blessedly brief) encounters with Detlev while he was still a Norsundrian. She remembered that little smile, as if everything going on about him were nothing more than a stage-play by traveling actors—as if whatever he did took no effort. Occasionally he would vary the program with a villainous frown, usually when someone like Senrid ripped back at him with a good crack.

All pretense, as it turned out.

Only when had the real villainy ended and the pretense began? And how did this relate to the twisting of truth that she had encountered in those reports?

Questions begat more questions as she considered the time of that vision, so long after the Fall. Who really was that morvende boy, and how did he match up with Ilerian's undisputed part in the Fall, which would have taken place centuries before that boy's birth?

"His first act," Theronezhe had said.

She contemplated Detlev's shopworn appearance. Those blood splatters had seemed real. She looked down at her uncombed hair, and the summer gown she'd worn all day before going to Wilderfeld to investigate. This place was timeless, she accepted that conditionally; everything else she was going to regard as lies unless they were proved true.

If that scene wasn't wholly manufactured, it was possible that she had seen Detlev when he was first released from deep in the Beyond.

She considered another memory, from five years ago: Detlev sitting in Erai-Yanya's study in Roth Drael, not long after he left Norsunder. Hibern had been studying, and came out of her room at the sound of voices, to find Detlev there.

She noticed his appearance only because it was the first time she had seen him wear civilian clothing instead of Norsundrian gray and black, though there was nothing remarkable about the plain undyed high-collared tunic, and commoner-brown long trousers, and soft mocs. He was talking to Erai-Yanya. *Yes, the Host will probably speak the truth—or whatever passes for truth in that instance. It's part of the game. But you must remember. When the Host in particular impart information, they are always telling you only the part of the truth that serves them best.*

Hibern was silent, for she had interrupted, and at that time, she'd held residual resentment against Detlev. The man very soon left, and as soon as he was safely gone, Hibern had rounded on the older mage. "'Whatever passes for truth.' So what he's saying is, there is no such thing as truth?"

"Absolute Truth is seldom reflected in the turmoil of human activity," Erai-Yanya had mused. "I think what he meant is only that."

"Which means?"

"It means that three people witnessing an event will see it three ways. And afterward—as time and experience alter the viewers—each will probably interpret the event at least three ways yet again. A little of the light of Absolute Truth, perhaps, would be shed on the original event when someone reconstructing it first recognizes and acknowledges the perceptual limitations, and then tries to provide all possible views. We're taught that we then see as the truth of the matter is symbolic of our finite apprehension of the absolute."

"Eh, all right, I'll accept that, for purposes of discussion."

Erai-Yanya smiled, then sighed when she looked down. The end of her long braid had smeared into her inkpot again. "All I'm suggesting," she said, dipping her braid in a nearby cup of water and wringing it out, "is that it's different from saying there is no truth. Which is what Norsunder maintains."

Hibern's sense of fairness had always been stronger than her prejudices. Besides, she had been raised a Marloven, and she had learned early on that assigning Evil was not always a simple matter. Over the next few years she came to value Detlev as an ally, and that sparked valuing him as a person; she liked his calm manner, his shared interest in history, and the breadth of his vision.

Another time, Erai-Yanya had exclaimed after reading an old record, "Oh, these Norsundrians think they are so much smarter than us hapless lighters, and love laying out the truth for us to trip over. But underneath that is their conviction that truth is so malleable that there is no truth. Were that true, we might as well all be barking at one another."

Hibern had discussed that with Senrid, one of their many conversations comparing the ways lighters saw the world, contrasted to what they had been taught. She remembering a hot day early one summer, as dusty wind brought in the voices of the academy rising in cadence, "How do you evaluate an enemy's words for truth?"

He'd shrugged impatiently. "I always heed threats. As for other things, eh, if I trust the speaker, I might accept their words as truth. Especially if it makes sense, or corroborates my own experience." Then he gave her his familiar toothy grin. "But you know how few I trust."

Trust as a component of truth. Hmm. She trusted no one in this place; but that brought her right back to the question of when Detlev decided to abandon Norsunder, and how would that affect what she found here?

What if his turning away from evil had happened *before* five years ago?

"After all," she whispered voicelessly as she scowled at the books lying with seeming carelessness about the table, "one can't say I took any harm of him during his days of Evil Deeds."

Definitely the worst had been sticking her with that ridiculous nickname Deheldegarthe. Historically it had been an honor, which made the use of it against her even worse. He was calling her a battle-maiden because she was so reluctant to take any kind of action—

Action.

She brushed back her hair and looked around more slowly.

I am on a stage. And my first dramatic scene was that business with Ilerian and Detlev. Designed to throw a timorous lighter girl-mage into horror and revulsion at the revelation of the "truth" at the core of every human being...

She had no idea what had happened to Detlev before he appeared in that glade, but this much she was sure of: that scene had been set up not by him, but for him. Certainty coursed through her nerves, a cool fire.

And if it was planned, then Ilerian wasn't corrupted, he was already corrupt. And corrupt people existed, certainly. Only why the elaborate charade?

And if it was a charade, had Detlev known? She considered the report book full of tiny, poison thorns—no, call them what they were: lies. Lies, written in his hand. Strewn among observations that corroborated her own experience. She needed to consider each lie carefully. But she was being watched.

Hibern put hands over her face to hide it. If she looked horror-struck, that was good, wasn't it?

They think me the same timid scholar that Detlev scorned all those years ago, when we first met. Probably wrote about my timidity in reports. Knowledgeable—but ineffectual, that's how he would have characterized me.

Not much of an advantage, but enough of one to act on.

And acting was just what was required.

Inside the shield of her mind she began reviewing each of her experiences since her arrival and what she knew of Norsunder.

Somewhere in Wnelder Vee

Diana scooted a little closer to the vagabond fire that Troy had made.

Bitter-cold air outside their hollowed-tree shelter stung their noses. She could smell snow in the air. That meant they could be moving soon. She pulled out her magic-note to check on the girls again.

Troy didn't seem to mind her writing every time they stopped. In fact, she didn't think he even noticed. He never wrote to anyone, she had observed, but of course she said nothing.

Instead, he sat there near the fire, his eyes wide and unblinking, as his fingers strummed his tiranthe. The music was soft, and made Diana think of sad thoughts. She warded bad moods by reassuring herself of Clair's and the girls' well-being. Especially Clair's.

CJ's responding note was terse, which meant she was worried. No details, though.

Diana did not ask for any. Except for her letter-writing forays, she worked hard on her inner story, just in case. You never knew. If any creepy mind-reading Norsundrian tentacled around, he'd think Diana was a bard's servant, meant to remind him of meals and things. Anyone who saw Troy would believe it.

She glanced at him again, and was startled to see him watching her.

"We're near the border," he said. "And I realize I don't know if I can go to Dthel Rendm after all."

Diana stuffed her paper into her pocket. "You can't?"

"Is it so odd?" His smile was more like a wince.

"No," she said. She hated personal talk, but for once it seemed important to fight for the right words. "I thought of that. Seeing the island all silent. Never again will they walk there. Laugh there. But I'd set fire to it first, before letting Norsundrians muck about where Dtheldevor and the gang once lived."

Troy sighed. "Everyone will say, it's just a place."

Diana shook her head, struggling to get her thoughts organized. "Not just a place. Freedom, it meant. To so many kids. If I hadn't had the girls, I'd have gone there. Some of the girls thought I was gonna join Dtheldevor's gang, but I never would have. Sail half a year with 'em, yes, and Clair agreed. Others, like CJ, were happy just knowing they were there. Kids. Freedom."

"It was my way of life." Troy closed his eyes, but the tears leaked from below his eyelids. "All gone. Tahra was the last link, and she's an adult, and I think she sees me the same way her parents did, a lazy fool. I don't have it in me to stay in one place, fussing with legal matters. The guilds do that. Why not let them? Why does my butt have to sit in that chair?"

"Clair would say, you're a symbol. Of order?"

Troy wiped his eyes on his arm, then looked out through the lightning-struck crack in the ancient tree. "I was put on a throne by birth, but all I understand is music." He shook his head. "When this war is over, they will tie me down by ribbons of guilt. Duty. Maybe I ought to go on alone, Diana. I very much fear that when I leave the island again I will walk here like a ghost, and my life will thereafter be a ghost's life as I try to do my duty, and fail."

Diana looked away. "All the more reason to see the island once more. My last time. Ever. I'll never go back. But I have to know they haven't destroyed it. Then I can be finished."

Troy sighed, and gave up, as he always did. He knew he always gave up, or gave in. Only music mattered. "All right, then, we'll go together, once we find passage. What is the report on the others? Any news?"

"Not bad," Diana said, thinking of Troy's tears of grief and regret. She herself didn't believe in crying. It made you weak, made your head ache, and fixed nothing. But the sight of someone's tears pained her heart just the same. "Mearsies Heili is safe, so what can threaten them? That's what CJ says. The harvests are coming in, and everyone will lock in for winter, and hope and plan. Relative quiet till spring."

"Everyone doing their duty," Troy whispered. "As they see fit."

He bowed his head, his fingers strumming slowly on the tiranthe.

Eleven

THE GRAY-SHAWLED OLD WOMAN with the battered basket of withered vegetables shuffled along the high stone wall, unnoticed by anyone. The few people on the wide Chandos Way hurried blinker-faced about their business—and they looked away when they passed the courtyard entrance to the old west end of the royal palace, which Bostian had taken as his royal palace—the eastern wing having been largely trashed while he was in Marloven Hess.

No one noticed the abrupt disappearance of the old woman.

A little later, on the other side of the courtyard, the two guards on duty at the huge oaken doors heard splashing strides as a young woman emerged from the rainy gloom of the adjacent stable (once the headquarters of the Sartoran Mage Guild) into the light cast by the torches mounted over their heads.

Neither recognized her, but as she snapped out the latest pass code—the one reserved for operations chiefs—they straightened up, and when she threw the basket at one and said, "Here, shitface. Watch that," the man did not respond, except to take the basket.

Elzhier slung her rain-heavy shawl across a dispatch-table

in the main hallway, relieved to get away from that disgusting wet-wool smell. To the flunky opening her mouth in protest she said, "Where's Bostian?"

"Sarendan. Asiarch's top of the stairs," the woman replied.

No one tried to stop Elzhier, but she knew, and relished, that word was making its way upstairs by back routes.

When she elbowed the command center's door open, Bostian's aide Asiarch was standing next to the relay desk. Two armed guards flanked her from the hallway as Asiarch said, "Who are you?"

She rapped out the necessary code words in a bored drawl.

When she was done, Asiarch made a gesture of dismissal to the guards, and for a moment they studied one another. He with interest at one of Connanre's best spies, granted independent status by Llyenthur; she with scorn at the tall, heavily built man bearing all the usual signs of a long military life. All brawn, no brain, that was how she summed them all up — the perfect definition of everyone in Theronezhe's branch.

She said, "I want a message sent to the Larkadhe relay desk. Now." Seating herself in Bostian's chair, she added, "Sealed."

"Very well." Asiarch spoke with no visible emotion, his pale eyes unblinking. "I understand we're to give you whatever you want. Bostian's due back at—"

"No aid. No questions. No interference. Paper. Now." She shoved existing paperwork away from her, smirking inwardly when two stacks fluttered to the floor, and picked up the quill.

She dipped it and wrote a quick report. One glance upward kept Asiarch on the other side of the room, ostensibly studying the pitch-dark view from the window.

"There." She folded the paper and held it out. "I'll wait."

He retrieved a black book from under the mess of papers that she'd made. He took her report, laid it on one of the familiar wooden trays, leafed through the book, and carefully read out the transfer-spell.

The paper vanished.

Elzhier sat back in the chair and shut her eyes. The hiss and rustle of paper as Asiarch and a flunky picked up and reordered the mess kept her amused. When that began to pall, she considered what she'd say about this mission to Red — and to Connanre. What a twisty irony! The perfect chance to teach the Little Shit a nice lesson in manners. Would she use it? He was so arrogant, but so ignorant, or he would never had given to her the crucial move of his current plan for subduing the restless lighters. For an entertaining moment or two she considered how silly he would look if she graveled it.

The image had to stay just that. It was too much of a personal coup to gravel it. Besides, she had to admit, if only to herself, that she had an interest in what he'd deem a suitable recompense.

Find Rel. Produce him for me at the proper moment. You do that, and I believe I can promise you a reward you will enjoy.

Yeah, no harm in continuing the pretense of the obedient servant a little longer, until either Connanre gave her the sign to slip in the knife — or until she saw an even greater advantage in backstabbing them both.

Asiarch said, "Here you are."

She opened her eyes and reached, aware of tired muscles reluctant to move, after being still for so short a time. Soon...Soon.

She opened the response, and read the two lines there: *Message received, Llyenthur not yet in.*

She didn't yet warrant one of his direct contact spells, even with this job. Perhaps it'd be diverting to wangle that status before squashing him.

Aloud, she said, "Tell Bostian he'd better be ready for some action. Soon."

Darchelde – Marloven Hess

Some hard riding, aided by willing, quiet and efficient Marlovens, and MV and his group arrived in Darchelde's hideout in time for supper a few days after leaving Methden. They hadn't seen Sveneric, Dirk, or Zairna Raadi again while on route, but on arrival found that the three had preceded them by half a day. Andri was delighted to discover that Siamis — aided by Arthur —had made more of his magic-papers, and there was a new one for him, brought by Sveneric. He sat right down to write to Liere.

Senrid still had not yet returned, but he had made ready for them by transferring all his resident refugees to different locations. Except for the original Methden gang of teens, who stayed to continue the southern border patrols, Detlev's team was alone. A welcome hot meal, warm bedrolls, and a cleaning frame awaited them. Mildred sniffed the air, past the clean smell of loam and the slight must of the tree roots overhead, past the lingering aromas of food, and a lot of young, active bodies, for the scents of anger, betrayal, fear. Anger's acrid trace existed, and she would discover who. But no betrayal or fear.

She relaxed.

Appreciation of these long-denied luxuries absorbed everyone else's attention for a time—everyone except Adam's.

Dirk was busy talking. Zairna Raadi's short explanation ("Yes, Sveneric is here, but he went up to take a walk in the forest") had been accepted by all. It was only superficially accepted by Adam. As food and liquid were consumed and the atmosphere charged to one of friendliness, laughter, and expectation, Adam watched for his moment.

The Methden teens were all intent on listening to any nuggets of wisdom that the infamous Detlev's boys might care to drop. Oh, Marlovens, you are so predictable, Adam thought, hiding his rueful amusement.

When, at length, they were settled in a story-telling circle, Mildred remarked, "That's a mighty long walk Sveneric's taking, eh." She was secretly proud of how much of her Geth accent she had trained herself out of. She was beginning to sound like a native! "Where's he going, back to the ocean to see the view?"

Dirk looked up. "Probably still in a funk. He thinks we've been wrong about the harvests."

Instant quiet as the newcomers shot glances MV's way. He set his cup down. "Yeah. No news to me. Let's hear your reasoning."

Dirk sighed. "I didn't think of this—I thought that the Norsundrians were going to jump soon's everyone got the harvest in. Take all the extra. But Sveneric says Llyenthur doesn't think like that, not with the world closed off, and his own people angling to see him fall while they wait for the Host to break through."

Adam watched the impact in the faces.

"Go on," said MV.

"Here's how he explained it to me," Dirk said, his light blue eyes wary. "Notice Senrid's semaphore system while you were crossing the country?"

"Me, I saw it," Mildred said, when no one else spoke. "Shutters on certain houses. Pastries in windows. Our guides paid too much attention to those details on certain houses for it to be accidental."

Dirk turned his back to the fire. It was harder to see his expression now. Adam sensed the inner cost to Dirk, knowing it was his own father who had bound the enemy to the world.

Dirk pointed upward, in the direction of the entry. "Sveneric says, despite the ban on travel. Communication. So forth. Or maybe because of it. News travels fast. Real fast. Not just here, but everywhere. Especially, it seems, in Sartor and its environs, because they have all those old geliaths and the Norsundrians have not yet managed to burn out the morvende and the other magic peoples." He stopped, and gave a short sigh.

Andri grimaced, thinking immediately of Enaeran, and MV whistled. "Certain kinds of news travels fastest, of course."

"Uh oh." Mildred propped her chin on her fist, her pupils slitted against the fire to thin vertical lines.

"We don't have anyone in Sartor right now," Adam said slowly. "We're spread too thin now. And Rel is so competent."

"Yeah. Too much." Dirk shrugged. "Sveneric says, a year ago Rel was just an adventurer. Oh, lots of people knew him. Knew of him, Rel the traveler. But that doesn't explain how, in a year, he suddenly became known everywhere."

Adam murmured, "Only Atan coming back herself could have the same effect."

Marend Ndarga spoke up suddenly, from the corner where the Marlovens sat watching. "Llyenthur told me himself he plays around with symbols. And Van confirmed it."

"Van being Senrid," Dirk clarified. "It was Darian Selenna who snouted this one out. He wrote last night to Sveneric 'cause he was penned up temporarily by a big thunderstorm. He's trying to get to Eidervaen in time. He's afraid—that is, he thinks he has to stop Llyenthur from using Rel to torch *all* the harvests."

"What?" MV sat upright.

"Rel?" Andri rubbed his jaw. "I'm lost."

Dirk went on in a gritty voice, "Not the obvious harvests, planted to draw Norsundrian attention. Everything. Leaving us hungry and desperate through another long winter."

"Not Rel, but using him. To torch the harvests?" Andri leaned his forearms on his knees, hands dangling. "That's rotten."

"I still don't get that," Crow said, turning from one to another.

"Catch him. Brandish him somehow. See that the blame somehow gets attached to his name," MV said to him. "Shit."

"Oh, I do hope he's wrong," Mildred muttered. "So cruel."

MV said to Adam, "Can we run a cave rescue?"

"No one near who has the necessary magic. And anyway Sveneric said this morning that Detlev insists on holding to the ban." Dirk rubbed his eyes. "If we pull Rel in through the cave transfer, it'll draw attention to the caves, and the Host will find a way to destroy them, or block them, now, instead of leaving them for later. Detlev said to ride it out."

"Ride it out?" Andri repeated. "Did he know?"

"No one knows what Detlev knows," Adam said dully. "Or why he makes the decisions he does. But I can tell you this. Painful choices are not new."

Andri slammed his hands down. "So, what, either people fight to save their harvests and there's a bloodbath in time for winter, or else they stand around and watch their summer's planting go up in smoke?"

MV said, "It's a gamble to force them all, on both sides, to submit."

"How? Oh!" Crow scowled. "I see it, I see it. If Rel puts out the word not to fight back, he loses his rep as a hero. Right?"

"And, perhaps, enough will obey and cease resisting," Adam murmured.

MV shot a glance at Dirk. "You boys thought to alert Rel, at least?"

"First thing," Dirk said, tapping his magic-note in his pocket. "But he's not answering."

While above, a long hike distant, Sveneric sat high in a tree, his eyes turned toward the canopy of stars.

Though Dirk knew him well, he didn't know him well enough.

It was true that Sveneric had begun grieving over the terrible destruction possible, the world-wide misery that, should Llyenthur choose to unleash it, they could not avert.

But then he had set it aside, because there was nothing they could do now. They had figured it out too late; they had misread the signs. The fact that the Norsundrians had not interfered with the secret planting anywhere had seemed to indicate at first that they were spread too thin to discover them all; at worst if they discovered extra harvests and storage here or there, they would take the surplus stores away. But as the autumn wore on and the harvests were brought in and stored, both regular and secret, and nothing happened anywhere, it was clear that there had to be another plan in place.

Sveneric wasted no time on wondering if his father had known from the start; Detlev's view was so long that Sveneric could not yet comprehend it all. Instead, he considered the individuals whose actions had brought about the circumstances, and he considered their past histories. Then he considered history from long ago.

And then he turned his mind to considering the next step.

Twelve

Mearsies Heili

"SHE SAID TO GO ahead."

Atan's thoughts broke when she recognized CJ's high, clear voice.

She set her needle with care into the tambour, and looked up at CJ in the doorway. The girl's direct blue gaze was emphasized by the whiteness about her mouth, her tense brow. And by her black clothing.

Atan laid aside her embroidery, and leaned over to pick up her candlestick. "You're dressed for night stalking. Going out with the Irregulars?"

CJ gave a firm nod. "Or else go loony."

"How is Aurora?" Atan moved to her writing table.

"Asleep. No nightmares. So far. And she was perfectly okay at bedtime and stuff. She seems to have accepted that Clair has to live in the jewel caves." CJ sagged against the doorway, closing her eyes. "Every time I think about that, I feel like barfing. I can't even tell Diana, because what can she do, on the other side of the world, guarding Troy?"

Atan set the candlestick down, lit another, and pulled her magic-paper forward. "Go chase Norsundrians. And remember—"

A small hand flashed up. "I know. If that stinkweed Ilerian

gets us ghosting around in fear all the time, he's winning. But—Clair hates that she might end up being a danger!"

Atan said, "With Siamis here, doing what he's been trained to do, nothing will happen. And I'll also give him this much credit, he never interferes with the ordering of life in the palace, or in the kingdom."

CJ rolled her eyes. "I know. I know." She lingered, watching Atan's swift pen-strokes. Then she said, "It's okay for *you*. *You're* in charge of everything. But Clair is tossed out of throne-warming once again. And it's not her fault!" She hesitated on the verge of saying more, made a face, whirled, and fled.

Atan knew what CJ really meant, and what Clair might be thinking, while sitting alone in that cave: she did not want any more adults taking charge of her kingdom or her life. Atan laughed at herself, aware that the Mearsieans regarded her as old, and yet when she was with other adults like Siamis, and Lilith, and Tsauderei, she felt as if she were five years old.

The Mearsieans saw her in charge, but she saw herself caught in a silken web fashioned by other hands, all the way down her ancestral line. Outside of that, she had become convinced that she had not obtained Detlev's cooperation so much as fallen in with plans already laid out by him. And yet she had seen … oh, not fear, precisely, in his gaze, but concern. *That* was what kept her awake of nights. If *he* got scared, they all should be scared.

She rubbed her arms, and hugged her elbows against her, fighting the harrowing feeling that the end was near. She wanted to be home to face it, whenever it came. She glanced at the clock, her eyes registering eight and her mind three in the morning in Sartor. As always, she tried to envision Rel safe in Shendoral, or at one of his bolt holes. He had stopped replying to notes, but that could be for any number of reasons, from losing the paper (as he always managed to lose notecases) or he might simply be asleep.

Atan looked around the map room. Her thoughts were not good company. She walked to the library to resume reading about the fall of the Colendi empire, which, typical of Colend, had been carried on by theatrical productions and street art on the walls, not by war.

Imry Llyenthur's HQ - Larkadhe

Duin's heavy blackweave boots reposed in the middle of the current-dispatch pile. On his stomach rested a bowl of hot buns with generous gobbets of honey smeared over the top.

He was savoring, one by one, the sweet top halves, and pitching the harder lower halves into the crackling fire behind him. The cook was getting better, finally.

He smiled to himself. He was alone—at Central HQ—eating and goldbricking. And ever since the shakedown last month, the sector relays had been prompt, circumspect, and cooperative.

Life was good, he thought as he reached to toss another half-eaten bun onto the fire—it being slightly dried out. He gloated at his ability to do that, remembering the days when he had been grateful to gnaw a dirt-covered bun far more stale. Whatever happened over winter, he would not go hungry.

Life was very good.

The door opened then, sprung wide by an impatient hand. Recognizing the style and then the step, Duin scrambled to his feet, to the detriment of both dinner and dispatches.

Llyenthur paused in the doorway, eyeing with some amusement his crimson-faced adjutant in his fluttering moat of honey-sticky papers. For once he was dressed in gray and black, and he was wearing that black-steel sword with the old fashioned handle that he'd taken off his brother. This meant he was going into the field to be seen.

As three or four aides crowded in behind, Llyenthur addressed Duin. "Time to reap the whirlwind." He twiddled his fingers in the air.

Duin promptly flung the papers onto the table—wringing his hand as two or three stuck—and reached for the spell-book.

"Never mind that. I've sent the General Alert. Be prepared to send the fire signal when I contact you. Should be in, ah, about two turns." Llyenthur flicked one of the sandglasses. His amusement increased as one of the other aides smirked and rubbed his hands, then he shut the door and was gone.

Most of the other aides left, for they all had their orders.

Bergan lumbered toward Duin, surveying the honey-smeared mess of papers and rolls, and guffawed.

Duin said, "Take a hike. Unless you know a spell—"

"—for removing honey from relays?" Bergan laughed

again. "You know, Duin," he said as he picked up a dispatch with thumb and forefinger, little finger outstretched. "You're good. Real good." He lowered himself to the edge of the table, adding as he perused the blotched work, "From Aldon, too!"

"Don't you have work to do?"

"Not until the start signal," Bergan gloated.

"Give me that." Duin twitched the paper away, and mopped at the honey-blotches with a besorcelled handkerchief.

"Three weeks ago," Bergan went on, "he would've used your empty skull for a trash bin."

So Bergan was still snouting out what had happened? Duin didn't know himself. No one knew. Excepting maybe Ilerian. Duin snorted. "Just you see that you do exactly as you're told, or it's you who will look even more stupid than usual with apple-cores staring out of your eye-sockets."

Bergan laughed, and sauntered out.

Duin flipped the sandglass. One turn, now.

A town in Sartor

With a gesture of generous invitation, Imry Llyenthur indicated the barred door across the rain-washed Sartoran street.

His companions surveyed the tile-roofed, ivy-walled house, indistinguishable from the rest of the street's houses. Like all the others, the windows were shuttered so tightly not a crack of light escaped.

"He's all yours," Llyenthur said. "But remember. We want him awake. And whole."

The squad-leader gave a short nod, gripped his sword hilt, and gestured to his men. They moved across the street, some fanning out to surround the house, others going to the door.

Llyenthur turned to Elzhier, who was just finishing an enormous yawn. "Want to watch the fun?" he asked.

"Only long enough to see the look on the hero's face." She spoke with the venom intensified by the weeks of boredom having to follow Rel, but not touch him or his companions.

The leader lifted his hand to a pair of husky men, who took their axes to the door. The wood splintered, they kicked the door in, and the squad rushed in. Shouts and screams emerged, followed by three or four running civs, who were cut down by the waiting perimeter guards.

A few Norsundrians sported with the ducking, squalling people first. No lighters to survive except Rel. Those were the orders. No one had said they couldn't play a little beforehand.

Llyenthur began to stroll across the street, noting the two or three faint lights in windows up and down the street flickering out. Total silence from the other houses as, with jingling harnesses and clanking swords, Bostian and his hand-picked mounted honor guard clopped up the street at a leisurely trot.

Elzhier at his shoulder, Llyenthur stepped with care over the remains of the front door and looked into a modest Sartoran home now in wild disarray. Broken furniture lay everywhere, and two or three as yet fitful flames licked at overturned tables and a half-finished tapestry on its loom.

In the kitchen corner Rel fought in grim silence against three Norsundrians. Weapons clashed, once shooting blue sparks; for a moment Llyenthur stood back and observed with undisguised appreciation the vertiginous flash of Rel's sword and dagger.

Bodies littered the room's periphery. Six or seven Sartorans, all adults, looked like. And near Rel's corner lay three Norsundrians. Some of the lumps were still alive, lying stunned or else twisting in agony. Llyenthur stepped over one of these last, in order to look down at the papers that had scattered where the big table had tipped over.

There was one partially burned paper of an odd size and color that had drifted away from the various little fires. He picked it up and studied it with interest, seemingly unaware of the battle three paces away. Two figures launched through a curtain-hung doorway, locked in bone-cracking combat. Elzhier hopped aside as they crashed across the last standing table then to the floor amid a shower of crockery. A hand clutched at her skirt. She jumped, and looked down to see a weak, blood-smeared arm, fingers groping. She gave it a sharp, hard kick.

Llyenthur paid no attention to either of the wild struggles. He folded the paper with care, and dropped it into a pocket of his gray jacket. Then he looked up at the Norsundrians still trying to disarm Rel. "Let's end this bout, shall we?" he suggested, waving a hand in a little circle.

The squad leader cut a fast glance his way—just as Rel's blade cracked down on his wrist.

Outside, the waiting mounted guard joked and laughed back and forth, as they waited for the locals to come out nosing, fearful, or affronted. All would afford equal entertainment. Even though the locals seemed to be disappointing them, there was a party atmosphere among the Norsundrians—finally, action, after weeks of holding tight.

Bostian, observing Llyenthur's approach, called out, "What? Didn't hazard a match with the great Rel?"

"Too fatiguing." Llyenthur smiled up at him. "However, if you think you can hasten things along—" He made a lazy gesture back toward the house.

Bostian leaped down—then remounted again, cursing in disappointment, as four figures heaved through the door. Rel, considerably disheveled, with his arms lashed tightly behind him, was being man-handed by three equally big Norsundrians. He looked dazed in the uneven torchlight, and his head and shoulders were copiously splashed with dark color.

"What's this?" Llyenthur asked.

Elzhier emerged from behind. "I flung a jug of hot mulled wine into his face. That ended things quick enough."

A flash of transfer magic riveted everyone's attention.

Efael and then Yeres appeared. The Norsundrians at once gave them wide berth, especially those who noticed the anger tightening Efael's sharp face in the leaping light. But he only glanced about and then transferred out again.

"Fire the house." Bostian raised his gloved fist.

Yeres smiled at her audience, then daintily picked up her skirts and trod around a puddle. She moved toward the group still muscling Rel toward the horses. The Norsundrians saw her approach, and stopped. The horse being held in wait stamped and rolled his eyes at Yeres' yellow draperies fluttering like the torch flames.

Yeres dimpled in mirth as Rel gave his head a violent shake. Then he seemed to become aware of Yeres for the first time, and though there was no trace of any human emotion in his burned, purple-smeared face, he transferred his gaze elsewhere.

Yeres said, in Sartoran, "What fun! But dear Rel. You do not look very heroic for the part you are about to play, do you?" She stood on tiptoe and reached up to brush his wet hair off his forehead. And as the faintest twitch of revulsion tightened his jaw, she put up both hands to straighten his twisted collar and flick a few soggy herbs from his soaked white shirt. "There!" She stood back. "That's the best I can do, I fear. I hope you'll enjoy the entertainment that Imry has gone to such trouble to arrange for you."

Rel's dark gaze moved from Bostian to Llyenthur and beyond. Slowing no disappointment at being thus ignored, Yeres gestured to the Norsundrians, and they resumed shoving Rel toward the horse being held for him.

Yeres looked around. "Elzhier!" She gave a glad cry. "Was it you who found Rel?"

Elzhier nodded, smothering another fierce yawn as Yeres joined her. "Yes. And I've had enough. He's about as much fun as a lump of mud." She cast a glance of loathing at Rel's impassive figure now seated on the horse. Around him Norsundrians were mounting up, one holding Rel's reins. Elzhier turned her back on them. "They'll be hours at this idiocy. Will you send me to Yaldar? I was promised a kingdom, and now it's time to collect."

Yaldar? That was Connanre's favorite place. Yeres shrugged: not her problem. She transferred Elzhier to the palace in Yaldar, then turned to watch the beginnings of the festivities. The Norsundrians were all either mounted or leaving the other way by then, and she consented to take one's horse, leaving him to walk on foot.

She rode with Bostian's column through the streets, urging her horse to trot so she could follow directly behind Bostian and Llyenthur, who rode at the front. It was unlikely she'd hear anything to the purpose, but you never knew. She certainly would get an unimpeded view of the fun.

Behind them rode Rel, his reins still held by a guard, and the column followed behind, two by two, at a leisurely pace. At the outside of the column rode torchbearers, so that Rel was clearly visible.

When Bostian gave the signal to halt before a long series of storefronts, the torchbearers rode forward to begin Llyenthur's autumn bonfire. Two torchbearers, however, remained with the column, so that Rel remained outlined in firelight for the Sartorans no doubt peering between shutters and door-cracks.

This first granary had been a community secret project. The back rooms of the six storefronts had been joined together to form one large barn. Over the recent eight weeks wheat, corn, rye, and barley had all been smuggled in, disguised as various types of goods.

First some window-smashing, punctuated by whoops and derisive calls from the watching column, before the torchbearers ran through. Flames winked, golden-red, in and out of the windows, and as everyone watched, the Norsundrians out in the street, the Sartorans from behind closed doors. Dark windows gradually filled with fire's warm glow. That light intensified as smoke fingered upward from broken windows, sending out a smell of singed biscuits; one roof exploded in a spiraling shower of sparks as flames roared up into the sky. Then another, and another, until all six stores were merely skeletons housing a bright, hot fury. Smoke billowed out, fogging adjacent houses. The heat drove the Norsundrians back, the horses restless and afraid, their rounded eyes reflecting the flames.

The Sartorans remained hidden. Rel was silent and expressionless, his eyes, like the animals', showing twin flames.

Bostian and Llyenthur seemed content to watch.

Then, as the growing flames licked out toward other buildings, a few cautious lighters emerged, buckets in hand. Bostian chuckled at the sight of them, and raised his fist to give the cut-'em-down signal, but Llyenthur stopped him with a shake of the head. "If they attack you, they're yours. If they fight the fire, let 'em."

That was it? No slaughter? What was the *point*?

Disgusted beyond measure, Yeres transferred out, leaving the horse to sidle in protest.

As the Norsundrians watched, but did nothing, more lighters emerged from the surrounding homes and stores and began trying to beat back the flames. Soon they were out in huge numbers, carrying buckets and spades and blankets, some forming lines to the nearest well.

Bostian sat his restive horse, trying to keep the animal still, and covertly watched Imry Llyenthur for signs. But Llyenthur wasn't giving any signs. He didn't even seem to see the lighters; he was watching his big bonfire. To all appearances he expected no trouble from the lighters.

And didn't look like much backup, either. Bostian was used to assessing circumstance in military terms, and the present ones weren't promising. He had twenty mounted, plus the torchbearers, surrounded by hundreds of angry lighters. None of them carried swords, but a lot of 'em had pitchforks, spades, and other handy tools that in strong hands could substitute as weapons. Did Detlev's ex-brat know what he was doing?

Bostian sidled another glance. Imry Llyenthur was half a hand shorter than Bostian and quite a bit lighter in build, and had at least thirty years less experience of exceedingly rough garrison life. But then, of his particular cronies, Bostian was the last one with a free hand left. Bartal had been the first to clash with Llyenthur, Aldon the latest. Alsaes hadn't even merited Llyenthur's direct attention—a distinction that no doubt would seem an asset to Aldon, whose slow and painful recovery still didn't keep him off a duty desk, though the signs were clear to anyone smart enough to see them that he'd just been making trouble everywhere else so that he'd finally get sent where he wanted—Marloven Hess.

So instead of inaugurating what had all the promise of being one of the most sporting routs of the season, Bostian sat and watched the lighters fight the fires that his torchbearers had started, and wondered what the point of it was.

Presently Llyenthur stirred. He glanced back at Rel, who was still astride his horse just behind them. "Rel?" he said, his voice carrying over the roar of the fires, and the voices of people fighting them. "No champions?"

Rel did not react. His eyes—one of them rapidly swelling shut—were focused on the fires.

Llyenthur gave Bostian a mocking glance. "Bored?"

"This isn't exercise, this is flushing sheep shit," Bostian said.

Llyenthur looked amused. "This is what is known as obedience. With their heroic leader on display to see them obey. For them to see him obey. Let's get on to the next stop. I have a long night ahead of me."

Two more secret stores were fired.

They arrived at last in Eidervaen, and made their way to three places.

The last place spread flames to nearby crowded houses. Again the Norsundrians watched until the residents were involved in their battle against the flames, and then Llyenthur said to Bostian, "That's it for Eidervaen. The rest is up to the gossips. Take him back to your place now, by as public a route as possible. And—Bostian." Llyenthur raised his voice, so that it carried to all corners of the street. "Remember. An orderly journey. No brandishing axes. Other places you might reasonably expect a riot, but our Sartoran friends are a good, obedient flock of sheep. They are to get their reward by remaining unmolested. And we don't want to distract them from admiring their heroic leader."

Bostian smirked, thinking, what was that about gossips? Then he shrugged it away: who cares?

"I'll be back for him when I'm finished," Llyenthur went on. Then he added wryly, "Unless Efael is bored and fetches him first."

He dismounted, tossed his reins to Rel's keeper, and transferred out.

Bostian said to Asiarch, "I'm changing the orders."

Asiarch slewed around, bushy eyebrows rising. "What?"

"Sartor needs to know who's now king," Bostian snapped. "All this stupid talk of Rel, Rel, Rel. It served Llyenthur elsewhere, but at *my* cost here. We'll keep brandishing Rel, as ordered, but every Sartoran who comes out their door is going to be treated as if they attacked us, see? Either they bow down to me and let the fires burn, or they die. Imry Llyenthur will never know once they are all dead, dead. Dead. Sartor needs to learn that *I* am king."

Thirteen

Norsunder-Beyond

HIBERN FIRMLY SAW HERSELF back in the library.

This time she found Theronezhe waiting.

She looked around and shrugged, keeping her face calm despite her slamming heart. *Remember, you are supposedly untouchable, so whatever he's doing has to be diversion more than real threat. You must find out from what he is diverting you.*

Out loud she said, "I found your Detlev books very entertaining. Not the trash written about him, but his scribblings. Are there any more?"

Theronezhe smiled. "There are indeed. But they are more recent. I thought you were interested in the days of Old Sartor."

"Yes. Before you destroyed it."

He sat back in a comfortable armchair. She watched, realizing that he was not—at this moment—intending to play bully. He was playing audience.

She walked along shelves, pretending to scan. A step, a slow scan, another step. Another. Another. Another even slower.

How can I bore him away? She remembered then that he knew these books. That meant he'd be interested in seeing which ones she selected, and how much she read. All right, then. Pick something.

Grabbing a thin book with an innocuous title, she walked with it toward a far armchair. She opened the book, and her insides griped. It was written by Efael. It appeared to be an excursion into foreign world-wrecking, written in an angry, bragging style that included detailed reports on what he had done to those he conquered. "Eh."

Theronezhe laughed when she shoved it back on the shelf rather than thinking it to its shelf. She knew how this worked now—he was baiting her. She carefully wiped her fake hands on her fake clothes to clean the metaphysical greasy stench of Efael's touch from her fingers.

Then she chose another report at random, and this time she let her eyes unfocus, and pretended to read. Locked behind her shield, she began to think, while mentally she retraced her way through those thorny reports of Detlev's.

She turned pages every now and then. After thirty-seven pages, Theronezhe vanished.

Time to experiment.

She formed an image in her mind, and reached—

And this time, when the nightmare struck, she was ready for it.

⸻

Sartorias-Deles

As nightfall wrapped the southern half of the world, fires licked at the darkness.

Barns, houses, even tunnels erupted into flame. In cities, in the countryside. The rosy glows silhouetted far hillsides and mountain slopes as carefully cultivated late crops, all ripe or ready for picking, were incinerated.

The attack proceeded step by step as the hours progressed. City, village, country. Desperate fighting broke out in some places—planned for, looked for, and efficiently put down. Those who were left alive, and could walk, were then sent home to spread word of defeat.

When the Norsundrians had finished with their tasks, they too disappeared.

And when shock, and anger, and grief eased a little, those who were in the habit of assessment began to perceive that the burnings were not universal—and they were not, except in a few places, extensive. Llyenthur had, in fact, been very selective.

But the choices of places, and the logistical execution, were all testimony to the extent of his knowledge. For those who thought in such terms, the attack displayed the care and precision of art; its theme (this was more generally apprehended) was humiliation.

Dei Manor - Imar

The prospect from the Imaran palace where the Host lived was winter-barren, the ground and bare-barked trees a muted gray, and the light seemed from a sun far more distant than Erhal.

Svirle of long-lost Yssel stood on the terrace facing eastward, his hands clasped behind him and his eyes half-shut. He smiled.

Efael, walking out, recognized the pose, and the smile, and endured the usual corrosive annoyance at Svir's ability to watch events from here, that Efael had to physically transfer to in order to witness.

Svir said, without opening his eyes, "Displeasure, Efael?"

Efael said with scorn, "It's the scale. Not exactly comprehensive. Instead he's playing games. What's he waiting for?"

Svir answered, "He's merely reminding the populace who has the firepower." And, as Efael glowered in silence, he went on, "It is what Ilerian wants. And I find the irony much more exquisite, to leave them a choice."

The rustle of silk across the flagstones announced Yeres. "Good morning! You were wise not to stay." She moved to Efael's side to caress his arm. "It was disappointingly dull after all."

Efael said, "It seems we are the only ones who thought so."

Svir smiled at them. "Then there is the image of Detlev sitting in the ashes somewhere and contemplating Imry's success."

Yeres was the first to perceive the oblique warning, but because she was in a sunny mood, and because Connanre had been boring enough to tell her not to speak to her own brother for a while, she followed Efael back in and teased and coaxed him into seeing the whole episode as nothing more than a joke.

She knew that the effrontery of using Norsundrian power just to make a gesture would cast him into black rage.

When he transferred out at last, she danced around in anticipatory glee. Now they'd see something entertaining, she hoped.

Llyenthur's HQ - Larkadhe

Below the high mountains with their burning grape harvest, the winds through the night and early morning were hot and eerie. The citizens of the city went fearfully about their business after dawn's light, often with looks over their shoulders southeastward, and even some of the Norsundrians at their guard posts gripped and regripped their weapons as they watched about them.

Llyenthur, however, was not around to see it. When he finally reappeared in the castle the fires above had long burned themselves out. He found a city wreathed in lingering smoke, the air quiet and still. The aides all were tired but in celebrative moods as he entered the map room where most had gathered, and indicated it was time to get to work. A mountain of reports was imminent—indeed, they began appearing.

He pulled the beige paper from his pocket, and examined it; sometime since he'd looked last, words must have appeared on it, for they were fading rapidly. He brought the paper close to his nose and squinted. It appeared to be signed "Atan" but he did not know her handwriting. There was little of import in what he could make out of the words—and yes, the ink was definitely fading as he watched. The prize was the paper itself. He was going to have to be very careful with it.

Just as everyone settled at their desks, and the hilarity began to die, the flicker of transfer magic caught their attention. Llyenthur pocketed the paper a heartbeat before Efael of the Host appeared.

Llyenthur stood before the big map while Duin and Bergan froze in the act of reading and sorting the mass of early reports. Llyenthur's arm dropped and he turned around.

"Carry on," said Efael.

Llyenthur's brows quirked a little, but he faced the map again, and said, "Latest?"

Duin read out subject headers, then sat at his desk to log them. As did everyone else. The fear pleased Efael, as always, as Llyenthur said, "What can I do for you?"

He was not the least afraid, which irked Efael, also as always. He stepped near the relay table, and glanced down at the tops of the aides' piles. Duin and Bergan rose and backed away, then looked to Llyenthur. No response from him; they remembered appointments elsewhere, and slipped out.

As Efael continued to sort, letting the silence build, Llyenthur dropped into a chair, fought a yawn, rubbed his eyes. "Well?"

Efael faced him. "Ilerian seems to have lost all interest in you. Did you ditch his quarry, or did it ditch you?"

"Why don't you ask Ilerian?"

"Because I'm asking you."

Llyenthur sighed, and steepled his fingers. "His quarry was a girl. Young. Sixteen or eighteen. Spoke Imaran. When I found her, she'd lost her wits, and Detlev snatched her away again before she regained them. I have no idea who she was, or why Ilerian wants her."

"You saw Detlev?"

"No. I showed Ilerian," Llyenthur said, his voice affable. "Would you like me to show you?" He tapped his head, enjoying the flinch that Efael didn't quite mask.

"But the report said *died in transit.* Yeres saw it. Does Ilerian know you lied?"

"Everyone lied," Llyenthur said soothingly. "We were all hoarding interesting prisoners, were we not?"

Efael flushed. "And if you had kept her—what then?"

Llyenthur's voice barely repressed laughter. "Well." He lifted a hand, palm up. "That depends on what you want to hear, doesn't it?"

Efael's rage flared white-hot. He controlled the response, though it cost a struggle. By his irritating, flippant attitude it was clear that Imry Llyenthur had no idea what that girl represented to Ilerian, whose mood had changed to expectation.

Efael looked down again at the relay desk as a paper appeared on it. He was closest. Llyenthur's hand dropped to the table when he saw Efael reach for it, pick it up, and smile. "One of your cap-list rulers seems to have been spotted on the border of Everon and Wnelder Vee."

"You're offering to be of use?"

Efael's smile increased. "Perhaps." He made the sign and vanished.

With the report, Llyenthur noted in mild annoyance. Probably Tahra Delieth. If it was something important he'd doubtless hear again.

He went back to his map.

* * *

Bostian's HQ - Eidervaen

Bostian's column of elites was the first to arrive back at their garrison. The rest of his command was out scouting for resistance to harass or kill, to be frustrated by empty buildings locked up tight.

His elite guard joked about the strangeness of the operation as they clattered into the courtyard before the stable and began dismounting. Bostian looked impatiently for the stable hands, and shouted, "Get out here!"

He waited with increasing impatience. Rel was important enough a prisoner to require Bostian to personally supervise Rel's removal to an appropriate holding cell. But before he could issue an order to roust and beat some alertness into the stable hands, all the horses went mad. The guards, caught utterly off-balance, struggled to catch reins, and some even ran—to discover themselves surrounded by pale, silent figures that seemed to materialize out of the darkness.

Knives flashed in the torchlight. Cries, and warnings, ceased.

Bostian found himself lying on the cold flagstones with a thin-bladed dagger held at his throat. Long white hair framed a marble-cold, pale face that whispered, "You will not get so easy an end."

Thin taloned fingers trussed him securely with rope from his own saddlebag. He could see nothing beyond this morvende crouched over him like an inimical ghost. The now-docile horses waited to be unsaddled by swift morvende hands, then they trotted free into the street and away. Bostian heard their hooves ringing far up the empty street, and further, distant shouts.

Rel loomed then, looking impassively down at him before he and the morvende walked toward the stable. Bostian began to shout until transfer magic jolted him.

Rel peered out of his good eye. Even in the blurry torch-light, he recognized Hinder, known since they were both boys.

Hinder wore a white headband with a peace mark on it, as did the rest of his team. Rel knew enough about the morvende to understand its significance: Hinder, and these others, had volunteered to join the resistance. But for morvende, the act of taking a life, for whatever purpose, put one outside the community for evermore. The headbands represented the peace symbol sketched by a family member on the brow of a deceased person before Disappearance. Hinder and his team had been memorialized as dead, and could never return to the morvende geliaths.

Rel knew that no words would suffice. So he did the only thing possible, he bowed low to his old friend.

Hinder closed his eyes, and then offered a flickering smile. "We will go into the hills to defend the refugees. When you need us, leave a sprig of loethe at the labyrinth." He turned his head, cobwebby white hair drifting, and made a sign. The morvende vanished with a whisper of bare feet and the tick, tick of taloned toenails on the stones.

Rel turned back, trying to marshal his wits despite his aching head. The rescue was scarcely real to him yet. At this moment, he was more concerned about Hinder, and the cost he'd paid. Rel hadn't seen Sinder among the team. It was likely she would have been obliged to stay, to carry on the family —

Something moved.

All of the events of the past few hours, and days, went out of Rel's mind when he saw the small, scrawny figure in the far corner of the stable retching miserably. Rel crossed the intervening space in three swift strides as Darian Selenna wavered to his feet and turned blindly.

"Rel?" Darian's voice was small, and tired, and so young. He trembled violently, his face pinched with shock and exhaustion.

"I'm here."

"I was too late." Darian choked.

Instinct extended Rel's arms, and he found himself holding the clinging boy. "I was — too late —" Darian wept into his shoulder.

Rel opened his mouth to assure him that he was all right, and then he remembered what had happened a year ago, and realized that Darian wasn't referring to him at all.

PART FOUR

One

Tove-Ne-on-Margren, mid-Sartoran continent

THE VILLAGES OF THE marshy lowlands east of Sholte in Holan look alike to outsiders. And indeed, Tove-ne has approximately the same number of small houses as the other villages built along the Margren River: round houses with conical roofs covered in overlapping, waxy big-ear leaves, built on stilts for the periodic high tides.

The villages are not known for wealth, and so visitors are rare. One possession the lowlanders have in quantity is music. It costs nothing, and brightens long, dreary wet stretches of days.

Tove-ne served as an unofficial provincial capital because of two things. One, the ancient, centuries-old Family Tree that grew on the upper edge of the village. A great, spreading oak, it had flourished all these years in an area unfriendly to trees. Custom from beyond memory gathered local families under its branches for Name Days, marriages, and memorials to departed folk. Holiday rituals were initiated there, and the rare royal proclamations that affected marsh-life were read out there, and afterwards affixed to its huge trunk for the requisite thirty-six days.

The second thing, or person, was reputed—and none laughed louder than she when she heard it—to be nearly as old as the Family Tree. The Old One was a short, scrawny, weather-beaten crone with eyes a bright pale gray, like clear water, in a face the color of the bark of the Family Tree. She had twenty-odd great-great grandchildren, all of whose names she knew, and rare it was in those parts that a child's lingering cough, or a brown-spotted crop that had been prospering, or a border dispute, or a family member's troubled spirits, were not brought to her for pronouncement on cause and resolution. The Old One's reputation for supernal wisdom was enhanced considerably by her blunt, "I don't know," the rare times it occurred — but then the marsh people were considered a contradictory crowd.

It was the Old One who looked into the face of a stranger the week before, and despite his inability, or his reluctance, to name cousins, village of origin, or business (beyond "traveler") had pronounced him welcome.

In fact he stayed at her house, and for some days worked alongside the family at harvesting the rice, and tending the winter-crops and the secret-crops up in the hills behind the villages. More curious villagers than usual found affairs taking them to the Old One's house at even-fall, and they saw the stranger and the Old One and the family laughing over the day's-end pot of chocolate, and then went away commenting on his hair the color of corn from the northlands, and his length, and his eyes the color of creamed chocolate. In a land of largely short, square people with marsh-colored hair and skin he was an oddity, and provided hours of pleasant fireside conjecture.

He was still among them the night the gray-coats rode thundering through the lowlands with their torches and fired the villagers' hill-plantings. On riding out, the last two tossed their torches high into the Family Tree.

The stranger worked all the night through alongside the Old One and her family as they fought the terrible fires, and he sang with the lowlanders. Even when the wind changed and the great billows of smoke and fierce orange glare kept families from seeing one another as they tried to save their homes. They could still hear the song, and the wind and the flames were woven into a night-long lament that echoed from field to field and from village to village.

Dawn brought bleak, pitiless light on the smoldering fires when people turned their steps at last toward their homes. Those who lived in Tove-ne were, at first, too numb to compass the glowing, tumbled remains of the Family Tree amid the ring of ash-strewn houses.

Those who were able to, or who could not resist, fell into bed, or onto grass, or into one another's arms, for a few hours' sleep. Others set houses to rights, or raked the ruins of their homes, looking for bits of their lives that might have been spared. The song was gone now. Everyone worked in silence.

The westering sun called fire to memory when folk began to drift toward Tove-ne again. Perhaps the silence at home was no longer endurable. Perhaps they saw others come out, and came forth too.

Once out they grouped together in uneasy clusters, looking toward the black-charred remains of the tree, and then turning their faces to the dark door of the Old One's house, which — among the few — had been spared. Some whispered behind furtive fingers, but stopped if approached by those not of immediate kin. Others stood, and looked, and said nothing.

Then the Old One emerged from her house. Her hands trembled and her steps were slow, but her back was straight. She walked to the dead Family Tree. People closed in behind, with lagging pace.

There among the ruins the surprised marsh-people saw their stranger. He looked down at something in his hands as he finished a slow, careful scrape, scrape, scrape with steel that occasionally reflected the red of the setting sun.

The Old One stood watching. No one spoke. Even the marsh birds were silent, as the stranger's fingers finished working a young branch that had escaped the conflagration of the Family Tree.

At last he straightened up and put away his carving knife. He picked up his carved wood, an object long and straight and narrow — but he had not made a weapon. He raised what he had made to his lips, and blew.

A sigh hushed through the watchers when they heard the two notes, one low and rich and clear, and one high and sweet. The last trembled a little in the air as he handed the thing to the Old One.

She took it, and played an experimental run of notes. She bowed. He bowed back, and she began to play. Once again the people sang, each aware that music was all they had, besides one another, and life. The song bound them together as they turned to the work of rebuilding.

The stranger picked up his pack, and walked away toward

the east.

———————⟨⟨⟨⟩⟩⟩———————

Outside Eidervaen - Sartor

The morvende tradition was firm, but considered fair by the community: though the defenders, having used weapons to take lives, were no longer a part of morvende society, they were permitted to enter any of the many abandoned geliaths left by their people over the centuries.

It was to one of these that they had taken Rel and Darian Selenna after the rescue.

After a long, desperately needed sleep, Darian Selenna drank deeply from a trickling fountain, then followed Hinder down the tunnel to a cavern with a pool. The water was dark, gently steaming at one end, the moving air smelling freshly of water and stone.

"Told you," Hinder said, perching on a rock.

Darian looked past the morvende to the cushioned low chair by the waterside. There, untouched food cradled by both hands in his lap, lay Rel. He was clean, and swathed in a magnificent morvende robe of exquisite weave. His head sagged gently to one side on the pillow. He was dead to the world, but the rise and fall of his chest testified to his being merely asleep.

"Happened when Arnadal was putting salve on his face where the Norsundrians burned him with the hot wine," Hinder murmured.

"You mean he hadn't woken since then?" Darian whispered back.

"Nope." Hinder snorted a laugh, unheard above the waterfall at the cold end of the lake.

The two retreated back up the tunnel, then turned off to the sleeping area. Hinder said, "He was on his feet, smelling of smoke and cloves and wine, until all the refugees who just had to talk to him had talked themselves out, and the word was in on the last of the outlying provinces that the attacks had ceased. Then he said he'd dunk in the pool, change, then eat, and, well, there he is. Two out of three, at least."

Darian looked around. Why was it that being surrounded by gray stone in morvende caverns was not even remotely like a dungeon? Was it the paintings? The air that moved, somehow, always fresh and cool? Or was it the occasional echoes of singing drifting along the stone tunnels?

In the geliaths where communities lived, he never thought of stone at all. Perhaps that was due to the light that somehow captured all the subtleties of the sun's color-spectrum, sometimes bright, where the beautiful plants grew straight and tall, unbent by wind, and sometimes the light was dim enough for one to perceive natural glows from the stone.

Darian sank gratefully down onto one of the pillows. His body still hurt from his desperate run. "Everyone says the damage was not as extensive as it could have been." He pulled his battered magic-paper from inside his tunic. He had checked it first thing after opening his eyes. "Sveneric says, even Detlev agrees. Said that Llyenthur plans are long."

Hinder crouched down. "He wants the Sunsiders hungry."

"Sveneric says, he wants them to obey. If no one has food, they have to ask for it, and he will give it only to those who are obedient."

"It's cruel." Hinder's amber eyes gleamed with twin reflections of the glowglobe behind Darian. "But not as cruel as Bostian. Who looked to no future, though he calls himself a king. People are toys, to him." He made a spitting motion, then said, "Detlev tells all to Sveneric?"

Darian closed his eyes. "Not everything. I don't think..." His voice drifted as his mind considered the tenor of Sveneric's letters, which had changed in the past couple of days. He didn't think Sveneric was telling him everything, either. But he would not say that out loud to anyone but Dirk, and maybe Lyren-Sartora, if she wasn't squabbling with Sveneric the way she used to squabble with Mac.

Darian sighed. If only he wasn't still so tired! Something was missing — something had changed. Only what? He tried to gather his thoughts. "We were afraid, you see, that some trouble between Detlev and Llyenthur a few weeks back would force Llyenthur into universal destruction. But Rel knows that it wasn't bad?"

"Yes."

"It must make it easier for him to bear." Darian remembered the sight of Rel being brought in surrounded by that column of smug, triumphant Norsundrians, his hands bound, his face red with burns. "It must be terrible enough, the memory of what they did and made him watch, saying it was in his name, and he the cause."

Hinder chuckled. "I do not read minds, and Rel is seldom one to tell his thoughts, but I have come to understand him a little, ever since he came to us first as a traveling shepherd's boy, all those years ago. I assure you, the rank, it means nothing to him. What did matter was what the Norsundrians did, not what they said. He will not forget that. Or forgive. Are you hungry? You have slept for two passes of the sun."

"Very." Darian nodded. "And what's more, I could sleep again. One more question. I saw that Bostian vanish. Is he dead?"

"Nothing so easy," Hinder said, his smile gone. "Bostian and those who did not die are under the eyes of the Loi in Shendoral. There," Hinder said, "their lives will be in their own hands. You know the law of Shendoral: any violence you commit, you receive. They will probably try to escape, but it will never happen."

Darian sighed with gratitude, his fingers brushing back and forth on his magic-note.

Hinder nodded at it. "You could help Rel by writing to Atan to let her know that Rel is safe, but his paper either burned or was taken by the enemy. He was not able to see what happened to it."

"I'll write her at once, and tell her to spread the word not to write to Rel," Darian said, and fought a yawn as he dipped his quill in the ink.

"Thank you," Hinder said. "I will fetch you something to eat."

He did so, making certain that the food was anything that must remain hot. Sure enough, when he returned, he saw Darian lying with his paper near his hand, letters fast fading on the paper. He was asleep.

⸺⸺⸺

Shiovhan - Enaeran

"I'm sorry, Aunt Liere."

Marga's contrite voice started Liere. A sigh of relief ballooned through her. "Marga," she exclaimed, the high voice of relief infused with exasperation. "You're back! Where were you? I was so worried!"

Marga smiled as she stepped into the dank shed that Liere and her party of resistors had ducked into to escape the rain. Beyond her, through the door, the hilly Enaeraneth countryside stretched up to the marching gray clouds.

Liere breathed a sigh of relief as she stared wordlessly at Marga, who was dressed in the generic laborer's tunic shirt, loose, baggy riding trousers, mocs, that Siamis had sent via the Selenseh Redian. Her very short hair, and the sash tied low on her hips instead of at her waist, more or less made her look like a fifteen-year-old boy. At least, once Siamis had transferred them to Shiovhan, no one had given Marga a second glance, though to Liere Marga looked so very … Fer Eider.

They'd barely had time to find Gared and insert themselves into Andri's resistance when Marten brought troubling news of Norsundrians marshaling the Adranis. That could only mean action. Yet there was no resistance fighting — who had the time, much less the strength? Everyone had been involved with harvesting, and readying for transporting and storing the secret harvests.

Liere shut her eyes, overwhelmed by memory of the previous night's panic. They'd come together in an attic to try to figure out what to do about the enemy. Nearly midnight, it had been. Everyone tense, tired, too many people sitting cramped in too small a space, debating things that everyone knew required time and thought but which would not get them.

Then — without any warning — the half-asleep Marga sat up in her corner with a loud, wordless cry. A couple heartbeats after, a messenger pounded up the ladder, too agitated to remember circumspection.

Slamming the hatch open, he'd cried, "They're firing our fields!"

Liere's first thought had been a sickened realization that Andri's prediction was true. The Norsundrians did know about the slope harvests.

Shouts and then screams echoed from the street. The gathered resistors turned to Liere, demanding action, reassurance, orders, and resolution as well as was-it-true?

And through it Marga had covered her face with her hands, crying in Imaran, "Ah, it hurts, it hurts, I can't stop it—"

Liere said, "They have a plan. That can only be bad for us. Let's get out there and caution everyone to get their buckets and get in line to the fountains, or to go back inside. You know

Norsunder won't be kind if we riot."

Then everyone moved at once, and Liere had lost sight of Marga. She tried to answer, to reassure, to make sense of the senseless, as her gaze searched the roomful of angry candle-lit faces. She glimpsed a large, flick-tailed tabby cat, but she couldn't be sure. All she knew was that Marga still lived, as she could sense her on the mental plane. But no words.

Two days she was gone. Liere blinked away memory as Marga plopped down next to Andri's friend Marten, gave him a sunlit smile, and reached for a seed-cake. "I'm so very hungry! Thank you, Brother Marten."

Liere drew a slow breath. "The cat. That was you."

Marga's smile dimmed, her expression wistful. "I could do nothing but run. As a cat I am big, and strong." She tapped her fingers on her wrist. "There is so much water within me. When I am a cat, most goes away."

"Where?" Liere asked, intensely curious. "I don't understand how you can do that. Does it hurt?"

"It tickles," Marga said, head tilted. "It is, oh, you take your components, and rearrange them. A bit like making dough? No, that's not right." She pursed her lips. "I believe I need to be a tree for a time, to understand it."

"A tree?" Marten gazed at her in fascination.

Liere trusted Marten not to talk about Marga. He had his own secrets—primary among them the fact that he saw ghosts. Or, what people called ghosts.

Marga's bright smile turned his way. "It will take time, though. Perhaps ten years, or longer. I must wait for… Oh, I distracted myself. The ones in gray, they only struck down those with weapons. They let the people put out the fires. I ran and I ran, and it was the same everywhere. Then I had to sleep, and then I thought I must come back—"

Marga's gaze veered to the door and her face smoothed to amiable vacuity as a courier appeared, staring into the shed's gloom. She took a huge bite of her cake. Amazing, how uninteresting she looked with all expression leached from her face. She had become a teenage boy with a sort of fading rash over his face.

Over the battered cap that one of the resistors had given Marga, Liere met Marten's dark, questioning gaze, and then she said to the courier, "Come in. Have some cake and pressed cider. How bad was it at Arbanion?"

Two

Darchelde – Marloven Hess

MAREND NDARGA WATCHED FROM inside the kitchen alcove as Detlev's son wandered through the main room and up the tunnel to the entrance and out. Sveneric's expression was pensive, but then it was always pensive, so that wasn't any clue.

She knew she hadn't been seen, though he might have used that mind stuff to scan everyone. You never knew when he was doing it. Oh, sure, he said he'd always let you know, but Marend flat-out disbelieved that anyone who had a skill no one else had wouldn't use it all the time.

The old anger surged through her. If she were big and strong, she'd be out there at Commander Stad's side, leading people against the Norsundrians, or killing the enemy herself, or...

She squashed wishful thinking. She wasn't big or strong. The disgusting truth had to be faced, and she faced it with angry determination because she'd almost gotten everyone killed when she'd tried on the pretense of greatness once before, nose-led by Imry Llyenthur. She was a girl. A short, no, be honest, a tiny girl, who despite considerable effort could only muster laughable strength compared to someone like Sveneric, three or four years younger than she was.

She sighed. The strange thing was, until she'd met him,

she'd equated strength and speed with size and muscle, but he actually wasn't all that much bigger than she was. She had seen him in action—she'd sparked the gang to test him, and he'd taken them all down. Easily. With considerate care, not hurting anyone. Control the entire time. The kind of control that could probably take down grown men—and more than one.

He was ... he was an *elgar*, a word her father had said used to mean hero, back in his great-fathers' days. It had gone out of use, except in the songs. "When terms get overused for political reasons, they fall out of favor," he'd said before the war—before he was killed. "But it will come back again, probably in your generation. The rest of the world says 'elgar' for hero, but we always know the real meaning. That's why there are so many Indevans, but they are always nicknamed Van, or Vana, because 'Inda' has special meaning for Marlovens."

He wasn't the only one. MV was also a real Inda. They all were; each of them had a martial style that caused the Darchelde teens to groan with envy. Why couldn't she get that kind of training, if size and muscle weren't so important?

Maybe she could. She hadn't been able to pressure Sveneric into training her and the others. Not that he ever swanked. Just the opposite. He just didn't seem to be interested in warfare, which made no sense whatever. Whenever she brought it up—or got one of the others to, when she realized he was avoiding her at free time—he'd always managed to turn the subject.

He also didn't talk about Detlev's gang. But before David left on his unnamed mission, he had said a couple of things, offhand-like, and Marend had treasured them up. David had only given them a couple of training sessions while he was there. After the last one, he'd said with that odd smile, "You really ought to meet MV. He's the one to give you a surfeit of steel."

And now MV was *here*.

As soon as Sveneric left the hideout, Marend slipped out, poking and jabbing the Methden teens awake—in Tdor's case, yanking off her blankets and pulling her out of bed as the others crowded into the small round cave-room that Marend shared with Tdor. Some protested. Some sighed. Kelsan rolled his eyes, muttering, "And what do you think the Great Warriors are going to eat when they wake up? Uncooked oats?"

"Who cares about food," Marend whispered. "We have to plan."

Ramond was the loudest protester—of course. "What is it

now, Marend?"

"Two things," Marend said. "Detlev's gang has to be here for a reason."

"They'll tell us when they're ready. I noticed they all know how to talk—" Sindan began.

"Shut up." Marend didn't even look at him. Jokes belonged to rec time. Otherwise they were insubordination. Not that she was the leader. She had to remind herself of that fact.

"They've got some other plan," Tdor said, giving a big yawn. "You can tell by how quiet they all go. Not just the assassin. It has nothing to do with us."

They had all decided that Zairna Raadi was a secret assassin. He was too quiet, too stealthy, and too fast not to be.

"Then why *here*?" Marend asked, folding her arms.

The gang exchanged looks, and hands opened, palm up in question.

"Does it have to do with the king, maybe?" Rom asked. "If so, Marend's right. Maybe we are going to be part of it."

"That means we have to be good," Marend declared.

That "good" was uttered in the low voice that meant deadly or maybe lethal. They all knew that to Marend, "good" meant only one thing: good at martial skills.

The others in the gang shifted, sighed, shuffled—all signs of agreement. Reluctant agreement, at least on the part of Ramond's old gang. Marend was aware that they were still a little wary around her. Couldn't be helped. An opportunity was here and she didn't mean to waste it.

"Sveneric won't tell us anything," Marend stated. "But that doesn't mean one of these other ones won't. Like the youngest one, Dirk. He also knows stuff. And he talks. I found out from him last night who it was Sveneric's been writing to so much all yesterday on that magic paper-thing."

"Detlev, of course," Ramond said, ink-stained hands out wide.

"Wrong." Marend adored telling Ramond he was wrong. "Dirk said, 'A friend of ours named Ian.' See? All we have to do is—"

"—is start getting nosy, and they'll leave," Ramond cut in. "Marend, you're enough to drive any sane person to leave, you and your—"

"Oh, let her be," Kelsan said blowing upward at a strand of his flyaway yellow hair. "We all want to get in on any action they have in mind, don't we?"

"Sure," Rom said, crossing his arms. "But let 'em tell us on their own."

"They might not want to," Kethadrend piped up, giving Marend a squinty look. "They might think Marend will blab it all to any Norsundrian who comes along and promises her a command—"

"Give it a rest," Tdor began.

"I can defend myself," Marend snarled, and advanced on Kethadrend, who glared back at her, refusing to back up.

Marend felt her control evaporating. She wanted so badly to strike that sneer off this brat's stupid face—

"Well, well."

They whirled around.

How could they not have seen him? Heard his step? Yet there he was, MV himself, leaning in the archway giving onto Tdor's and Marend's room. He was almost too tall for the rounded arch. The top of his straight black hair brushed the magic-smoothed mud. He'd ghosted up as quiet as a cat.

For a moment Marend just stared, her anger whirling away into an impossible tangle of fear and admiration and teeth-gritting determination not to show any of it.

Why was life so unfair? He was tall, lean, dressed entirely in black, and you could just tell he was as strong as thousand-fold Marloven steel. His eyes were a weird light brown that in certain light somehow looked like they were on fire, and there was nothing even remotely soft in the planes of his face, or in his features.

He smiled. It was a smile to make whole armies cut and run.

"Well." He said it a third time, drawing it out.

Sindan started biting his nails. Kethadrend's babyish jaw jutted out.

"So you worthless shitbirds think you know something about using your hands?" His voice was low, and slightly husky, and very, very sarcastic.

Instant protest rose to Marend's lips, but she gritted her teeth even harder.

Ramond—blushing to his ridiculous ears and pointy nose—said, "We've done all right so far. King thinks so. I mean, none of us are big, but Rom there's pretty good with a knife, and Marend and Tdor and Keth are all decent with the bow—"

MV's teeth showed. "Hah."

With that, MV turned away, and sauntered back up the tunnel.

They all followed, drawn irresistibly as if by invisible strings.

As they all emerged into the big room, Marend had just enough time to see that the one with the long curly hair was there at the desk, writing. What was his name? Adam. He had a nice face and she'd wondered if he was their cook or servant, because he couldn't be any good, not with that mild manner and kindly voice.

"You?" MV said, poking Rom with a long forefinger. "Good with a knife?" His hand flattened, sweeping down and then up, and now there was a blade in it. "Adam."

MV threw the blade right at Adam, who didn't even drop the pen. His left hand came up. He nipped the blade by the handle as it flew toward his ear, then sent a look of mild reproach at MV. Without setting down his pen, he tossed the knife whirling up into the air, caught it by the blade — and flung it back.

Whoop! The Marloven teens flattened against the wall, but MV caught it mid-flight and whish, it vanished up his sleeve again.

"Ah." That was Sindan.

"Yeah." Kelsan fanned himself with his hands. "I wouldn't even do that with vegetables!"

MV turned around then, and crossed his arms. "Because you're lazy. All of you. Lazy, no-good, bumbling, mouth-flapping yakkers, and I don't know why I'm going to waste the time running you. Maybe it's because I feel so sorry for Senrid, but I'm going to see if I can drum a little elementary learning into those thick skulls before he gets back."

Ramond had just enough time to send an exhilarated grin Marend's way, *Of course that's why they're here!*, before MV pointed up the tunnel. "Move!"

And back in the hideout, Adam gestured Andri, Sveneric, Crow, Rolfin, Mildred, and Dirk into a circle. "We've practiced contact as individuals," he said seriously. "Now we're going to learn how to pass strength between contacts — while shielding identity. Two skills at once. Let's see how far we can pass a mental image of a sun-ball around the circle before someone slips."

A week later, after news of the burnings reached Darchelde: "Crow! Get your worthless hide up here!" MV ordered in a field command voice down the length of the dark tunnel.

It never ceased to amuse him, the mysterious vagaries of human nature that would inspire the likes of Prince Marseth Ghandorjien, otherwise known as Crow—heir to a fiercely independent island, and effective leader of an underground resistance group that Llyenthur had felt enough of a bother to turn his attention to personally—with zeal and gratitude to be treated as MV's personal dogsbody.

Any time the Marloven teens showed signs of arguing, he gave them a rough run and then, when they were exhausted to the point of nausea, he favored them one of his most inspired dressing-downs, well-punctuated with choice insults.

He'd meant to instill some self-discipline while keeping the Marloven teens out of the way during Adam's lessons in melding into a circle, but what he got was unwavering hero-worship. The more sarcastic he became, the more they lapped it up. He shrugged and accepted it because he knew that he could keep the peace much easier as leader than as a visitor.

He'd resisted it as long as possible with Crow, though. The Marlovens were already loyal to Senrid right down to the bone; they regarded MV in the light of a training master. Crow was a different problem. He really was looking for a hero, and MV resented Detlev for convincing Mildred to bring Crow along. All very well to blab about powerful untrained talents, and the desperate need for same. MV hated posing as someone's hero.

But that second night in Darchelde, Adam drifted up next to him, seemingly absorbed in loading pan-fried potatoes and onions onto his plate, and murmured, "It could so easily have been Imry. Would have been, without Mildred."

Adam was always right about these things, damn him.

MV thought about it all night, and the next morning decided, all right, if he had to be hero, the teenage tough was going to sweat for it.

As soon as the light was up, he assigned Crow as his own partner, and they embarked on an exhausting set of chores and exercises that were going to eventually straighten out that warped body. The mis-healed bones couldn't be helped—at least, not now—but mind and muscle and finally tendon could only benefit. And at the same time, channel that enormous strength, both physical and mental, into better training.

After a few days of this, Crow's squinting eyes were open in expectation when MV glanced his way.

He jabbed a finger at Crow, Marend, and Rom. "Cam sent word. Delivery ready, but Norsundrian action is up since the burnings. We're going to scout the border garrison. And if they so much as sniff one of you, I'll gut you first."

Crow was the first one up the tunnel before the threat had died away.

When they returned, each loaded down with supplies, they found a hot dinner and a row of eager faces waiting in anticipation. Scrapping had become the after-dinner activity ever since that first run.

MV lounged back, pulled one of his own knives to trim his nails, and heaped abuse on the sweaty, fatigue-swimming heads of Ramond and Crow as they squared off for their second session of unarmed combat. They were grunting through some tricky holds when, unexpectedly, Senrid walked in, and lifted a hand in greeting.

A great clamor of welcome went up from the Marlovens, and for once they abandoned their joy in lethal endeavor to plop down before the fire and demand his news. Kelsan thoughtfully brought him a loaded plate, and Senrid smacked into it before saying a word.

After he'd taken the edge off of what had obviously been an appetite of appreciable size, he said, "Goes like this." Talking in a nasal, gossipy voice, "Have you heard the news? It's not just us. It's everyone. And you know, they're saying that the king of Sartor was forced by the Norsundrians to start the first fire. Not that *I* believe it, but that's what *they're* saying. What're we going to *do*?"

Mildred nodded. "Yes. Me, I think this is not a new plan."

"Started in spring," MV drawled. "Soon's one of those damned birds spotted the first fields cleared out in the middle of nowhere."

Dirk said, "I didn't think Llyenthur was that smart—Kessler thinks he's an idiot."

"Everyone says," Andri repeated. "Bets on who got those rumors about the King of Sartor going?" He frowned. "Is it Rel or Sartor getting this kind of treatment?"

"Both," Adam and MV said at the same time.

Dirk glowered. "Are people so desperate for rescue because they've given up on rescuing themselves?"

"Maybe." MV leaned over, carefully selected a slice of carrot from Senrid's plate, and popped it into his mouth. "What's definite is that Imry set Rel up as a straw figure." He turned to Senrid. "What about the forge?"

"They trashed it," Senrid said. "We got some ore out first. Not nearly enough, of course."

"Getting weapons is next?" Dirk asked. "Ore isn't going to turn into swords without fire, magic, and banging hammers."

Senrid shrugged. "For now, back to the old plan. Raid the garrison armories ahead of the general attack, whenever that happens. The problem with that is, some of 'em don't keep weapons stored there, just in case. Magic transfer brings 'em when they need 'em. We break in, find nothing. And meanwhile they know where we are, and that we're about to act." He waved a hand. "But that's for later. MV? What's first for us?"

Sveneric, who had been watching them all with his impenetrable gaze, drifted toward the writing table. Adam watched from the kitchen archway.

MV sat back and resumed trimming his nails. "What we have," he said, "is time. That is, it's our sense of time— something we're used to. What the Host has is the burden of time, which they are not at all used to. That means they're going to strike sooner than later, and we're going to have to be ready when it comes. Which is why we're here." He pointed at them, then drew a circle in the air.

Silence.

"Time-malaise is hitting our friends from Norsunder hard," MV went on. "Not that we can count on any weakness, not from Ilerian. Or Svir. The others—" He shrugged. "David thinks Efael, who is already way outside the boundaries of what even Wan-Edhe of the Chwahir would call sane, is worsening fast. To ward it, he's got to find action, or make it—currently he's assing around Everon."

Adam said, watching Sveneric, "Detlev concurs."

"Where is David in all this?" Senrid asked. "Isn't he supposed to be here, with us, learning this Dena Yeresbeth attack circle?"

MV tossed the knife up into the air, and caught it with the other hand. "He's far beyond you shitbirds, so he's running his own plan. He thinks Efael's next mad action will be to go after

Imry's command. David plans to be there when it happens, if he can."

"Where?"

"Why?"

"How?"

Three voices spoke at once—none of them Sveneric's.

MV grinned. "Where? Not in Imar, don't worry. David's reckless, but he's not witless. As for how and why, I can't tell you, but I suspect the answer goes back ten or fifteen years."

Sveneric lifted his head. "It goes back four thousand years." Then he went back to writing.

MV tossed his knife, watching the fire gleam on its edge before catching it. He sent an glance Adam's way, then said, "What we can be sure of is, it won't happen here. So our job is to get ourselves in shape for our attack on Ilerian. That's covert. No one to know—*no* one. More overtly, we're here in case Aldon does turn up in Marloven Hess. If Efael turfs Imry out, he'll let Aldon come here and chew up the kingdom while he builds another army. As for long-term..."

"War with the Host," Dirk said.

MV snapped his fingers, then drew a circle. "Now that Senrid's back, let's get busy on that."

Three

Darchelde – Marloven Hess to Erdrael Danara's Border

CLOSE TO THE END of Tenth-month, Sveneric went out to do warmups on his own. Nothing unusual in that. But he did not return that day. Or that night. There was no sign of a struggle anywhere in the vicinity — but far more telling, Sveneric was tightly shielded. He clearly did not want to be found.

A couple days later, MV and Adam finished a run, and entered the Darchelde hideout.

With a practiced flick of his hand, Adam sent his hat sailing across the main room to catch on one of the coat pegs. It spun once or twice, then stilled, looking like a decrepit specimen from a bad dream. "We're going to have to keep Zairna and the teens apart at knife drill," Adam said. "They keep sneaking behind to watch him."

MV grunted. "There's a lot of the Ildareth style in what he does, eh?"

"Except it's a different form."

MV shrugged. "Close-in fighting is going to have similarities. Thing is, I noticed Rom and Marend trying to mimic."

"I'll talk to Zairna; I don't think Senrid wants his youths turning into, ah, duelists."

"Go ahead and say it, Zairna's an assassin. A prince trained to be an assassin. Even Ramond noticed, and he's got the focus of a butterfly." MV collapsed full-length on the floor, and crossed his hands behind his head. "I wonder what his story is? Eh, we've got maybe half an hour. What are we going to do about the shrimp?"

Adam looked up, thinking of the Marloven teens still running through the forest. Senrid had left abruptly two nights ago, the day after Sveneric vanished, having received a message from Jan Senelac about resistance matters. And sure enough, last night, the two Methden gangs had begun to split again over some internal squabble.

MV had sauntered into the room where they gathered, saying with cheery brutality, "I hear you squabbling like five-year-olds. You must be bored. Certainly look flabby. Tell you what. We'll all have a brisk forest run come morning. Always clears the head. I'll set the course tonight. So I suggest—" A sinister pause. "—you fade now and rack up while you can."

Midway through the night, Andri, Dirk, Rolfin, Adam, and MV rousted them out of bed and chivvied them out into the freezing air and over a course that would have daunted grown men, all at a murderous pace. Zairna Raadi, Crow, and Mildred split the Marlovens' patrols and supply and message runs between them as the Marlovens were driven until it felt like their brains rattled in their heads.

And at just the right moment for maximum demoralization, MV and Adam had pulled ahead and finished the course at a dead run.

"Hat's got to go," MV commented, staring up from the floor at the offending object.

"I just got the brim good and flexible. It'll serve for at least ten years. You don't believe Sveneric is on some sort of short errand?"

MV rose to his feet and lounged over to the table which was generally regarded as Senrid's desk. Sveneric and Adam were the only ones who regularly used it. MV's fingers rummaged for a moment among the neat piles of papers that Senrid kept there. "Ah. Here," he said, holding up a long, beige piece of paper. "I assume you didn't see this."

Adam's gut chilled. "Sveneric's?"

MV grunted an assent. "Senrid searched his stuff before he left. Found it at the bottom of the trunk, under his clothes. Said no clothes are missing, either, other than what he was wearing."

Adam sank into a chair, and pushed his sweaty, overlong hair off his forehead. He gazed at a point in arm's reach before him, and then looked up. "He's still blocked. Can you track him?"

"Maybe." MV shrugged. "Tough, unless he wants to be found. Got to remember, this past couple years while you were off world, Detlev made certain the shrimp was even with the rest of us on the run. Gone's gone, unless we can piece together why and where. You got anything from him at all before we left?"

Adam was silent for a time. Sveneric had never been easy to parse, even when he was very small. In the years that Adam had been away, the boy had changed little outwardly, but his mind, interests, and perceptions had altered to an astonishing degree.

Adam considered Sveneric's behavior through the past few days. Something had changed about the time of Imry's fires. The day before Sveneric disappeared, Adam remembered seeing him writing at Senrid's desk, as always on his magic-paper. Dirk had made reference to frequent communication with Darian Selenna, and Adam had assumed that if anything were extraordinarily amiss, Sveneric would correspond directly with Detlev.

Adam said: "He was watching me."

"Then he thought you might niff whatever's bouncing between his ears. Damnit! That ends the debate." MV snapped his fingers. "When I do catch him I am going to thump him good for bailing out the very day after we were lamenting our lack of numbers—and after he watched me sweating over my little lessons in cooperative teamwork."

Despite his concern, Adam smiled at MV's breezy inaccuracy about who was actually doing the sweating.

MV stretched, then cracked his knuckles. "Nothing to do but tell Detlev. Here." He slapped his hand on Adam's paper. "You do that. I'll start the meal. My guess is those brats'll want to chow and then crawl right into the sack after we finish with them this afternoon."

Adam sat down and swiftly wrote, as from the kitchen-alcove various bangings, thumpings, and crashings sounded forth. Adam sat back to await an answer as the tantalizing aroma of braised shallots drifted out.

Adam shook out the paper, watched the ink vanish—he

always enjoyed that—and saw the paper fill with swiftly written words.

> *Sveneric last communicated with me, by this method, on the 24th. More food riots here between the haves and the have-nots. Imry's coverts are more than willing to help tear down the ancient and corrupt systems of oppression. I am on my way to persuade Erai-Yanya to forsake her solitude.*

Adam studied this note for a time, then he took it into the kitchen. MV tossed down his wooden spoon, scanned the note, and then resumed his stirring. "Didn't say he didn't already know," was his only comment.

Adam said, "Sveneric wrote a number of notes on that day. Perhaps to a number of people, rather than to one or two." He frowned over the implications of this conjecture.

MV tasted his concoction, then tossed the spoon across the little room into the cleaning-bucket. "Done. Cornbread, soon. Nah," he said as they walked back into the main room. "Out of our hands. Detlev didn't tell me or Rolfin to go out and hunt him down, eh? That's as clear as he ever gets, when it comes to the shrimp: hands off." And to all appearances he thrust the matter from his mind.

Adam was thinking, whether Detlev knows where Sveneric is, or not, he doesn't like it.

There was no time to ponder this observation. A slam from above, followed by the thuds of tired feet, moans, and sighs, and the room filled with the staggering remains of the Methden gang.

MV clapped his hands, grinning. "Well! Fun's over! We'll grab a bite and get in some serious work."

Both were wondering if and when David would turn up, while David himself trudged up the last of a goat trail leading to Terry of Erdrael Danara's bolt hole high in the crags bordering Erdrael Danara and Chwahirsland.

The Danaran sentries on night duty were surprised—and alarmed—by the appearance of an unknown civilian proceeding up the lower road. By the time David reached the gates, the word had filtered from the sentries to the gate-guards, who issued out, swords drawn and torches held high.

The fitful reddish light revealed a tall, blond young man

whose tired brown eyes were quirked in humor despite the ring of steel hemming him, despite the late hour, and despite his own sodden state.

The guards took in his empty hands, the mud-soggy clothes, the rain-drenched, shapeless pack, and the leader's point lowered.

"Who are you and what business brings you here?"

"My name is David. I'm a friend of Senrid Montredaun-An, who I understand is your king's ally. He told me I might find an extra bed and a meal here." He gave the password, and the gate opened.

A day later, the gates opened again, and David exited with a young woman and two ponies. Right on their heels a stocky gray-haired woman came up, and all the Danarans saluted, palms to chest.

The woman, Terry's outpost captain, said to the guide, "Go back. I'll show him the path."

"Thank you." David kept his voice polite, and hid his reluctance.

The guide slipped inside, and the captain mounted one of the ponies. David knew what it meant: questions. Probably the sort he would not answer, at least not truthfully.

But the questions were not immediate in coming. As they rode the high trails and through the occasional narrow, black tunnels, David ran through his mind several potential and likely lies.

The sun followed its course as they toiled through the difficult mountain terrain. The questions still had not come; they travelled in silence, except for occasional comments about the trail, until the light began to fade with typical mountain swiftness and they found a good place to camp in a narrow pass sheltered somewhat from the cold west wind.

After they saw to the ponies, the captain turned her attention to dividing up the food she'd packed along. She said, "Had enough to eat?"

"Yes, thanks."

"Weather holds, tomorrow noon'll find us in sight," she commented next.

"Great."

She then wrapped up in her cloak, put her head on her saddlebag, and went to sleep. David, watching the top of that gray-streaked head, conceived a rueful fondness for the surly captain. You got what you saw, a quality he was coming to deeply appreciate. Jilo. Erol.

The remarkable Marga.

Before dawn he rose and stretched his muscles by doing Detlev's warmup. He'd thought she slept, but when he finished, he found her eyes open. She watched without moving, then got to her feet and packed her cloak away. They took care of the ponies, and set out.

The sun's light grayed in great, shadowed jags as they rode down a dangerously narrow mountain trail. Impossible to see the depths of the canyons yawning seemingly just beyond the curve of his sturdy pony's round belly.

Ahead, the captain's short, square form jolted along matching the pony's gate with the comfort indicative of someone who had spent forty-odd years, night and day, war and peace, riding pony-back along mountain trails. David, who liked the mountains, found some of these crumbling trails unnerving, but ahead his guide only looked around in pleasure, and once she glanced back to comment, "Pleasant ride when the weather's fine, eh?"

The sure-footed ponies wound down a treacherous incline, across an old landslide, and came upon a vast valley stretching many miles to the east, then bearing north as a result of what had to have been a tumultuous rupture. It looked as if some giant hand had plucked three or four mountains out of the range's midst and flung them away. To the northwest, on a high, black crag, crouched the mighty bulk of an ancient castle. Totally inaccessible except for a steep switchback trail, it nevertheless possessed massive towers and crenellations, as if all existence was defined only in martial terms.

"There y'are," was the laconic comment in the high, grandmotherly voice.

David gazed, but said nothing.

The captain leaned out, squinted down the trail, then pointed. "Ten days, it'll take ya, walking. Wish I could spare a mount."

"But not to that place. I understand. I'd rather not risk borrowing one, in fact. Thanks again for—"

Humor quirked one of her gray brows. "Just you?"

David gave a rueful laugh. "If I can."

"Your style." She picked a burr off the pony's mane and dropped it over the edge of the cliff half a pace from her pony's front legs.

David, distracted, watched the burr tumble into the canyon; he was certain it wouldn't land for half a day.

"Not a Marloven style," she continued. "I know. I teach it—we were taught by Retren Forthan, the best of the best. One of Detlev's, aren't ya?"

"As it happens."

She grinned, then looked across at the big castle, and grunted. As if everything now fit to her satisfaction.

She said, "Jass gave ya the signal in case you need backup?"

"Yes, he did. Thanks." He didn't tell her he would never use it. Terry's mountain rangers were good—they dealt well with bandits and badly led Chwahir—but Efael's Black Knives would carve them into pieces.

He dismounted, hitched his pack over his shoulder, and looked back up at her.

She said, "Jilo's rovers insist Efael of the Host lurks there, but none of us've seen him, mind. Maybe he comes and goes by magic, or maybe it's just rumor. I don't say I don't believe 'em, but I thought they were based over the sea somewhere."

"Imar. That's true. But the main part of them prefer to emulate a semblance of civilization. Efael prefers the essence of dungeon for his pastimes."

She thought that over, then turned her head and spat into the road. Then she took the pony's reins. "Fare well."

She clucked to the animals, and rode back up the trail.

Four

ON MIDWEEK MORNING, NEAR the end of the month, Sveneric slipped into the main courtyard behind a hay wagon, an easily overlooked little boy carrying a basket of apples.

Shortly after noon, he entered the map room, which was—a very rare occurrence—empty. He was standing before the map, relays in his hands, when Duin and another aide entered the room.

"Get out of here, you little turd," the aide exclaimed. "Jenk! You're supposed to be on the desk here!"

"I was getting more ink, which you should've—"

Duin gasped as the boy turned their way, his face immediately recognizable to anyone who had ever met Detlev. Duin had.

"That's—Detlev's brat," Duin croaked, stopping in the doorway.

"It's not my job to—what?" The aide swung about, and blundered into Duin, and Jenk lunged and tried to make a grab.

Sveneric moved so fast that Jenk didn't see the knife-hand strike to the side of his neck that felled him with a thud. Sveneric darted past him, and as Duin also tried to grab him, his elbow slammed with lightning speed to Duin's midsection, which disinclined the latter from entering the ensuing chase. An enthusiastic chase; groaning as he clutched his gut and tried to get his breath back, Duin heard shouts and clangs echo up the stairs as word spread as fast as sound.

As soon as he could wheeze out a word he gabbled the Detlev-alarm spell to alert Llyenthur.

Llyenthur appeared at once. "Where?" he rapped out, scanning the map for Detlev flags, and the relay desk.

Duin pointed at the stairs.

"*Here?*" Llyenthur looked around, his hair pressed in a mat against his skull in back, his shirt wrinkled and smelling of stale sweat from across the room. Puffy eyes. He'd obviously been asleep—and soundly, too. And in his clothes? Duin grimaced, wondering if that was the real price of command. "Detlev. Here?"

"His boy," Duin wheezed.

"You mean Detlev is not here, but his boy is?" Llyenthur said, sounding somewhat more like himself—and then he was taken by a violent sneeze.

"Yes. You didn't—" Duin whooped in a painful breath. "Have a code-spell for him..."

"If I'd wanted one, I'd have—" Llyenthur sneezed again.

At that moment the chase entered the courtyard below, and noise rose up to rattle the windows.

Llyenthur sniffed as he moved to the casement and flung it open. Duin joined him, and together they watched Sveneric outrun a group of guards who singly outweighed him more than twice. To Duin's eyes Sveneric seemed to move with dreamlike slowness as he emerged from a far window, landed running, and crossed with two neat dodges to some horses being led toward the stables.

One of his hands arced away from his clothing, holding a knife. He slashed at the Norsundrian who held the animals' reins. Then in a movement nearly dance-like in its precision he kicked at the knee of his closest pursuer, whirled and leaped to slam the side of his hand across the nose of another, and then vaulted to the nearest horse's back. He kneed the mount into springing directly toward the group of pursuers. They scattered, three running for the gate—

Llyenthur turned away to sneeze again. He said with rather hoarse humor, "Better control than I had at that age. And a mirror for Detlev's style in action." He squeezed his eyes shut as he fought another sneeze. When the danger was past, he said,

"You might spread the word, the next shitbird who sneezes on me is going to wind up wearing his ears stuffed up his nose."

Duin was still back one mental step, struggling with astonishment at Llyenthur's lack of reaction—of interest. "But it *is* Detlev's brat. He looks just like him."

"So he does," Llyenthur said dryly. He yanked his shirt straight, and as an afterthought, stepped through the cleaning frame installed in the doorway to the inner room where they took their meals when they had to work extra watches. "If there's anything left of him, I suppose we'd better have him up."

Duin turned toward his desk.

"Duin."

He turned back, his brain still refusing to work.

"The Detlev-sign means Detlev. Got that?"

"Got it," Duin said nervelessly, and plopped in his chair.

Mearsies Heili

Erai-Yanya was talking, her voice earnest, her hands gesturing.

Arthur, sitting with them in the Mearsiean library, realized that Detlev was not listening; the gray-green eyes held an inward look that was quite unlike his usual focus when others spoke.

Arthur nudged his mother. She faltered, and sent him a look of question.

The silence recalled Detlev's attention.

"Something wrong?" Arthur asked.

"Yes. But not here," Detlev said. "Go on."

Llyenthur's HQ

Llyenthur put down a mug of hot coffee and scowled at the beige paper. No messages had appeared on it since the words from Atan had faded. Nor had he been able to determine the magic. He was hesitant about writing on it; he sensed formidable protections.

How to break past those? He pocketed the paper and winced against a headache as the door slammed open.

Two grim sentries entered, shoving a small figure before

them. Sveneric was bent nearly double, his arms twisted savagely up behind him and bound there. The sentries stopped in the middle of the room and jerked the boy upright.

Long brown blood-stickied hair was flung back, and Llyenthur stared down into a face that, despite blood-smears and the fast-growing discolorations and swellings of myriad bruises, did indeed belong to Detlev's son.

He smiled. "I suppose you had a reason for allowing yourself to be taken?"

Sveneric jerked his head again to fling his hair back out of his face, though how much he could see out of one fast-swelling eye and the other with a long knife-cut above one eye would be difficult to surmise. "I have to talk to you," he said.

Llyenthur grimaced with comical dismay, and gestured toward the sentries who were holding the boy up. "What price did we pay for this visit?"

"Eight," was the curt answer. "Four dead — soulbound. Medics with the rest of them."

Sveneric smiled as well as he could with a split lip. "Why should I make it easy?"

Llyenthur stepped forward, reached down, took hold of the boy's chin, and forced his head back. The strain on Sveneric's arms must have been excruciating, for the two sentries did not alter their grip, but Sveneric's bloodshot and swollen eyes were intent and unwavering. Llyenthur studied that gray-green gaze, and then said, "You're a very pretty boy, but I think I can dispense with your decorative company, and — "

Transfer magic zapped stale air through the room. Efael appeared.

" — with your words of wisdom," Llyenthur finished, and sat on the edge of his desk, hands folded.

Efael's sharp face altered to cruel pleasure when he saw Sveneric. He flicked a dismissive hand at the two sentries without taking his gaze from the boy's face. As the pair let go and Sveneric began to fall, Efael took Sveneric's arm in a harsh grip.

"What has he said?" Efael demanded of Llyenthur as the sentries effaced themselves and closed the door.

"Merely that he wished to pass the time of day with me. We hadn't yet progressed beyond that point."

During all this Sveneric never once glanced Efael's way, but kept his gaze with a kind of desperate intensity on

Llyenthur, who picked up his coffee again and gave him a benign smile.

Efael said, "I'll take him."

Llyenthur raised his coffee in a flourishing toast. "You want to run him to Imar? Help yourself."

"Imar." Efael's face tightened at this reminder that anything to do with Detlev was on the Host's own short list. Which meant Llyenthur would be immediately tattling to them in order to claim credit for the bag. No time for fun.

He transferred Sveneric, then himself, to Imar to claim credit for the grab, leaving Llyenthur alone. He stayed long enough to finish drinking his coffee and to consider Efael's prompt appearance, and then he too disappeared, to resume his interrupted sleep.

Five

CJ WAS TIRED OF playing monster in the chase games. Sometimes it was fun, but the little ones always wanted her to be the monster. Not fun. She preferred hide and seek to chase games anyway. And sometimes she just wanted to run, with no sounds but the wind and the rustling of leaves on the ground. Not little kid shrieking.

If she was in the underground hideout they called the Junkyard (Junky for short), she started from there. But if she was in the white palace, and had to transfer down, she'd discovered that the lake below the Selenseh Redian was the shortest distance, which meant the jolt hurt less. Running from there to the Junky was a good distance, making a satisfying run, with plenty of leaf piles to kick up.

She transferred, and skirted the lake, as always looking down to see if any of the beings were around, visible as moving lines, rather like the facets of a diamond. The water was smooth. It was getting colder outside, which meant they moved deeper into the water, and closer to the hot spring in the mountain. She leaped over a boulder — and stumbled to a stop when she nearly fell over Retren Ndarga, who lay on his stomach, elbows framing a book. Jilo sat nearby, with his old, grubby book that Kessler had given him.

CJ let out a squawk of alarm, then halted. She sniffed the air, and promptly sneezed. "You're doing dark magic lessons?" she accused Jilo.

Jilo said, "No. Yes." He blinked, then said, "Not lessons. Working on a project."

"I'm comparing light spells," Retren said. "Light magic, dark magic, vagabond."

CJ forgot nearly being tripped, and perched on the boulder. "That's kind of interesting. I know that dark magic can make fire really dangerous if you're not super careful."

Retren nodded.

CJ looked from his gray eyes to Jilo's light brown, and then shivered as a gust of wind rattled the pages in their books, and drove leaves skittering toward them. "Isn't it kind of cold out to be doing lessons here?"

Retren looked toward Jilo, who flushed, then said, "It's quieter."

CJ was going to make a sarcastic comment, but she remembered why she had come down to run. "Even the library?"

Jilo said, "People are always coming and going. Even if they don't speak to me, I hear them. It breaks my concentration. I'm so used to being alone, with no noise."

CJ thought of Wan-Edhe's nasty castle with its poisonous murk. That was quiet, all right. More like dead.

She said, "What are you working on, anyway? It's definitely dark magic."

Jilo shrugged awkwardly. "It's actually to break a dark magic lattice ward. Wan-Edhe forces all his commanders to have this ward on them, so he can kill them if they betray him." His voice drawled the word *betray*.

"Right," CJ said. With Wan-Edhe, that could mean having the wrong type of bread at breakfast.

"Exactly," Jilo said. "I'm close. I think. It's … complex."

"You don't have to tell me that. I heard about lattice wards once, from Leander. I didn't even understand the definition, much less the magic itself. But, if you get the spell, how are you going to tell the evil commanders from the good ones?"

"Everyone will get it," Jilo said.

"But…" CJ bit off her protest. Supposing he was going to hand the spell only to the good ones, how would he even go about determining that, especially in this horrible war, where Chwahir were getting it from both sides? Anyway, Chwahir things were none of her business. She said, "But it's cold out here. Why don't you work in the Junky? Nobody goes there except for us." She considered what he'd just said, then added, "I could tell the girls to stay in the white castle for however long you need. They wouldn't mind. There's still plenty of room. And even if the rooms in the white palace did get all filled, which would take a long time, we'd just make a blanket fort in my room, and camp there. It'd be fun—and you can take over the Junky. How's that?"

Jilo's lips parted, but no sound came out. CJ did not understand the intensity of his stare; she had no idea what the offer meant to him. Nor did Jilo, who had longed during so much of his early life for an underground hideout. No, he'd wanted *that* underground hideout. No—he had come to realize—he wanted that one, but with all the companionship, laughter, and fun.

He got hold of himself, and as she was giving him a weird stare, he said, "Are you sure?"

Retren looked from one to the other.

"Of course! Oh, I'll ask Clair. Since you could say it's hers. Since she made it. But I know she'll say yes. In fact, I'll go do that, after I tell Falinneh to spread the word. How's that?"

Jilo swept his papers together and got to his feet. Retren also rose, his skinny shoulders high. He was definitely feeling the cold, CJ thought.

"Go on over there," CJ said. "You know the Destination, right? If you don't want to hoof it?"

"We'll walk," Jilo said.

CJ transferred before he could thank her—she could see the gratitude coming, and it always made her uncomfortable.

She knew where Clair was. And knew she'd be welcome, or Clair would have said so. But she didn't want to come unless she had something spirit-cheering. She knew that Clair would endorse her decision about the Junky, but thought she might enjoy hearing about it. She appeared outside Clair's new retreat, the rocky ledge above the rainbow-filled waterfall into the magic lake, one of the many fissures leading to the Selenseh Redian.

Clair sat nearby with her chin on her knees as she gazed down into the rainbow-glory mist. Her beige paper lay next to her toes, pen and ink beside it.

"Clair!" CJ plopped down next to her. "I've turned the

Junky over to Jilo."

"Oh?" Clair's smile was perfunctory, but it relaxed a little by the end of the tale.

CJ ended, "Isn't it weird how some things can turn around completely? It seems like a week ago that we had to sneak in and out of the Junky because we didn't want him to find it."

CJ watched that smile's incremental alteration, her own gratification measured against its change. "Nightmare last night?"

"No. Don't even have that excuse for this mood. Just a very, very bad mood. I don't know why."

CJ grimaced. "Too bad! If I had someone to pocalube—"

Clair's smile widened at their code word for insults, then faded. "I might be feeling guilt for being a creep to Siamis."

"Argh!" CJ's grimace was even more sour. "You have not been a creep." She grinned. "Believe me, I would know about that! You've just ignored him."

"I've been thinking. Remembering the day, just before Siamis came, and we got the word about that fire attack in Sartor, and what they did to Rel. The way Atan didn't react at all."

CJ rolled her eyes. "Yeah. But we've always known how good her control is."

"But did you ever realize that she does it all the time?"

"What do you mean?"

"Only coming into Morning Court when I've asked her to. And every time someone who has not liked some judgment of mine asks for the Queen of Sartor to hear their problem again, she always backs me up. Even if—I've found out since—she might have disagreed under other circumstances. They're so careful to adapt to our life."

"As they should be," CJ stated. "This is *our* country. Just because we're not stupid grownups—"

"It's the cost," Clair said in a soft voice. "Don't you see? Atan makes it look so easy. Much easier than we would, if we went to her place and tried to adapt to her ways. They don't feel at home here. It's constant diplomacy."

CJ's brow puckered.

Clair went on in a low, tired murmur, "I prided myself on how easy life is here, with us. But it's not, for some. Like Atan. Worse, she seems to have to hide how she feels. That makes me feel like a big baby. Double that for Siamis being so unfailingly nice all the time. And so very careful not to interfere. Like the palace is made of glass, and we are all fragile porcelain. Did you know, he doesn't even get his meals from Janil, because she already has so much going on?"

CJ shrugged. "They know we don't want anyone pulling any adultery around us. That is, they can *be* adults, but they can't take over. So? I don't think you ought to feel bad."

"But that's only part of it. Not all. No nightmares. And Aurora is safe. So I don't know why..."

Clair's silvery green gaze moved restlessly over the Magic Lake, as though any pleasure she had ever had in the place was gone. "And I can't go—or even mind-seek—to check. But since yesterday, I've felt rotten."

"Danger to one of the girls?" CJ remembered that the only one not home was Diana. But she didn't say her name, lest it bring bad luck. Her hand crept to her shirt, under which lay her medallion. All the Mearsiean girls wore them, made painstakingly by Clair.

Clair's fingers rose, an absent gesture, and brushed at the chain that lay over her collarbone. "I hope not."

"Have you written to Diana?"

"No."

CJ saw the pain in Clair's forehead, and knew she didn't want to lie to Diana, and make her anxious from so far away.

CJ's breath choked in her throat when she saw Clair's eyes go wide and dark, her complexion going chalky.

"Diana..." Her lips formed the word. And she raised a hand.

CJ patted her pocket, where she kept her beige paper, thinking she would sit right down and write to Diana herself. But then the import of Clair's gesture struck her—preparing for a transfer—and she lunged forward to grab Clair's wrist. "Don't. You can't. I'll go."

Clair shook her head. "But you can't get there—"

"Oh, yes, I can. The cave transfer. Detsie wanted it secret, but this is important."

Clair turned to stare at CJ, her face mute with misery. That terrible expression did not leave Clair's eyes; in fact, she did not seem to comprehend. CJ snapped her mouth shut, and since she was still holding Clair by the wrist, she magicked them both back to the palace, to the library. They stumbled forward, the reaction from a double transfer even so short a distance like being kicked by a horse.

Siamis and Atan both stood before the map. They fell silent at their appearance.

The moment she caught her breath CJ said, "I'm going to Wnelder Vee. We think Diana is in danger. I can find her by this." She yanked her medallion from her shirt. "Wnelder Vee is even sort-of close to a cave. All I have to do is sneak out. And I can do that."

CJ promptly transferred out before the grownups could interfere.

Atan moved forward, her face sympathetic, her intention to try to comfort Clair, whose burden was already more than anyone ought to bear. Siamis looked silently from one to the other, then left in search of Dhana.

CJ transferred from the Selenseh Redian in Mearsies Heili to the one above Wnelder Vee. The transfers left her nauseous, covered with cold sweat. The crisp autumnal air helped dissipate the reaction. Standing well inside the cave, she held her medallion with still-shaky fingers, concentrated on Diana, and transferred once more.

This time she fell down, onto soggy, mossy ground. Where was Diana? The night-forest of Wnelder Vee seemed unreal, its smells like something out of long-ago memory, and she did not feel the cold rain driving down through the bare branches. Blue lightning beckoned to the left as she stepped cautiously toward a pair of trees whose trunks had confusing, jumbled outlines, as though a person leaned against each.

Lightning flared, and CJ's wits fled when she saw revealed in stark blue-white light the two small, limp figures held against two straight young trees by knives rammed through their midsections.

And standing between them, his hand reaching for one of the knives, a tall figure. A male figure, in dark clothes.

A scream ripped from CJ's throat. She ran to the attack. Her voice blended with the thunder; she reached him as more lightning flared. The male face looked down at her, and she recognized her old enemy Laban. The years between this meeting and their last vanished and she launched herself onto him crying, "IRENNE!"

She never felt the fingers press the side of her neck that sent her sliding into the darkness.

Darchelde

Dirk's ears strained into the silence of the main room in the Darchelde cave. It was dark. Everyone was asleep. He breathed slowly, sniffing the air for scents and for displaced currents.

Soundless, swift steps. The beginning of the exit tunnel, just there. Ah. Reached it, and—

Five steel-strong fingers closed on the front of his shirt.

Blindly Dirk struck, a blow meant to maim, to be blocked hard enough to hurt.

A short, violent struggle ended with Dirk slammed down to the dirt floor and pinned there.

Behind, with a whooshing sound, the vagabond fire flared into existence again.

Dirk looked stone-eyed up into MV's face. Through completely free of rivalry in the give-and-take of practice sessions, he hated to be bested for real. He said, unwisely, "You can't keep me here."

MV's teeth showed in a smile of little humor. With his straight black hair hanging in fanged lines across his forehead, his bony face side-lit and his eyes glowing in the orange firelight, he didn't look mean, he looked malevolent. "If you want to leave, feel free." The smile increased. "But first I'm going to break every bone in your body."

Dirk made one focused effort to free himself, and winced as the implacable grip tightened. Pain shot stars across his vision. "Sveneric is in Imar," he gasped. "They have him."

"Yeah, and?" MV retorted.

Others emerged from the darkness, Rolfin crouching down to fill the hot water kettle and swing it over the fire that Andri had restarted.

Andri spoke much less trenchantly. "We know. But not why, or what happened."

MV added, still harsh, "If he'd wanted you he would have taken you along."

Andri coughed, then said with contrasting charity, "Dirk, questions of what is going to happen next aside, if any more of us bail out on disastrous personal quests, then we may as well give up backing Detlev on the Ilerian attack. Leaving him to do it alone." He ambled over to stand behind MV, who'd at least managed to pull on a pair of pants. Andri clutched around himself a blanket whose colored zigzags marked a bizarre counterpoint in the flickering light to his tousled yellow hair and red nose.

Some of Dirk's resentment seeped out of him, and MV freed him with an abrupt move.

Dirk got to his knees, silent with conflicting emotions. He dusted himself off and muttered, "Imar. I hate Sveneric being there."

MV's response was blunt. "Better he's there than with Efael."

This seemed to reassure Dirk a little. He nodded once, a reluctant nod. Then he glanced toward the tunnel down to the sleeping rooms. No witnesses in sight. "But. Imar. With *them*." He had trouble controlling his voice.

"That means your place is here," Andri said.

MV added, "Don't lose sight of the real goal. We desperately need all our strength. More, actually. And the shrimp does have one or two other people interested in his welfare."

"But Detlev hasn't said anything," Dirk whispered. "I didn't think he cared."

"Wrong." MV's mouth was derisive.

Rolfin glanced up. "Detlev's been prepping Sveneric since he was knee high, in case he doesn't survive this war. Might be he doesn't expect to."

Dirk looked appalled. "Then he *is* going to give himself up in trade for Sveneric? Like he did with Siamis?"

"No," MV snapped. "Remember, they lied. They didn't let Siamis go. He won't fall for that twice."

Adam sent a reproachful glance at Rolfin and said sympathetically, "None of us know what Detlev's thinking, but he won't act without consideration, and the Host will enjoy the wait, knowing how much it hurts him." He smothered a coughing fit, then added, "Go back to bed. While you can."

⸻⸻ ◆ ⸻⸻

Wnelder Vee

CJ came to, her head aching.

Memory hammered her into awareness. She opened her eyes to Laban's moonlit face above hers. She tried to suck in her breath to scream, and realized that she was held against the ground by a knee, and that a hand covered her mouth.

Laban murmured, "I did not do it. I found them just before you did. Morgeh Troiad just died, but your friend is alive. Barely."

The hesitance of the last word stung her eyes, her heart. He said, "Make it easy."

His face started to blur.

A fierce effort. CJ nodded, a jerk of her chin. Whether Laban lied or not, Diana came first.

Laban lifted his knee and CJ sat up. The two lay on the mossy ground a little ways from the trees. Laban had wrapped Troy in his own cloak. Diana lay next to him, her head turned toward CJ, her eyes open. She lay loose-limbed, the terrible wounds obscured by darkness.

CJ started to say something, to exclaim, but bit hard on her lower lip. She bent instead. As her face moved into Diana's line of vision, Diana's brows lifted, her expression weary, puzzled, at the blocking of light—and then relief relaxed her face. "CJ," she breathed, her whisper barely audible. "It is you. Clair?"

CJ swallowed rocks. "Home. Do you want me to get her?"

Diana's lips twitched in the tiniest smile. But it was there. "Let's—go home."

"Sure," CJ said, taking Diana's sticky hand in hers. Diana's blunt fingers twitched, briefly gripping CJ's, then her strength gave out. CJ held her limp hand with both of hers and she fought against the pain constricting her throat, and her voice came out in a whisper, "We're going home."

Diana's dark eyes gazed up at CJ with mild contentment for the space of two, three, long breaths, then drifted shut. Her breath went out, and stopped.

Six

LABAN KNELT BETWEEN THE two, his profile somber as CJ looked up with aching eyes, telling herself fiercely not to blub in front of a poopsie. Laban had already straightened Troy out in the ruined cloak. Only Troy's hands showed, holding his beloved instrument.

Teeth gritted so hard her jaw ached, CJ carefully smoothed Diana's beautiful dark hair, a thing Diana had rarely done herself. She straightened Diana's clothes, then sat back on her heels, refusing to look at Diana's face with all the life gone. She did not want that to be her last memory of Diana.

"Ready?" Laban said.

CJ knew what he meant. She swallowed the cannonball in her throat and jerked her head in a nod: Clair, and the girls, would want to know that CJ had done the spell of Disappearance for Diana.

They each said the words, and the bodies vanished, now a part of the world into which they had been born. CJ felt as if her insides had gone along with Diana, leaving only a shell of skin and eyes and clothes. And dripping hair. But she knew the pain would come. That much she'd learned when Irenne died.

She realized she was shivering, and within her cold, sodden skirt, she brought her knees up and hugged them hard, grinding her chin into one knee, her glowering gaze turned away toward the drips of rain from the silent trees. She tried not to think, or to feel, but the memories came anyway, and grief uncurled inside her like a flower made of darkness.

Presently, Laban said, "Time to move."

"I..."

"Don't give Clair two to mourn for."

It was the right thing to say. CJ swallowed again. It took effort, and it hurt. "Troy?"

"Three."

"Who?" she demanded. "Who did it. *Why*."

"If I understood Troy, he and Diana were not the target. The Black Knives found them, and assumed they were with Tahra Delieth. Who is rumored to be raising a resistance on both sides of the border. Efael turned up, and decided to play with them even though they had no idea Tahra was even in Drael."

Laban ran his hand up over his forehead, slinging long black wet hair back. "I was trying to catch up with a pair of Black Knives on the ridge above." He tapped his bow and a quiver of arrows. "I heard ... screaming. When I got there, Efael was gone. He left Troy and your friend alive. For others to find. I did what I could, but it was already too late."

"For others. To find?"

Laban said, his reluctance obvious, "Efael was, ah, making a gesture."

"At Clair?" It hurt so much to talk. But she had to know. The girls would want to know.

"I don't think he knew who your friend was. In fact, I'm sure of it, or she would be in Imar now, probably in even worse shape. You have to realize how important Clair is right now. His gesture was aimed somewhat at Tahra, in case there was a connection, but mostly at Imry."

At first CJ said nothing. Laban cast her another look, trying to find the right words for this girl he'd thought intolerably annoying so long ago. She hadn't changed. He had.

"Im—oh yeah." Her voice took on a little strength. "That Llyenthur skunk. Imry—that's what David and Detsie called him." Her fingers plucked at the hem of her filthy skirt. "Efael. Host scunje. Pl-playing." CJ looked up, her eyes fierce. "You don't mean like in a regular chase, like they did with Dirk'n me last spring, you mean—" But she didn't say the T-word, or wait for it. "I don't care what anyone says. Host or not, I'm going to *get* him for that. You just wait and see."

Laban said, "I hope you do."

CJ took a surreptitious swipe at her nose with her skirt, leaving a wide mud-smear across her tear-stained face. "But first I better get home." Her voice thinned with shock and grief. She looked around as though dazed. "I forgot. I don't know how to get back to the cave, and the medallion only worked to take me to Diana."

Laban hesitated a moment—a long moment—then said, "I can show you the way."

Royal Palace at Yalda

Elzhier surveyed her domain, and was pleased.

She turned from the window to Connanre. Her smooth, round face showed not the slightest trace of regret as she said, "No."

Connanre glanced over at Yeres, who perched with grace on the arm of an old, tall-backed carved chair. Her chin was propped on her fist and her head cocked as she surveyed Elzhier with a mixture of exasperation, and amusement.

Yeres said, "You have discovered after all a taste for thrones."

"A taste for power." Elzhier's smile was wide, but there was no smile whatsoever in her wideset, lashless eyes.

From her earliest moment she had enjoyed initiating trouble and standing back to watch. When Connanre found her, at the age of nineteen, she'd prided herself on being able to enter an unfamiliar village and within three days set everyone at everyone else's throats.

Ruling, she'd always thought, went to the conquerors—a role at which she'd never seen herself excelling. Connanre had never disabused her of this notion during those early days of training, and so she'd turned her attention to what she could—and did—excel in. Until Little Shit Llyenthur, as the promised reward for the long and tedious Rel exercise, had placed her in charge here in Yaldar

Oh, she'd hesitated at first, until, after he made known what he had in mind, he looked at her with his obnoxious smile and said, "Doubts? And I thought you knew something about the organization here."

She opened her mouth to deny familiarity with the

cumbersome maze of military hierarchy, but then she remembered some interesting info she'd nosed out the winter before, when she'd joined Red on his frustratingly unsuccessful search for the rulers of Hael Morvendreon. That search had remained a waste, but in tracking down a related item, she'd discovered two traitors to Llyenthur in his organization, busily working away midlevel and looking for their chance to strike and move upward.

Of course she'd said nothing at the time.

When Llyenthur made his offer she had looked back at him, and realized he knew. She laughed at his overtly smug expression and said, "Your occupation force really is answerable to me?"

"No one else. Unless I'm here. And, of course, any of the Host. If you find the company's enthusiasm for their duties a little slack, use your imagination. Try, however, not to shoot too many. Not until we do manage to retrieve Theronezhe and his minions. We're a trifle shorthanded."

She'd taken a night to think through some plans. The next day she'd issued half-a-dozen orders, beginning with the expiration of two careers—now that they were working against *her*—and by nightfall as she walked through the castle and listened to the breakers outside crashing against the rocks, she knew that she was in control.

Now she sat down in the chair opposite to Yeres and said, "Until the day, therefore, that the Little Shit decides to retire me, I'm going to stay here. If—when—he pulls me, I'll be happy to resume pursuing his bony back with a rusted knife. Unless—?"

Connanre shook his head. "No better offers. Not yet, anyway."

Elzhier lifted her hands. "Then here I stay. Working for you has been fun. And I've said nothing about your plans, nor will I. But until hypothetical is as real as this—"

Yeres said, "You did know that Imry's favorite trick for assuring quick allegiance is something like this? Put potential problems in charge of one of his better-regulated units, and let them play king or commander for a time?"

Isn't that one of your favorite tricks, too? But that's life in Norsunder. Elzhier mentally shrugged. "You think that's news to me? Anyway, it works. And it will, until the moment, and not a heartbeat beyond, he takes it away again. Or tries. Incidentally if that was his main motive it rather suggests he's onto you, doesn't it? Except for you telling me about Efael's imminent takeover—and everyone seems to be expecting that—I don't know anything that he hasn't already read in a report."

"I had thought of that." Connanre smiled, signaling Yeres with a glance. "But I wanted to hear what you'd say. Shall we leave you to it, then?"

They vanished, and Elzhier laughed, and rubbed her hands, as Connanre and Yeres transferred to the lovely summer palace in Yaldar that he had taken over as his own particular retreat—one of many royal retreats. If Elzhier discovered he was there, he'd move. The world was full of palaces.

There, in the tower room, he sank down onto the window seat and reached for his tiranthe. Yeres lit on the hassock at his feet. She was close, within touching distance, but he occupied his hands with the instrument. If he reached for her, she would spin out her games, watching him watch her. Was it the pull of real time, of inexorable day and night that made him just a little tired of her tricks?

Not, not tired. No. He wanted to bury his face in her hair. Sex and then sleep would banish, for the briefest respite, the increasing malaise. How long could they endure the excruciating weight of time?

Yeres leaned against his knee, and smiled up at him, her eyes too bright. In the strengthening light he made a discovery: she was drinking a poppy tincture against time malaise. He'd wondered how she escaped the languorous effects, but now he had it. She was combining poppy-essence with the poison called pepper-sweet by the Chwahir, and deathbrew at Norsunder Base. It was produced by a species of pine that only grew in high mountains. A drop or two added to coffee, it imparted a sense of warmth and vigor, enabling long marches, though the result was terrible thirst and the need to sleep through a couple of days. Dungeon masters dipped their instruments into a diluted mixture to heighten sensations, in particular pain.

Combined with poppies, it was very dangerous long-term. Interesting. She obviously expected the impasse to be resolved soon—and as usual was hugging her secret to herself.

Well, so was he.

She ran her dainty fingers through her long ribbons of shining hair. "Elzhier's out, then. What next? Another spy? Or shall we speed things along and help Efael?"

Connanre glanced down into her face, suppressing the

urge to take it in both hands and kiss her until she bruised. How could he love someone who was so profoundly incapable of love? Ah, yes, as one of his lovers had said once, it was because he was even more twisted than she. He laughed inwardly at the thought, and picked out a rapid, minor-key melody that shimmered on the heavy air. "It's not enough. Do you not see?"

She sighed, brow furrowed with annoyance. "No. I can't. Especially when I still do not know what it is that you plan to do when we finally get them running after one another's blood."

"We have one chance, Yeres. Just one. When Ilerian finds that girl he's looking for, he'll be putting all his attention into using her shredded soul to break the world bindings. Then we have one chance, and Norsunder-Beyond can be ours. We have to be ready."

"Oh, that girl again. Idiocy! And my brother is another idiot. Efael really believes Imry's plotting with Detlev. Why don't we make use of that?"

"Because somehow Imry seems to have figured out that he was being set up. We can only succeed if we manage to inspire everyone to action, but without involving us directly. Everyone. And Svir and Ilerian know that Imry is not plotting with Detlev. The connection—if there is one—is more subtle than that. Yes. There is one, or they would not watch Imry with such lingering interest." His fingers left the strings, and lightly brushed the top of her head. "Can't you wait, just a little longer?"

"While they find that girl and use her to break Kessler's spell?" She leaned away and tucked back a straying lock of her silky hair. A deliberate taunt.

He shrugged and smiled. She answered the implied question with a brilliant smile of her own, and then she transferred away.

And appeared in her boudoir in the Imaran palace. She sat down to gaze into her mirror. At first anxiously, then with contentment when she saw that it was still too early for signs of age to show. She might have to resort to non-aging spells, but they told on a person, and the idea made her furious with them all for their inaction.

"I have waited long enough," she told her reflection, watching the perfect shape of her lips. "What better way to hurry things up than by delivering Imry as a present for Efael?"

She smiled, then turned her head from side to side, admiring the smile. Thinking about how that smile made lazy, cold Connanre warm with passion. What a fool he was, to be so predictable. But he was fun to dally with. These days, he was much more fun than Efael.

"Imry is going to die," she said. "And then watch the scalded ants scurry."

She laughed at the image, and then again at her reflection, admiring her laugh. "Including you, my very dear Connanre. I've waited long enough."

Seven

Below the Seleseh Redian at Wnelder Vee

CJ AND LABAN WALKED for several hours, until at last she said, "You grew."

Laban did not mistake that for a compliment, but he treated it as mere observation. "So I did."

Silence fell for a little while as they made their way up the muddy trail. CJ looked behind her once at the disappearing valley under its long, low, broken rain cloud. "I guess this would be pretty country, when the leaves are green." She brushed aside a wide, delicate-fronded fern, and said, "Some of these plants I've never seen before."

"More rainfall here than in Mearsies Heili," he replied, wondering why she was yakking. But he'd humor her; he could feel her grief, so very near the surface still. The raw pain, her frequent unshielded thoughts about how much she dreaded telling the other girls—their bond—reminded him of the old firejive. Dead, he said to himself. Dead. "And some spots in the forestland here contain trees that are the oldest in the world."

She sucked in a breath. "Smells good." Then she sidled a quick look in his direction. "Easier to fight off creeps, I suppose."

Laban smiled. "When one is grown, you mean? Yes, it is."

Silence again.

Their footsteps were the only sounds, that and trickling

water hidden in the underbrush as they worked their way up the misting trail northwards.

Then she said, "Makes sense. I guess."

Laban turned to observe CJ's small figure toiling sturdily up the trail, bare feet caked to the shins with mud. Her head was bent, her long straight black hair swinging limply with each stride. They shared similar coloring, though no shared ancestry. What was she hinting around at?

CJ said, "How far is it?"

"About two days, by foot."

He was wondering why he'd been foolish enough to feel an impulse to waste two days on this errand, much less give in to it.

She said in a surly voice, "They must have had no luck in— I mean, they must have not been able to find a boat to take them to Dthel Rendm."

"I think they were not able to break the perimeter Efael established along the coast. So, yes, perhaps they were heading for this trail."

And that was the extent of their conversation for a long time.

He was hungry. And tired. There had been nothing edible to forage in the rain-soaked late-autumn landscape. He wasn't too bothered. So far, the transfer spell he'd lifted from a spy seemed to be holding.

He was surprised at CJ's lack of complaint. The air was bitter, she was barefoot, and she had on only her skirt, shirt, and vest. His clothing was much heavier, and he felt the cold. But his cloak had Disappeared with Troy, who had been muttering *It's cold, so cold*, nearly until the end. All those years of unreserved contempt for Morgeh Troiad's vacuous stupidity, his being such a waste of a person in a rank and responsibility he ought never to have remained in, and irony sank its fangs into them both when Troy had no one but Laban to hold him when he died.

A movement on CJ's part broke his reverie. A relief. Her face was visible now, pale and solemn. Her thin shoulders twitched earward. Bracing herself? For—?

"Makes sense," she said again.

He thought back, identified the comments and a question as a specific topic, though as yet he still didn't know what motivated it.

He said, with wry humor, "I did not release the Child Spell

in order to better swing a sword."

She said, with an accuracy that silenced him, "Less disappointing, then?"

The squash-plod of their steps, and the hiss of her skirt brushing past a wiry bush, were the only sounds. Her gaze was now turned up toward the jumble of rocks and wind-twisted trees on a distant cliff.

He said, "What do you mean by that?"

Spots of color flared in her cheeks and her shoulders hitched up another notch. "Cuz you don't expect to trust other adults. Much. Alliance, I mean. You guys probably never— ugh!" She made a horrible grimace, then whirled around to face him, her shoulders now right up alongside her jutting jaw. "I'm sorry about that time. In the Junky. About my part. I've felt like a double skunk for years. Especially." Her eyes widened, their blue intense, their expression earnest. "Since you never came back and told me I was one."

Surprise made him laugh; she had not gained some miraculous penetration into the pointless ruin that he called a life. She was feeling guilty over an incident he had nearly forgotten.

CJ's face was crimson by then, and her mouth began to thin into a line that he recognized from those half-remembered old days.

"I'm sorry, too, CJ," he said in haste. "A most handsome apology, but quite undeserved. In truth, I'd forgotten that episode."

She said stiffly. "We acted like you guys. I did."

"Perhaps," he agreed.

She looked up, startled. "Then it wasn't me?"

"Do you mean, that incident did not inspire me to leave childhood behind?"

"Yeah."

"Nope."

She sighed. "I've promised myself never to be a rockskull again, but it's so hard to keep it when people who've no excuse for rockskullery act like rockskulls!" She snorted, and added less trenchantly, "I did want to ask ol' Detsie, during that rotten mess last summer, but I never had the guts. About you, I mean."

"Awful business with Detlev?" Laban asked.

She gazed at him in surprise. "When Caris-Merian almost killed David. And then that hose-nose Llyenthur got his tentacles on him. You didn't know about that? I thought you poo—guys knew everything each other did!"

"I've been busy. Out of touch," he replied. "I didn't know. What happened?"

CJ told him, her voice taking on some of its old vigor. She added an increasing variety of adjectival coloration against the Norsundrians. That led, in turn, to mentioning her run with Dirk from Efael and Yeres, and her just-in-time rescue by MV.

At first she faltered, reminded of Diana by the connection with Efael, but a musing repetition on Laban's part of one of her better insults, and the comment, "Why don't you tell me? I'd forgotten how much I used to enjoy your storytelling—though I would have died rather than admit it in the past."

CJ gave him a brief, watery smile, and though grief made her voice break, he pretended not to notice, and gradually she got a grip on her emotions. MV presented through her descriptive style made Laban laugh. Before she was done she stopped in the middle of a sentence, her hand going to her skirt pocket. "Oh! A magic-note." And she yanked out the beige paper, and held it up to read the close-written words.

Then she uttered a gulping, unsteady laugh. "Good old Pilo! He's in the Junky. How Diana would laugh if only she—" A gasp and CJ flung about. She ran back down the trail.

Laban dropped onto a convenient rock to wait for her. He looked out over the valley, and watched for a time the march of clouds eastward. Other darker ones were trundling in behind. Rain again, soon.

His gaze transferred to the pale brown and silver-touched bare treetops stretching away below, to melt into mists further south. He thought about Fortnyal Roth, away to the west, and its empty throne in the dusty, neglected palace. A half-deserted city, once-thriving.

Home.

That dreadful sense of exile burned inside his heart. *Shall I revive the old claims now?* He smiled at a vision of himself dodging Norsunder on one side, and Delieth-adherents on the other. And—Detlev? What would he do? When Laban had been small, Detlev had been assiduous about keeping him from the area, not that his efforts had mattered. From the first moment Laban had stepped onto Wnelder Vee's mossy soil, he had known, body and soul, that he was home. Everon, the same. A feeling he had fought against ever since.

Laban thought about CJ's story, and (for CJ, in tiredness and grief, had forgotten to shield her vivid memory images) David's fading whisper, *I wish it was light*. And he saw the defeat in Detlev's face that had so horrified CJ when he said, *He will not last an hour*.

Laban shook his head, knowing that Adam could have used that episode to disarm him. Why hadn't he? His gaze dropped to his hands. CJ reappeared a short time later, face red-blotched, tears and dirt smeared over it, her expression solemn and determined.

"More notes," she said, raising the beige paper. "It gives me the creeps."

"This paper?" He rose to his feet and fell in step beside her.

"What was on it. Well. Did you know about Sveneric?"

"What about him?"

"The Host got him," she said.

Sveneric. No one had told him that, either.

Suddenly sick with worry, he wanted to shout, "Then is this Siamis all over again?" Sveneric was even the same age! But CJ wouldn't know. He bit down hard on rage, fear, worry, a painfully vivid image seizing his brain: Detlev walking deliberately into Imar to surrender. And the world would be lost.

But in those old days, Detlev had been alone. He wasn't, now. *Surely* the others weren't sitting on their hands? Laban wanted, no, he needed to talk to David. MV. And smothered a bitter laugh at this sudden self-awareness: he could rail at Adam all he wanted, but the firejive was still there, damn, damn, damn. Or it wouldn't hurt so much.

"Yuk!" CJ exclaimed. "What bugs me is, Sveneric wrote to me a few days before he musta been bagged, saying, if I wanted to get into action again, to remember my plans to go help out Erenlara of the Venn. It's like he knew. Course, at least he's big." Her fingertips whizzed to a point just above her own head—which was somewhat below chin level on Laban, not that he smiled. "And he's smart. And has plenty of Norsunderish background so he probably won't find it as nasty as Aurora would, or Kyale, or Randon, or—"

Laban interrupted. "Can you write to anyone with those papers, and the transfer is immediate?"

"Um, I can write back and forth with anyone who's got one."

"Can you write a note for me when we reach the Selenseh Redian?"

Pink-blotched blue eyes rolled up toward him in surprise. "Sure," she said.

He smiled. "Shall we try to make it in one day?"

They did—barely ahead of a sudden, howling, ice-hailing storm on the last day of the month. It slid down from the mountains above Helandrias, whirled around the bowl of the Sea of Storms, then smashed its way southward between the two continents, buffeting everything. Picking up speed and fury over the belt of the world, it smashed over the Olaran Peninsula, causing flood surges, then howled down the strait, the last storm before the current reversed for the winter, sending all living things, on both sides, into hiding.

Tornado-force spin-offs ripped apart the skies from Elchnudaebb to Toar, and from Seth Aron to Erdal. And then the storm moved majestically northwards, drenching the huge forests of the Nadeyv countries. It finally resolved into picturesque rain by the time it retired from public life in Peaceland.

The warring humans thus had a respite forced on them. Those driven to confrontation despite contending elements were limited to personal encounters. Others, on both sides, began to contemplate the advent of a second winter, this one having come upon them far too early.

The two who had caused this eruption in the usual weather patterns—Wan-Edhe and Efael—both withdrew to brood in the safety of their respective lairs.

The weather suited the moods of the Mearsiean girls.

On CJ's return, they closed ranks for a week.

Clair declared a period of mourning, and the Mearsiean people throughout the kingdom—to the surprise of many refugees—respected it. Though the mourning had been declared for a girl of no rank or birth, who had done nothing that heralds and poets would laud. But Clair had made it clear years before that her group were sisters, and so it was as a princess that Diana was mourned.

Atan and Siamis saw almost nothing of the Mearsiean girls, who respected Jilo's privacy in their underground retreat. At the invitation of the elderly governor of mountainous Ceram Aru,

Clair and the other girls transferred there. Siamis assured Atan that the indigenous peoples of those high mountains could effectively ward Norsunder. Even Ilerian, as long as he still could not get physical access.

Elsewhere, those with longer vision hiding in that little kingdom began to reflect on what might happen if the magical protection was to break. Some organized different sorts of fighting practice, and others organized dances and plays that people attended with a kind of desperate hilarity that underscored the fear closing them in, like the cold weather.

Atan and Siamis saw the girls again when CJ, who found real release only in action, turned up in the kitchens one day, announcing that she was keeping her promise to Erenlara of the Venn.

Atan watched without understanding these girls at all, as Clair herself helped CJ to pack a knapsack. "You have to take shoes," Clair told CJ, her hair blue-white in the low winter sun streaming in the window.

"But ... isn't it going to be early spring up there?"

"According to everything I've heard and read, spring in Land of the Venn is little different from winter down here. It might even be colder."

"Shoes it is," CJ sighed, as if condemned to prison.

Tall Seshe murmured for CJ's ears only, "We will watch over Clair."

CJ blinked and nodded, and transferred herself to the Destination Erenlara had given her, at the northern borderlands of the Land of the Venn.

Clair saw her off, then retreated to her lair in the outer cave of the Selenseh Redian, overlooking the waterfall into what the girls called the Magic Lake. She looked around, and then walked back inside, and called softly, "Siamis."

"I'm here. Enter."

This was their polite way of knocking, as no one wanted to rap on the gems whose edges were dagger-sharp.

"I was thinking," Clair said. She was a short, pale figure dressed little differently from her friends. "In Ceram Aru, maybe it's the high mountains. Maybe it's the innate magic of the people. You know they, I mean, the Arusians, who don't live in the towns, they're related to the Geres of the Fereledria?"

"I did know," Siamis said. "They were there back in my day."

"Oh." She might have asked more, but she was reticent around adults by habit, and her heart still ached for Diana — and for Irenne. "I sent CJ north because I knew she'd be blaming herself."

Siamis had been writing, but at this confession, he set aside his quill. "I thought that might be it."

"Erenlara will keep CJ busy, and the hurt will be bearable," Clair said. "As for me, I think I need to go back to Ceram Aru. Just for a few days. It seems to help. I can … see clearer." She tapped her forehead, a revealing gesture.

Siamis said, "That is an excellent idea. I doubt there will be much in the way of court interviews with the weather turning bad. And you know Atan will carry out your wishes. As well as let you know if there are problems."

Each thing he said was obvious, no more than she already knew, but he saw the words reassure her.

She nodded, but didn't go. After a moment or two, she said, "Thank you for being forbearing. With us. And for guarding the coast — I hadn't understood until I began to see wider, how much you have been doing, and no one seems to notice. It's the act of a friend."

He understood how much it cost her to say that, but it would never do to point it out. "My friendship is there for the taking," he said, and then grinned. "Your cousin Puddlenose has been making all kinds of demands — up to and including my scouting out the better harvest ales and sending them to the *Lheit*."

Clair laughed soundlessly. "That's Puddlenose's kind of friendship, oh, yes." She transferred, and Siamis returned to his letter.

The shore of Shevraeth - Remalna

Tiny snow pellets blew up the beach and over the remnants of tough grasses, toward the ice-edged stream. Darian Selenna shivered in his coat. Rel tried to block the frigid wind, but he could see how skinny little Ian shivered, bent with his head down.

"Are you sure they'll come?" Darian tried not to let his teeth chatter.

"I know that his usual patrol is oldsters." Rel had to raise his voice against the wind. "He might not want them out in this weather—"

Before he finished his sentence, a shrouded figure emerged from the blur of flying pellets, and resolved into a wizened face. Rel shouted the latest password he'd had, and to his considerable relief, was beckoned to follow.

On this side of the Sartoran Sea, time was measured by candles of different colors. They had changed from green to blue when Vidanric Renselaeus himself appeared, dressed, like Rel, in fisherman's clothing, his long, pale hair clubbed at his nape. Vidanric's imperturbable face cleared with unhidden relief. "Rel," he said on an exhaled breath. "Rumors about you have been dire. Also conflicting, which was slightly comforting."

"I'm alive, as you can see," Rel said. "How are things with you? My communications have been spotty, and ended altogether at the attack on the harvests."

Vidanric waved him and Darian to cushions around a low table, where a couple of young people were setting down hot cider and freshly baked bread. "Please. Warm yourselves. Eat. We can talk the while."

Darian plopped down between the two tall young men and grabbed up the cheese-stuffed bread with the ready appetite of the young, as Vidanric said, "You're not the only one. We had to cease communications for a time, and go covert."

"The mysterious big search?" Rel asked.

"Yes—rumor was consistent they were looking for a teenage girl, though no reasons were given. That had scarcely ended when they came back at us with the harvest burnings."

"Was it bad here?"

"Not as bad as it could have been. I'd been skeptical from the start, largely because of the word about the birds forced to spy. As a precautionary measure, we cleared and planted cabbages and carrots in some remoter areas, but our real harvest was conducted on the sun side of the upper slopes beyond Hill Folk territory. Meliara thinks the Hill Folk had a way of warding the spy birds. We didn't do badly."

"Excellent." Rel said nothing about Sartor, but Vidanric knew that the brunt of the burnings had been borne by them, and next by Colend and Khanerenth. When he perceived that Rel was not going to say anything, including about how he got so battered-looking, Vidanric mercifully changed the subject.

"We've not had any rescues since Seventh-month, except for two false ones, but both times Siamis's Ferret surfaced in time to warn us, then vanished again. He's not been here since. I hope he's safe?"

Rel opened his hands. "I never saw him, not once. I just know that Siamis promised Atan he would be effective, watching your relay from afar. It seems to have been true."

"Indeed," Vidanric said, his gaze straying to Darian.

Rel interpreted the unasked question. "This is Darian Selenna of Sarendan. I came to ask if you could hide him for a time. In trade, he will be able to keep you apprised of the latest plans. He has a magic-paper that will reach Atan. Among others. Darian will explain."

Vidanric raised his voice to summon one of the youngsters, who was much of an age with Darian. At Vidanric's behest, she took Darian off to another part of the low, rambling house they'd been brought to.

Vidanric said, "He'll get a bath if he wants one—there's a hot spring in the basement—and some rest. We'll leave later tonight, under cover of the last of the storm. Selenna. Relation to the ruling family?"

"He's the last of that family," Rel said.

Vidanric lowered his gaze, shaking his head. "Something we'll hear too often."

"You and your relay have saved more than we'd hoped," Rel said.

"Not enough," Vidanric replied. "Never enough."

"Darian could have gone to the morvende—he has the passes—but his friend Dirk Sonscarna doesn't. He'll tell you more if Dirk does come."

"We'll find room for him," Vidanric promised.

"Also, on a personal note, Atan wished me to congratulate you on the birth of your child, and asked me to gather any details you wish to pass on. She could use some good news."

Vidanric smiled. "Her name is Oria, and she flourishes." He paused, considering what else he could say. Oria had been odd from birth—a very good baby, unnervingly so. They were fairly certain that she had that Dena Yeresbeth that seemed to be showing up in some of the younger generation, and she definitely knew the Hill Folk in a way that no one else did, young as she was. Meliara was convinced this was a result of Oria being immersed in a magical pool not long before she was born.

But there was no proving any of that yet, and anyway, people really did not want a long catalogue of infant accomplishments unless they specifically asked. He finished by saying. "I hope Atan will meet her, sooner than later. Which is my subtle way of asking what plans are being discussed?"

Rel said, "I'm not really at the center of things."

Vidanric laughed. "You are far more than I am."

"But not in magical affairs, and those are becoming increasingly important. One thing Atan has passed along through Darian: those mages I mentioned believe that a significant action must take place within the next year. Perhaps will be forced on us. We need to be ready."

Vidanric's brows flicked upward. "I had to ask."

Rel rose, aware that vagabond magic was at its peak at the moment. He would be able to transfer himself, at least as far as Ryadas, the north coast of Sartor. "I think I can sum it all up in these words: stand by."

Eight

Darchelde

WINTER HAD ESSAYED A first, early blast when Laban walked into Darchelde hideout.

He ignored the strange faces and looked straight at MV, reaching on the mental plane: *Detlev's not going to surrender himself, is he?*

: Not so far. We're talking contingencies.

The Methden teens took one look at that dashing figure, and at the unfeigned welcome expressed by Detlev's Own, and their martial anticipations kindled the fiercer.

MV surprised his admirers by his sudden, gleeful talkativeness. Most of it insults, of course, but he couldn't seem to shut up. Adam said nothing, but everyone felt his elation—whether they were aware of it or not.

When the noise died down, MV said, "And just in time. I hear sleet."

"Noooo!" Sindan cried, ahead of the rest—by now they knew what was coming.

MV widened his eyes. "Is Svir going to ask us if the weather suits us when he attacks? I think not." He scowled at Laban. "Let's see what kind of shape you're in. You can lead." And to the rest, "Everybody, out!"

Larkadhe to Imar

Well into the eleventh month, as the storm-caused lull in action created a lull in administrative reaction, Llyenthur looked at his empty desk, and out at the muddy, melting slush in the empty courtyard, and decided he may as well get it over with. There had been no messages whatever from Imar. No contact, even. The lack of information about Detlev's boy meant he was to find out himself.

Svir, he suspected, had limits to his patience.

He threw down his pen and transferred to Imar, arriving in the parlor room that served as Destination for any who sought—or were brought—to interview with the Host.

The time was early evening. A scene of domestic coziness met his eyes. Sveneric and Svir sat in two wingchairs before a leaping fire. A rug had been spread over Sveneric's knees. Ilerian stood behind Svir's chair, his attention wholly on Sveneric, who was talking. Detlev's brat appeared to be quite animated; his hands were up and gesturing, one bandaged, the other with long tapered fingers that called his cousin Siamis to mind.

As Llyenthur came forward, he saw one of the thin hands tremble, and he looked again at Sveneric's face. He was now close enough to perceive that what he'd taken as animation was in fact a high fever.

Svir appeared to be enjoying himself very much. His black eyes narrowed with expectant humor. "Imry. Welcome."

Sveneric's hands dropped into his lap, and he leaned back silently in his chair.

"Have you met Sfenaraec? I do not think you have."

"My name is Sveneric," Detlev's brat interrupted. "Slightly modernized version of my aunt Sfenrael's name. Why would my father name me for an ill-natured fool?"

Svir's quick, appreciative laugh made Llyenthur suspect some private joke.

"Why would he indeed," the Lord of the Host said. "Imry. You have missed some singular discussions."

'Perhaps, but you'll have to remember that I've heard years' worth of the original that the brat is no doubt parroting." Llyenthur stopped by Sveneric's chair in order to better study his face; though the room appeared to be well lit, the lighting was distorted, a physical testimony to the steady drain of power that Ilerian exerted in order to ward time malaise.

Llyenthur looked down at Sveneric's wasted flesh, his bruised-looking eyes, and the hectic coloring of continual fever. His lips were dark and cracked. "By the way," he commented, casting an ironic glance at the two on the other side of the fire. "Have you put your mark on him?"

Svir's brows slanted up. It was obvious that this particular escape had bypassed him completely.

Llyenthur, seeing the question, said, "Judging roughly, I'd say you've got about two weeks' entertainment value here, and—" He snapped his fingers.

Sveneric had wrapped a thick strip of white cloth around his head, low on his brow, covering the still-bleeding cut over his eye. Llyenthur reached to yank the bandage off, revealing the purple, still oozing wound. "—And then you'll lose him to either fever or these various contusions that don't seem to be healing."

Svir smiled. "We do not want him to die, do we?"

Llyenthur shrugged.

From behind, Ilerian spoke for the first time. "Not yet."

Svir still smiled. "What do you suggest we do?"

Llyenthur sensed danger, but one always sensed danger in the presence of the Host. They were impossible to parse; the only survival strategy was to keep their interest. "Take him—or send him—away from here for a few days. That should suffice."

"Send," Svir repeated. His amusement seemed to be increasing by the moment. "Would the place you selected to house David be suitable?"

"Detlev found that one." Llyenthur grinned. "I think not."

"But you've since found, no doubt, equally remote locations for your sporadic burrowings?"

Llyenthur spread his hands. "Obviously." And made as if to leave, but Svir stayed him with a gesture and then turned his attention to Sveneric. "Shall we send you with Imry to his hideaway? Did you not express a wish to talk to him?"

'Yes," said Sveneric.

Svir uttered a soft laugh. "Well, we will not know what is on his mind until you take him, then, will we?"

Llyenthur merely looked resigned, and dropped a hand onto Sveneric's shoulder for the transfer. The place he sent

Sveneric to, then transferred himself, was a small, plain, one-room house on a tiny island, furnished only with a bed and table and chair, constructed by a hermit mage long ago. Its one—open—window looked out over a rocky bay, the shore too far to swim even if it were not winter. The back of the house tucked into a cliff side, so no windows existed there. Cedar soughed on either side, the aroma blending with ocean salt.

Sveneric cast one glance about, his focus hazed from the transfer and from his own weak state. He collapsed full length onto the bed, and drew in a long, unsteady breath of the cold, pure air. And another, as his eyes drifted closed.

"Sveneric," Llyenthur said.

Sveneric opened his eyes with a visible effort.

"You do understand I'm going to ward this place? Attempting a transfer would be a bad idea."

"You're leaving?"

"I have one or two other things to do."

Sveneric shut his eyes again. "I'll stay. No magic on me, please."

"No, or you might as well have remained in Imar. Transfer ward only." Llyenthur hesitated, testing: as expected, sick as he was, Sveneric's mind-shield was utterly impervious. "Contact anyone you wish, but like as not you'll have either or both of them listening in at any given time."

Sveneric gave a soft sigh. "May I have another blanket?"

Llyenthur disappeared to one of the storage sites, and soon returned with a heavy brown quilt, a hunk of fresh-baked bread, cheese, a few apples, some spring carrots brought in from Goerael, and a big stone jug of fresh water. He put the food on the table and, seeing that Sveneric was curled in a ball and deep in sleep, draped the quilt over him, paced around the house laying down the transfer ward, then left.

The same day, on a northern mountainside, well above the line where most trees grew, Yeres appeared, shivering inside her warm woven yeath-fur cloak. She paused to look down at the blue-white fuzzy hem brushing over the snow, and she regretted that no one was about to see what a beautiful picture she made there. She could see herself: the long soft folds, among which her hair hung in waves, black against white. Her own face the focus against those ugly trees.

Alas, it was important that no one see her.

She turned her attention to the fine silver embroidery along the edges of the cloak, idly wondering how long it had taken to do the work—and what the intertwined symbols meant. Then she lost interest in remembering how much she'd enjoyed taking the cloak away from that red-haired fool before killing her.

Now her face was cold. How she loathed weather! But the trees she sought had to be winter-bound. And there was a cluster of them. Black, thick trunks, squat, no leaves. Drifts of snow piled up against the boles, shadow-blue. This was not fresh snow.

She stepped with care toward a likely specimen, her distaste at cold feet making her shudder. She bent close to a branch and sniffed. Her nostrils twitched, burned inside, and she sneezed out the strong scent of pepper-sweet. Then she laughed as she brought from beneath her cloak a heavy, black-handled dagger of singular make. Holding it with both hands, she plunged the steel hilt-deep into the tree, then slowly pulled it forth.

The blade gleamed with oily streaks in the cold light, but as she watched in delight, the wetness began to congeal. This, right here, was pure, undiluted poison; if diluted it would make at least a barrel of strong deathbrew.

It was oily, so it would take more than a day to dry. Best to leave it near fire for several days, to concentrate its potency. And then she'd see some fun at last.

Nine

HIBERN HAD LEARNED EARLY that there was a pattern to everything. You just had to find it.

So it was in this place.

She experimented again, this time relaxing the pressure of
timelessness around her, an effort a little like reaching
(handless) to loosen a cloak that has become too warm, and
sensed Theronezhe passing by. Ah. So they had to remain on the
same plane of timelessness to see one another. That was
unexpectedly easy. No, logical. *Nothing* here was easy.

She put her fingers up to rub her temples. It was more to
reassure herself of the existence, somewhere and sometime, of
skull, flesh, and hair than because she expected to ease the
peculiar tension due to too much mental juggling. She had to
think within the concept of timelessness and placelessness. She
felt as if she'd learnt it all an hour ago — too short for practice —
and had been using it without cease for twenty years. Juggling
too many objects to count, but if she dropped one it would turn
into flame and engulf her.

However, I am doing it. Enough twittering, Battle-maiden.

Hibern smiled to herself. She'd never played games as a
child, for she'd wanted to read from the time she first saw a
book, and then had wanted to learn. Yet here she was involved

in a hunt-and-prey game with Theronezhe. He did not yet know what she knew, surely, or he would not have let her have access to that library.

But now he knew she'd found the trick of moving about in this place of damnation, and he was exerting himself to find her. And she had to prevent it, and at the same time she could not stay on the run. She had yet another game to play, and again its stakes were death and worse than death.

Bereth Ferian... Eidervaen... Ferdrian... Thand-Ator.

If you thought of the cities with the poison thorn additions as they existed on the world map, there was another pattern.

She shifted time and place again, turning possible meanings over in her mind.

Then she mentally slapped herself. If she took the pattern made by that map and superimposed it...

Here?

Near Efael's lair – Chwahir border

David eased his stiff, cramped legs a trifle by shifting position a bit at a time, taking care that the branch he crouched on did not shiver. Then he sped up his heart-rate, again, in order to force his limbs to warm.

Snow. Months early. As if he needed any further discouragement.

He raised his spyglass and focused again on the inner courtyard, doing a brief mental sweep to count living souls. No change, as usual.

He settled in for a long watch. A week of spying, and waiting, and not the slightest hint of trap-laying, or perimeter reinforcement. David had been wondering all week if he had been wrong about Efael and Imry battling it out on Efael's turf. Except that Detlev had suddenly agreed to let David embark on this watch, when he was needed in at least two other places, in addition to working with Adam and the others on the Dena Yeresbeth circle. But Detlev could not watch this place. Even if he hadn't been trying his best to investigate ten hot spots at once, he was warded all the way to the border. Efael hadn't warded David or the boys, which indicated he still believed they were a bunch of twits, only worth grabbing for entertainment purposes.

Detlev seemed to believe that *something* was going to happen.

David sighed, wishing again that there was some way in. But there wasn't. And the air was freezing.

He forced his mind to clear of conjecture.

He would watch until Detlev let him know he was on a futile mission.

Above Mesendre Bay – northwestern Goaerael

Llyenthur transferred to the cottage on a lovely spring day, and found his charge present and accounted for. Sveneric still lay on the bed, eyes closed. Mind unguarded. Instinctively he reached for Sveneric's surface thoughts, and found music.

Llyenthur banished the contact.

Sveneric opened his eyes, which were now the gray-green of returning health.

"How are the ribs?" Llyenthur asked.

"Better." Sveneric passed a hand lightly over his middle; better in that he could breathe without so much pain, if not actually "better."

They studied one another as leaves rustled in the ocean breeze outside the open window. Llyenthur veered between amusement and annoyance; Sveneric tried to read David's half-brother, and though he'd become adept at sensing David's moods, and his intentions, Imry was opaque.

Llyenthur sat down on the window ledge, hands folded on his knee. He said, pleasantly enough, "Svir will want to know what reason you could have for an act of such monumental stupidity. And he seems to want me to ask."

Sveneric thought, here it is at last. He said, "It's Larkadhe."

"It's Larkadhe," Llyenthur repeated. He sounded patient, which meant he must be restless. Or wary. "Speak your piece."

"It was better in the old days, of course. I've seen it. Heard it, in Detlev's memories. The winds are right maybe once every fifty years now, if that, for everyone to hear, but it's much more frequent, isn't it, on the sub-audial level? The City of Enchantment. The people used to think it was the visual beauty that affected them so remarkably, back when there was more than the tower—"

"Irrelevant ancient history is what you wanted to talk to me about?" Llyenthur sounded incredulous, but what he felt was annoyance.

"But it's not just the visuals. Or the sounds. I mean, it *was* them, right?" Sveneric persisted.

Llyenthur lifted his hands. "Whatever you want to think! Was that it? Shall we return?"

The healing ribs made swift words difficult for Sveneric, but he tried. "I knew all along about Larkadhe. I said nothing to anyone because I didn't see the connection between you and it. But the harpwinds were the beginning, yes?"

"If you like to think so," Llyenthur said, and raised his hand for the transfer magic.

Sveneric moved, a flash of his father's lightning speed. He caught Llyenthur's wrist so he could not make the sign. Reaction, quicker than thought, made Llyenthur snap his arm free. And then, for the first time in years, color heated his face.

Sveneric said, "I was born in spite of, not because of, your defection."

"How reassuring. I was so very worried." The mockery was back.

Llyenthur raised his hand again.

Sveneric started in conclusion, "My father's gift —"

The magic swept them both through space and just enough time for the disorientation to wrench through mind and body. A double transfer was harsh. The magic flung them into the decorative parlor in Imar, with its weird, muted light. Bent light. And its still, scentless air. Sveneric collapsed on the floor, his complexion ashen; he was only superficially improved. Llyenthur blinked away the pangs of transfer reaction.

Svir sat in his chair before the fire, as if he had not moved. Ilerian was nowhere in sight. Svir said to Sveneric, "You look a little better." And to Llyenthur, "What did he have to say?"

"He wished to assure me that his father did not intend Sveneric to replace me in his affections. And I believe he was threatening to expose my secret vice."

"Vice?" Svir repeated, amused. But the atmosphere sharpened.

"Harpwinds," Llyenthur said.

Svir regarded Sveneric with a shade of complacent condescension. "I liked them myself. Ah, that was before weather and erosion marred the purity of the sound."

Sveneric climbed shakily to his feet, bracing for one last try. "My father's gift is clarity of vision, and he saw in you the makings of a—"

"Musician?" Llyenthur interrupted, before Sveneric could say the word *healer*. "Whereas I see in you the posturing of a promising dramatist. Perform for your hosts. I've things to attend to." With a careless flick of his hand, he was gone.

Sveneric sighed. It seemed that he'd failed after all. Of course Imry had to have figured out that latent talent, he just didn't care. Sveneric knew he'd been stupid, but at least—so far—he wasn't dead. He knew he would be safe enough just as long as he kept Svirle Treloar, Lord of the Host, interested. The press of time as they waited needed diversion, but the moment Svir became bored, Sveneric would be handed over to Ilerian to be brandished—as excruciatingly as possible—as a lure to Detlev, before he died.

It was his responsibility therefore to postpone that as long as he could.

He turned about, and climbed into the empty chair. He sat cross-legged, straight-backed, his hands resting on his knees. A mirror for his father. He looked up, and registered amusement and cruel awareness in Svir's steady gaze.

"Entertain me." Svir smiled.

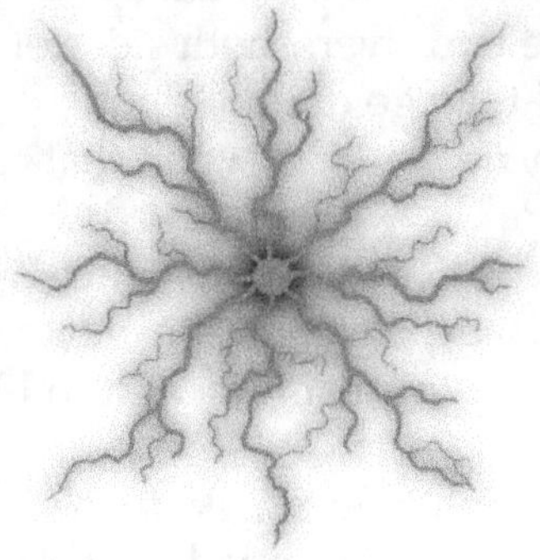

Ten

Ralanor Veleth

I MUST RETURN TO the day that Sveneric first entered the fortress at Larkadhe, and began to make his way up to the map room in the tower. At that time, on the continent of Goerael, a tired, filthy scout was passed through the hidden perimeter in the heavily wooded mountains of Drath.

When he finished his report:

"It worked?"

Those who knew Markham Glenereth best saw the briefest lift to his eyelids, the first sign of life in his flatly impassive face since his son Lexan vanished one night.

Flian Elandersi, widowed queen of Ralanor Veleth, held her breath. Besides proving to be a formidably effective resistance leader, he had been her husband's closest and most trusted friend outside of his brother Jaim, in whose thin, pain-lined face Flian glimpsed a hope equal to hers.

Jaim could sit now, after months of recovery from the terrible wounds he had taken when Norsunder sent that army under the black and gold fox banner. Though it was unlikely he would ever sit a horse again, he had made himself chief of logistics—a surprisingly effective one.

"Our Lathandra ruse really worked?" Jaim whistled.

Their scout, still covered with mud to the eyebrows,

bowed. "After I heard the grumbling about the new orders, I waited long enough to see Banth Fortress actually ride out before I slipped away." His exhaustion-red eyes widened in wonder. "All. Five fortresses. Called out to make a line-of-sight search between the two rivers, both sides of Lathandra, to close in on the city. And then go door to door."

Flian said worriedly, "Oh, won't that create danger for the people of Lathandra?"

Markham turned her way, his gaze less flat, though she could not read his expression; she never had been able to, though she had come to trust him, and to like him, as much as Jason had.

Before Markham could speak, Jaim said with some of his old insouciance, "Nope. We spread the word to make sure they sit tight, and keep those damned papers to hand. You can trust Pearl Vargan. She'll spread the word to be extra cooperative and helpful, but very, very busy. They'll find ways to make the search frustrating, but they won't find a thing."

Markham crossed to the trunk where he kept his weapons. "Then let's go." As he began arming himself, he spoke over his shoulder to a fresh scout. "Get word to the Dantherei volunteers to stand by. I'll lead that one myself."

Flian couldn't help herself. "Markham, can't someone else rescue their queen and consort? It's so far, which puts you in more danger. And you're so needed here."

Markham bowed, as always patient and polite toward her. "I'm afraid that if I don't, once the Dantherei contingent get their queen back into their hands, they will abandon us. We need them too much."

She wanted to argue. Her lips shaped the word *but*, then she relented when she saw her brother shake his head slightly. Maxl wasn't all that much more of a fighter than she was—he might even be less, after her years of marriage among the martial Velethi, who made training a sport—but he was here so that Lygiera's volunteers would not slip back to their homeland.

Garian Herlester, Prince of Drath, was their nominal host, as this series of caverns threading his mountainous principality had served as their rallying point since the beginning of the war. It was now full of refugees.

Garian strolled over to Jaim, and addressed him in a low voice, his usual drawl pronounced. Flian caught a couple of words: "...arrows ... horse cakes?"

Jaim wheezed a laugh. "Oh, Erishu has been waiting for weeks, with all her gang, to raid Banth. Prason!" He raised his voice.

"On my way." A young man called over his shoulder, bag swinging from his hand. "I'll reach Mom in four days, see if I don't!"

Markham's deep voice followed: "Wait until they are a day's ride out."

"She knows!" Prason was gone, and within a short time, so was everyone else who had been waiting for word, leaving Flian, her young family, and the other non-combatant refugees to another agonizing wait.

The same day that Imry Llyenthur brought Sveneric back to the Dei Manor in Imar, in Dantherei, north of Ralanor Veleth, Markham's rescue party brought out the aged queen and her consort from where they had been kept imprisoned.

The Fhlerians on guard, unaware as yet that this was only one operation of several, gave hard chase, knowing what would happen to them if they lost their charges, old as they were. Markham had counted on that, and as the chase showed no signs of abating, he and four volunteers — all without family left alive, and professing themselves ready to die in the cause — peeled off to help him to deflect the chase.

Markham had chosen the site in a very hasty reconnaissance. At a specific rockfall, when the pursuit lost sight of them due to spring growth rising from the old tumble of rock, they galloped on ahead while the escort took a sharp turn down a narrow path and pulled under a bridge, where they waited, hands to bridles to keep the horses quiet, as the Fhlerians thundered overhead.

The rescue party proceeded up the stream and away to safety, as Markham and his four raced down a gorge. One, two, three possible turns passed by, but the pursuit could not be shaken. They ended up at a dead end, on a cliff overlooking a deadly drop next to a waterfall.

"We'll make our last stand here," Markham said, pulling his sword, his heart bleak. He had not let himself hope that Lexan was alive, but now that death rumbled down the path toward them in the form of a troop of Fhlerians, he wished Lexan was beyond life only so he would not grieve. At least he had never spoken his heart to Flian Elandersi: he would never burden her...

The four, who had fought together under Jason Szinzar, spread out to give each other swinging room, and had enough time to draw a couple of readying breaths as the Fhlerians drew rein. The Fhlerians, trained fighters all, saw their quarry standing in a line, ready to fight to the end. There was no surrender here.

Five? Their leader, furious at being deflected, sent one of their number to race back up the gorge to report. But first the captain meant to obliterate the five before him. He gestured his troop into an attack formation that left so space to get by. Then they charged.

Markham led the defense. Though he had resigned his mind to death, his body stubbornly fought on. The world had reduced to the arc of steel, the shift of horse, the shouts and outcries around. Two enemies tried to hack him from the back, and one got in a glancing blow above his lower ribs before he nearly took the man's arm off in a powerful backswing.

One of his defenders went down. Markham fought on, though pain was leaching his strength; the enemy, seeing victory ahead, crowed and laughed.

It was then that a lone horseman galloped down the mud-churned path. The Fhlerians ignored him at first, all assuming this had to be one of their own, until two powerful swings — left hand, right — decapitated one man in the middle of a taunt, and took the Fhlerian captain's right arm off, sending it flying into the gully.

As quick as that, the balance shifted, the newcomer fighting with two swords. His horse was as tired as all the other animals, but that did not slow him as he fought with a skill that everyone on both sides perceived as a level beyond their own. It was the last thought for most of the Fhlerians. The rest were wounded badly.

Markham and one of his volunteers dismounted to check on their fallen man. He was still breathing. The newcomer went around to the Fhlerians' horses, still shivering from their exertions in a war not of their making, and stampeded them back up the gorge as Markham and his least wounded man threw their fourth over the saddle of his horse. Markham took the reins in one bloody hand, and they followed the newcomer back up the gorge, leaving the wounded Fhlerians to a long walk. Not far up the trail, they came across the Fhlerian sent to report, lying beside the path, his horse gone. Dead or alive, it was impossible to tell.

Markham, his volunteers, and the stranger rode a short distance farther, then the stranger halted.

"We'll go this way," the stranger called, and led them down a steep incline that no one had noticed on the earlier chase.

They caught up with a trail as spring rain began to fall, filling their prints, Markham hoped, before fugue set in. When it lifted, he found himself in a very tiny village of no more than six houses, bounded by ancient forest.

An older woman stood by his stirrup, looking up into his face. "We need to get these animals rubbed down now," she said, in Dantherei's language.

Markham tried to dismount and nearly fell. It was then he discovered a sword cut in one thigh, as well as two on his right arm, and one on the left. Besides blows uncounted. Inside a house, the wounded man was taken away, and everyone else sat dripping bloody water as people of all ages helped the wounded out of wet, muddy garb and brought out bandages and salve.

Markham turned his head as footsteps approached, and he looked into the brown face of the stranger who had rescued them. He was a husky young man, totally unfamiliar. "Name is Leefan," this young man said in an unrecognizable accent. "You are Markham Glenereth?"

Markham was going to deny the family name that he had lost long ago, then he remembered that Jason had restored his name, though he could not give back the lands or title that had gone with it. "I am."

"I came from your son Lexan," Leef said simply. "He's safe."

At first the words made no sense, and then the pain struck, sudden and harsh, driven by the cataract of hope that Markham thought he had vanquished. He stared, unable to speak.

"He came to Sartor, looking for Liere Fer Eider—ah, Sartora. I was the one who got him out before Norsunder could grab him. We took to the ocean. Landed on the north shore. Had to go to ground."

"Where is he?"

"In hiding," Leef said. "I'm sorry I was late. I had to find this bolt hole, then your trail. Anyway, I thought you might not believe me—I'd be wary of a stranger who turned up suddenly—so I asked Lexan to write to you." Leef flushed as he pulled a very crumpled letter from inside his tunic.

Dazed, Markham took the paper, which was damp with sweat. He struggled with trembling fingers to get it open, then cast his eyes down the page. At first nothing made sense. It didn't have to. That was Lexan's hand, and he was safe.

Lexan was safe. Markham looked up, emotions a chaos of hope, regret, and the dawn of belief that after all, his son lived. After jaw-locked silence for months, words tumbled out of him. "We parted angry—I did not at first even know he was gone. I wouldn't let him fight. He's not strong enough yet, and I couldn't bear—we left him with the young ones, and on our return, he was gone. No word since."

"He told me." Leefan dipped his head in a short nod. "We had the time, floating there in the Sartoran Sea. I tested him a little. Showed him that, yep, he has a ways to go in his training. And to get some size on him. I left him with friends. Came to find you." Detlev had said, *Keep it simple*.

"You did find me," Markham said, and now the questions began to proliferate.

Leefan tapped his forehead. "I found you this way."

Markham stared, understanding igniting more questions. Through them piped little Jaimas Szinzar's voice in memory, *You have to think about being a brick! They will hear you, the way I do!* And they had tried to concentrate on bricks, or rocks, or trees—but not while fighting, when all concentration had to be on avoiding getting killed.

Leefan said, "You did not ask for my advice, but I'm going to offer some: it's time to go to ground for a while, because the next one who comes will probably be able to track you down the way I did."

"And then?"

Leefan grinned. "And then get ready to join the counter-attack."

By the time Markham had recovered enough to read Lexan's letter, reports were going out from observers on both sides.

Having magic, the enemy got their reports first.

Up in Efael's citadel, when he heard that a major supply cache at Banth Fortress had been systematically emptied while his line-of-sight search was closing in on Lathandra, he knifed the captain who had come to explain that they had strictly followed his orders. Then Efael stood there looking down at the body, aware that he had not heard the rest of the report.

He turned away, shrugging it off; it was all Ilerian's fault. No one could think past this constant headache, and when was he going to gain access to the Beyond? He scowled at the nearest Black Knife. "Go find those supplies. That big of a caravan cannot vanish into thin air."

The Black Knife saluted and left while Efael flung himself into a wingback chair to brood.

At the same time, in Larkadhe, Llyenthur read the two reports that had come in so far. While he was studying the map of Ralanor Veleth to remind himself of locations and terrain, a third came in with yet another report of a raid.

He cursed steadily, then said, "It looks like I'm going to have to go take a look."

All the aides side-eyed Duin, who said, "But these cap-list sightings in Sartor. And Marloven Hess."

"The Marloven Hess sightings we can leave. Every infant and doddering granny there appears to resemble Senrid, these days. Aldon… Yes. Back to old habits. But I need to look around Ralanor Veleth before I kick some obedience into him. Supplies are tight over in Goerael, due to whoever this is biting at our heels."

Bergan, knowing how angry Efael would be at Llyenthur countermanding his orders to the Fhlerians, said, "Any of us can track down the raided supplies."

Llyenthur flashed him a derisive glance. "If the locals conveniently keep them tidily grouped, that would be true. But tidy caravans are for the conquerors. I expect those supplies are now spreading in twenty directions, the weapons disguised as beer, or wool, or sacks of rice. Are you going to go open every barrel to see if it contains arrows? I thought not."

He turned back to study the map.

Duin said, "Seems to be getting bolder. Three attacks."

"Four," Colleron spoke from the relay desk, where he was back now that he was more or less convalescent. "One just came in. Dantherei, prison break. They got away with the old queen and her consort. It's not Ralanor Veleth, but the timing seems non-coincidental."

"Dantherei is rising, too?" Bergan said, thinking of how to report that to Efael.

Llyenthur scowled at the map, then tapped the locations of the raids. The timing was no coincidence—three raids early, tying up three key bases, drawing possible reinforcements away from this fourth, whose rescuers would have to move more slowly, burdened with two elderly people. One of them disabled.

That suggested this leader had succeeded in spreading their organization over three kingdoms. Four, if you counted in Drath.

Bergan spoke again, trying to elicit something he could report to Efael, "Looks to me as if the leader is in Lathandra. That search…"

Llyenthur shut him out. The Lathandra raids were consistent, but all of them were small. A lively group of six, say, could compass all those. And every one of them likely a local with proper identification papers and alibis.

He transferred to Banth Fortress, and surprised the very few guards, who came stiffly to attention, guilt and fear emanating from them. Llyenthur waved them off; no use in dealing with them when he knew that Efael had interfered with his latest orders.

He only had to walk over a section of the supply buildings — while noting the lack of corpses — to see that this had been a job carried out by smugglers or thieves, whose entire lives were lived covertly. A military raid would have left the guards dead, and more clues.

He looked up at the sky. Spring here in the north.

Instinct insisted that the unknown commander was somewhere west of there. But the only way to be certain was to shove aside an already overcrowded list of emergencies, and spend a week there himself. As he braced himself for the return transfer, he mentally rearranged his day, beginning with landing hard on Aldon, then perhaps stopping at his latest hidey hole to pick up David's black sword, the sight of which always had a suitable effect on these Fhlerians.

Eleven

WHEN LLYENTHUR RETURNED TO the command center in Larkadhe, he found Yeres waiting for him.

He looked at her sitting in his own chair, posed with careful grace, and he didn't have to scan the muck of her mind to know that she'd tried several postures, selecting the one she'd think most provocative. Were she to sense that he found her as repellant as her twin, she'd never let him alone because that, and only that, would make him irresistible to her — and if she didn't succeed she would never cease trying to kill him.

He said, "Come to lend a hand? Things are somewhat slow."

"Slow. Very funny." She rose, and spun around. "Boring, yes. So very dull, the both of you. Efael is ranting and raving about supply trains. Come. Distract yourself. Have some fun with us."

"Fun?" he asked, sitting down and leaning the chair back.

She nodded, fingering her hair and watching his eyes. "Everything is so very boring. Before you took him away, I even spent a night playing with that whey-faced little boy. How could our wolfish Detlev have produced such a rabbit? It was too easy to make him squirm for breath."

"I expect that was due more to the four broken ribs, which

wouldn't heal in Ilerian's salubrious atmosphere, than to your nightmare carousels."

She wrinkled her nose. "I hadn't thought of that sort of thing. He didn't say anything. Well, next time—he seems to be back. But meanwhile Efael and I are tired of one another's company, and Connanre is rummaging about somewhere in Bereth Ferian, being drearily dutiful. Come. You must divert us."

Llyenthur's first thought was that Efael was moving against him already. No, he'd want to lay an elaborate trap to make sure of winning, which would take time, and he knew that Efael had been in Imar a lot lately, fretting and bootlicking alternatively, as if that would speed Ilerian in breaking Kessler's ward over the world. It was more probable that Yeres was amusing herself in hopes of playing one against the other, her favorite form of recreation. But there was the mess Efael had made, commandeering the eastern sector of the Fhlerians for his grand search, when anyone but an assassin would know you don't sent everyone away from a base unless that base is absolutely secure.

Llyenthur laughed as he let the chair crash to the floor. Maybe it was time for some elementary lessons in strategy before he left for Ralanor Veleth.

"Lead on."

Mearsies Heili

From an upper window Siamis watched the Delieth children playing on one of the white palace's garden terraces. He made certain that he was not observed, for he did not want to create any problems for them.

It was a shame that these candid, happy children were already finding ways to get around Hatahra's determination to bind them to her particular hatreds. Siamis foresaw grief ahead, for both Tahra and her offspring as their communication became increasingly constrained. He could not prevent it, for Tahra clung to old grudges so tightly that they had shaped her life, and now provided its purpose as much as did her sense of duty. She would not listen to anyone who could help her.

Detlev had said, "Look at her absence as a gift. She can do

the most good rallying her people in Everon. Use your influence to make suggestions for the education of her children, the twins in particular."

"But not directly. I can't even make suggestions through the tutor Tahra left, for she reports everything to Tahra, in exhaustive detail."

"But you are still tutoring Aurora," Detlev replied. "If you make the lessons interesting enough, she will share them with at least one of the twins. What one reads, the other reads."

Siamis had already begun in a sense, but now he made that a deliberate practice, with instant results, at least with Tahra's oldest twins. The smaller twins were too much like puppies; they were more interested in running about than in sitting in a boring room with papers and books. The girl between the twins, Madelon, veered between long stretches of reading and of playacting with Aurora, Clair's daughter.

A little while ago the elder twins had consented to take a break and play seek-and-find in the garden. Carl's version of playing was to hover over the others, providing comfort when the younger ones teased one another or gloated in triumph and provoked tears. Siamis watched, a strong sense of regret suffusing him. That frail, plain little Carl was only happy when her siblings cooperated. How was her life going to reshape when she had again to live with Tahra's unbending hatred?

A mental tug dissolved the dismal conjectures.

His patience had been rewarded. Detlev was back.

Siamis transferred directly to the Selenseh Redian, knowing that they would remain unobserved, with Clair still in Ceram Aru. Detlev had arrived, looking tired and disheveled.

"Report?"

"Roy is still covert in Fhleria, doing his best to disrupt the new chain of command."

Detlev gave an absent nod; it seemed he knew that. He glanced around. "The Mearsieans?"

"Spirits recovering as steadily as is possible. They closed around Clair, who is in the Arusian mountains again, though she sent Aurora back to continue her tutoring. Dhana still balks at acknowledging her connection to the magic here."

"A shame about Dhana. She could ward Ilerian from Clair more effectively than we."

Siamis shook his head. "Last summer, possibly. No longer."

Detlev considered this news, his mouth grim. "A new influx of refugees. Desperate. Running mostly from fear of a hungry winter, despite savage Norsundrian harassment all along the borders. Every local commander is cycling his troublemakers through to the border to run off their restlessness in lighter-hunting sport. Efael is making himself a nuisance in Ralanor Veleth, where I expect Imry will feel obliged to go next."

Siamis looked up at that. "If he's there long, I don't hold any faith in Markham Glenereth remaining undiscovered."

"I've put Leefan there to do what he can. What's the border situation here?"

"Puddlenose's Irregulars have been dealing with it. Any success with Erai-Yanya?"

"I convinced her that we'd had nothing to do with Hibern being sent to Norsunder-Beyond. But it took time, and had to be done in person."

"You know," Siamis commented. "I can't help wishing we'd trained Hibern to the treasure hunt. Or at least pointed the way. On her own she has outrun David in lattice studies, and she's a digger."

Detlev was too tired for should-have-beens. "Hibern comes of tough Marloven stock, and she's got brains, unlike her ass of a father. I'm sure she will survive. Anything else, we cannot plan for." He sat down, back against the cave wall. Siamis summoned the fresh food that he had paid a local eatery to keep on hand for his meals.

The summery scent of Sartoran steep infused the cold cave air with promise, and some of the tension in Detlev's brow relaxed. Siamis poured steep for them both, and Detlev held the shallow little bowl in both hands, a remembered gesture from Siamis's early childhood, so far away in time, if not in distance.

Siamis gazed at the spot where Detlev had stood. Of course he would not discuss whatever desperate action he was contemplating in order to rescue Sveneric: last time, Siamis had been the other half of the excruciating choice.

Sorrow, regret, even grief struck with unexpected strength. But Siamis was no longer a twelve year old boy escaping his tutor. He forced himself to turn back to duty.

Twelve

IN WAN-EDHE'S PRIVATE CASTLE perched on the Chwahir side of the border, Efael was drinking alone, brooding about the failure in Ralanor Veleth.

It was all Imry Llyenthur's fault, of course. Efael scowled into the fire, arguing with himself about when to make his run on Imry Llyenthur. He wanted to do it now. Yesterday. But it would take so much of just the sort of tedious preparation he least wished to do, while they were still stuck in the drag of time. And it would be a mistake to try anything while Svir had Detlev's brat—when Svir got bored, which should be soon, Efael very much wanted to get the brat next, and make it last. But making a move on Sveneric before Svir gave him the nod would almost insure that Ilerian would get to have him, and then there would be nothing left.

It was better to consider what to do about Llyenthur.

The room Efael liked best was one of those huge, windowless Chwahir stronghold chambers, dark and still air closed in by bare stone, impossible to adequately heat. Efael lounged back in a great blackwood wing-backed chair that had to be at least five hundred years old, one boot propped on an equally ancient table, and the fire to his right, as he contemplated plans that required the least effort on his part.

His surprise when Yeres appeared with Llyenthur himself was replaced by annoyance.

It was clear to Imry Llyenthur that Efael had not expected anyone. So whatever was going on was Yeres's idea.

Avoiding the chairs, Llyenthur sat on a corner of the great table and watched Yeres begin fussing around her brother, pulling the goblet from his hand and setting the wine decanter farther down the table. He sat where he was, only turning his face toward her. They held a short colloquy in their home tongue; her voice was too swift and giggly to be heard above the fire, but Llyenthur caught *Where have you been, Ereis?* from him, and at the end, *What's he here for?*

That was loud enough to require a response.

"Diversion," Llyenthur replied in Norsundrian. "Her idea."

"Admit you're bored." She addressed them both, posing with her hands on her hips. "I certainly am."

"Of course I'm bored," Efael said, sending a look of acute dislike at Llyenthur.

"Well then." Yeres threw up her hands—and Llyenthur missed the next sally from her fluting, tittering voice because he felt the faintest, briefest brush of mind quest.

Here? Impossible. Close by, maybe. Efael would not permit anyone with Dena Yeresbeth within his citadel, convinced that they needed proximity to rifle through the midden-heap of his mind. Llyenthur shut brother and sister out as, rapidly, he scanned the castle on the mental realm. Guards. Prisoners. Outside: nothing.

He looked up when something was pressed into his hand. His uncomprehending gaze dropped, and as his fingers closed around a worn, heavy hilt, he recognized an obsidian dueling dagger, in the old Ildareth martial arts style. Surprised, he turned his attention back to the others, and saw a twin to his blade lying on the table next to Efael's hand. Yeres had just laid it down, and she was carrying the pewter goblet and decanter to the mantle.

"So dull, Efael. Any more of that and you'll drown. How very tedious people are when they sot themselves. Now, you need the practice. Both of you. And I require the entertainment—I love to watch men fight..."

Llyenthur hefted the knife with unthinking habit. Yeres was trying to provoke them—to what purpose? Efael appeared to be in the dark as much as he was. Why this kind of contest? It was well known how Efael disdained the futility of practice. All his fights ended in death, or at least serious wounds.

Efael had once descended on the Den to instruct the group in the intricacies of Ildareth form; they'd hated him so much they made a game of being clumsy and stupid, until he left in disgust. Imry had secretly been impressed, but when he decided to learn it later, he discovered that the style Efael favored was an assassin's skill, mostly flashy speed moves meant to cut up prey before killing. *Cat-kill* was another name for it, just Efael's sort of game. But it was nearly useless against attackers from either side, behind, or mounted, and Imry had abandoned it.

He'd tried it again, just to pass the time, with the boy Yeres had brought around four or five years ago. What was his name? Lyal. Though the teen was fast—superlative training—he'd been too mind-blurred from Yeres's magic bludgeoning, and too angry from Efael's attentions, to tolerate for long. A successful switch meant a useful one to Imry Llyenthur. A mind-cripple might be a testament to one's power, or tenacity, but was worth little else beyond that.

These thoughts raced by as a counterpoint to his question about Yeres's present intention, but when his ears belatedly registered the word *lesson* from among her irritating titters, he forced himself to pay attention.

Efael shed that stinking coat of his, picked up his knife, and stood up in shirt and breeches and boots. Llyenthur watched as Efael strolled into the empty part of the room, his boots scraping over the uneven stones of the floor. A rotten floor for any kind of contest, much less this sort. And Efael's black clothing made him difficult to see. Were they supposed to grope about for one another in the dark?

Yeres muttered a fire spell and wall sconces high up on the walls blazed with new flame. Not much of an improvement— red, fitful light making the shadows jitter and writhe.

But without forewarning Efael attacked.

The fight did not last long.

Llyenthur shut out the bad floor, the uneven, smoky light, cold air, and Yeres' excited, shrill laughter as they exchanged feints and moves. Within a short time Llyenthur realized that for whatever reason—time malaise, or drink, or both—that he had, this time, the edge on Efael.

Then events fell out with near simultaneous rapidity, as his own instinct collided with Yeres' urge to assure the desired outcome by cheating.

Perhaps she assessed the situation as rapidly as he had. At any rate, the sequence went like this: Llyenthur saw an opening, and impatient of the intricate rules of Ildareth dueling, he shifted his knife to his right hand for a feint as he brought up his left to sock Efael a good solid smack on the jaw.

Yeres yipped a spell, blinding Llyenthur by a flicker of glaring white light in his eyes. He flung up his left hand in a gesture of warding-by-magic, and Efael's blade sliced neatly across from armpit to directly over his heart—and checked.

Llyenthur glimpsed blank shock in Efael's face before the sun devoured him; with the last shred of awareness he got himself out of there.

Efael looked in silence at the place where Llyenthur had been standing, then, hearing at last the cascades of gasping laughter from his sister, with fastidious distaste he tossed the knife so that it jammed into the back of a chair. "I know that stink. You poisoned it."

"Don't tell me you didn't smell it first." She danced forward. "What fun, oh, I loved it. Now at last we'll see some action."

"I didn't smell anything—it's too cold in here. You cheated in a duel with the black blades," he said with increasing annoyance. "And I didn't kill him. It was only a dragon-claw mark. You nearly blinded *me*."

"I had to do something, you lazy sot, or you would have lost. Go find him! He can't have gotten far," she shot back with angry scorn.

He shook his head. "I wasn't mad. You know I fight best when I'm angry. And I am not drunk, either. Just sick of this world—"

"Why are you *waiting*," she shrieked. "Fool! Stupid, stupid, *stupid!* I don't care if he's Svir's pet. Svir will do *nothing* if you take Larkadhe fast. I'm sick of this world too, and none of you are capable of any *action*."

As her temper rose Efael's rare sense of humor was tickled. He laughed out loud at her red face, realized she'd had a plan, and all unknowing he and Imry had ruined it—and laughed louder as he sauntered to the mantle to fetch his goblet.

In a fury she transferred out.

During their exchange, not far outside the castle walls, David ghosted down off a crag to investigate the flash of magic transfer he'd felt more than seen.

What was that? Fifty paces down the incline a human form lay, a silhouette in the softly gleaming snow. Another dozen paces, and he saw a faint red gleam on a belt buckle, reflecting the high battlement torches.

Mind keyed for a trap, David approached with care, to look down into a face he recognized even in the darkness. He saw the bloodstained shirt, and one outflung hand loosely clasped around the hilt of a knife. And as he dropped down to check the slow but steady heartbeat, he smelled deathbrew poison. He picked up the knife, and thrust it through his belt as he looked back up the crag. He calculated time, distance, and possible searches.

Then he said to his brother's unconscious body, "Want to take a little hike?"

Thirteen

Imar

YERES BLAZED INTO THE palace, her fury pushing back a colder atmosphere than ever before.

She looked around in dissatisfaction. Both Svir and Ilerian were gone—probably looking for that tiresome girl they'd been yammering about.

How could Efael be so perverse? Now nothing would happen. Nothing. They'd all go blundering on like this until they either went out of their minds, or dwindled into ugly old age. She was too angry even to watch herself being angry. What she needed was an audience. No, what she needed was a victim.

And she remembered there was one to hand.

It being late at night, Sveneric was in his room, stretched out on the bed. Exactly as he'd been the other times that Yeres had sought him out to have some fun. She did not hear the difference in his breathing this time, for she was much too furious. She remembered only those broken ribs, and grinned, because the brat appeared to be asleep. What better way to get rid of her frustration than to watch his reaction when she heralded her presence with a good, hard blow to those ribs?

She tiptoed up to the bed, raising her hands high.

Imagine her surprise when, just as she began her strike, ten boyish fingers closed around her throat.

Mearsies Heili

Jilo had given up trying to get his legs to fit under the desk in the Mearsiean girls' underground cavern. That desk was made for short people, so he'd ended up lying sprawled on the brightly colored patchwork rug in the center of the main room floor, his papers and books spread around him.

Retren was off somewhere studying. Jilo was alone as he looked down at his wrist in a daze of exhaustion and euphoria. Of course he'd used drips of his own blood to partially test his solution to Wan-Edhe's poison spell—after he'd attempted to poison himself and then try the antidote. But he'd only succeeded in knocking himself out, following which he'd had to sleep for two days, while Seshe and Retren insisted on sitting with him.

He'd sent them both off for much-postponed sleep, promising to sleep himself, but his restless brain would not let him until he'd risen, lit the glowglobes, and worked out on paper the lattice sequence he'd been half-dreaming.

"I think it works," he said to the empty room, breathing deeply.

"I think it works," he said louder. And then hunted through his pockets for the second magic-paper Siamis gave him, the other still being with Shontande Lirendi. If only there was some way to get word to him that he could use it…

Jilo shook his head, ignoring the headache that never seemed to go away. He'd better eat something. When had he eaten last? His mouth tasted like iron. Oh yes, Seshe had come down, and brought him food. When was that? Didn't matter. He ought to test the spell first. But how? He wouldn't use another person. But there was always himself.

He balked at laying the poison spell on himself, gritted his teeth, and began it—and the room turned white as he slumped to the floor, bleeding from the nose.

Fourteen

Near Efael's lair - Chwahirsland

THUNDER ROLLED OVER THE rocky cliffs and rumbled south-ward. A couple small rocks clattered by David's knee, followed by a brief hiss of sandy soil. Miraculous that the searches were sent out so late. He wondered exactly what had happened in the castle barely visible from the ancient crevasse he crouched in.

For now, he was grateful that he'd had the time to lug Imry up into this rocky cliff, smooth his footsteps, and get water boiling over the vagabond fire before he'd sensed the first search party crashing through the brush in the next canyon.

David tossed a few leaf-fragments into the tin cup he'd hooked onto his belt and settled back. Ironic, how his and Imry's situations had reversed since their last meeting. Not that they were completely comparable. Imry was not a prisoner in a stronghold, and despite the heavy dose of deathbrew, he was not in danger of dying, though for a time he might wish he could.

David took the cup off the fire, and set it on a rock to cool a little. Moving nearer to Imry, he smelled the poison again, sharp enough to burn the insides of his nose. Deathbrew, when very diluted, was often used by armies on long forced marches through wintry conditions.

From the smell, David guessed that Imry had been nailed

with an undiluted dose. The slightest movement would be unbearable for some time. Ideally one sweated it out, with gallons of hot drinks until the poison had weakened to the heat stage, then one could work it out fairly quickly. But David had no doubt that Imry would be gone as soon as he could maintain consciousness long enough to endure the transfer.

He had one chance. Best make it good.

Imry's face was still, his chest—already slick with moisture—barely moving. David pulled the remaining laces from Imry's shirt so that he could examine the wound, then thoroughly searched him. David removed his weapons, and was considerably surprised to discover one of Siamis's beige papers in his pocket, the creases indicating that it had been unfolded and refolded many times. No doubt experimented with, probably in secret, or orders would have gone out about the papers.

David had figured it was inevitable that his brother would find out about the papers, and maybe even crack a level or two of the spells, but why make it easy? He pocketed the paper, and stashed the weapons on himself. Then he leaned over and examined the knife cut more closely. A neat, superficial cut through the first layer of muscle. It was one of those Ildareth-style duel marks. David forgot the fancy name for it. Didn't matter—all of them basically meant the same thing: *I could have killed you.*

And that meant that Imry had lost the fight. Interesting. David sat back, tried not to think of his food freezing and soggy under its blanket of snow, and instead considered what to say, and how to say it, for in the intervening years since Imry left the boys, David had had plenty of time to reflect on how their early experience could not have been more different; David had been surrounded by companions from the beginning, whereas Imry had been alone, except for their shit of a father, until age four.

David eyed the still figure. Imry hadn't moved. Not even an eyelid twitch. But David sensed that he was awake. "What happened?"

Imry breathed the word, "Efael."

"Made his try? It was inevitable. You got yourself out of there. But by the time you recover from the poison, he's going to have you edited out of command." David clasped his hands around his knee. "I expect you can fight your way back. Depending on the whims of them in Imar, of course. For what?"

David watched Imry gather what little remained of his

strength. He whispered, "Why did Detlev go over?" Sweat sprang out on his forehead; the muscle movement involved in speaking five words had to feel as if he'd swallowed fire.

"Still don't see it? Here's what I find pathetic. Strive and fight, but you'll always be on the outside. Never mind. Whatever you end up doing, stay out of Marloven Hess. To the end of his life, Senrid will be hunting your blood for killing that little girl."

"Efael or me."

David stared down at Imry, considering the distorted memory he'd gleaned from Imry before he even understood what he was seeing. It had happened early on, when emerging Dena Yeresbeth tangled with the marsh sickness on Geth, and David was getting memories and thoughts and dreams from everyone, until Detlev helped him learn to shield.

But some of those impressions remained. Imry was four, the memory was distorted, the adults monstrously huge as Imry climbed into the lap of a grandfatherly man, chosen no doubt at random by Kedran Llyenthur as a practice target, in place of Imry's and David's grandfather, the king of Marloven Hess. Imry pulled a thin-bladed knife from his sleeve, and sliced across the old man's neck before the latter was aware. Then tumbled down when startled by a sudden spurt of hot blood right in his face.

In Imry's memory their father had laughed and laughed, but Imry didn't get a beating. For once. He got a honey-cake! He was all ready for more honey-cakes.

"Senrid. Saw her off," Imry breathed.

David grimaced when he realized what Imry meant: he'd placed the killing stroke in such a way that the child had not died at once. David was going to retort that anyone sane would see that as torture. But Imry wasn't sane, empathy beaten out of him, and trained to kill at a younger age than Senrid's little daughter had been. David had forgotten that dealing with Imry was like trying to pull a whole image out of a cracked mirror.

That didn't mean he shouldn't try. "No, if that's meant to be an excuse, it's shit. You could have tossed that brat into a cell, and Efael wouldn't have found her. And the effect on Senrid's concentration would have been exactly the same. Unconsidered expedience or mere spite, there's no coming back from that. Ever."

Imry closed his eyes, and David sensed that any more on

the subject would be a waste of effort. Change of subject. "What happened with Efael?"

"Yeres," Imry murmured. "Cheat." His lips were already dry from the effort it took to speak.

David reached for the steep. "Can you lift your head? You'd better have a slug of this."

When Imry lay flat again, his hair was soaked with sweat. David watched him fight for consciousness, win, and his breathing slow. Time for a guess. David said casually, "Do they know you've got the old magic?"

Imry's surprise was brief. He murmured, "Svir suspects."

"So now?"

"So now?" Imry echoed, his voice faint.

David smiled gently. "No one except me knows that you are here. And since, possibly, anyone on either side finding out would as soon slit either of our throats, no one will. Why not finish our conversation?"

Imry made another tremendous effort. "Why. Detlev go over?"

It was the same question that had occupied the others in the group for the past six years.

David refilled the cup with melted snow, then searched his brother's pain-hazed green eyes. "Detlev never explains his past to anyone even now," he said. "But I'll tell you what Adam thinks. Every action Detlev's taken since he let us loose has been toward the destruction of Norsunder. You might call it a monumental act of revenge, if you like. What the real joke is—" He smiled. "—you are an instrument of his vengeance, in everything you do, just as surely as I am."

Imry lay breathing for a time, his eyes hazing and then focusing again after sharp blinks. Finally, "Siamis," he whispered hoarsely. Sweat beaded on his forehead from the effort.

"Adam has a theory about what was going on with that very public falling out. But you'll have to ask him." David dug in his pack for the last bits of steep. "The snow layer is too thin on this slope. It'll be dirty, and I won't be able to sweep my prints. I need to get more water. Here, drink the last of what I fetched, and I'll range farther and get more."

Imry drank it too hot, but he was too thirsty to care. When he was done, his eyes closed in unfeigned exhaustion from his relentless pace as well as the pain, the rest of him drenched in sweat that smelled sharply of pepper.

David waited until his breathing was slow and deep, then slipped out. Wishing he'd thought to bring a bucket, he suspected when he returned it would be to an empty cave, and he was right.

He sighed, pulled out the beige paper, and wrote to Detlev.

Up in the castle, Efael prowled around as he thought it all through.

His frown kept his Black Knives disinclined to come anywhere near. Thus no one disturbed him until he summoned a guard, and gave orders for a search to be made in the environs of the castle. He gave no explanations, but, knowing the orders would be carried out, he then left for Imar.

They were all in the library, which was Ilerian's favorite room.

At first he perceived nothing wrong with the tableau. Svir sat adjacent to the fire, his long legs crossed at the ankle under his fine linen robe, his narrow feet neatly shod in kidskin; it was Efael who had brought the concept of wearing animal skins to this world, with his prized manskin coat. Yeres slumped in another chair, and next to her, Connanre. Between them, slightly behind, stood Ilerian, one of his hands resting on Connanre's shoulder in what appeared to be a benevolent gesture. No, a possessive gesture.

Efael said, "Imry's gone—"

"We'll forget Imry for a moment or two," Svirle interjected.

Though his light, drawling voice was precisely as pleasant as ever, Efael knew that Svir was angry.

Efael took a step into the circle of light, and then he saw Yeres's face, which was half-hidden from the firelight by the curve of the chair arm. He'd assumed her posture was a sulk. In the light she appeared shaken, even ill. Bruises dappled the pale skin of her neck. "What happened to you?"

"Just found her in the garden," Svir said. "It appears that Detlev's boy did not desire her company when he constrained her to transfer him past our wards, and out."

Yeres winced, and shivered. "Don't."

Svir continued, his gaze still on her, "He seems to have amused himself with rifling through the closet before discarding her."

Mind-raid, Efael realized, with hatred. No matter how

much magic he learned, how vicious his kills, he would never be an equal in the eyes of the two lords of Norsunder, because of Dena Yeresbeth.

Further, he saw by the tightness to Svir's smile, and the intensity of Ilerian's whole aspect, that her mind-shield had not withstood the boy's efforts—that she had revealed all her secrets. Including whatever-it-was she'd been doing with Connanre behind everyone's back. And now Svir knew it. But that would be just the usual amusing game to Svir and Ilerian. Yes?

No.

Svir turned his smile on Connanre. Firelight gleamed, twin glows, in his black eyes, and they all felt the force of his anger. "Well, Connanre? What precisely is this secret blunder of Detlev's that Yeres has been trying to hide?"

Connanre faced Yeres. She met his look of utter betrayal listlessly, and without any trace or remorse or regret. Of course she'd babbled in order to shift attention off her own blunder.

Accepting his final—ineradicable—defeat in her indifference, Connanre said, "Detlev has tampered with some—perhaps all—of the lattices of the mirror ward in Norsunder-Beyond, Ilerian. I don't know how he found them, but the last time you left Norsunder I checked a few. He'd keyed the enchantments through his field reports, a slightly different method for each update. But he forgot that there are actually some of us who read that material."

"I read everything," Svir said softly.

"But you don't do field work. I do," Connanre said, his languid voice becoming forceful for the first time in anyone's memory. Why was he reminding them of his value? They all knew what he did, Efael thought impatiently. "I'm the one who does enough field work to recognize, and—given enough time to investigate, once we get back—connect the deceits."

Ilerian said, "Detlev forgets nothing."

At that moment, he and Svir remembered the Marloven girl who, with Detlev's covert aid, had defeated Ilerian's first attempt to open a portal to the Beyond, just before Kessler closed that route: Hibern of Roth Drael. Who was in Norsunder right now, untouchable by either of them.

Svir and Ilerian looked past Connanre's treachery, and past the world-closing that coincided with so many disastrous re-awakenings.

They looked past the brilliantly trained fighters cavorting so absorbingly on either side, to the times when those field reports had been written, and beyond to when the work was done, and beyond that to the fundaments of Norsunder's great mirror ward, built over hundreds of years. Longer.

Svir contemplated for a time how the weapon aimed at his heart had been fashioned before his own eyes, with his own tools.

Within his own citadel.

Svir smiled at Connanre. "You do not appreciate the magnitude of the tribute."

"He will," said Ilerian.

Fifteen

TWO DAYS LATER, DETLEV and David stood on the prow of a fishing boat that one of Detlev's watchers plied off Khanerenth's east coast. Snowflakes drifted out of a white sky, ignored by all. Visibility had blurred the ocean around the little boat.

Distrusting the weird sphere that Detlev held in both hands, the fisher's captain stood well back, by the wheel. She motioned her crew to keep a circumspect distance as well.

Detlev turned to David. "Would you like to do the honors?"

"No." David rubbed absently at his chest, and said, "Right now, I suspect you can throw farther. We do not want to be swamped."

Detlev gave a soft laugh, cocked back his arm, then whipped it around, hurling the weirdly glowing sphere in a high arc to drop into the sea.

Which boiled and surged. Every one of the small crew gasped as a sight unseen for eight hundred years materialized: a three-masted, black-sailed Venn drakan ship, its dragon-head affixed to the high curved prow, its rails etched with intertwined leaves. It rocked on the waves ringing out.

David had known what to expect, but still his heart slammed at the sight of the drakan's captain, a tall, knife-lean man with silvering dark red hair, hammered hoops with rubies glinting blood-red at his ears, symbols of a long-ago, barbarous time. He lounged toward the rail to gaze down at Detlev in the fishing boat.

"Eh, Ramis," observed Savarend Montredavan-An, otherwise known as Fox. "It seems I'm back."

About the Author

Sherwood Smith writes fantasy, science fiction, and historical fiction. Her full bibliography can be found on her website at https://www.sherwoodsmith.net.

About Book View Cafe

Book View Café is an author-owned cooperative of professional writers, publishing in a variety of genres including fantasy, science fiction, romance, mystery, and more.

Its authors include New York Times and USA Today best-sellers as well as winners and nominees of many prestigious awards such as the Agatha Award, Hugo Award, Lambda Literary Award, Locus Award, Nebula Award, RITA Award, Philip K. Dick Award, World Fantasy Award, and many others.

Since its debut in 2008, Book View Café has gained a reputation for producing high quality books in both print and electronic form. BVC's e-books are DRM-free and distributed around the world.

Book View Café's monthly newsletter includes new releases, specials, author news, and event announcements. To sign up, visit https://www.bookviewcafe.com/bookstore/newsletter/